Caledan drew his dagger from his boot as the three magical mastiffs howled, an eerie sound of fury and bloodlust.

"Please don't tell me that pig-sticker is all you've got, scoundrel," the Harper said caustically. Her movements were fluid as she unsheathed the curved, gleaming sabre belted at her hip and assumed a battle-ready stance.

"As you wish." Caledan gritted his teeth.

Mari shot him a hard look, but there was no time for a reply. The hounds were rapidly closing the distance between them. Caledan could hear the crackling of the fiery auras that surrounded the beasts. The air was charged with an acrid, sulfuric odor. He let his dagger fly in a precise arc. It struck the lead hound directly between the eyes—and then bounced harmlessly off the creature's skull.

Caledan and Mari traded desperate looks.

"These are enchanted beasts," he shouted. "I don't think mundane weapons can harm them."

"Now you tell me," Mari said disgustedly, thrusting her sabre back into its sheath.

THE HARPERS

A semi-secret organization for Good, the Harpers fight for freedom and justice in a world populated by tyrants, evil mages, and dread concerns beyond imagination.

Each novel in the Harpers Series is a complete story in itself, detailing some of the most unusual and compelling tales in the magical world known as the Forgotten Realms.

THE HARPERS

FORGOTTEN REALMS

FANTASY ADVENTURE

CRYPT OF THE SHADOWKING

Mark Anthony

TSR Inc.

CRYPT OF THE SHADOWKING

First Printing March, 1993.
Printed in the United States of America.
Library of Congress Catalog Card Number: 92-61086

9 8 7 6 5 4 3 2 1

ISBN: 1-56076-594-1

TSR, Inc.
P.O. Box 756
Lake Geneva, WI 53147
U.S.A.

TSR Ltd.
120 Church End, Cherry Hinton
Cambridge CB1 3LB
United Kingdom

This novel could not have been written without the help and inspiration of a number of people. I would especially like to thank:

My indefatigable editor, Pat McGilligan, for continued belief in my ability as a writer.

TSR editor Jim Lowder, for patience and encouragement above and beyond the call of duty while reviewing early stages of this work.

Carl and Carla Schnurr, for improving this book in countless ways with their insightful comments—and also for general silliness, which was always much needed.

Enya, for the beautiful and inspirational music of the recording, Shepherd Moons.

And most of all my family, for their love and support.

This one is for the Scribbling Primates!

Prologue

The thief made his way through the dark, labyrinthine sewers far beneath the city of Iriaebor. The foul, murky water swirled around his thighs, sucking at his boots with every step. He hugged the tunnel's slimy tiled wall as he moved. Darkness was a thief's best friend, and he wore it like a soft, enshrouding cloak.

The tunnel ended in a vaulted chamber, a junction where several pipes spewed their filthy contents into a larger passageway. A few wan beams of light filtered down from a narrow iron grating above, and the thief froze. His small, close-set eyes glittered like hard, black stones. Voices drifted down from above with the torchlight.

"I tell you, if we don't find the little thief there's going to be the Abyss to pay."

"Worse than that, there'll be Bron to pay. The city lord won't take kindly to hearing a prisoner's escaped his dungeons. Gods know, it'll give every rat in the whole bloody place the notion to try to escape." The raspy voices

1

drifted away with the sound of booted feet, and the thief relaxed.

He saw now that one of the tunnels opening into the junction was dry inside. Perhaps it led to some unused part of the dungeon, or maybe even beyond. At any rate, it would be better than forcing his way through the stinking swill that flowed through the rest of the sewers. He climbed up into the empty tunnel, relieved to be where it was dry. The tunnel was tall enough that he could run in a hunched position, his fingers lightly brushing the sides, warning him of any turns. He quickened his pace, sensing freedom ahead.

There was no way in the blackness that the thief could have seen the wide, jagged crack that crossed the tunnel before him. When his foot struck the crack's edge he nearly managed to catch himself, but then the rotting tiles beneath his feet crumbled. The thief screamed once. Then he was falling, down into endless dark.

* * * * *

How long he had lain there on the hard stone, the thief did not know. A day, maybe more. His tongue was parched and swollen, and the blood on his face had dried into a hard, painful mask. That he was dying was certain. He could not feel his left leg, and his right arm was shattered. The ragged breaths he drew were labored, shallow, tasting of blood. Each one was agony.

He didn't think he was in the sewers anymore. The stone beneath him was rough and jagged, not hewn by human hands. More likely it was some natural cavern, far below the city. He wondered if anyone had ever come this way before. Perhaps, he told himself. Perhaps not.

With great effort he managed to crack open his eyes. It was several minutes before he realized that he could see. Here, where there should have been only darkness, there was light. Welling up from the stone some distance before him was a dull, red glow. Hope flared in his heart. Was there someone there, someone who would get him out of this blasted hole? Somehow, using his one good leg and his unbroken arm, he managed to inch his way at a snail's pace toward the light. The pain was dizzying, threatening to tear him apart, but he went on. He would do whatever it took to survive.

Finally, after what seemed a lifetime, he reached the edge of the ruddy illumination, and his head sank to the stone in despair. He had reached the edge of a chasm. He could see the other side, a dozen feet away in the dimness, but it might as well have been a league. There was no going onward. There was nowhere he could go, except down.

He peered into the chasm. It was from here that the faint, red glow rose, like a fine vapor on the still air, but from what source the illumination sprang he could not say. The chasm seemed to delve down into the earth forever.

He felt a sharp pain in his hand. He turned his head and found himself gazing into the bright crimson eyes of a rat. It was chewing ravenously at his thumb.

"Curse you," he croaked, trying to brush the rat away. The creature simply sidestepped his feeble motion and continued to gnaw at his battered flesh. The thief could not defeat it. He laid his head down, willing the darkness to take him.

The rat squealed in agony.

Startled, the thief cracked his eyes open once again. The rat writhed in pain before him, bathed in the dull red glow emanating from the chasm. In moments its struggling ceased, and it lay dead. That was when the voice spoke.

Serve me, and you shall be made whole.

It was a dry voice, as dusty as old death. The thief shrank from the sound of it. He could not tell where the voice came from, only that it was there.

Serve me, and I shall make you whole, thief.

The words came from the chasm itself, he realized, rising up from the unthinkable depths with the haze of blood-red light. The voice was ancient, enormous, and the thief shriveled beneath it. Yet its words lit a spark of dark hope in his heart.

You are dying, thief. Will you accept?

He tried to wet his lips, but his tongue was as dry as sand. Finally he managed to croak a few words. "Who are you?"

I am darkness.

The thief shuddered at those words. For a moment his mind caught a glimpse of something vast and terrible, ancient yet alive, and hungry, so enormously hungry. He realized this voice reaching up was just a thin tendril of the entire being that waited, down there in the darkness. The thief felt his soul withering. His whole being screamed to let death consume him.

But he had vowed to survive.

Do you accept?

With agonizing effort the thief lifted his head and peered unblinking into the endless depths of the chasm. "Yes," he croaked. There was a vast rumbling deep below, almost like laughter.

Then be made whole, thief!

From the depths of his broken body, the thief screamed. His back arched rigidly, lifting him off the cold stone. White-hot fire seared through him, burning away all that he was. But then cool darkness quenched the fire, drowning him, and he knew no more . . .

. . . for a time.

One

The purple gloom of twilight was deepening into night as the traveler rode toward the gates of the city. Torches flickered on the high stone wall that stood on the far bank of the slate-colored river, and beyond, on the dark crag looming above the city's center, a thousand spires rose like silent sentinels into the leaden sky.

The hooves of his mount—a pretty gray mare with a fine, noble head—thudded dully against the damp stones of the road. She was weary, her flanks stained with the sweat and mud of a long journey. Her rider leaned forward to scratch her roughly behind the ears, an action which brought a soft nicker of appreciation.

"Not much farther, Mista," the rider told her. "We're almost home." As if she understood the words—and in truth the rider was not at all certain that she didn't—the horse quickened her pace, lifting her delicate legs a bit higher off the rain-slickened cobblestones.

The rider took a deep breath of the moist air. The fine,

steady rain had ended only an hour ago, and his midnight blue traveling cloak was dusted with tiny, pearl-gray droplets. The cloak was worn and faded, stained with long years of travel, and in places it was more patches than anything else. But it was a good cloak, its wool still thick and warm, and in this it was much like the man who wore it. He was not a young man. Seven years of wandering the Realms had carved their mark upon his angular, almost wolfish face, and though his green eyes were clear, their color was as faded as the cloak thrown over his broad, sharp-edged shoulders.

But despite the rider's frayed appearance his dark hair bore no trace of gray, and the muscles knotted about his rather large and bony frame were surprisingly strong and quick, as more than a few highway bandits had learned to their dismay over the years. The rider's name was Caledan, and once, before his years of wandering, he had been a Harper.

The Harpers were the meddlers of the Realms. Troubadours and mages, warriors and thieves numbered among their ranks, along with men and women of all races and crafts. Theirs was a small, secret fellowship whose members vowed to work against villainy and wickedness. But instead of relying on brute force, the Harpers used more subtle means to accomplish their aims. Often single agents were given the task of slipping stealthily into areas that had fallen under shadow's sway, from the halls of kings to the dens of thieves. There they did all that one being alone could do to loosen evil's grip, and not a few had given their lives in the course of their missions. But the sacrifices were not in vain. These days more Realms shone in the light beneath the banner of freedom than festered beneath the dark cloak of evil.

Caledan had once been a bard of great ability, but he hadn't played a note of music since the day he left the

Harpers, and he didn't suppose he ever would again. He'd begun his wanderings long ago, and he considered the Harpers a good riddance.

A narrow wooden bridge of five separate spans crossed the great serpent of the River Chionthar, and Mista's hooves thumped hollowly on the stout wooden planks. A dozen ships drifted on the dull water, looking like ghosts in the dusky air. Iriaebor was the farthest point that trade ships sailing from the Sword Coast in the far west could travel up the Chionthar. Here merchants were forced to unload their goods and transfer them to overland caravans traveling to the great kingdoms of Cormyr and Sembia to the east, and in this lay Iriaebor's fortune.

Mista stepped off the last planks of the bridge. The south wall of the city loomed in the dimness above Caledan. The great iron-bound gates stood open, as they always had, for commerce kept no set hours in a trade city this large. A torch burned brightly to either side of the gates, and thick coils of smoke rose up against the soot-blackened stones. Caledan guided his gray mount toward the great, arched portal.

"Too important to stop for the guards, are we, lordship?" a coarse voice taunted. Caledan reined Mista to an abrupt halt as a man clad in a leather jerkin stepped from a dim alcove to stand before him. He was an unsavory fellow, missing the better number of his teeth. He reeked of sour sweat mixed with the unmistakable odor of strong drink.

"I beg your pardon," Caledan replied, assuming a cheerful, almost simpleminded manner. "I don't recall that the gates of Iriaebor were ever guarded in the past."

"Well, they are now. Leastwise since Cutter's been in the High Tower, that is. Now you'd best be telling me who you are and what you're about. 'Tis a cold night to be a corpse."

"Indeed," Caledan replied dryly. He noticed the glitter of torchlight reflecting off a pair of eyes in the shadows by the gate. It seemed the guard had a friend there. He would have to keep that in mind if things went awry.

"I'm Symek of Berdusk," Caledan lied smoothly, "a merchant of jewels by trade."

"A *jool* trader, eh?" the guard said dubiously. "You don't look like a *jool* trader, friend." He squinted suspiciously at Caledan.

"These are hard times for all, aren't they?" Caledan lamented with a dramatic sigh.

The guard seemed to consider this, rubbing his unshaven jowls with a grubby hand, and then he nodded. "All right, Symek of Berdusk. I suppose yours is the sort of business Cutter wants in the city, though watch you mind the rules, unless you want to meet Cutter face-to-face in the dungeons. And I'm telling you that's not something you want to do."

"I can pass then?"

"Aye," the guard answered, and then a sly smile crept across his scurvy features. "But first you've got to grease the gates, if you know what I mean, *jool* trader."

Caledan cast a distasteful look at the guard, who held out a grimy paw. This was getting tiresome.

"You really should wash that hand, my friend," Caledan said in a conspiratorial tone, leaning down toward the guard. "It's much healthier that way, you know."

The guard's expression darkened. "I've had just about enough of you, Symek," the guard said, reaching for the hilt of his sword.

"I wouldn't do that if I were you," Caledan replied pleasantly. The guard's eyes widened, and he looked down to see the sharp, glimmering point of a knife just pricking into the chest of his worn leather jerkin. Caledan smiled broadly at the trembling man. "Like you said, it's a cold night to be a corpse."

The guard nodded wordlessly, and Caledan touched his

heels to Mista's flanks, slipping the sharp dagger back into its sheath in his boot. The horse walked forward, and as she passed the guard she bared her big teeth, nipping his shoulder. The fellow cried out in pain and stumbled backward. The other guard took a hesitant step forward, unsure whether to draw his sword or not.

"I wouldn't recommend it," Caledan advised cheerfully.

"Milord!" the guard said in a quavering voice, apparently deciding he was safer with his blade firmly sheathed. Caledan passed through the arched portal and into the dim, torch-lined streets of the city.

"That was hardly necessary, you know, Mista," he told his mount. "That fellow wasn't much of an opponent."

The horse nickered defiantly.

"I know," Caledan said with a grin. "I enjoyed it, too." He frowned then. What in Milil's name were guards doing bothering travelers at the gates of the city? Iriaebor had always been a free and open place in the days when Caledan had dwelt here. Merchants and wayfarers came at all hours of the day and night. There had never been any need for guards.

"Perhaps there have been more bandits on the road of late," Caledan said aloud, and Mista snorted softly as if to question this.

"True. Those two were hardly the sort I would want to depend on to keep me safe from marauders. If you're going to go to all the bother of putting guards at the gate, why use a pair of buffoons?"

But Caledan was weary, and his throat was in sore need of a mug of ale. He resolved to think about it later.

Horse and rider made their way through the open avenues of the New City. Before them, in the city's center, loomed a high, rocky hill. The Tor, which was perhaps a half-league long, rose a full three hundred feet above the rest of Iriaebor, and Caledan could see the lights of the Old

City flickering like golden stars in the darkness above him. Over the years, space on the narrow hilltop had been at a premium. Within a hundred years of the city's founding, the only direction left in which to build upon the Tor was up. The result, after several centuries, was a profusion of tall, spindly towers stretching toward the sky, bound together with countless bridges that arched precariously between them like so many spiderwebs.

Caledan guided the gray mare to the narrow road that wound back and forth up the steep southern face of the Tor. The presence of guards at the city's gates still nagged at him, but that wasn't the only thing that seemed different about the city. The torches that guttered in the air along the streets were few and far between, casting more shadows than light. The streets themselves were grimy and littered with trash, and foul-smelling water flowed darkly in the gutters, pooling into black, stagnant puddles in the middle of every intersection.

Yet even more disturbing was the city's silence. The streets were empty of all but a few individuals, and these walked quickly past Caledan, their eyes cast down toward the dirty cobbles as if they were in a hurry to be inside, though the sun was no more than an hour set. When Caledan had last visited Iriaebor, the bustling trade city's torch-lined streets had been nearly as full at midnight as they were at midday, crowded with merchants and jongleurs, nobles and thieves. But these dark and sullen streets seemed to have little to do with the cheerful, brightly lit avenues he remembered. Of course, it had been seven years since he left, and he supposed his memories might have become overly fond. Still, he couldn't shake the growing impression that something was amiss.

As Mista steadily ascended the narrow road into the Old City, the tall towers closed over the streets so that riding through them was like riding through a tunnel. They passed an ill-kept tavern, the ruddy light of its fire spilling out of its doorway like blood onto the street. The sound of raucous laughter drifted out with the light, but it was a sinister rather than merry sound, and Caledan chose to ride on.

He considered going to see if the Sign of the Dreaming Dragon still stood on the very western edge of the Tor. He thought it likely he might find an old friend or two there. But Caledan was not certain he was ready for the memories that came with meeting old friends. Instead he guided Mista toward another inn called the Wandering Wyvern, where he knew he could find good drink and good rest.

Just then a shadowy form shambled from the dark maw of an alley, and Caledan's hand slipped to the knife in his boot. The form stepped into the dim circle of illumination below a sputtering torch. Seeing it was an old woman, Caledan relaxed. She was clad in tattered rags wrapped about her shapeless form, and her white hair was filthy and matted against her head. She didn't seem to see Caledan riding toward her, and she stumbled before Mista so that he was forced to rein the mare hard lest the old woman be trampled.

"Good evening, old mother," Caledan said as the haggard woman gazed up at him with dull, rheumy eyes. "Shouldn't you be home on as chill a night as this?"

The old woman shook her head, moving her lips silently, mumbling to herself as if she was trying to remember something. Then her eyes cleared for a moment, and her gaze met Caledan's.

"I have no home, sire," she said finally, her voice cracked and hollow. Caledan reached into the pocket of his cloak and pulled out a gold coin, which he pressed into the woman's gnarled hand.

"Then find one with this, old mother, at least for tonight."

She looked at the coin for a moment as if puzzled by it

and then nodded as she turned down the street. Caledan watched her as she shambled away, mumbling to herself. He shook his head as he nudged Mista onward. He didn't remember that the elderly had ever been turned out onto the city's streets before, either. It seemed there was a lot he didn't remember.

He soon found himself before the Wandering Wyvern. To his relief it looked much as it had on the day he left, a blocky, comfortable-looking building with the High Tower of the city lord looming above it. "I was beginning to think I had come to the wrong city, Mista," Caledan said to his mount.

In the small courtyard Caledan called for the stable boy, who appeared moments later, bleary-eyed and with straw in his hair, apparently having been asleep in the barn.

"I'm sorry, milord," the lad said. "We don't usually have travelers after dark."

"Take this," Caledan said, flipping a copper coin to the boy as the lad led Mista toward the stable. "And if you tell her several times over what a lovely horse she is, it's likely she won't even try to bite you."

"Aye, milord!"

The interior of the inn was comfortably warm, but there were few patrons, and most of these cast mistrustful looks at Caledan before huddling back down over their food or drink. Caledan took a place on a bench at one of the long wooden tables, and when the innkeep, a nervous little man, came to him, he ordered a plate of whatever food there might be in the kitchen and a mug of ale.

"I'm sorry, milord," the innkeep said fretfully, "but there's no ale served after sundown."

"What?" Caledan said, completely taken aback.

"It's in the rules." The innkeep gestured furtively toward a large, crudely drawn placard nailed to one of the walls. The placard was filled with line after line of writing scrawled too poorly to be legible at a distance, though the large words which headed it were clear enough. They read: Lord Cutter's Rules.

"Since when are there rules about drinking ale in Iriaebor?" Caledan asked with growing annoyance.

"Since that lout Cutter came, that's when," a rough voice growled next to Caledan. He turned to see a burly, red-faced man sitting nearby. The comment seemed to make the innkeep uncomfortable, for the nervous little man looked hurriedly about, as if to make certain no one was watching, and then disappeared into the kitchen. "Every day there's another of Cutter's rules come down from the tower," said the big man, who from his dress and size appeared to be a dockhand.

Cutter. That was the name the guards at the gate had spoken. Curious, Caledan moved over and sat next to the man, whom the other patrons seemed to be purposefully ignoring.

"Just who is this 'Cutter'?" Caledan asked, trying to make his tone as sympathetic as possible. "Is Cutter the city lord?"

"Aye," the dockhand said glumly. "Ever since good old Bron disappeared a year or so ago. Wasn't so bad at first, but that didn't last long. Seems old Cutter never runs out o' rules, and all of them boil down to the same thing—there's nothing worth having or doing that's allowed no more. And you learn quick enough all right not to break any of 'em. You do that, and Cutter's guards haul you away, and no one ever sees you again." He paused for a moment, taking a reflexive pull on his mug and frowning when he realized it was only water. By the look of him, he must have swallowed as much ale as he could possibly hold before the sun had set. "You just come into the city?" he asked.

Caledan nodded. "I've been traveling for a long time."

"Well, you shouldn't 'ave come here," the dockhand said,

and after that he fell into a gloomy silence. Caledan left him in peace.

The nervous innkeep came back not long after with a plate of food for Caledan. The fare was good—a thick stew, cheese, and brown bread—but there wasn't much of it. He had just finished eating when the door of the inn opened, and a tall, fierce man clad in the livery of a city guard stepped through. A tense hush fell over the common room. Conversations halted in midsentence, and forks froze in midair.

The guard scanned the room slowly with hard eyes. His countenance was harsh and proud, his sharp cheekbones each outlined by a thin white scar. His hand rested with practiced ease on the polished sword hilt at his hip. This man was a warrior, and a dangerous one at that, Caledan thought.

"Innkeep, bring me food," he barked in a guttural voice. "Make it your best, and make it quick. Otherwise I might get angry." A cruel smile touched his thin lips, and his dark eyes glittered perilously. "You wouldn't like me when I'm angry."

The innkeep swallowed hard and bobbed his head, scurrying off to the kitchen like a frightened mouse. The guard sat at a table in a dim corner, a leer on his face. His hand never strayed far from the hilt of his sword.

Gradually, the conversation in the common room started up again, though now it was even more subdued than before. The nervous little innkeep brought a steaming platter of roasted meat for the guard and received only a harsh glare in payment.

"Friend," Caledan said softly, turning to the nearby dockhand who was scowling at his mug, "you wouldn't happen to know who that cheerful-looking fellow in the corner is, would you?"

"Him?" the dockhand grunted. "He's one of Cutter's captains, he is. Let me tell you, stranger, you don't want to have no trouble with him. He'd gut you as soon as say good-day to you. You'd do best to keep out of his way, you would."

"Thanks for the advice. Here." Caledan slipped a few coins toward the fellow. "Wait until dawn, then buy yourself a mug or two."

"Say! Gods be with you, lordship," the dockhand said. His bleary eyes glimmered as he pocketed the coins, but Caledan had already moved away toward a shadowed alcove where he could watch the guard without risk of notice.

The guard's black leather jerkin was emblazoned with the traditional symbol of Iriaebor—a silver tower above an azure river. However, Caledan noticed that a crimson moon had been added to the insignia, rising behind the tower. No doubt that was Lord Cutter's touch. Caledan found he cared for it as little as the other changes which had befallen the city.

When the guard finished his food, he roughly pushed his plate away and stood. His chair clattered to the floor, and the inn fell deathly silent.

"What are you maggots staring at?" the guard snarled. The patrons in the room quickly averted their eyes. The guard snorted in disgust and then swaggered out the inn's doorway.

Pausing a few moments, so as not to appear as if he were following, Caledan stood and walked casually out of the door into the night beyond. He espied the guard in the distance, striding jauntily down the dimly lit street. Caledan followed, keeping to the shadows.

The guard made his way down the Street of Jewels and then turned onto the Street of Lanterns, disappearing from view. This had not been a particularly savory part of town even seven years ago, and now it was worse. Bold, red-eyed rats scurried in the refuse-lined gutters, and wicked laughter drifted down from open windows above.

Caledan turned the corner and then paused. The guard was gone. He must have entered one of the doorways that lined the street. Caledan muttered an oath, but there was nothing he could do. He turned around to make his way back toward the Wandering Wyvern.

He found himself facing the tall warrior with scarred cheeks.

"Don't you know, friend," the guard said with an evil grin, "it isn't safe to be about on the streets at night." The guard's sword glimmered dully in the dim light. "I'd best see you to Lord Cutter's dungeon. Trust me, you'll be much safer there."

Caledan started to back up, but the grating of a boot heel on the cobbles behind him brought him to a halt. He looked quickly about to see two more guards step out of a shadowed doorway a dozen paces away. He was outnumbered.

Caledan swore under his breath. This wasn't the sort of homecoming he had envisioned.

Two

The two guards advanced on Caledan from either side, short swords drawn. The captain watched with a satisfied leer, his dark eyes glittering.

"Don't worry, friend," the captain said with a coarse laugh. "I'm sure you'll find Cutter's dungeons most inviting."

"I'm afraid I'm going to have to be rude and turn down that gracious invitation," Caledan replied cheerfully. He had already developed a serious dislike for this fellow.

The captain nodded almost imperceptibly to the guards behind Caledan, but Caledan was ready. He feinted a lunge at the guard to his left, a pot-bellied fellow whose stupid grin displayed a half-dozen jagged yellow teeth. The guard swung his blade wildly with enough force to cleave Caledan in two, but Caledan dodged to one side. The force of the guard's swing carried him forward, and his companion screamed as the sword bit deeply into his side. The snaggle-toothed guard watched in confusion as his companion slumped to the street, a rivulet of dark blood trickling into the gutter to mingle with the filth.

"Kill him, you idiot!" the captain snarled. The pot-bellied guard roared in rage, rushing at Caledan and shaking his bloodied sword.

In a flash Caledan dove for the dead guard's sword, rolled, and came up standing. He thrust the blade out before him just in time to meet the guard's rush. The man's eyes went wide. He slipped backward off the sword, the blood-smeared blade making a sucking noise as it pulled from his chest. Like a felled tree, the guard toppled to the street.

The captain regarded the bodies of his fallen men dispassionately for a moment, then turned his glittering gaze toward Caledan. "You're full of surprises, friend," he said, stepping across the corpses. "It appears I'll have to deal with you myself. It will be worth it, however. Lord Cutter will be most interested to meet you, I think." He lifted his gleaming sword, his stance practiced and ready, his eyes deadly.

"I'm afraid I'll have to disappoint your master, then," Caledan said wryly. He dropped the bloodstained short sword and tensed as if to run. Victory glimmered in the captain's eyes as he lunged for Caledan, but he was far too slow.

In the space between heartbeats, Caledan reached down, drew the knife from the sheath inside his boot, and let it fly. For a frozen moment the knife spun in the air, glinting in the light of a nearby torch. Then the captain stumbled backward, his dark eyes filled with dull astonishment. He clutched weakly at the hilt of the knife buried in his chest and slumped wordlessly to the cobbles.

Caledan quickly surveyed the shadowy street around him, but it was empty. Apparently there were no more city guards nearby. He knelt beside the staring corpse of the captain and retrieved his dagger. He pulled the black leather glove from the captain's left hand and then swore softly, his suspicion confirmed. The captain was missing the tips of his last two fingers. It was an age-old sign of loyalty and devotion to cut off a fingertip and ritually present it to one's master. But Caledan knew of only one group in the Realms that still practiced that barbarous tradition.

The Zhentarim.

"I suppose they're after the caravan routes," Caledan muttered in disgust as he stood up. He had dealt with the Zhentarim before, in his days as a Harper. Those were not memories he cherished.

The Zhentarim were members of a dark, secretive society based in Zhentil Keep, a city on the edge of the Moonsea far to the west. Made up of warriors and sorcerers, renegade clerics and thieves, the Zhentarim's goal was to bring as many of the Realms as possible under its control, and then to bleed the lands dry. Now it appeared that Iriaebor—along with the lucrative trade routes it controlled— was the Black Network's latest prize.

This Lord Cutter was probably a Zhentarim himself. It would certainly explain the pall that had been cast over the city. The Zhentarim cared nothing for life or beauty. Only gold meant something to their black hearts—gold and power.

Caledan cleaned his dagger on the dead man's cloak and resheathed it. "It's good to be home," he said bitterly, staring at the three corpses, then he started off through the canyons of the Old City, back toward the Wandering Wyvern.

Moments later a shadow separated itself from the blackness of a doorway to slip away through the darkened city. The street was silent for a time. Then the first of the rats came upon the corpses and squealed over its grisly discovery.

* * * * *

"Play us another one, Anja!"

The cluttered little cottage was filled with golden candle-light and the sound of laughter. Anja, a plump woman with bright black eyes and ruddy cheeks, smiled at the small audience of coarsely clad farmers gathered about her.

"All right. One more, Garl, and then it's home with you louts." She lifted the wooden flute to her lips. It was a simple instrument, worn with long years of playing. Anja had made it herself when she was barely more than a lass, and it had been her truest companion through three husbands and a half-dozen droughts. Life was hard here on the sun-parched plains so close to the vast desert of Anauroch, but it was not without its pleasures, and music was one of them.

Though her hands were toughened and calloused from years of toil, Anja's fingers moved nimbly over the flute. She played a carefree, lilting air, and the farmers stamped their dirty boots and clapped their hands in time to the music. But it wasn't the music alone that had brought her friends to her cottage.

Even as Anja played, the shadows cast by the candles began to dance upon the whitewashed walls.

The shadows seemed almost to bow and whirl to the music of the flute, their outlines suggesting dancers at a fancy ball. A slender shadow, hinting at a young maiden, flickered and seemed to spurn the advances of a decidedly rotund shadow. The men laughed as they watched the shadowplay.

Anja didn't quite know how she made the shadows do her bidding with the music of her flute. She had always been able to do it, even as a child. Some had told her it was magic, and while Anja didn't know about that—magic was more for wizards in their towers than for farm girls on the dusty plains—she did know she could shape the shadows on the wall however she wished with the notes of her music.

She finished the song with a flourish, and the shadows all seemed to take a bow. Garl and the others thundered their applause as Anja lowered her flute. "One more song, Anja! Just one more!" they called out.

She never had the chance to say no.

The cottage's wooden door burst apart in a spray of splinters. All turned in shock to see the figure of a man standing in the doorway. At least they assumed it was a man. The form was tall and clad from head to toe in a heavy black robe.

"Hey, now!" Garl growled in protest, advancing on the stranger. "You can't—"

With eerie speed the stranger reached out with a black-gloved hand, snapping Garl's neck with an almost casual motion. The farmer slumped lifelessly to the floor as Anja watched in frozen horror. Shouting and swearing in outrage, the other men leaped into action, but to little avail. The black-robed stranger batted aside a glowing poker with an easy gesture and threw a burly farmer through the sod wall. He smashed one young man's skull against the stones of the chimney and with a quick blow crushed another's windpipe. In moments only Anja was left standing, shaking her head in terror. The stranger walked slowly toward the one he had come for.

"Please," she whispered. "Please don't." The stranger lifted a gloved hand, and Anja's scream was lost in a gurgle of hot blood. The wooden flute slipped from her hand to the dirt floor. It would never make the shadows dance again.

The black-robed stranger left the cottage then, slipping into the night. His mission had been accomplished. The woman with the shadow magic was dead. Now there were but two more left in all the Realms. Soon there would be none at all. The stranger turned to the wind, testing the cool air. The trail led southward.

The wind hissed through the dry grass, and suddenly the night was empty.

* * * * *

Caledan rose early the next morning. He retrieved Mista from the stable of the Wandering Wyvern and rode off through the cheerless streets. Even with the coming of dawn Iriaebor seemed wrapped in gloom. Many of the city's once-proud towers slumped precariously above the narrow avenues, the bridges that spanned the distance between them crumbling and treacherous where passable at all. The light of the sun was dull and tired by the time it managed to filter its way down past the ancient spires, and even as the sullen light filled the streets so did the people, pouring out of countless peeling, weathered doors to pursue the day's affairs, their faces grim and wearied. Caledan could only shake his head. Perhaps that drunken dockhand had been right. Maybe he should never have come back at all.

Why *had* he returned? Did he really think he could find some sort of peace here after all this time? If so, he was a bigger fool than he thought. There were too many memories here, he now realized. Every street, every tower, every stone reminded him of a time when he had been happy, when he hadn't been alone.

Absently he twirled the braided copper bracelet he wore on his left wrist. That happiness had died seven years ago. He had laid it cold and dead in the earth alongside a woman with summer-gold hair. All he had now were ghosts. Maybe no amount of wandering would be enough to leave such memories behind.

He supposed an old friend or two might still live in Iriaebor, but he feared his one-time companions would be as changed as the city was. Besides, he had grown used to loneliness these last years, and he could live without friends.

"Anyway, I have you, Mista," he said, slapping the pale mare's neck with a friendly hand. She tossed her head and

pranced haughtily, her hooves ringing against the cobbles.
"Vain beast," he said with a laugh.

It was time to leave this forsaken place, Caledan decided.
He had heard there was good pay to be had guarding caravans on the roads north of Waterdeep. He was as handy
with a sword as any man, and he could use the gold. He
guided Mista onto a wide avenue that led down the Tor and
out of the city.

The avenue widened as it made its way past the tower of
the city lord. The tower stood atop the very highest part of
the Tor, soaring above all the city's thousand spires. Its
walls were wrought of dark stone quarried from the very
hill upon which Iriaebor rested.

Much blood had been shed in the tower's construction,
and those who had laid its foundations were long dead by
the time the last stone of the turret was set in place. One
could still see the faint line a third of the way up the tower's
height where the color of the stone changed slightly. Every
child in Iriaebor knew the tale of how the wall of the first
quarry had collapsed, killing a score of workmen as well as
the first city lord, Eradabus, who often labored beside them
as a symbol of good will. After that a new quarry was begun
by the second city lord, Melsar, but it was the third city
lord, the Lady Saresia, who saw the tower completed and
first held Argument in its vast great hall.

Guards patrolled the battlements atop the wall that surrounded the tower, and a full dozen stood before the great
iron-banded gates. At least a dozen among them had the
battle-hardened look of Zhentarim warriors. Caledan kept
his distance from them. He was a Harper no longer and
doubted anyone would recognize him, but the Zhentarim's
hatred for the Harpers was no secret. There was no sense
in taking chances.

He veered Mista onto a less-traveled side street, then
brought her up short. A band of mounted city guards rode

toward him down the street, waving their swords and barking at the cityfolk to make way. Hurriedly, their eyes wide with fear, the citizens of Iriaebor complied, pressing against the buildings that lined the street.

"That way doesn't look so good after all, Mista," Caledan noted drily. He spun the mare around and headed back for the broad avenue. A similar scene greeted him there, only this time with about three times the number of guards. Quickly the throng of people crowded along the gutters, keeping the center of the avenue clear. Caledan tried to nudge Mista out of their way, but in moments he found himself trapped in the middle of a tight knot of people, livestock, ramshackle carts, and horse-drawn wagons. There was no way to escape without causing a scene.

"What's going on here, friend?" Caledan quietly asked a rotund merchant next to him. The merchant was perched on the bench of a wagon that looked as if it might fall to pieces at any moment.

"City lord's coming this way," the man answered, his harsh voice more than a little bitter. "You've always got to make way for the city lord these days. Too good to mingle with the rest of us, I suppose."

"I suppose so," Caledan replied wryly. Suddenly he didn't mind the crowd. He found he was curious to get a look at this notorious Lord Cutter before he left the city.

A brassy trumpet blare shattered the morning air. Eight black chargers trotting in formation rounded the corner of the side street and turned onto the main avenue. Astride them were men clad in the black livery of the city guard, swords raised and glittering in the sun. The guards did not need to warn the onlookers to keep out of their way. Behind them came a standard-bearer, holding aloft the banner of Iriaebor: the tower, river, and—now—crimson moon.

A small, wiry man clad in robes of a sickly, poisonous green came into view, riding a soot-colored gelding. The

man's dark hair was cropped close to his head, adding to
the severity of his sharp features. His eyes glittered in the
ruddy sunlight like small black stones. Folk bowed their
heads as he reverently passed them by.

"That's Lord Cutter?" Caledan asked the merchant in a
low voice, but the fellow shook his head.

"Naw, that's the lord steward. They call him Snake.
Name suits him, I suppose. There's venom in that one's
heart, no doubt. But he's more Cutter's lapdog than he is a
viper."

Caledan nodded, but before he could ask another question there was a second fanfare of trumpets. A tall figure
clad in dark leather and a cloak of deep crimson rounded
the corner and rode down the avenue astride a glossy, jet-
black palfrey. Shoulder length hair of pale spun gold shone
brightly in the sun.

"Now that," said the merchant, "is City Lord Cutter."

Caledan felt his heart lurch in his chest. A loud rushing
sound filled his ears, and he gripped Mista's reins tightly
with white-knuckled hands. He couldn't believe his eyes.

The woman called Cutter was beautiful. Her eyes were a
dusky blue like the evening sky, and her face was smooth
and moon-pale, her strong, fine features better hewn of
marble than flesh. But it was not this revelation that made
Caledan's heart stop in his chest.

"Ravendas," he hissed through clenched teeth.

"Hey, friend, you'd better bow your head if you don't
want the guards to notice you," the merchant whispered
hoarsely. "They'll haul you off to the dungeons, they will."

Caledan didn't move. He could only watch as the woman
who now called herself Cutter rode with her lord steward
through the waiting gates of the tower. The gates swung
shut with a sound as vast as thunder. She was gone. As
though suddenly released from a spell, Caledan shook his
head, trying to swallow the hot bile in his throat. Somehow

he had always known he would meet her again. His old
enemy. The Zhentarim, Lord Ravendas.

* * * * *

"It looks like we'll be staying a while after all, old friend,"
Caledan said softly, stroking the gray mare's silky mane.
Dusk was drifting down like fine, purple dust among the
towers as he rode toward a shadowed section of the Old
City. Seeing Ravendas had changed everything. Caledan
couldn't leave, not now. He had to find out what his old
enemy was up to, and there was an old acquaintance of his
on the Street of Jewels who just might be able to help him
find out—for the right price, of course.

He had nearly reached his destination when he realized
he was being followed.

Caledan had to admit, his dark-cloaked pursuer was
skilled, walking down the street after him with a perfect
imitation of aimlessness. However, Caledan had played the
game enough times himself to know all the tricks.

He rode onward casually, keeping watch on his pursuer
out of the corner of his eye. If he remembered this part of
the city correctly, he knew of a place where he might be
able to arrange a little surprise for his mysterious shadow.
He guided the mare down a narrow side street, for the
moment cutting off his pursuer's line of sight. He nudged
Mista's flanks, and she leaped into a canter, her hooves clattering metallically on the crumbling paving stones.

"Run for a short distance, then wait for me," Caledan
whispered into Mista's ear. The horse snorted softly, her
ears twitching. Whether it was his words or tone she understood, Caledan could not say, but he knew that she would
do his bidding.

As the horse raced on he stood up in the stirrups. He
tensed his body and sprang upward. His big hands caught

on to a stone ledge jutting from a low bridge that spanned the narrow street. Mista trotted on, disappearing around a corner. Caledan hung for a moment and then heaved himself up onto the bridge with a grunt of effort.

"I am definitely getting too old for this," he groaned, his shoulders throbbing dully. He rolled over to peer down the alleyway. At first he could see nothing. Then out of the murkiness came his pursuer, padding lightly but quickly down the alley, hooded head moving from side to side, searching. When the figure was almost directly below him, Caledan stood up, throwing his cloak back over his shoulders.

"Looking for someone?" he called out. Before his cloaked pursuer could react, Caledan leaped from the low bridge. The two went tumbling to the street. His pursuer was strong and wiry and almost managed to twist out of his grasp, but Caledan had the advantage of size. After a few moments of struggling his shadow was pinned beneath him.

"Let go of me!" his captive shouted, taking a swing at him, but Caledan caught the blow before it landed.

"Not until I find out why you were following me," he said through clenched teeth, holding the person tightly by the wrists. His pursuer was silent for a long moment, then finally spoke in a low, husky voice.

"I am seeking Caledan the Harper."

Caledan grunted, not missing a beat. "What makes you think I know him?"

"Will you let me go?"

"Only if you tell me who you are."

With a curse his captive angrily shook back the cloak's concealing hood. Caledan drew in a sharp breath. His pursuer was a woman. He scrambled quickly to his feet. The woman fought to disentangle herself from the voluminous cloak, then stood to face him. She gazed at him hotly, fire dancing in her dark, smoldering eyes. She angrily brushed her dark auburn hair from her face and planted her hands firmly on her hips.

"I'm Mari Al'maren," she said in her low, rich voice, "sent by the Harpers to find Caledan Caldorien. Satisfied?"

Caledan leaned nonchalantly against the brick wall bordering the street. His heart was beating rapidly in his chest. What would the Harpers want with him now, after all these years? His face remained impassive. "Really? So why were you following me?"

The Harper woman angrily shed the remains of her tattered cloak. Beneath she was clad in a green velvet jacket and breeches of soft buckskin that matched her boots. A small silver pin, wrought in the shape of a crescent moon encircling a harp, glistened on her collar—the sigil of the Harpers.

"I'm beginning to wonder the same thing myself," she said disgustedly. "I thought there might be a chance you were the one I was searching for."

"This . . . er . . . what did you say his name was?" Caledan asked casually.

"Caledan Caldorien," the woman who called herself Mari answered, kicking away the cloak and pacing the narrow alleyway in agitation. "Call me crazy, but with the way you dealt with that Zhen—er, that captain on the Street of Lanterns, I thought you might be Caldorien. He's supposed to have been a great hero, you know. At least, that's what all the stories tell."

"Oh, really?" Caledan asked, raising an eyebrow. No doubt they had sent Al'maren here to spy on the Zhents— that would be standard procedure—but Al'maren looked so wet behind the ears he was almost tempted to offer her a handkerchief. "So what makes you think now that I'm not the fellow you're after?" Caledan went on.

"Oh, please!" Mari said with a husky laugh, halting for a

moment to stare at Caledan. "No offense, friend, but now that I've seen you up close you look more like a vagabond cutpurse than a hero of renown."

Caledan spread out his hands. "No offense taken," he replied amiably.

"Besides, if you really were Caldorien, you'd have a set of reed pipes with you," she continued wearily. "You don't happen to play the pipes, do you, scoundrel?"

"I wouldn't know which end to blow in," Caledan said, lying smoothly.

"I didn't think so," Mari said, sighing. "Caledan Caldorien was supposed to have been the finest piper in the Realms and one of the bravest men as well. We could use his help in dealing with the . . . the city's new ruler."

Harpers, Caledan thought derisively. They send one agent on what was probably her first mission to counter a city crawling with Zhentarim. That was just like them. They were idealists almost to the point of idiocy. Mari Al'maren no doubt thought that a few old, tired ballads and a few lofty, outdated ideals were somehow enough to end all the suffering and darkness in the world. Caledan knew better. He, of all people, knew that music—and the Harpers— would never be enough.

"Well, I'm sorry to have caused you trouble, friend scoundrel," Mari continued, "though you seem to have paid me back for it." She rubbed her shoulder. "I've got to keep searching. This city is supposed to have been Caldorien's last known home, though gods know why anyone would live here." She looked distastefully around the dingy street.

"It wasn't always so bad," Caledan said, taking a step toward her. "It was beautiful once. You know, legendary Iri-aebor of the Thousand Spires."

She smiled crookedly. Mari was not a woman who would ever be accused of being pretty, Caledan thought, but there was a warmth to her smile that made him grin back. "I'll let you know if I run into this 'Caldorien' character."

"Don't bother," she replied wryly. "It's going to take me a while to heal my bruises from our first encounter. So do me a favor, friend scoundrel. Let's say farewell."

Caledan performed a stiff mock bow. "As you wish." He straightened up—and his eyes widened in shock.

Mari frowned at him in puzzlement. "What is it, scoundrel?"

"Don't look now," he whispered, "but I don't think you were the only one who has been doing a little following."

Mari spun swiftly on her heels, and the blood drained from her face. Not a hundred paces away three black dogs were loping down the alley. Each was as large as a pony, and all of them were covered with flickering crimson flames. Their eyes glowed with a deadly golden light, and their huge maws hung open, baring their fangs.

Caledan gave a low whistle. "It looks like you should have said good-bye when you had the chance, Harper."

Three

 Caledan drew his dagger from his boot as the three magical mastiffs howled, an eerie sound of fury and bloodlust.

"Please don't tell me that pig-sticker is all you've got, scoundrel," the Harper said caustically. Her movements were fluid as she unsheathed the curved, gleaming sabre belted at her hip and assumed a battle-ready stance.

"As you wish." Caledan gritted his teeth.

Mari shot him a hard look, but there was no time for a reply. The hounds were rapidly closing the distance between them. Caledan could hear the crackling of the fiery auras that surrounded the beasts. The air was charged with an acrid, sulfuric odor. He let his dagger fly in a precise arc. It struck the lead hound directly between the eyes—and then bounced harmlessly off the creature's skull.

Caledan and Mari traded desperate looks.

"These are enchanted beasts," he shouted. "I don't think

mundane weapons can harm them."

"Now you tell me," Mari said disgustedly, thrusting her sabre back into its sheath. "May I be so bold as to suggest we turn tail and run?"

"We'll never be able to outrun them."

"Well, maybe we can outclimb them."

Caledan nodded. He made a running leap onto the alley's wall and began scrambling up the crumbling, uneven stone surface. The Harper did likewise on the opposite wall. Just as Caledan was heaving himself over the top, the flaming mastiffs were upon them. One of the beasts let out a feral snarl as it leaped upward, its jaws snapping. Caledan felt its hot, scorching breath even through his boots.

Somehow he managed to heave himself onto the sooty rooftop. His heart was thumping wildly in his chest, and his breath came in searing, ragged gasps. "What in the Abyss did I ever see in this battling evil business?" he groaned as he dragged himself to his feet. He saw that the Harper had reached the rooftop across the narrow alley, no more than ten feet away. The three magical hounds circled below, snarling and growling. Hot, sizzling spittle drooled from their maws, pitting the cobblestones where it dripped.

"What now, scoundrel?" Mari called across the gap, hands on her hips.

Caledan saw a large oaken barrel perched on the rooftop a few feet away from him. It was a rain barrel, filled to the brim with cool, dark water. An idea struck him. "Harper, is there anything over there that holds water?"

Mari frowned in confusion, but she looked around the rooftop all the same. "There's a trough here with some sort of swill in it," she called across the alley. "But I wouldn't recommend it if you're thirsty. I think more than a few pigeons have been using it as their personal bath."

"It'll do. Drag it to the edge of the rooftop, and when I tell you, dump it into the alley."

Mari glared at him. "You want to give the dogs a bath?"

"Just do it, Harper," Caledan growled.

She muttered something under her breath but did as he asked all the same. The fiery mastiffs were scrabbling at the walls, getting higher with each jump. It was only a matter of moments before one of them successfully made the leap.

"Now, Harper!"

Caledan pushed over the heavy rain barrel. At the same moment Mari grunted, heaving the wooden trough onto its side. Cold water rained down on the three mastiffs. There was a deafening hissing sound as a thick cloud of steam billowed up from the alley. The hounds yelped as their flaming auras were doused and extinguished.

Caledan readied himself for a dash along the rooftops. He hoped the trick with the water would give him and the Harper a few moments' head start before they were forced to climb back down and take to the streets. Suddenly Caledan halted. He watched the magical beasts in fascination.

The mastiffs were continuing to yelp and whine, but their movements were growing slower, stiff and jerky. Steam ceased to rise from their sodden pelts. Abruptly the hounds froze in their tracks. They stood motionless for a heartbeat, and then, with a sound like breaking glass, the beasts collapsed into three heaps of jagged black shards.

Caledan shook his head in amazement. The magical beasts were dead, shattered like hot crockery immersed in cold water.

The Harper arched an eyebrow. "Not bad, scoundrel. Did you know that was going to happen?"

"Of course," he lied.

The two climbed back down into the alley. With his boot Caledan kicked apart the piles of broken shards. They rang like chimes as they skittered across the cobbles. He found his dagger and stuffed it back into its sheath in his boot.

"Well, it looks like this time it's farewell for good,
Harper," Caledan said thankfully. He had forgotten how
much trouble Harpers could be.

"And good riddance, scoundrel," Mari replied, her eyes
blazing. "Let's make certain we never—"

The Harper didn't get the chance to finish. She cried out
as a crackling bolt of crimson brilliance streaked out of a
shadowed doorway and struck her in the shoulder. The
force of the blow threw her hard against the opposite stone
wall. Her eyes fluttered shut as she slumped, motionless, to
the ground.

Without hesitating, Caledan reached down, grabbed his
dagger, and threw it spinning into the darkened doorway.
There was a soft moan, and then a sharp-faced man clad in
red robes stumbled out of the doorway and sank to the cobbles, the dagger buried deep in his chest.

Caledan swore under his breath. It seemed he had
grown stupid as well as rusty with the years. After an attack
by enchanted beasts, he should have known the wizard
who had conjured them would not be far behind. He put a
boot on the dead wizard's chest and pulled the dagger free.
Blood flowed forth, spreading its dark stain across the
ground.

"So who sent you, sorcerer?" Caledan spat, but the dead
man could not reply. Caledan was about to search the body
for some clues as to the wizard's identity, but immediately
the corpse began to steam and bubble. The wizard's body
burst into flame, and in moments there was nothing left but
ashes. Caledan muttered an oath, turning his attention to
the Harper.

She was alive, but just barely. Her skin had a deathly pal-
lor to it; her breathing was rapid and shallow. He could
barely detect her pulse. He heard the clatter of hooves
behind him and turned to see Mista trotting down the alley.

"I don't suppose I could just leave her," he said hopefully.

The mare snorted in agitation, laying her ears back. He sighed. "I didn't think so."

He lifted the Harper as gently as he could onto the gray's back and climbed into the saddle. She needed a healer, and there was only one place in the city he knew where he could take her. He spurred the mare into a brisk walk. "If I never have dealings with Harpers again, Mista," he growled as he rode, "it'll be much, much too soon."

* * * * *

Caledan took a deep breath of relief when he saw the old three-story inn at the end of the small lane. He had half expected to find it gone, what with the rest of the changes that had transformed the city. However, the half-timbered, gable-roofed inn still stood at the very western edge of the Tor. Half of the building actually jutted precariously out over the precipice, hanging in thin air where it was supported by a mazework of stout oaken beams anchored deep in the sheer rock of the cliff-face. A brightly painted sign hung above the intricately carved door, depicting an emerald green dragon dozing peacefully on a mountain of golden treasure. Caledan smiled despite himself. It was good to lay eyes on the Sign of the Dreaming Dragon again.

He dismounted and carefully lifted the Harper from Mista's back. The gray mare flared her nostrils and shifted nervously from hoof to hoof. Caledan bent his ear to the Harper's chest, then grinned at the horse.

"Fear not, friend. She still lives." Caledan carried the Harper to the stout, iron-banded door. He pushed through the doorway and into the inn.

His heart sank.

Everything was different inside. In his memories, the common room of the Dreaming Dragon was a warm place filled with firelight and the clinking of mugs, reverberating with garrulous voices, laughter, and song. This dim, sullen room was just the opposite.

The great fireplace was cold and dark, and only a few smoking oil lamps offered their wan illumination. The polished wooden bar that had once stood against one wall was now covered with dirty cloths. Lord Cutter's Rules were posted in plain view.

A handful of sour-faced cityfolk looked up from the bare tables, staring at Caledan with suspicious eyes. Grimly, he laid the limp form of the Harper down on a long bench and surveyed the scene. The longer he looked, the worse it seemed. This place had been his home once. Now it was almost as inviting as a dungeon, but not quite.

"Listen, stranger, we don't want any trouble here."

Caledan turned around and found himself looking down at a stout, curly-haired halfling. The halfling's nut-brown eyes glittered warily, and his broad face was drawn down in a scowl. He stood firm, raised to his full four feet, gripping a cudgel in one hand. "This is a respectable establishment. At least as respectable as you can find these days. We post the city lord's rules for all to see. You'd best be off, ruffian. Work your mischief elsewhere."

Caledan winced. Ruffian? He rubbed the dark stubble on his chin. He was going to have to do something about his appearance.

"Friend," he said wearily, "I have a lady here who's been gravely hurt. Once there was a healer who lived here, a woman who would never have turned away one in need. Has she vanished as well, like everything else of good in this city?"

The halfling's gaze took in the limp form of the Harper, and his wide-spaced brown eyes softened somewhat, though they remained resolute. "Come back in the morning."

"Gods, man, she may not have until morning!" Caledan

bellowed in exasperation. He took an angry step forward. A half-dozen chairs scraped against the floor as an equal number of burly men stood, glaring at Caledan. He froze. It looked as if this was about to turn nasty. He crouched, ready to give his best before he was dragged down.

Suddenly a halfling woman clad in a gray homespun dress entered the inn's common room from the kitchen, a startled expression on her kindly face. "Jolle, what is it?"

"Stay back, wife!" the halfling man told her, lifting his cudgel, but before he could swing it the halfling woman let out a cry and dashed forward, throwing herself at Caledan. Caledan nearly tumbled backward from the impact. Then he caught himself and returned her embrace.

"By the Lady above, Caledan!" the halfling woman cried, caught between laughter and tears. "You've come home. You've come home!"

Caledan cast a wry grin at the halfling man in answer to the fellow's look of bewilderment. "It's good to see you after all these years, Estah," he said, hugging the halfling woman tightly. "Especially when so much has changed. But I've someone here who needs your attention more than I."

"Oh, by the Lady!" Estah said, letting go of Caledan and only just now seeing the still form of the Harper lying on the bench. Concern flooded her deep brown eyes and touched her broad, rosy-cheeked face. She laid a small hand gently on the Harper's pale brow. "My pretty child," she said, and then she assumed an air of briskness. "How like you, Caledan Caldorien, to drag a poor lass about when she's hurt like this. Now don't be in my way. I've work to do."

Estah promptly began running her hands over the unconscious Harper, expertly feeling for injury. Caledan looked at the halfling man—evidently Estah's husband—and shrugged.

"We're old friends, Estah and I," was all Caledan said.

The halfling man whom Estah had called Jolle simply nodded and lowered his cudgel. "Then you're welcome here, friend."

As if on cue, the room suddenly burst into action. "Coast's clear!" a man keeping watch out the window called. With a swiftness and efficiency that suggested the movements were well rehearsed, the inn's patrons proceeded to transform the common room. Bright cloths were spread across the tables, candles were lit, and a fire sprang to life on the hearth. The dirty cloths were snatched from the long wooden bar and quickly stowed away. The board bearing Lord Cutter's Rules was turned around to reveal a notice that read: Ale, Two Silver Pieces. Stout mugs clinked together merrily as they were filled to the brim with foaming brew.

"Welcome to the Dreaming Dragon, stranger," a grizzled fellow said as he handed Caledan a tankard.

The only answer Caledan could manage was an amazed smile. It looked as if some things hadn't changed so much after all.

* * * * *

It was well into the morning when Caledan awoke. Pale, golden sunlight streamed through the small round window of his third-story room—the same room that had been his when he had lived in the inn, in the days when he had been a Harper, and Estah had been his oldest and truest adventuring companion. He rose, washed his face in a tin basin, and scraped the dark stubble from his chin and cheeks with a straight razor he found in a drawer. He laughed, and the reflection in the mirror laughed silently back at him, green eyes dancing.

Last night Estah had tended to the Harper woman, Mari, in her efficient, caring manner. Mari's shoulder had been dislocated by the wizard's magical bolt, and the shock had jolted her into unconsciousness. However, the halfling healer had inspected the wound and announced that it was not dire. She had deftly pushed the joint back together—Caledan was rather glad the Harper was not conscious for that—and then from beneath her own blouse had drawn a small, intricately wrought silver amulet.

It was engraved with the flowing symbol of Eldath, the Goddess of the Singing Waters. Caledan had seen the amulet on too many occasions, when he or one of his other traveling companions had been wounded in battle. It had been given to Estah by her mother, and while in most hands it would have been but a pretty, lifeless piece of metal, Caledan knew that in the hands of a true healer the amulet had impressive powers. When Estah laid it on the Harper's shoulder Caledan thought he heard a faint musical humming. The Harper's brow—furrowed in pain, even in unconsciousness—relaxed, and her breathing grew deep and even.

They had carried the Harper upstairs to sleep, and then Caledan and Estah, along with her husband Jolle, had sat by the flickering fire, talking late into the night. They spoke of the seven years since Caledan and his band of companions had separated and gone their different ways.

He had met them, one by one, in his missions as a Harper agent, and each—for his or her own reasons—had chosen to throw in with him. Their journeys had taken them across the length of the Realms, fighting tyranny wherever they found it, and over time they had become more than simply friends. They were a family. They had called themselves the Fellowship of the Dreaming Dragon, for the six of them had all resided in this very inn that Estah still owned.

But all of that had been before Lord Ravendas, before Caledan had buried hope and music in the hard earth and had left the Harpers behind him. Seven years ago the Fellowship had disbanded, and all Caledan had tried to do since was forget the past.

"But you didn't forget," Estah had said, placing her hand on Caledan's. "And now you've come home."

Caledan sighed. Home to what? Estah married Jolle a few years after the Fellowship had disbanded. Now the two of them spent their time struggling to keep the city guards from harrowing the inn, not an easy task in these difficult times. They did their best to foster the illusion that they obeyed Cutter's rules, all the while secretly maintaining the inn as a refuge for the cityfolk, a place where they could still find a pleasant hint of the days when Bron had ruled in the tower. "I'll choke on her rules before I take a single word of them to heart," Estah had said, her eyes flashing.

Ravendas and her Zhentarim servants had taken over Iriaebor about a year ago and had been steadily sapping the life out of the city ever since. If Ravendas caught sight of Estah, the Zhentarim lord was bound to recognize the halfling healer from her encounter with the Fellowship seven years ago. That would spell the end of the Dreaming Dragon.

"But not if I can help it," Caledan growled to no one in particular. Then he laughed grimly at himself. That sounded like something Caledan the Harper would have said. He had always been so ready to play the hero. Fool was more like it.

He pulled on his black leather breeches and the matching jerkin over his white shirt. He jammed his feet into his boots, checking to make sure his dagger was in its sheath. He was about to head downstairs when the door to his room burst open.

Two very small people bounded through the doorway, laughing and giggling. They were Estah's children, Pog and Nog. Caledan had been surprised when Estah had introduced him to them the night before.

"It's time for breakfast, Uncle Caledan," said Pog. She was the elder of the two, pretty yet impish.

"Eth, geckfebst!" echoed Nog. He was the younger, a tiny, round-cheeked boy who spoke in a language only Estah and Jolle seemed capable of deciphering.

Caledan let Pog and Nog lead him down the back stairway that led to a private chamber situated behind the common room. Neither one of them stood higher than his knee, and he felt like a great behemoth towering above them. Deciding Estah would be angry if he stepped on one of them, he grabbed both children and stuffed one under each arm. They squirmed and squealed a great deal, but he let them go when he reached the foot of the stairs. They promptly forgot their big new friend—much to his relief—and scampered off, probably to torture each other, or whatever it was children did. This uncle business was going to take some getting used to.

Jolle had suggested that both he and the Harper keep to the back room in the wing of the inn that jutted out over the edge of the Tor. Given yesterday's incident, it seemed best for Caledan and Mari to keep a low profile.

Caledan saw that the Harper was sitting in a chair pulled close to a small fireplace. She was wrapped in a patchwork quilt, and still seemed a bit pale, but otherwise looked little the worse for wear. Estah was with her, and Caledan found himself slightly perturbed to see the two talking animatedly. He ambled over and sat next to them. The Harper's smile quickly vanished as Estah looked at him worriedly.

"You might have told me, scoundrel," Mari said sullenly.

"Would you have believed me?" Caledan asked her with a wry expression. He winked at Estah. "I seem to remember someone saying I looked more like, let's see . . . what was it? Ah yes, more like a 'vagabond cutpurse than a hero of renown.'"

Mari frowned at this, but after a moment she began to

laugh. "It's true, you know. Though you are looking a bit
more presentable today. I see you actually have a face
beneath those mangy bristles."

Estah smiled hopefully at Caledan and then left them
alone to discuss their "Harpery business" as she had
always called it.

"You still look more like a highwayman than a hero,"
Mari added stingingly after the halfling was gone.

"Listen," Caledan said, anger suddenly flaring in his
chest. "I'm sorry that I'm not the storybook knight you
were expecting, but let me set one thing straight. I am not a
Harper anymore. Nor do I wish to have dealings with them.
When I left the order seven years ago, it was final. Is that
understood?"

"Really?" she asked archly. "If you cared so little, why
didn't you simply leave me there in the alley, Caldorien? It
would have saved you some trouble."

"Gods, woman. I saved your life, and all you can do is
mock me for it?"

She lifted her square chin defiantly. "For that I thank
you," she said stiffly, "but from now on you needn't concern
yourself about me. Next time you may be the one who
needs rescuing."

"Is that so?" Caledan sneered. "Well, maybe you wouldn't
find yourself on the wrong end of a wizard's magic if you
tried to be a little less conspicuous. Didn't the Harpers have
the sense to teach you to keep that blasted sigil under
cover? Or did you think that if you wore it in plain view all
the Zhentarim agents would simply flee in terror? Who is
your prime master, anyway?"

Mari's eyes smoldered, but she did not flinch beneath his
harsh words. "Belhuar Thantarth, Master of Twilight Hall,
gave me this mission."

Caledan grunted. He remembered Thantarth. Seven
years ago Thantarth had been a journeyman Harper, but

even then he had the kind of ambition and staunch—if overly idealistic—values the Harpers treasured so much. No wonder Thantarth had risen to the highest seat in Twilight Hall in the city of Berdusk, to the west of Iriaebor. It didn't surprise Caledan that Mari had been sent by Twilight Hall. That bunch believed in giving their new agents a trial by fire. The Harpers of Shadowdale were a more impromptu and secretive lot. They would never have let someone as green as Al'maren journey alone to a city crawling with Zhentarim.

"Let me guess," Caledan said flatly. "This is your first mission." Mari said nothing, her hands clenched into fists. Both of them knew he was right. "You know," Caledan went on a bit smugly, "you still haven't told me why you were searching for me in the first place."

The Harper looked away, gazing out a window into the morning light. On the plains below the Tor sprawled the New City like the shining but deadly web of some vast spider. "It's simple enough," she explained, turning to regard Caledan once more. "You don't think that the Harpers would simply stand by idly while the Zhentarim enslaved the richest trade city between the Sword Coast and the Moonsea, do you?"

"No, I suppose that would be too much for a bunch of meddlers like the Harpers." Caledan laughed grimly.

Mari shot him a fiery look. "These 'meddlers,' as you call them, are all that stand between the Zhentarim and the Realms. If not for the Harpers, the Black Network would not stop until it ruled every land. Would you be a slave to the Zhentarim, Caldorien?"

He had no reply to that.

"Anyway," Mari went on, "the Harpers sent me here to spy on Lord Cutter—that is, Lord Ravendas—and the Zhentarim. We need to learn how their operations work here, discover what their weaknesses are, and devise a way to help the people of Iriaebor drive them from the city. At the same time, I was supposed to search for the *legendary* Caledan Caldorien, even though he had not been heard from in seven years." She eyed his frayed and road-worn clothes disapprovingly. "But it seems I've failed in that part of the mission."

"Why? You found me, didn't you?"

"Really?" Mari scoffed. "I was searching for a Harper, Caldorien. What I found was a worn-out drifter who doesn't seem to care about anything, least of all himself."

Caledan winced. That one hurt, especially because it came dangerously near the truth.

"I don't know the reason you left the Harpers, Caldorien, and now I find that I don't particularly care. I thank you for your assistance yesterday, but I won't bother you again." She shrugged off the quilt and rose stiffly.

"Sit down, Harper."

"What?"

"I said *sit down*," Caledan growled fiercely, and in her surprise Mari complied, sinking back down into the chair. "Maybe you don't want my help anymore," he went on, "and I don't want yours, either. But there is something you should know. Lord Ravendas and I have . . . encountered each other in the past." He laughed darkly. "This was during my last mission as a Harper. It was not a pleasant meeting. Someone . . . a friend of mine . . . died that day. But I think I always knew that someday I would face Ravendas again. Now it seems that the time has come, and the meeting is destined to be here."

He stared fiercely at the Harper, as if daring her to question his resolve. "I had the chance to be happy once, you know. Ravendas stole that from me. I won't let her do it a second time."

Mari regarded him carefully for a long moment, her expression guarded. "So you will work with me then, Caledan Caldorien?" she asked finally.

He let out a twisted laugh. "Oh, no, Harper. *You're* going to be working with *me*."

*   *   *   *   *

The crescent moon was just rising over the city's spires when Caledan and Mari slipped out a side door of the Dreaming Dragon and into the walled garden Estah kept behind the inn. Caledan searched along the high stone wall until he found what he was looking for—a small wrought-iron gate overgrown with morning glories. The secret portal led into a narrow alleyway behind the inn.

"Are you going to tell me where we're going, Caldorien?" Mari asked as they made their way down the shadowed alley. "Or is this supposed to be some sort of surprise?"

Caledan grimaced. Why did the Harper always have to make such an issue out of everything? "We're going to see an old acquaintance of mine. His name is Cormik. In fact, I was on my way to pay him a visit when I had the misfortune to cross paths with you."

The alley opened onto a larger avenue. Making certain no guards were about, the two headed on foot deeper into the heart of the Old City. The streets were deserted. It was the hour for thieves and murderers. And Harpers and scoundrels, Caledan thought wryly.

"And what does this Cormik do?" Mari asked softly.

"You might call him an entrepreneur," Caledan whispered back. "Then again, you might call him a greedy, self-centered, crooked-hearted swindler." He laughed quietly. "It just depends on how much you like him . . . and on whether he likes you."

"Sounds enchanting," Mari muttered. "So how many daggers are we going to get stuck in our backs?"

"You worry too much, Harper. Cormik and I have been

friends for years. If you really want to learn something about the Zhentarim operations in the city, there's no one better to talk to. If Cormik doesn't know about it, it isn't happening." *If he's still alive, that is,* Caledan added to himself. Cormik's line of business was not without its risks.

Mari shot him a skeptical look but said nothing the rest of the way. Finally they turned onto the murky, refuse-lined Street of Lanterns. They halted before a dark storefront. The building looked as though it had been abandoned for years, but Caledan knew better. The place was a discreet gambling establishment called the Prince and Pauper.

"Just follow my lead," Caledan said jauntily. Before she could reply, he opened the door and stepped through. Mari followed on his heels.

Inside was a large room. The light of a few torches was mostly lost in the haze of smoke they gave off. The Prince and Pauper was crowded. It appeared this was one establishment that had lost little of its trade since Cutter had become lord of the city. True to the place's name, nobles in fine but threadbare clothes, opulently attired merchants, and every manner of rabble crowded about the gambling tables, shouting, laughing, or crying as best suited their luck.

Caledan ignored the gamblers. He spotted a heavy velvet curtain in the back wall and began wending his way through the crowd toward it. Mari followed, a look of disapproval on her face. Caledan reached the curtain and flipped it back. He and the Harper stepped into the quiet hallway beyond.

"Stop right there," a huge, bull-necked man clad in crimson leather rumbled. "I don't know you two, do I?" He stood blocking the hallway with a companion who was similarly dressed and likewise massive. Both wore short swords at their hips, and there was no doubt that they knew quite well how to use them.

"Name's Caledan. I'm a friend of Cormik's. And this here's my lady, if you know what I mean." Mari opened her mouth in protest, but Caledan elbowed her hard in the side. She threw him a venomous look but held her tongue.

"A friend of the Master, eh?" The big man leered down at Caledan. "Well, you'd better hope to the gods that you are. Follow me." The huge man led Caledan and Mari to a small but plush room.

"The Master will see you when he has a minute," he said with an unpleasant grin. "He's a busy man, you know." He left the room, shutting the small door behind him. Caledan didn't have to try the latch to know that it was locked.

Mari crossed her arms, pacing the small room in agitation. "Now what?" she demanded.

"Just wait, Harper. Just wait."

Scant minutes later a key rattled in the lock, and the door opened. A man, who might have appeared nondescript if not for his ostentatious clothes and black velvet eye patch, stepped through, followed by the two muscular bodyguards. "Well, well," the man said in an oily voice as he examined the prisoners with a critical eye. "So Jad was right. It truly is Caledan the Harper."

"Cormik," Caledan said, smiling broadly. "I knew you'd remember me. I have a favor to ask of you."

"Oh, I remember you quite well, Caledan," Cormik replied. He approached slowly, moving, despite his large girth, with the predatory grace of a cat. "In fact, after that last time we met, I remember that I wanted you dead."

Caledan laughed, as if he had just heard a good joke. "I would have thought you had forgotten that little misunderstanding by now, Cormik."

Cormik returned the laughter. "What a curious notion, Caledan. Gentlemen." He made a brief motion with his hand. Before either Caledan or Mari could move, each was grabbed by one of the bodyguards, and their arms were tightly pinned behind their backs. Both Caledan and Mari struggled, to no avail, while Cormik's laughter filled the room.

It appeared that they were prisoners.

Four

 "I thought you said the man adored you."

Cormik's hulking bodyguards had chained the two of them to a cold stone wall in a dim, squalid little chamber beneath the Prince and Pauper.

"Everyone's entitled to a few mistakes," Caledan muttered. His hands were chained over his head; his shoulders were throbbing painfully. His joints were getting far too rusty for this kind of abuse, and his brain must be getting rusty as well. He should not have assumed that Cormik would have forgotten their little "misunderstanding" of seven years ago. The proprietor of the Prince and Pauper was well known to have a long, keen memory. One had to in his business.

"So what did you do, scoundrel, that he still holds a grudge against you after all these years?"

"I saved him from being murdered by one of his patrons, that's what," Caledan replied angrily. "A nobleman named Maderon owed Cormik a king's ransom in gambling debts,

and he was going to have Cormik killed rather than pay up.
I did Cormik the favor of doing away with Maderon first,
though I had my own reasons. All Cormik knew was that I
had slit the throat of his richest patron. Cormik's an intelli-
gent man, but he has me figured all wrong."

"What do you think he's going to do with us?" she asked.

"Kill us," Caledan replied flatly.

They were interrupted by the sound of the lock once
again being turned. The iron-banded door flew open, and
Caledan squinted as brilliant, golden light flooded the small
prison chamber. After a moment his eyes adjusted, and he
saw Cormik standing before him wearing an unsavory grin.
He was flanked by his two bodyguards, as well as by a
lanky young man with black hair and eyes.

"I trust my retainers treated you well in my absence?"
Cormik asked.

"But of course." Caledan rattled his chains, smiling face-
tiously. "You're too good to your guests, Cormik."

Cormik bowed his head in acknowledgment, his one eye
glittering. "Nothing is too good for an old . . . friend."

Caledan took a deep breath. "Cormik, if you'd just let me
explain—"

"Silence!" the man snapped. The bodyguards took a step
forward, hands on the hilts of their short swords. Cormik
held up a neatly manicured, ring-covered hand. "No, I shall
deal with him in my own manner." The hand dropped casually down to the hilt of a stiletto at his belt. The knife was a
delicate, beautifully crafted thing with pale opals set into
the hilt. "You may leave me, gentlemen. Dario and I will
attend to business here." The two bodyguards lumbered
out of the room, shutting the door behind them.

"Cormik," Caledan tried again, forcing an expansive
smile, "if you would just give me a chance to tell my side of
the story, I'm sure—"

"Spare me your lies, Caledan. I haven't the time, and

frankly neither do you or your friend here." He smoothly slipped the jeweled stiletto out of its sheath. "Be so good as to help me with this, Dario."

The dark-haired young man grasped Caledan's shackled wrist firmly. Caledan's eyes widened. Mari stared at the scene in horror.

"Cormik, please. If you'd just—"

"That's the trouble with Harpers, Dario. They never stop talking, even when you desperately wish they would." Cormik poised the blade inches from Caledan's wrist. "That's good, Dario, hold it steady."

Caledan clenched his jaw. He was determined not to beg. Then he watched in amazement as Cormik deftly turned the knife, pressing one of the polished opals. There was a small click, and a thin piece of metal popped out of the end of the hilt. It was a key.

Caledan's jaw went slack. He stared as the man he'd just thought was going to kill him removed the shackle instead. Quickly Cormik unlocked the rest of the chains, and in moments Caledan stood free, absently rubbing his sore wrists. Cormik released Mari next, chuckling. Then he slipped the dagger into his belt once again.

"You old wolf, it's good to see you," Cormik exclaimed. He grasped Caledan's hand firmly between his own beefy palms and squeezed it warmly.

A smile slowly crept across Caledan's face.

Cormik's eyes glittered. "Come drink a cup of wine with me while I explain." His gaze turned to Mari, and a sly smile crept across his lips. "And perhaps you'll introduce me to your charming companion."

A few minutes later found them in a richly appointed chamber hung with expensive Sembian tapestries. Cormik bade them sit down while Dario poured them each a goblet of deep red wine from a crystal decanter.

Caledan swirled the ruby-colored liquid a bit suspiciously. "Nothing unpleasant at the bottom, I trust?"

"Not unless my good Dario put it there. However, I may simply be an old fool, but I believe the lad's loyal to me."

"One of his many delusions," the young man said with such perfect seriousness that Caledan was almost taken aback. Then he saw the mischief dancing in the young man's dark eyes.

The wine proved to be cool and delicious, and Caledan took the liberty of refilling his goblet as Cormik talked.

"I hope you'll forgive my rude treatment," he said, his attention directed more toward Mari than Caledan. "I'm afraid it was necessary to protect myself, and both of you as well. I couldn't let it look as if I was consorting with Harpers. It's a well-known fact that Cutter—or should I say Ravendas?—is not overly fond of Harpers. Except for dead ones, of course."

"I'm afraid you're mistaken," Mari said with an expression of disarming innocence, "but I'm not a—"

"Don't be coy, Harper Al'maren," Cormik said with a low chuckle. "I'm afraid neither you nor Caledan has been terribly inconspicuous these past few days. I've intercepted reports concerning both of you that were bound for the city lord's tower, and I'm certain Ravendas knows of your presence."

"I agree," Caledan said grimly. "I had the misfortune of being too close to the Harper yesterday when a wizard, probably Zhentarim, loosed a trio of magical hounds after her. We came very close to being incinerated and eaten."

"Actually, Caledan," Cormik said gravely, "I don't think that attack was directed at Harper Al'maren."

A startled look crossed Mari's face. Caledan frowned. "And what tells you that?"

"This." Cormik drew a piece of parchment out of a pocket of his voluminous embroidered silk tunic and laid it on the table. "It was posted down in the New City, in the free market, along with dozens of others like it. It's a notice offering a reward for any information concerning your whereabouts, Caledan. And the reward is not an inconsiderable sum. Surely you didn't think your duel with Cutter's captain went unnoticed the other night."

Caledan grunted.

Mari took the parchment and studied it carefully. She looked up and regarded Caledan with concerned eyes. "What would Ravendas want with you, Caledan? You've said it yourself. You're not a Harper anymore, and no threat to her."

Caledan shook his head. "I can't read her mind, Harper."

"Well," Cormik went on, "I hope you can see that I was simply protecting myself by treating you openly like enemies. Since Cutter took over the city a year or so ago, mine is one of the few businesses that's avoided any trouble. And it's not because I've been pandering to Cutter or that new lord steward, ah, what's his name?" Cormik looked to Dario, then snapped his fingers before the young man could answer. "Snake, that's it. Odd name. Odd fellow. He gives me the chills just to look at him."

Cormik sipped his wine. "Luckily, that old 'misunderstanding' of ours was public enough that folks won't think it odd if I still consider you an enemy, Caledan."

Caledan nodded. "But you're not still angry over all that, are you, Cormik?"

Cormik gave a rumbling laugh. "I know very well—and always have—that Maderon meant to kill me. He simply owed me too much money to let me live. I had everything planned and taken care of. And then you had to meddle in my affairs. How like a Harper."

"What does it matter who killed him?" Caledan asked with a shrug. "Dead is dead."

"Quite," Cormik said dryly, sipping his wine. "Except that I had devised a little scheme to relieve him of the rest of his fortune before I relieved him of his ability to go on breathing. You cost me quite a bit, you know. And don't try to tell me you only did it to protect me. It would be very touching, but it would also be untruthful. You had your own reasons for doing away with Maderon. I know that, even if I don't know what those reasons were."

"Believe me, it's a tale you don't want to hear." Caledan sighed, fidgeting absently with the braided copper bracelet on his left wrist.

"Fair enough," Cormik said, then he changed the subject. "Perhaps now you can tell me what brought you to my doorstep this time. I'd like to think it was because you've missed me, but I suppose that would be another one of my 'delusions.'" He looked at Dario pointedly. Cormik motioned his apprentice over, and whispered something into Dario's ear. After a moment the young man nodded.

"It was nice to meet you," he said, smiling as he bowed to Caledan and Mari. Then he exited the chamber by way of a secret passage concealed behind a bookcase.

"Very well, Cormik," Mari said after Dario had gone. "We came because we need information about Ravendas and the Zhentarim."

Caledan rolled his eyes. There went their chances of getting anything out of Cormik for free. The Harper was going to have to learn how to be more clever when bargaining with someone like Cormik.

"All right, Cormik," Caledan grumbled, "how much is it going to cost us?"

"For you, Caledan, the standard fee." Cormik's gaze swept over Mari. "But for the enchanting Harper, there's no charge."

"Why, thank you," she said huskily, treating Caledan to a look that was insufferably smug.

They spent the next hour listening to Cormik describe the steady decay of the city since Ravendas had ensconced herself in the tower. "Things are dire enough as it is, and I'm afraid they're only getting worse by the day," Cormik said grimly. "The stalls in the free market are practically bare. Half the folk in the city are bordering on starvation. Almost everything that comes to Iriaebor by ship goes out again in caravans to the east. And there isn't a business that's not under her control. She keeps the Council of Lords in her pocket and has the Merchants' Circle dangling by their purse strings. The terms of her trade agreements are anything but profitable, but inexplicable things keep happening to the ships and caravans of merchants who don't sign on.

"There's only one rule in Iriaebor these days. Serve Cutter or perish." Cormik sighed. "None of it is good for business. And it gets even worse when your customers keep disappearing daily."

"Disappearing?" Caledan asked. He felt his hair prickling on the back of his neck.

Cormik nodded. "Every day dozens of cityfolk leave their homes in the morning and don't come back at night. Men and women, even children. Anyone out on the streets, especially at night, seems to be fair game. The Zhentarim are kidnapping them and spiriting them away to the dungeons below the tower. Why, I'm not entirely certain. There are rumors that Ravendas is pressing them into work gangs and forcing them to toil on a series of excavations deep in the heart of the Tor itself. However, if that's really the case, I have no idea what she thinks she'll find by digging beneath the tower."

"Gold?" Caledan ventured.

Cormik shrugged. "Maybe."

Mari stood up and began pacing on the thick carpets strewn across the floor. "This can't go on," she said, striking her palm with a fist. "Why have the people of Iriaebor put up with this for so long? There can't be more than a few hundred Zhents in the city, but there are tens of thousands of citizens. Why don't the people of Iriaebor rise up against Ravendas?"

Cormik shook his head ruefully. "I wish it were that simple, Harper. At first a few people—merchants, guild masters, and lords of the council—did stand up to Ravendas. It didn't take long before every one of them was swinging by the neck from a gibbet. Ravendas makes an example out of anyone who opposes her.

"Of course, there are still a few bands of folk who are trying to work against Ravendas," Cormik went on, his tone purposeful. "I hear reports about them from time to time. They meet in secret here and there about the city, in basements and abandoned towers. But there are only a few of these groups, and they're small. They need weapons, hiding places, a way to transport messages and supplies, and more recruits. These things cost money. Lots of it."

Caledan stood up, a roguish expression on his face. "All right, Cormik. Use your scouts to start making contact with a few of these resistance bands. The Harper and I will get you the gold you need to arm and organize them."

"That sounds well and fine, Caldorien," Mari said in a scathing voice. "But how do you propose we get this gold? Shall we just go begging at Ravendas's money house?"

Caledan snapped his fingers. "That's not a bad idea, Harper."

"Careful, Caledan," Cormik said seriously. "You'd do well if you didn't underestimate Ravendas. Or the Harper here. Get the gold if you can, and I'll do my part. But try not to get yourself killed in the process."

Caledan was about to reply when a light knock came at the hidden entrance behind the bookcase. The shelves swung to one side, and Dario stepped through. Caledan gaped at the young man. He was dressed identically to Caledan, in black leather breeches and jerkin over a white shirt.

"Ah, I see you're ready," Cormik said, smiling.

"What's going on?" Caledan asked suspiciously.

"You're going on a little trip, Caledan. You see, in my eminent mercifulness, I decided not to run you through on the sole condition that you leave Iriaebor—and don't come back. That should keep up my appearances."

"But I'm not leaving Iriaebor," Caledan said angrily, clenching his big-knuckled hand into a fist.

Cormik groaned. "Must you be so dense, Caledan? That's where Dario comes in." He eyed the young man critically. "You're not a bad match for size, Dario. Of course, you're not nearly as ugly as Caledan is, but that would be almost impossible, wouldn't it?"

Mari laughed with amusement.

"I'll pull my hood up," Dario said with a wink at Caledan. "Assuming you'll allow me to borrow your cloak to complete the disguise, of course."

"Here, take it," Caledan growled petulantly, handing Dario his patched, midnight-blue cloak. The young man donned the cloak and pulled the hood over his head.

"Perfect," Cormik pronounced. "Are you ready to ride? Excellent. Have Jad and Kevrek throw you out—not too roughly. Just enough to let my patrons see how much I still despise Caledan the Harper. There's a gray mare similar to Caledan's tied out front. Make certain the guards see you riding out of town. I want all who might be interested to believe Caledan Caldorien is gone for good."

"As you wish, Master Cormik," Dario said, bowing with a flourish. He turned and disappeared through the hidden doorway.

"Do you trust him?" Caledan asked after Dario had gone.

"Better yet, I care for him," Cormik replied. "He's the son I never had, Caledan. But then, I don't suppose you'd care about such sentimental things."

Caledan grunted but said nothing.

* * * * *

"I want the Harpers out of my city!"

The Zhentarim Lord Ravendas was not in a pleasant mood. She prowled like a cat about the topmost chamber of the tower of the city lord. The chamber itself was a den of luxury. Snow white furs were strewn across the floor of dark, polished marble. Exotic tapestries woven with gold and silver draped the walls, and expensive incense scented the air. Ravendas spun to fix the lord steward with her ice-blue gaze.

"Do I make myself clear?" she hissed, her voice as chilling as her eyes. "I will not have their meddling undermine my control. I want the head of any Harper that dares to set foot within the walls of this city delivered to me on a silver tray."

"Including Caldorien's?" the lord steward, Snake, asked in his dry, sibilant voice. His tone was utterly deferential, but Ravendas's pale cheeks flushed with sudden rage.

"I should have you flogged for that impertinence, my lord steward," she snarled. She sat upon a velvet divan, smoothing the wrinkles from her crimson gown. "And perhaps I will do just that," she mused. "You know very well that I want Caldorien delivered to me undamaged."

Snake's expression remained impassive. "But pain is acceptable, my lord?" Snake inquired.

"Oh, yes," Ravendas crooned. Sudden fire sparked in her eyes. "Pain is quite acceptable when dealing with Caldorien." Her delicate hands clenched unconsciously. It had been seven years since she had last faced Caledan Caldorien, but the memory had if anything grown more vivid with the passing of time. Seven years ago she had raised an army to conquer a town called Hluthvar, but Caldorien and his Harper friends had defeated her, making a mockery of her power. That was an affront she would dearly love to repay.

Fate must favor her, she thought, to have brought Caldorien back to Iriaebor, practically to her doorstep. At first, when the reports of a troublesome stranger reached her, she had not thought of Caldorien. Then came the sudden, violent death of one of her captains on the Street of Jewels. Her lord steward was not without his uses, and by means of a magic created from the dead warrior's blood, Snake had conjured an image of the captain's killer. She had recognized the angular, wolfish face instantly. It was Caldorien. He was in the city—*her* city. But where?

She would find him. The intervening years had made her more powerful than she would have once dared to imagine. Caldorien would not defeat her again. No, this time he would become her slave.

"You are dismissed, my lord steward." She spoke harshly. "Do not forget your orders." The thin, almost skeletal man bowed deeply, then turned to leave the chamber, his green robes hissing against the marble floor. "And, Snake," Ravendas called after him, "send my son to me. I wish to hear him practice his music."

"Of course, my lord. I shall send for him immediately." The door shut, leaving Ravendas alone. She poured herself a goblet of crimson wine and gazed out the window, surveying the city that she had vanquished. Every building, every stone, every *life* down there was hers, hers to exploit or destroy as she saw fit. But even that was nothing to what was next. Soon, very soon, the other lords among the Zhentarim would quail before her. It was Ravendas's destiny to rule them all.

She heard the door open softly behind her and set down her goblet, smiling with lips stained red by the wine. She turned to see a boy standing in the doorway, his skin as pale as moonlight, his hair as dark as shadows. He regarded her with wide green eyes, clutching a set of reed pipes in his small hands.

"Come in, my son," Ravendas whispered. "Come in."

* * * * *

Dario rode through the pearly, predawn light. The dim silhouette of Iriaebor rose behind him in the misty air, like a spectral city. Cormik's plan had gone well. The little scene with Jad and Kevrek had caught the eye of a Zhentarim officer who had followed Dario until he rode out the city's north gate. After that, the guard had turned around and ridden back into the city. Dario had no doubt that a message would make its way to Lord Cutter's tower that Caledan Caldorien had been driven out of Iriaebor. Dario would ride a bit farther and lie low for a day or so before returning—without his disguise, of course. There was a small village a few leagues to the north. Dario had made the acquaintance of a certain farmer's daughter there a few years back, a fair-haired young woman named Adalae. Dario wondered if she would remember him.

"Caledan the Harper?" a voice spoke suddenly from the mist.

Dario's mare spooked, rearing. He fought with the reins, managing to bring the horse to a stop. Its hooves skittered nervously against the cobbles of the road.

"Who's there?" Dario called into the thick fog. His dagger was ready in his hand.

A tall figure, clad head to toe in a black, concealing robe, stepped out of the swirling mist.

"Caledan the Harper?" the stranger asked again, in a voice that was both cold and dry. It sent a shiver up Dario's spine.

"Who wishes to know?" Dario asked, confused at the fear he felt rising in his throat.

"*I* wish to know," the black-robed figure said. Dario began to lift his dagger in alarm, but with dizzying speed a long arm reached out and, with terrible strength, pulled Dario from his horse. The mare neighed in terror and galloped away. An icy, strangely smooth hand closed about Dario's throat. His eyes widened in terror, but he was unable to move.

Another hand pulled the hood of Dario's cloak away from his face. A cold finger traced a line down his cheek. Dario tried to scream, but no sound escaped his throat.

"No, you are not the one," the attacker hissed.

Cold fingers closed about Dario's neck. There was a wet, snapping sound, and the young man fell limply to the ground, dark eyes staring lifelessly into the silvery light.

The black-robed stranger hesitated a moment. This was odd. The man's cloak had smelled right, but there was no scent of the shadow magic.

Of course—there could be only one answer. This man was a decoy. Caldorien must still be within the city's walls.

This was troublesome. The stranger dared not enter the city. No, the stinking streets were too much. Their scents were too overpowering. They would cause torment, resulting in sure madness. There was nothing to do now but wait. Yes, wait. Eventually Caldorien would set foot beyond those walls, and when he did, the stranger would be there to greet him.

Silently the black-robed figure drifted back into the veils of mist from which it had emerged just as the first rays of sunlight set fire to the tops of the city's towers.

Five

The crimson fire of sunset was fading to ash-gray behind the dark silhouette of the Tor when Mari heard the clatter of horses' hooves and the creak of wagon wheels. She waited in the shadows to the side of one of the New City's broad, tree-lined avenues, trying to slow the beating of her heart. She could only hope that Caldorien was ready. He had done little enough to inspire her trust these last days.

Mari had been elated when Belhuar Thantarth, the Master of Twilight Hall, had given her the task of finding Caldorien in Iriaebor. It was her first important mission as a true Harper, and she had been anxious to prove herself. Now she was having second thoughts. This cynical, ill-mannered, scruffy-looking scoundrel was not the legendary Harper she had been led to expect.

Old Master Andros, the Harper who had been her mentor, used to tell her stories of Caldorien's adventures: how he had destroyed the Cult of Bane's plan to seize the throne

of the Empire of Amn; how he had freed an army enslaved
by a bloodthirsty Calimshite sorcerer; how he had rescued
hundreds of children who had been kidnapped from Waterdeep and forced to work in a goblin prince's mines. As a
child, such tales had enthralled Mari. But she was no
longer a child, and Caldorien obviously was not the hero he
once was.

A wagon appeared on the dusky avenue, drawn by a pair
of dark horses. On it sat two men. One held the reins, the
other rested a hand comfortably on the hilt of his short
sword. Zhentarim soldiers. The wagon itself was a box-
shaped rig, like a gypsy wagon, and Mari knew that within
it was a valuable cargo. Mari and Caledan had met with one
of Cormik's countless spies that morning. The woman had
told them that a wagon entered the city's east gate every
evening bearing stiff tariffs that Cutter's men had extracted
from caravans that tried to bypass the city on their journey
toward Cormyr.

Unfortunately, the information about Cutter's tax collec-
tors wasn't the only news Mari and Caledan had learned at
the Prince and Pauper. The body of Cormik's apprentice,
Dario, had been discovered that morning on the north
highway outside the city.

"I suppose it was brigands," Cormik had said, his round
face haggard. "Gods know the roads are crawling with ruffi-
ans these days, what with no guards riding out on patrol.
It's Ravendas's fault the highways aren't safe anymore."

Caledan felt responsible and tried to say something, but
Cormik had waved his words away. "No, Caledan," he said
wearily. "It was I who devised the little charade, not you.
Besides, the culprit couldn't be Ravendas. You and I both
know that Ravendas would prefer you alive, not dead. No,
Dario has always been lucky—until now."

Despite his grief, Cormik had been ready to help plot
this night's adventure. He was eager to help organize a

resistance movement against Lord Ravendas. And for that
they needed gold.

As the wagon drew close, Mari lifted the hood of her tattered gray cloak and gripped her stout walking stick tightly
in one hand. Back bent, she hobbled out onto the avenue,
directly in the wagon's path. The driver swore loudly,
pulling back on the reins. The wagon clattered to a stop just
short of Mari's shambling form.

"Hey there, old woman!" the driver shouted. "Make way,
unless you want to spend the night in Cutter's dungeon."
Mari just stood there, muttering under her breath as if she
were some simpleminded old crone.

"Gods, Brim, get the old witch off the road, will you?" the
driver snapped. "Cutter'll have our heads if we're late to the
countinghouse."

"All right, all right," the other Zhentarim said in annoyance, climbing off the wagon. He swaggered toward Mari.
"You're in our way, hag. Be off with you, before we do
something to you that you wouldn't like." He flashed a lurid
grin at his partner, but in the moment his head was turned
Mari hefted the gnarled walking stick and swung it in a
whistling arc. It struck the Zhent's jaw with a resounding
crack, and the guard sprawled to the ground.

"I guess that will teach you to respect your elders," Mari
said with a grim laugh.

"By all the bloody gods!" the driver shouted in shock.
"You'll pay for that, you crazy old witch!" He stood up, drawing his short sword, but he never had the chance to swing
it. A dark form leaped from the overhanging branch of an
oak tree, landing nimbly on the roof of the wagon. The driver turned around in surprise—just as Caledan's boot
caught him square in the face, shattering his nose. The
Zhent tumbled out of the wagon and rolled into the foul
muck of the gutter.

"Care for a ride, old woman?" Caledan asked with a

smirk. Mari smiled back. The two took a moment to strip the dead Zhents of their dark leather uniforms.

"You're enjoying yourself, aren't you, scoundrel?" Mari hopped up into the wagon as Caledan flicked the reins.

"It never hurts to take pride in your work," Caledan remarked as the wagon bounced along into the night.

Before guiding the horses onto the steep road that led up the face of the Tor, Caledan halted the wagon. Quickly he and Mari donned the uniforms of the dead Zhents. Then they continued up the Tor, winding through the dim streets of the Old City. Both tensed when a trio of city guards rode by on horseback, but the guards simply saluted and continued on their way.

Caledan brought the wagon to a halt at the base of a tall spire in the shadow of the city lord's tower. Cormik's multifarious eyes and ears had learned that this was Cutter's primary countinghouse. The lion's share of the money that her guards extorted from Iriaebor's ships and caravans passed through here on its way to her coffers.

"Are you ready?" Caledan asked Mari as he brought the wagon to a stop in the courtyard.

"Worry about yourself, Caldorien, not me," she said crisply as she stepped down from the wagon. Caledan merely shrugged, following suit. Mari opened the wagon's rear door. Inside was a jumble of swords, shields, bolts of cloth, and pieces of ivory, but after a moment Caledan found what he was looking for—a small iron-banded casket filled with coins. He lifted, grunting with effort.

Mari's heart was beating swiftly in her chest, but she forced herself to walk boldly alongside Caldorien to the tower's stout wooden door. She rapped on the portal with a black-gloved hand. After a moment the door swung open. A meaty-looking guard glared out unpleasantly at them.

"We've got a delivery," Caledan said.

Mari was surprised at his suddenly brisk military

demeanor. It was a convincing act. She nodded, doing her best to imitate Caldorien. "It's the caravan gold," she added harshly. "We had a good haul today."

"Avdis has been waiting for you," the massive man said gruffly. Then suspicion glittered in his eyes. "Say, I don't know you, do I?"

Caledan shrugged. "Your loss, friend. Brim got sick tonight, and his partner, too."

"Sick?"

Caledan nodded grimly. "Plague. But it's all right. I don't think he coughed on me. How about you?" he asked, turning to Mari.

"Oh, not more than a couple of times," she replied flatly. "He was almost dead, after all."

Swiftly, the massive guard retreated several steps, his meaty hand pressed to his mouth. "Gods, get on with you!" he said, waving them past quickly.

"Thanks, friend," Caledan said. "We'd hate to keep Avdis waiting."

He and Mari strode past as the doorkeeper repeatedly made the sign against the evil eye. They reached the floor of a spiral staircase and proceeded upward. They passed several floors where they caught glimpses of city guards gambling, sleeping, or sharpening weapons. Mari and Caledan exchanged concerned looks. The message was clear: getting out might not be as easy as getting in had been. The stairway opened up into a circular chamber.

The chamber was lit all around with bronze oil lamps. Windows faced in all four directions. The ceiling was a high tiled dome. There was little furniture in the room besides a large table and a chair, on which sat a flabby middle-aged man with a pointed ratlike nose and beady ratlike eyes. The man was counting gold coins, muttering to himself as he piled them in neat, precise stacks. He looked like a child hoarding his favorite toys and seemed to be enjoying himself immensely. After long moments, Mari cleared her throat.

"Blast it!" the rat-faced man—apparently Avdis—squealed. "You've made me lose my count!" He looked up, but he barely noticed Mari and Caledan. Instead his eyes locked immediately upon the small chest Caledan held. "Well, what are you standing around for?" he snapped impatiently. "Bring that over here. Hurry!"

Caledan did as he was bid. Avdis pulled out a silver key he wore on a chain around his neck and unlocked the chest. He eagerly flipped back the lid, then let out a sigh of delight at the gold and silver within. He reached out with eager fingers to scoop up some of the precious metal, but a black-gloved hand on his wrist stopped him.

"Not so fast, friend," Caledan said. He smiled nastily. Avdis stared at him in dull confusion, then his eyes widened in comprehending horror.

"Not my gold!" he gasped. Caledan nodded solemnly. The little man drew in a deep breath as if to scream, but when he saw the threatening glimmer of Mari's knife he stifled the impulse.

Caledan picked up some of the gold and let it tumble though his fingers as Avdis watched, licking his rubbery lips. "You know," Caledan mused, "gold and silver are so heavy. Why don't you show us something a bit lighter, Avdis?" Avdis groaned. "Something in jewels, perhaps?"

Within minutes the sacks Mari and Caledan had tucked inside their uniforms were bulging with jewels. It represented at least a half-month's income for Ravendas, Mari was certain. There had been no need to tie up Avdis. He had slumped to the floor, quivering there as Mari and Caledan riffled through various chests and boxes, relieving them of their valuable contents. Concealing their burdens as best they could, they started down the stairs.

"I hope no one notices we've put on a little weight all of a sudden," Caledan commented wryly.

They were halfway down the staircase when suddenly a small, unnoticed rip in one of Caledan's sacks opened wider. A single, brilliant emerald slipped out of his jerkin and tumbled down the stairs. The gem bounced brightly down the stairwell and came to rest on a stone step, right at the foot of a Zhentarim warrior who had been walking in their direction.

Mari and Caledan froze. The Zhentarim was a grizzled fellow, an officer of some sort. Slowly he bent down and picked up the shining emerald. He stared at it thoughtfully for a moment, then looked up at Mari and Caledan, baring his yellowed teeth in a grin. The two grinned back weakly.

"Robbers in the tower!" the Zhent shouted. "To arms! To arms!" The thunder of booted feet and the ringing of drawn swords echoed up the stairwell. The Zhentarim officer lunged at Caledan, managing to grab his leg out from under him. Caledan fell, trying to kick away the soldier's tenacious hold. Mari grabbed a torch from an iron sconce on the wall and brought it down hard on the Zhent's head. He groaned and fell backward, bowling over the first of the guards who had come dashing to the scene.

Mari pulled Caledan to his feet, and the two scrambled back up the stairwell. "Now what?" she shouted.

"I was just about to ask you that," Caledan returned.

Once again they burst back into the topmost chamber. Avdis, who had just managed to gain his feet, stared at them in renewed horror and then promptly slumped back to the floor. They slammed the chamber's door shut and slid home the bolt just as the first guards reached the landing. Immediately the door resounded with forceful blows.

"That's not going to hold them for very long," Mari said, eyeing the door nervously.

"Then you'd better think of something fast."

"Me? This was all your idea," she retorted hotly.

The door shook under additional pounding.

Mari glared at him angrily. "A window, Caldorien," she said flatly. "Try a window."

Unfortunately, the outside walls of the tower offered only a sheer drop to the ground far below. The only chance lay with the west window, where there was a decidedly crumbly-looking bridge about twenty feet down, spanning the gap from this tower to the next.

"We'll never make it to the bridge," Caledan said after peering out the window. "Even if we don't break our legs, the impact would probably destroy that rickety thing."

"What's the alternative?" Mari asked in exasperation.

The door shuddered violently. One more blow and it would fly apart.

"All right, let's try it," Caledan snapped.

Mari threw her arms tightly around his neck. The door burst open in a spray of splintering wood, and a dozen guards charged into the room, swords drawn. Gripping Mari tightly, Caledan jumped out of the window. With one hand, he grabbed a handful of the tangled ivy that snaked up the west face of the tower. The tendrils could not support both his and Mari's weight, and the vines ripped from the wall as the two fell.

They landed hard on the narrow stone bridge that arched between the two towers. Mari felt the stones shift beneath them with the impact, but the derelict old bridge withstood the shock. Though winded and bruised, the two scrambled to their feet. Guards shouted angrily from the window above, but Mari and Caledan dashed across the bridge.

They froze in midstep.

The door in the next tower flew open. A half-dozen guards stood in the opening. Mari and Caledan spun around, only to view a similar obstacle behind them. They were trapped.

Something hissed past Mari's ear. She looked up to see one of the Zhent officers above, reloading a crossbow. From both directions the guards began to edge their way carefully onto the bridge. Mari felt the stones shudder beneath her.

"This thing is about to collapse," she whispered to Caledan.

He nodded. "Do you see what I see?" he asked, not daring to point.

She peered down into the moonlit dimness. At first she could see nothing, but then her eyes adjusted, and she nodded jerkily.

"When I give the signal," Caledan whispered, reaching down and gripping her hand. She squeezed back tightly. She supposed it wouldn't hurt to be nice to the scoundrel. They were going to die together, after all.

Another crossbow bolt whistled by, this one putting a hole in Caledan's stolen cloak. The guards drew closer. When perhaps a dozen stood upon the bridge, Mari heard a low groan and felt the bridge lurch beneath her feet.

"Now!" Caledan shouted. Without hesitation they both ran and leaped off the bridge. The guards stared after them in dumb amazement. Then the bridge broke apart, and the guards went crashing to the street below along with several tons of bone-crushing rock.

For a moment Mari felt as if she were flying. She heard the noise of the crumbling bridge behind her, but their leap had carried her and Caledan clear. They landed, hand-in-hand, in a cloud of dust and chaff.

"You couldn't have picked a wagon with *clean* straw, could you, scoundrel?" Mari said in disgust, spitting out an unpleasant mouthful. Her sore shoulder throbbed painfully. The two quickly slid off the back of the wagon that had been passing under the bridge.

"I wouldn't complain," Caledan countered, eyeing the

rubble of the stone bridge and the bodies buried beneath it.

They started off swiftly through the city's shadowed streets and were nearly back to the inn before they remembered to argue about whose fault this had all been.

Six

The priceless statuette shattered into a thousand pieces as it struck the dark marble wall of the tower's topmost chamber.

"I want them strung up by their necks!" Ravendas, Zhentarim lord and ruler of Iriaebor, demanded through clenched teeth. She was pale and lovely despite her rage, or perhaps because of it. "No, I want them run through, left to the rats, *then* strung up!"

A young boy sat in a chair before the fireplace, a dulcimer lying in his small hands. Ravendas's son. His green eyes were focused on the fireplace, watching the flames, as if he were oblivious to his mother's fury. The lord steward, Snake, stood serenely by the door, watching his mistress's tantrum. "You're being unreasonable, my Lord Ravendas," he said in his low, almost droning voice.

"*I'm* being unreasonable?" she thundered, turning upon Snake, her deep blue eyes flashing like lightning. "First two intruders raid my countinghouse and make off with a fortune in jewels, not to mention managing to kill a half-dozen of my guards. Then one of my best warships catches fire and burns to the water. Now I learn that—despite my orders against drinking—someone has been selling cheap casks of tainted wine to my guards and poisoning them sick in the bargain. More ships and caravans are passing through the city every day as the weather warms, and a quarter of my soldiers are flat on their backs puking their guts up."

Ravendas's golden hair glimmered in the torchlight. Her beautiful face was as hard as marble. "Did you not tell me that a sorcerer had been sent to deal with the Harper in my city, my lord steward?" The honorific was twisted into a sneering insult. "Did you not tell me that Caldorien was run out of Iriaebor by some underworld filth he had made an enemy of? Tell me, Snake, am I imagining these reports?"

"No, my lord, you are not," Snake replied deferentially.

This time it was a crystal vase that succumbed to Ravendas's wrath. "Then who is to blame for these outrages against me?" Snake started to speak, but Ravendas lifted a hand, silencing him. "No, I will hear no more excuses. Inform my captains that I want the perpetrators of these offenses found. Otherwise, it will be my captains' heads I will have. Is this perfectly clear, Snake?"

"Of course, my lord," Snake said, bowing deeply.

Ravendas lowered herself onto a silk-draped lounge and lifted a glass of wine. She drank deeply, and gradually the livid rage melted away. "Come, Kellen," she crooned to the boy. "Come play for your mother."

Without a word the boy slipped from the chair and sat at Ravendas's feet. His small fingers plucked at the dulcimer, and a sweet, sorrowful music filled the air. Ravendas closed her eyes for a moment, drifting with the music.

It would be a pity if Caldorien truly has fled Iriaebor, she thought. I would like to give him a taste of my power. He spurned me once. But no one, not the Harpers, not even those fools in Zhentil Keep, can stand against me now.

Her eyes opened and she regarded Snake, still standing subserviently near the ornately carved door. "How fare the excavations?" she asked him, her voice languid now.

"Very well, my lord. Soon you shall have what you desire. Every soul in Iriaebor will belong to you, and even those beyond."

"Excellent." A small black kitten crawled into Ravendas's lap, and she stroked its soft fur absently. Her cheeks were flushed with the wine, with thoughts of power. And of Caldorien.

The boy's music had stopped. The chamber was silent. Ravendas ran a hand over his dark, glossy hair—hair as dark as shadows, such a striking contrast to her own golden tresses. "Go with the lord steward, my son," she said to him. "It is late."

The boy nodded silently and stood, kissing her once upon each cheek. Snake turned to leave, and the small boy padded after him. They left Ravendas alone in her chamber, petting the black kitten, a smile curled about the corners of her deep red lips.

"Do you require anything, Kellen?" Snake asked when they reached the boy's room. The boy shook his head, clutching his dulcimer tightly.

"Do you think she will keep me when she is done with me?" Kellen asked then, with the utter seriousness of which only a child is capable. "Or will she break me when she is through?"

Snake regarded the child for a long moment. The boy was just eight years old, but he always struck Snake as being older than his years. There was a wisdom about him that was odd in one so young. But then, with a mother such as Ravendas, there were many sights this child had witnessed which other children never dreamed of, not in their most terrible nightmares.

"Go to sleep, Kellen," he said finally. The boy shrugged and stepped into his room, shutting the door behind him.

Snake turned and descended the tower's central stairwell. He had orders to give.

* * * * *

Caledan and Mari sat at a table in the Dreaming Dragon's private dining chamber. A map of the city lay unrolled before them, its corners weighted down by mugs of ale. The two of them were arguing, as usual, this time about a possible raid on a weapons warehouse in the New City.

"Either you're feebleminded or you're mad, Harper," Caledan barked, thrusting a finger at the map. Disagreeing with Mari was getting to be a habit. "There's no route of escape. Ravendas's guards would have our backs to the wall and their swords at our throats in a second."

Mari opened her mouth to say something, but suddenly Estah hurried into the room, slamming the door behind her. Her brown eyes were wide with fear.

"Estah, what is it?" Mari asked in concern.

"City guards!" the halfling healer managed to gasp. "They're searching every house and business on the lane. And they're headed this way."

Mari shot a worried look at Caledan. "Do you think we can slip out the garden and into the alley without being seen?"

Caledan laughed grimly. The Harper's inexperience was showing again. "You don't have a clue how the Zhentarim work, do you, Harper? They'll have someone keeping watch on the back door of every place they search."

He stood and pushed the heavy oaken table aside. "It's still here, isn't it, Estah?" He stuck a finger through a knothole and pulled. A small panel opened up in the floor. This part of the inn jutted precariously out over the edge of the Tor. Through the trapdoor Caledan could see the maze-work of beams that supported the structure and beneath them nothing but air and space until the jagged bottom of the Tor three hundred feet below.

Jolle hurried into the room. "You'd better hurry. They're nearly here."

"Let's go, Harper," Caledan said. He didn't wait for a reply but lowered himself quickly through the trapdoor, clambering onto one of the beams below the inn. Mari's eyes widened as she stared at the dizzying drop. She started to protest.

"Surely there must be another—"

"*Now*, Harper!" Caledan growled. "Unless you'd rather explain to the Zhentarim where you got that fancy moon-and-harp pin you're so proud of wearing."

Mari's eyes flashed fire, but she bit her lip and lowered herself through the opening. "Be careful, Estah," she told the healer.

A stern look crossed the halfling's face. "Don't you worry about Jolle and me. We can handle a few of Cutter's men. Now you two stay quiet." She shut the trapdoor, and there was a grating sound as she and Jolle moved the heavy table back into place.

"Comfortable, Harper?" Caledan asked patronizingly.

Mari gave him a scathing look. With white-knuckled hands she clung to one of the oaken beams. Wind whipped at her dark hair. A trio of swallows lazily spun and dove below them.

Caledan rather enjoyed the view himself, but he knew his was an unfair advantage. He and the other members of the Fellowship had used this hiding place on more than one occasion in the past.

Both of them tensed when they heard the heavy thumping of booted feet on the planks above their heads. A growling voice drifted down through the boards, but Caledan couldn't make out the words. A gentle yet resolute voice spoke then. Estah.

The booted feet departed, and for a long time the only sounds were birdsong and the voice of the spring wind. Then there came that same dull scraping sound, and a moment later the trapdoor opened. Estah's broad face was framed in the square.

"They're gone," she said in a relieved voice.

Minutes later they were once again safe within the inn's private dining chamber. Mari's face was pale, and she fairly gulped down the cup of spiced wine Estah offered her. However, she was none the worse for wear. Caledan had to admit to himself, albeit grudgingly, that the Harper had been brave.

"At least this should keep Ravendas's attention away from the Dreaming Dragon for a while," Caledan said. How long that might be was another question.

It was evening when Cormik arrived at the inn. He had traded his normally fastidious, opulent attire for a disguise consisting of the patched, mud-spattered garb of a peasant farmer and wore a wide-brimmed straw hat pulled down low to conceal his eye patch.

"You know, I think it suits you," Caledan told him with perfect seriousness.

"I've killed men for much less than that," Cormik snapped, plucking at his threadbare attire with a look of profound distaste. "What necessity can make us stoop to," he lamented in a pained voice, but then his manner grew businesslike. "I didn't come here for compliments, Caledan. I came to warn you and the lovely Harper Al'maren. I just received word that the lord steward, Snake, has ordered a door-to-door search of every habitation in the city."

"We already know," Caledan said matter-of-factly, enjoying the startled look on Cormik's face. The owner of the

Prince and Pauper wasn't used to others learning things
before he did.

Caledan and Mari spent the rest of the evening deep in
conversation with Cormik. Estah brought them a plate of
good but simple fare—bread, cheese, and a jug of pale
wine. Cormik eyed everything with a sense of novelty.

"So this is how the masses live," he remarked, picking up
his earthenware cup and studying it carefully. "How interesting. How peculiar." He sniffed the wine, and his bulbous
nose wrinkled. He quickly set it back down. "How revolting."

Not possessed of such delicate palates, Caledan and Mari
enjoyed the repast while Cormik talked. The efforts to try
to wear Ravendas down and, more importantly, to discover
her weaknesses were going well. A few small opposition
bands under the direction of some of Cormik's agents had
scored several hits against Lord Cutter's city guard.

"We've been a thorn in her side, to be sure," Cormik
said, "but we have a long way to go. We still need to find
more people who are willing to fight the Zhentarim. And
then we have to arm them. You two came away from the
countinghouse with a fair sum in jewels, but I can't simply
sell them openly on the market here. Ravendas is bound to
notice. Besides, she has a lock on the weapons trade, and
there isn't a blacksmith in a dozen leagues that isn't firing
up his forges to arm her men. However, agents of mine are
currently making deals in Berdusk and Elversult, though
it's going to be a slow process smuggling weapons into the
city."

Mari sighed deeply. "Let's hope she moves even slower
than we do."

Cormik chuckled deeply. "Don't despair, Mari Al'maren.
I have ways of sowing problems among Cutter's men." His
one good eye gleamed wickedly. "As a matter of fact, I sus-
pect that even as we talk new reports are making their way

to the tower, telling how the leaders behind the insurrection are in truth captains of Ravendas's own city guards. More than a few of Cutter's men who don't swear their complete loyalty quite fast enough will be swinging by their necks before morning."

Caledan shook his head. "You're a devious man, Cormik. Remind me never to get on your bad side."

Cormik stared at Caledan flatly. "You *are* on my bad side, Caledan."

Mari laughed after Cormik had left. "You know, I'm really beginning to like that man," she commented.

"You would," Caledan replied sourly.

* * * * *

It was late. The inn had closed for the night. Its shutters were drawn, giving Mari and Caledan the freedom to sit in the glow of the fire in the common room with Estah. Jolle was upstairs. He said he wanted to check on a leak in the roof. Mari didn't remind him there hadn't been a drop of rain in days. She knew the halfling was keeping watch.

"Despite Cormik's deceptions, it's still only a matter of time before Ravendas discovers us," Caledan said in a low voice, gazing into the flames. He twirled a dagger absently in his hands.

Mari started to reply, but just then two pairs of small feet came thundering down the stairs. Pog and Nog burst into the common room and dashed to Estah, clinging to her desperately.

"My bonnies, what is it?" Estah asked them, hugging the two tightly. "You should be long abed." Nog tried to explain in whatever language it was that he spoke, but Pog interrupted.

"It's the shadows, Mother," she said gravely, her brown eyes wide in her small, round face. "The ones in the closet.

I woke up and saw them moving, and Nog did, too. They want to eat us!"

Estah laughed, hugging her two children tightly. "Why, that's nonsense! Even if the shadows could move, how in the world could they step off the wall to eat you? And if they did eat you, where in the world would they put you? Shadows are awfully thin, you know." Pog's little forehead wrinkled a bit as she considered this information. She didn't seem entirely convinced.

"Well, if you're still worried," Estah said, "perhaps I could have your Uncle Caledan here speak with the shadows. He's a friend of theirs, you know."

"You can talk to shadows, Uncle Caledan?" Pog asked. Mari looked at Caledan, raising an eyebrow. He shifted uncomfortably in his chair.

"It's just an old trick, nothing more," he explained. "I haven't done it in years."

"An old trick?" Mari asked curiously.

"Oh, a bit more than that, I'd say," Estah said, her brown eyes twinkling. "Why, with the music of his reed pipes, Caledan can make the very shadows dance upon the wall."

Pog's eyes lit up then, and Nog squealed in glee. "Oh, please, Uncle Caledan. Make the shadows dance on the wall for us! Please?"

Caledan shook his head. "I don't suppose I even remember how." He turned to Mari in explanation. "It was just an old parlor game—an odd talent that ran in the family." He looked at Pog and Nog and grinned, tousling their straw-colored hair. He picked them up, one in each arm, much to their squeals of terror and delight, and headed up the stairs. "I may not make them dance on the wall, but I will talk with them. Maybe I can convince them not to eat all of you. Perhaps just a few bites . . ." Pog and Nog squealed in horror and delight.

"Can he really do that, Estah?" Mari asked when they

were alone. "The trick with the shadows, I mean."

"Indeed he can. Shadow magic, I always called it. He could make the shadows on the wall move and act as he pleased with the music of his reed pipes. Of course, he put little stock in it. He regarded it simply as a minor talent that ran in his family. But however small a thing it was, it was *magic*." Estah's eyes glimmered in the firelight, then she sighed. "Now, of course, he won't play a note of music at all, not for any reason."

"Why, Estah? Why did Caledan forsake his music, and the Harpers?"

"You don't know, lass?" Estah asked softly. "I thought you knew about Ravendas."

Mari shrugged. "Only that Caledan had met her before. That's all I know."

Estah sighed deeply. "It's a long tale, but I think it's one you should hear. I suppose I should start by telling you about the Fellowship of the Dreaming Dragon." She poured a cup of fragrant tea, scented with mint and camomile, for each of them. Mari leaned forward, listening intently.

"I'll never forget the first time I met Caledan." Estah smiled with the memory. "It must be more than a dozen years ago by now. He was a young man then, on his first mission for the Harpers. As it happened, his travels brought him to Iriaebor, to this very inn, which I had only just bought. Over the next year or so his journeys frequently brought him to the Dreaming Dragon, and we became friends. And then one day, before I really had a chance to consider what I was doing, he told me he had need of a healer, and the next thing I knew I was off on one of his missions with him!"

Estah shook her head and laughed. "If I had known what adventuring was like, I doubt I would have ever left the warm comforts of the inn. But once enlisted, I knew I could never let Caledan go off on his journeys alone again. They were simply too dangerous. He needed a healer with him."

"But you weren't the only one to journey with him, were you?" Mari asked.

Estah nodded, sipping her tea. "That's right. One by one, others that we met on our journeys joined the Fellowship to help Caledan. The first was Morhion, a mage of considerable power. After him came Ferret, who was always more rogue than hero. And then there was Tyveris, a great warrior but also a gentle soul. Over the years, and through our travels, we became almost like a family." Estah smiled fondly. "No, I think we *were* a family." Her broad face grew solemn.

"Where are the others now?" Mari asked gently.

"Last I heard, Tyveris lived north of Iriaebor," Estah replied. "As for the others, I'm not certain. No one could ever keep track of Ferret for long. Morhion may still live in the city, but if so I don't know where. I haven't heard from him since the day we went our separate ways. Even when we traveled together he was a strange, secretive man."

"But you still haven't told me why Caledan left the Harpers, Estah, why the Fellowship disbanded."

"Let me finish the tale," Estah said with a sigh, setting down her teacup. "I think you'll understand then. You see, there was one other who joined the Fellowship. Her name was Kera, and she was a Harper, too. I once heard it said about Kera that her hair made sunlight seem pale, and that compared to her eyes the morning sky was colorless. But it was her heart I remember most. She was a woman of true beauty, within and without."

How lucky for her, Mari almost found herself saying, but then she bit her tongue. Why should she care what Caldorien's old friends looked like?

"You should have seen Caledan in those days," Estah said with a laugh. "You wouldn't have recognized him, Mari. He was young and handsome, full of humor and hope. I think that was Kera's influence on him. Never have I seen two people more in love than Kera and he. They used to sing the most marvelous duets."

Estah rose to put another piece of wood on the fire. She stirred the coals with a poker, and sparks flew up the chimney. She sat back down and gathered her thoughts for a moment before going on. "It was seven years ago that Caledan and Kera finally decided to wed. They were going to take their vows in Twilight Hall in Berdusk itself, before all of the Harpers. But on the eve of our journey to Berdusk, word came from Twilight Hall that a Zhentarim lord was raising an army of goblinkin outside the walls of Hluthvar, a town some leagues to the north of Iriaebor. As it turned out, the Zhent's name was Ravendas.

"Caledan and Kera accepted the mission. The wedding was postponed."

Mari edged forward on her chair, her tea forgotten, as Estah described how Caledan and the Fellowship managed to ruin Ravendas's plans to usurp the town.

"Goblins are clannish creatures," Estah explained, "and goblin tribes are constantly feuding with each other. We discovered that Ravendas's army was comprised of goblins from two different tribes. We managed to plant rumors among each of the tribes that the other tribe was planning to betray them. Driven nearly mad with suspicion, the leaders of the two tribes attacked each other. The rest of the goblins quickly followed suit. Ravendas's army actually destroyed itself. The town of Hluthvar was saved.

"In the chaos of the battle Caledan managed to capture Ravendas, and he threw her in chains," Estah went on. "However, when he was off routing a few straggling bands of goblins, Ravendas managed to escape."

"But how?" Mari asked.

Estah's face hardened. "Ravendas was always a sly one. She could don a look of remorse as easily as you might don your cloak. At the time it happened, Kera was the only one in camp. Ravendas spoke to her, pretty words I'm sure, and finally she convinced Kera that she was truly repentant, that she wished to begin a new life. Kera believed her, and she unlocked Ravendas's chains."

Estah's voice trembled and her eyes grew distant, as if she were reliving it all over again. "By the time we rode back to camp, Ravendas had escaped. We found Kera, her fair face pressed to the cold ground. The chains that had bound Ravendas were wrapped about her neck, wet with her blood." She shook her head in sorrow. "Kera was dead. Ravendas had strangled her."

"But I don't understand," Mari said, angered by what seemed Kera's pointless death. "Why did Kera believe Ravendas? It should have been obvious that she was lying."

"True," Estah said with a nod, "but Kera wanted to believe. You see, Mari, Kera and Ravendas were sisters."

Mari stared at the healer in silent shock.

"Caledan blamed himself, of course," Estah went on sadly. "And he blamed the Harpers as well. He broke with the Harpers that day, and that was when the Fellowship disbanded. We each went on to lead our separate lives, and as far as I know Caledan has not played a note of music since. I think it reminds him of Kera far too much."

Mari did not know what to say. The healer's tale made her regret a few of the harsh things she had said to Caldorien.

Estah shook her head, regarding the small hands resting against her gray homespun skirt. "If only there had been enough healing in these two old hands," she said softly. "Perhaps Kera might have lived."

Mari reached out and took the healer's hands in her own. "But you can't fault yourself, Estah, no more than Caledan can."

Estah pulled her hands away. "Oh, yes, I can," she said

sternly. "I can, and I do. But while Kera's death shattered
Caledan, it made me strong, Mari. I vowed that day never to
let another person I love die. Never." She rose to her feet
abruptly.

"I'd best see if Pog and Nog are in bed yet," Estah said,
then left Mari alone in the flickering light of the fire.

* * * * *

It was quiet in the Dreaming Dragon. Mari sat at a small
table in the corner of her room, bathed in the light of a
single candle. She unrolled a piece of parchment and
dipped a quill in a small pot of ink. Her hand wavered for a
moment as she thought of Estah's tale. Then she swallowed
hard and began to write. She had her duty. When she was
finished she read over the brief missive, written in her flowing hand:

> *To Belhuar Thantarth*
> *Master of Twilight Hall*
>
> *Greetings!*
> *I have made contact with Caldorien as ordered. He*
> *has agreed to help counter the Zhentarim in Iriaebor of*
> *his own will, and all goes well. He has learned that Cut-*
> *ter is in truth Ravendas, but he does not suspect our*
> *knowledge. More importantly, I have confirmed the*
> *rumors concerning his shadow magic. I shall make con-*
> *tact again in one tenday.*
>
> > *Milil's Blessing!*
> > *Mari Al'maren*

Mari deftly folded the parchment and sealed it with hot
wax from the candle. She would find a rider tomorrow who

could deliver it to Twilight Hall in Berdusk. For a moment she watched the shadows cast by the candle's light flicker on the wall of her room. It was almost as if they were dancing, she thought, and then she blew out the flame.

Seven

It was midmorning two days later when Estah returned from a trip to the free market in the New City. The few patrons in the common room looked up in astonishment from their tables. Most had known the innkeeper for years, but few had ever seen her angry.

"She has gone too far this time!" Estah exclaimed furiously.

Jolle hurried into the common room. He took one look at his wife and, sensing something was terribly wrong, gave the signal. Instantly the inn's occupants leaped from their tables. The shutters were closed, the door locked, and lookouts headed upstairs to keep watch. Caledan entered as Jolle was trying in vain to calm down the healer.

"She has gone too far!" Estah repeated, her cheeks flushed. She snatched the board bearing Lord Cutter's Rules from the wall and flung it to the floor.

"Ravendas?" Caledan ventured, his expression grim.

"Look at this," Estah said, her voice trembling as she

87

thrust a crumpled-up piece of parchment toward Caledan. "I saw it just a few minutes ago, posted in the free market." Caledan unfolded the parchment. It was an official notice. Quickly he read it, his heart sinking.

"What's going on?" Mari asked as she descended the stairs. She and Caledan usually kept out of the common room, but the commotion had brought her down. Caledan handed the parchment to her, and she read the declaration with a solemn face.

"It looks like Ravendas has arranged a bit of entertainment for the city," he said, gritting his teeth. "There's going to be a public hanging tomorrow afternoon. One of the criminals to be executed is an old friend of ours. His name is Ferret."

Estah sank down into a chair. All the spirit seemed to go out of her, and she buried her face in her hands.

"It's all right, wife, I'm here," Jolle said, holding her shoulders tightly. "All's going to be well. You'll see."

Estah wiped her eyes with the corner of her skirt. "I'm sorry, husband. I'm weary, that's all. I'm just so weary of Ravendas ruining everything that I care about." She shook her head. "She's wounded this city so deeply, I wonder if we will ever be able to heal it."

Mari looked at Caledan, her face tense. The message was clear: We have to do something.

He nodded. There was no question about it. Ferret had once been one of his best, if not most trustworthy, friends. He was not about to let Ravendas claim another member of the Fellowship.

"Estah," Caledan said gravely, kneeling down to talk to the healer, "Ferret got us out of more scrapes than I can count during those years we all traveled together. We both owe our lives to him, several times over. This is the time for us to repay him. We can't lose hope.

"Still, a little extra help wouldn't hurt," Caledan went on, standing up. "Estah, you said once that Tyveris still lived near the city. Can you tell me how I might find him?"

"I think so," Estah ventured, "but . . ."

"No buts," Caledan said, striking his palm with a fist. "If we're really going to rescue Ferret, we're going to need that warrior's sword."

* * * * *

Caledan rode through the New City toward Iriaebor's north gate, keeping the hood of his blue traveling cloak drawn over his head. It seemed as if city guards were more common than rats these days, and he had no doubt they were still searching for him and the Harper. It had felt a little strange donning the old cloak that morning, knowing that Cormik's young apprentice, Dario, had died wearing it. But Cormik had given it back to Caledan after Dario's body had been returned to the city for burial. And Caledan couldn't bring himself to throw the cloak away. He had worn it for too many years, on too many journeys.

A trio of guards were keeping watch over the city's north gate. They might have given Caledan some trouble, but they were distracted by a flock of sheep being driven into the city for slaughter. The sheep balked as a red-faced peasant man tried futilely to herd them through the gates. The scene erupted into a cacophony of bleating and cursing. Caledan took the opportunity to slip through the gates unnoticed.

"Remind me to be grateful the next time I eat mutton stew," Caledan commented to Mista as they left the walls of the city behind. The gray mare replied with a snort that sounded uncannily like laughter.

The day was fine and clear and the midday sun warm. Caledan breathed deeply as he rode across plains that were in the midst of taking on spring's brilliant hues. It was good to get out of the city.

To Caledan, Iriaebor looked like some vast, dark toad-stool looming on the Tor, a blight on the land, a thing of disease and decay. Every day the city's streets were growing dirtier, its buildings shabbier, its people poorer and more desperate. And every day the streets grew emptier, as well. Soon it was going to be more ghost town than city. The Zhentarim continued their mysterious abduction of able-bodied cityfolk, forcing them to dig into the hard rock beneath the city lord's tower. But for what purpose? That was a secret even Cormik's agents were unable to fathom. Caledan sighed, putting the troubles out of his head for the moment.

It was early afternoon when he found the standing stone Estah had described, marking a road branching off from the main highway. He followed the road up a low, rounded hill, finding himself before an edifice of gray stone, its ornately embellished spires rising above a walled court-yard.

"This must be the place, Mista," he said with a frown, dismounting.

Caledan pulled the rope that hung next to the wall's stout oaken gate and heard the clang of a bell. After several moments an ancient man clad in a simple robe of drab brown opened the door. When Caledan explained that he had come in search of his old friend, Tyveris, the man smiled and bade him enter.

Caledan left Mista in the courtyard. The old man led him inside to an entrance hall, gestured that he should wait, and then shuffled away.

The entrance hall was a high, narrow room paneled in mahogany. Faded frescoes decorated the ceiling, and dappled light from an intricate stained glass window fell to the floor like so many scattered gems. The hall was silent.

Suddenly that silence was shattered.

"Caledan Caldorien!" a deep voice thundered, the sound of it rattling the stained glass. Caledan spun on a heel to see a man clad in a brown robe stride into the room. The man stood no taller than Caledan himself, but he took up considerably more space. His monumental shoulders looked ready to split the brown robe he wore, and the homespun cloth did little to conceal his thickly muscled arms and chest. The man's skin was a dark, coppery color, and his eyes were as black as obsidian, encircled by a pair of gold wire spectacles. He grinned broadly as he crossed the room, enfolding Caledan in a bear hug.

"It's good to see you, too, Tyveris," Caledan gasped, wondering how many of his ribs were cracked.

"I thought old Ebrelias was seeing things again when he said someone had come asking for me," the big man said merrily, releasing Caledan. "How long have you been back in these parts, old friend?"

"Not long," Caledan said, rubbing his chest. "I've been staying at the Dreaming Dragon in the city, with Estah."

Tyveris smiled broadly. "How is Estah? I haven't seen her in years. I'm afraid I don't really get to the city these days. Maybe you can tell me something more of the dark rumors I've heard about Iriaebor. Can you stay awhile? I can send to the cellar for a bottle of wine." He winked slyly. "I still have some of that Sembian red. You know, from that time we raided the caravan of that Amnian merchant who was running slaves to Thay . . ."

Caledan laughed at the memory. "That was a good vintage, wasn't it? As I recall, the grand finale to that evening was when you sang Chultan war songs on the roof of one of the caravan wagons, then slipped and fell on your head."

"Actually, Caledan," Tyveris rumbled, "that was a *duet*. And it was *your* head that I fell on when we hit the ground, not mine."

"Oh, that's right," Caledan said, wincing as the details

came back to him. "But I don't really have time for wine now, Tyveris." Quickly, Caledan told Tyveris that the city's new ruler was their old nemesis, and about the notice Ravendas had posted that morning. Tyveris listened carefully, his face grave. When Caledan finished, he sighed deeply.

"Of course I'll help you free Ferret, Caledan," the big man said. "The gods know we all owe our lives to that little scoundrel a dozen times over. But there's one thing I think you don't understand. Didn't Estah tell you?"

"Tell me what?" Caledan asked.

"I gave up my sword more than five years ago," Tyveris said slowly. "This is an abbey, dedicated to Oghma. Caledan, I'm a monk now, a loremaster of Oghma, not a warrior."

Caledan stared at the big man in amazement.

"I think we'd better go have that wine after all," Tyveris said, gripping Caledan's shoulder and steering him out of the entrance hall. Caledan could only nod dully. Seven years ago Tyveris had been the most fearless and ferocious swordsman Caledan had ever known. Now he was a . . . monk?

They spent the next hour talking intently in Tyveris's small, spare chamber, furnished only with a low bed, a chest, and a table with two chairs. A coarsely woven mat of rushes was the lone covering for the cold stone floor. The single window looked out over a garden, perfectly framing a small pear tree just coming into bloom. Tyveris had sent a young boy—an orphan and refugee from the city taken in by the abbey—for that bottle of wine, and it was every bit as delicious as Caledan remembered.

They spoke of old memories for a while, but finally, after a long silence, Tyveris explained what had led him to trade his sword for a loremaster's robe. "You remember how I came to these lands," he said, gazing out the window thoughtfully. "The ships traveled from Waterdeep across the Shining Sea to my homeland, to the jungles of Chult. They promised much gold and glory to those young Tabaxi men and women who would come with them, to train with the sword and become mercenaries. Despite our parents' tears, both I and my sister went with the ships, leaving our homeland behind, never to return."

Caledan nodded. He recalled the familiar tale. "You lost your sister on that voyage, didn't you?" he asked gently.

A flicker of pain passed briefly across the big man's face. "The ship was crowded and filthy. Almost half of my people died of sickness before we reached the Sword Coast. Tali was one of them. That was when I vowed to become the greatest warrior I could, to make her spirit proud of me." He lifted his cup of wine, draining it to the bottom. They both knew the rest of the story. Tyveris and the other Chultans spent many years as mercenary fighters in the service of a wizard from Calimshan whom they could not escape. It was the Harpers—and Caledan—who had freed them. That was when Tyveris joined the Fellowship.

"But I was living a lie, Caledan. I realized that, after you left and the Fellowship disbanded. For a long time I had made your purposes mine, and that was enough to sustain me. But for the first time since I had left the jungles of Chult, I was faced with my own purposes, not another's. Killing held no true joy for me, and no glory. I realized that I could no longer honor Tali's spirit by acting as a warrior. Killing only mocked her death.

"That was when I found this place, the Abbey of Everard. The loremasters here let me work for them and sleep in their stable. Abbess Melisende herself taught me to read, and soon I learned that there was a whole different power besides swinging a sword. Finally, I asked if I could join the order, and the other loremasters agreed. That was four years ago." Tyveris paused, pushing his spectacles up higher on his nose. "It's a good place, Caledan. The loremasters take care of the poor and sick as best they can, though these days far more come from the city than can fit within these walls. And there's a library, filled with books." His dark eyes gleamed as he smiled, and Caledan couldn't help but return his expression. "I think Tali would be pleased with my choice."

"I think she would be, too." Caledan stood up. "But sword or no sword, I would still like to have you by my side, Tyveris."

The big man stood and gripped Caledan's hand tightly. Caledan winced, hoping that none of his bones would break. "Then you can count on me tomorrow," Tyveris said firmly. "Ferret deserves our help. And Oghma knows, there is no love lost between myself and the Zhentarim."

Tyveris promised to be at the Dreaming Dragon early the next morning, and Caledan bid his old friend farewell. The gloom of dusk was just beginning to gather as he rode back toward the waiting city.

*   *   *   *   *

It was full dark when the stranger caught scent of the trail, but the black-robed one did not need any illumination to follow the prey. The call of the shadow magic was strong. The other was still within the city's walls, still beyond his reach. But not Caldorien. Caldorien was outside the city— in the stranger's territory.

Heavy robes billowed out like dark, fantastic wings as the stranger sped across the shadowed land. An evening wind hissed through the grass. There was no moon, but the stranger did not know this, did not care. All that mattered was finding Caldorien, finding him and tearing the life from his body.

All with the shadow magic must die. All. The master had decreed it.

The scent grew stronger, the trail fresher. Caldorien was close now, very close. No more than a minute or two ahead. The stranger's black-gloved hands opened and closed in anticipation of the flesh they would crush.

Suddenly the stranger faltered and slowed. Caldorien's scent dwindled, faded, was lost in a roar of other odors, pungent and overwhelming—the city. Caldorien had reached its walls, eluding the stranger's grasp once again. The figure reeled, turned, and slipped back toward the plains, letting out a high, blood-chilling shriek of fury.

Then the night was silent.

* * * * *

Caledan rose in the gray light before dawn. There were preparations to make. He found Mari and Estah already in the kitchen. "Can you shoot a bow, Harper?" he asked gruffly.

She set down her cup of tea and looked him straight in the eye. "Try me."

Dawn was just breaking over the city's towers as Caledan and Mari strung a pair of longbows in the garden behind the inn. Jolle had brought the two bows down from the attic, along with a longsword now belted at Caledan's hip. There was quite a store of weapons, armor, and traveling gear up there, left over from the days of the Fellowship. Estah had thrown nothing out.

Caledan nocked an arrow and aimed at an apple dangling by a string from a tree branch across the garden, a good hundred feet away. His hand steady, he pulled the arrow back until the fletching brushed his cheek. Then he let it fly. The arrow hissed through the air. A heartbeat later, the apple spun on the string.

Caledan was smug. "Beat that, Harper."

He watched as she carefully selected an arrow and

nocked it, lifting the bow with a sure, easy grace. The morning mist clung to her green velvet jacket like translucent pearls, and the first rays of the sun seemed to set fire to her dark auburn hair. She looked almost beautiful in this light, Caledan suddenly thought. Almost. Not that he particularly cared.

Mari paused for a moment, then the arrow raced through the air. The apple dropped to the ground.

"Damn, you'll have to try again, Harper," Caledan growled, walking toward the target. "The string broke."

"It didn't break, scoundrel," Mari said, a hint of mirth in her rich voice.

Caledan frowned in puzzlement. What was she talking about? He bent down and picked up the apple. Then he saw. The end of the string had been sliced cleanly through. He looked at her, a smile spreading across his angular face.

"It looks like you've got the job, Harper."

"Good," was all she said.

Tyveris arrived at the Dreaming Dragon a short while later. Caledan had feared that the guards at the city gates might give him trouble, but they had let the monk pass. The Zhentarim had taken one look at the massive Tabaxi Chultan and had thought better of bothering him.

At the first sight of Tyveris, Pog and Nog squealed in terror, running upstairs to hide. However, despite his booming voice, which seemed to rattle the very timbers of the inn, there was a gentleness about Tyveris that eventually drew Pog and Nog from their hiding places. Before long they each sat upon one of Tyveris's broad shoulders.

"Come on, Tyveris," Caledan said finally, helping the huge loremaster disentangle himself from the tiny halfling children. "There's someone we need to pay a visit to, someone in need of holy guidance, I think."

"Really?" Tyveris rumbled, his dark eyes gleaming behind his wire-rimmed spectacles. "Well, don't let it be said I'm one to turn my back on a soul in peril."

The two slipped out the garden gate behind the inn and down the dank, narrow alley that led deeper into the Old City. Tyveris had to turn sideways to make it through the cramped passage. When they reached the alley's end they had to wait for a city guard on patrol to pass by. Then they made their way through the city's grim streets.

Caledan had paid a visit to the Prince and Pauper the night before to get some information and to make a few arrangements for today. Cormik had been happy to oblige.

"Anything to put a little vinegar in Lord Cutter's wine," he had said with a raucous laugh. He gave Caledan the name and residence of the priest who was to speak the final rites over the prisoners before the execution. The priest was a disciple of Cyric, a god devoted to murder and lies as surely as Oghma was the deity of knowledge and illumination. Cormik had learned that many of the Zhentarim in the city worshiped Cyric in secret, abominable ceremonies of blood and fire. Ravendas herself was rumored to be a follower of the dark god, though Caledan doubted that. Ravendas was not the kind of woman who would kneel before anyone, even a god.

The priest's tower stood on the east side of the Tor. Caledan rapped on the door, and a scar-faced guard answered. Scant moments later Tyveris was muttering a prayer over the guard's body while Caledan quietly shut the door. He bent down and pulled his dagger from the man's chest, cleaning it on the guard's uniform.

They found the priest of Cyric sleeping in a lavishly decorated bedroom high in the tower. They had encountered a few servants on the way up, but these had hurriedly scurried away after one look at Caledan and Tyveris. Apparently there was little bravery among followers of the evil god.

The priest was in for a rude awakening.

"What in the Abyss!" he cried, throwing off his bedclothes and trying to scramble to his feet. "In the name of Cyric, I command you to—"

"To what?" Tyveris asked a moment later, standing over the priest's limp body. The big Tabaxi's fist hadn't left much of the man's now-bloodied nose intact.

Caledan regarded Tyveris curiously. "I thought you said you had given up fighting."

"The gods didn't give us swords, Caledan, so I won't use one," Tyveris said solemnly. "But the gods did give us fists," he added slyly.

They bound and gagged the groaning priest of Cyric, then rummaged through a cherrywood wardrobe until they found his dark purple ceremonial robes. Luckily the priest had led a soft life, and his garments were rather roomy. Tyveris tried on the garb. The fit wasn't perfect, but it would do.

"Let's get out of here," Caledan said, stuffing the priest's robes into a sack.

* * * * *

The sun stood high overhead in the azure sky. It was time for the execution.

Caledan lay low against the stones of a weathered, lichen-covered bridge that spanned from tower to tower high above an open plaza. Thirty feet directly below him stood the gallows, a tall platform reached by a set of narrow wooden steps. A half-dozen nooses dangled from the stout crossbeam. It was to be a multiple hanging. Ferret was just one of the unlucky ones.

Seven years ago the plaza had been called the Fountain Square, but it had been unofficially renamed under Cutter's rule. Now it was called the Scarlet Square, for all too often the gutters ran, not with water, but with blood.

Two gigantic statues carved of ancient gray stone stood

facing each other at opposite ends of the square. These, too, were Ravendas's additions. Each of the statues stood at least fifteen feet high on a basalt throne. The Gray Watchers, Caledan had heard them called. One was carved in the image of a stern-looking man, the other a regal woman. The king and queen of cruelty, both wore circlets of stone upon their brows. Rumor had it Ravendas had discovered them in the ruins of an ancient keep in the Sunset Mountains to the west and had them transported here to keep watch over her executions.

Caledan turned his gaze away from the forbidding statues. They chilled his blood just to look at them.

A crowd was beginning to gather in the square. Eight guards led by a Zhentarim captain stood before the gibbet, keeping the folk away. The crowd's mood was hostile, and it was clear they would have torn the gallows down but for Cutter's guards standing there, hands on the hilts of their swords.

Caledan squinted up at the sun. It was almost time. Cormik had made his promised arrangements. Even now, a man—one of Cormik's agents—stood by one of the three archways leading into the square, hawking ale for the hanging. Several wooden casks were stacked around him, though he did not seem to be doing a very good business. Perhaps it was because he was closer to the guards than to the cityfolk.

An angry murmur rose up from the crowd as four heavily armed guards led a half-dozen shackled prisoners into the square. One woman counted among the unfortunate prisoners, all of whom looked pale and wan. The last prisoner who came into view was Ferret.

The old rascal hadn't changed a bit. A small, wiry man, his dark, beady eyes glittered sharply, and his thin nose almost visibly twitched as he looked from side to side—obviously searching for a means of escape. One of the guards shoved him brutally from behind. A grimace of pain crossed his face, but despite the hobbles about his ankles Ferret managed to keep himself from falling. Caledan swore under his breath.

The prisoners were pushed up the narrow steps of the platform. A monstrously obese, black-hooded executioner covered their heads with hoods of sackcloth and slipped nooses about their necks. The guards returned to the plaza to help keep the crowd away.

A startling figure strode into the square then, a massive man clad in the thick, deep purple robes of a disciple of Cyric, his face lost in the shadows of his cowl. A pall fell over the crowd. Even the guards exchanged nervous looks. Caledan bit his tongue to keep from laughing aloud. He hoped this little masquerade wasn't going to get Tyveris in trouble with his god.

The massive figure made his way through the crowd and ascended the steps of the gallows ceremoniously. He paused before each of the prisoners in turn, weaving his hands in arcane patterns and whispering strange words.

Finally Tyveris arrived at his place next to the executioner. He turned and spread his arms out to the crowd in a gesture of benediction. "Let this be an example to you all!" he boomed to the crowd. "In the end, the gods will punish all transgressors, and there is but one punishment!" The cityfolk murmured with fear. Taking this as his signal, the executioner reached for the lever that would drop the floor of the platform out from beneath the prisoners.

Only his hand never reached it. With a swiftness impressive in one so huge, Tyveris grabbed the executioner by the belt and heaved him off the platform. The man's scream ended in a wet, sickening thud as he hit the cobblestones fifteen feet below. Shouting, several guards clambered up the steps to the platform. Tyveris gripped the top of the steps and pulled, his straining muscles ripping through the

purple ceremonial robes. Nails groaned. Tyveris wrenched
the steps loose and with a grunt heaved them to the pave-
ment. The guards fell in a tangle. The crowd erupted in
screams as people tried to flee the plaza.

Abruptly a hissing sound cut through the air. A flaming
arrow sped from the window of an abandoned tower on the
edge of the square, striking one of the ale seller's wooden
casks. The ale seller himself was suddenly nowhere to be
seen. Caledan looked up in time to see Mari, her face hard
with concentration, loose a second arrow from her perch
high in the derelict tower. The Harper's timing was as good
as her aim.

The second flaming arrow struck another wooden cask.
For a moment the arrows burned into the wood as the
guards nearby stared in puzzlement. Then the casks
exploded in a blossom of brilliant, fiery light. The towers
around the square swayed on their foundations. A half-
dozen guards flew through the air like strange, dark birds,
and when they landed they did not rise again. The square
plunged into chaos. Half of the guards were dead, the
others stunned. Tyveris was cutting the prisoners free of
their nooses and lowering them down to the ground, where
they escaped easily in the confusion.

Caledan looked up to make a sign to Mari, but the window in the tower was empty. The Harper was already gone.
Now it was time for Caledan's part.

Quickly he tossed down a coil of rope he had securely
anchored to the bridge's balustrade. He slid down the line
and landed on the platform. Tyveris, hood fallen back and
robe in tatters, had just one more prisoner to free—Ferret.

"You know, this probably makes you a heretic in the
Church of Cyric," Caledan commented.

"I can live with that," Tyveris replied. With his bare
hands he snapped the rope around Ferret's neck. The little
man snatched away the sack that covered his face, then his

beady eyes went wide. He stared at Tyveris, his nose twitching. "I must be dead already. Tyveris, you look like a monk!"

"I *am* a monk, you weasel," Tyveris bellowed, reaching out to catch the small man in an embrace. Ferret's eyes nearly bulged out of their sockets.

"You're breaking me," he gasped. He wormed his way out of Tyveris's grip.

"Let's save the joyous reunions for later, all right?" Caledan told them. "We're not out of here yet." Some guards were regrouping and were getting ready to charge the platform. "All right, everybody, up the—" *rope*, he was going to say, but the pounding of hooves interrupted him.

Five iron-shod chargers thundered into the square. Astride four of them were Zhentarim warriors clad in the livery of the city guard, their short swords drawn and ready for violence. On the fifth horse rode a figure both Caledan and Tyveris recognized, a massive man with blood soaking through the large bandage covering his nose. The priest of Cyric.

"I guess I should have hit him harder," Tyveris grumbled darkly. Ferret, who needed no further prompting, scrambled nimbly up the rope.

"I'll bring up the rear," Caledan said. The big Tabaxi nodded and followed the thief, swiftly pulling his bulk up the rope.

One of the square's three exits had been blocked by rubble from the smoke powder blast. Now the four mounted Zhents moved to guard the other two arches leading from the plaza. As they did, the priest of Cyric gripped a hideously twisted amulet of dark, wrought steel that hung about his neck. He began shouting something in a harsh, foul-sounding tongue.

Ferret and Tyveris had reached the bridge above. Caledan leaped onto the rope and began hauling himself up, arm over arm.

A low groaning sound shook the air when Caledan was only halfway to the bridge. Suddenly there was a deafening crack. Caledan briefly wondered if it was another smoke powder explosion, then heard Tyveris shouting frantically. Caledan looked away from the rope and nearly lost his grip in his utter shock.

The Gray Watchers were moving.

The priest's chanting had mounted to a triumphant crescendo. The two massive statues slowly, ponderously pushed themselves up from their thrones of basalt. The circlets around their brows glowed vile purple, the same color as the magical aura surrounding the priest's amulet.

"Caledan, watch out!" Ferret called down.

The words spurred Caledan to action. He scrambled farther up the rope barely in time to avoid a startlingly swift blow from the statue of the ancient queen. For a moment he found himself gazing directly into the soulless eyes of the statue. He kept climbing.

"No offense—I mean, I appreciate this and all—but you two didn't plan this escape all that well, did you?" Ferret asked.

"Well we don't all have your extensive experience with escaping," Tyveris rumbled angrily. The big monk stood on the edge of the bridge and spread his arms in a mirror image of the priest of Cyric. He began chanting in a flowing, musical language, trying to drown out the evil priest's dark prayers. The gigantic statue stepped closer to Caledan, wounded guards crushed unnoticed beneath its feet. The statue of the king was still rising from its throne, reaching toward its full height, five times that of a man.

"Andebari al Oghma, al d'bai altan!" Tyveris roared. "In the Name of the Binder, may evil's enchantment be shattered!"

Suddenly the priest of Cyric let out a strangled cry. The

circlet about the stone queen's brow flared brilliantly, shattering into countless splinters of stone. The statue halted. Then slowly, almost gracefully, it toppled to the street, smashing the cobbles as it struck, shaking the very foundations of the city.

But the statue of the king showed no such reaction. It continued to move toward Caledan, who dangled halfway up the rope.

"Hurry, Caledan!" Tyveris shouted down. His face looked ashen and haggard. "I dispelled the magic coursing through one of the statues, but I don't think I can break the enchantment in the other!"

Meanwhile, the priest of Cyric had regained his composure, and his chanting rippled forth once again as he gripped the steel amulet.

"Allow me," Ferret said. He took the knife Tyveris had used to cut the prisoners' ropes and hefted it experimentally, testing its weight. Then he let if fly with a precise, expert throw.

The priest's chanting abruptly stopped.

The flabby disciple of Cyric slipped from the back of his horse, Ferret's knife embedded deep in his throat. Blood flowed out to pool with the grime of the street. The purple glow of the amulet flickered, faded. The statue of the nameless king slowed to a halt.

Then a rivulet of the dead priest's blood trickled across the steel amulet. The dark blood hissed and steamed. The purple aura strengthened and grew brilliant once again. Blood flowed more quickly toward the amulet now, defying gravity as it rose from the cobbles to the evil symbol.

The stone king began to move, once more, toward Caledan.

"Uh-oh," was all Ferret said.

The statue of the king reached out a hand of granite to crush Caledan.

Caledan's arms were going numb. He wasn't going to make it.

"Break the king's circlet, Caledan!" Tyveris bellowed. "It's the heart of its power!"

The stony fingers, each as thick as a tree branch, began to close about Caledan. There wasn't time to think. Holding on to the rope with one hand, he drew his sword. Just as the cold, hard fingertips brushed against his chest he swung the rope forward and brought the hilt of his sword down on the circlet resting on the statue's brow.

His hand was thrown back painfully with the force of the blow. The sword clattered to the street far below. The stony fingers closed about his chest, tightening until he could barely breathe—before shuddering to a stop.

His blow had cracked the king's crown. Brilliant purple sparks flared about the dark fissure, sizzling like lightning. The violet glow wavered, then vanished. The gigantic statue lurched precariously to one side. Caledan tried to free himself from its grip, but he was stuck in its grasp. The stone king started to topple.

"Oh, no you don't," Tyveris growled. The loremaster, his chest against the bridge, reached down, just managing to grab Caledan's collar. Caledan felt himself pulled roughly from the stone king's grasp as the statue fell next to its queen. With a grunt Tyveris hauled him up onto the bridge.

Caledan groaned. His shoulders and chest felt as if they were on fire. "I am really far too old for this," he managed between gasps.

"So are we all," Tyveris rumbled wearily, rubbing his aching temples. Breaking the priest's enchantment had left him exhausted.

"Speak for yourself," Ferret replied in his raspy voice, his dark eyes shining.

If Caledan could have, he would have strangled the little thief.

The trio made their way westward along a mazework of bridges far above the city streets. Some Zhentarim tried to follow, but the smokepowder blast had blocked the western exit from the plaza. The three companions quickly left the turmoil of the square behind.

Finally they descended to a quiet side street. Estah, clad in simple peasant garb, sat on the bench of a farmer's wagon filled with straw, holding the reins to a pair of ponies. Mari was with her.

"Ferret!" Estah cried out in joy at the sight of the thief. He bowed deeply in response.

"What took you so long?" Mari asked, her eyes flashing.

Caledan and Tyveris exchanged a weary look. "I really don't think you'd believe us, Harper."

She laughed. "You're probably right."

"We'd better go," Estah warned. "The guards will be coming this way soon enough."

No one argued with the healer. Caledan, Mari, Tyveris, and Ferret burrowed themselves deep into the concealing straw in the bed of the wagon, and Estah flicked the reins. The wagon clattered down the street.

Estah was right. Minutes later a pair of hard-faced Zhentarim warriors pounded on their chargers down the street. However, all they saw was a halfling farmer driving her wagon to market. They swore as they continued on, knowing that if they didn't find the troublemakers Lord Cutter was going to have their heads.

Eight

Twilight crept on soft, padded feet into the garden behind the Dreaming Dragon. Mari sat on a stone bench, watching as the pale crescent of the moon rose above the city's spires, its silken light glimmering off the moon-and-harp pin she wore on her jacket. The faint, sweet scent of the first crocuses hung upon the cool evening air, and the mourning doves that nested in the branches of an ancient oak tree sang their gentle song. She folded the piece of parchment she held and slipped it into her pocket. It was a missive from the Harpers.

She had managed to slip away to the free market in the New City that afternoon to meet the messenger, but later Caledan had nearly caught her reading the secret communication. That would not have been good. The missive came from the hand of Belhuar Thantarth, from Twilight Hall in Berdusk. *Continue your close contact with Caldorien,* the missive had instructed her. *However, he is not to discover from you what we already know. His resentment of the*

107

Harpers runs far too deep for him to believe what we have learned. He must discover the importance of the shadow magic himself.

Mari heard the sound of heavy footsteps approaching and looked up to see the big loremaster, Tyveris. He smiled broadly as he walked toward her, his teeth white in the moonlight, and Mari could not help but smile in return. There was a gentleness about the priest of Oghma despite his size, and he seemed perpetually good-natured.

"Estah would not be pleased if you caught a chill out here, Mari," Tyveris said reprovingly, though as always there was a kindly note in his voice. He held out a midnight blue cloak and wrapped it about her shoulders. Mari tensed for a second when she realized that the cloak was Caledan's, then she relaxed. Tyveris meant well, and besides, he was right. The air was chilly, and she had been shivering.

"Thank you, Tyveris," she said, pulling the cloak tightly about herself.

"It really isn't safe to be out here so long, you know." Tyveris's dark eyes were concerned behind his spectacles. "The Zhentarim are combing the city for us after our exploits yesterday. Ferret's already . . . er . . . disposed of one guard who ventured too near the inn. You should come inside."

"I will," she said. "I was simply . . . thinking, that's all."

"Are you well, Mari?" Tyveris sat next to her on the bench. It groaned alarmingly beneath his bulk.

Mari smiled at the massive Tabaxi. "Oh, it's nothing really," she told him. "This is just a day for memories, that's all." She took a deep breath of the purple air, sighing. "I was raised by a Harper, you know. Master Andros was his name. When I was a child, in the city of Elturel, both of my parents died of the fever. After that, I lived on the streets for several months, finding food where I could. But then winter

came. I don't know if I would have survived. Or, if I had survived, what I might have become. That was when Master
Andros found me."

Mari thought back to that cold day, to the small, thin girl
she had been, shivering in her rags in a storm drain
beneath an abandoned building. She had been so afraid at
first when the man had stopped and peered in at her
through the grating. But his blue eyes had been so kind
that finally she had reached out and taken his hand.

"He took me in, like you take in children at the abbey,
Tyveris. We lived in a small, rambling cottage, filled with
books, and maps, and musical instruments. He was growing older and didn't travel for the Harpers anymore. We
spent our evenings together by the fire, reading, making
music, or talking about ancient days. But Master Andros
was more than just my teacher. He was my father, Tyveris,
and my friend."

The loremaster laid one of his big hands gently on Mari's
own. "How long ago did his spirit move on?" he asked her
softly.

"Three years ago today," she said, surprised at the tight-
ness in her throat and the trembling in her voice. What
would Master Andros think of her? He had always taught
her to be strong. "I joined the Harpers after he died," she
said, clenching her jaw and forcing her trembling to stop. "I
want more than anything to make him proud of me."

They sat in silence for a time while the doves sang their
sorrowful song. Finally Tyveris squeezed her hand and
then stood. "Why must you make him proud of you, child?"
he asked her softly. "Was he not already?"

Before Mari could reply Tyveris turned and walked back
into the firelit glow of the inn, leaving her alone in the darkness of the garden.

* * * * *

Caledan headed down the narrow back stairwell and joined the others in the private dining chamber.

Tyveris and Mari were helping Estah set supper on the board as Ferret entertained Pog and Nog with a copper coin the thief had borrowed from them. The weaselly little man sent the coin dancing about his knuckles, the penny disappearing in one hand only to reappear in the other. The two halfling children watched in rapt delight, and Nog squealed when Ferret seemingly pulled the coin right out of the boy's ear.

"All right, that's enough," Estah scolded the three of them. "To the supper table with all of you." Pog and Nog groaned in disappointment but shuffled off, dragging their feet, to obey their mother. Ferret, of course, pocketed their coin as he followed.

"So are you ever going to tell us why Lord Ravendas wanted to string you up, Ferret?" Caledan asked the thief as they broke bread.

Ferret shrugged. "All you had to do was ask, Caledan. It isn't as if it's a secret. I was making plans to escape from Ravendas's work gangs beneath the city, along with the other prisoners who were going to be hanged." He scratched at the dark stubble on his pointed chin. "But then one of the prisoners in on the plan got scared and betrayed us to the Zhentarim. That's when Ravendas decided to make an example of us. Oh, by the way." He reached into his pocket and pulled out a small object. He handed it to Mari. "I believe this is yours."

"How—?" Mari started. He had handed her the moon-and-harp pin she always wore on her jacket, the sigil of the Harpers.

"Just trying to keep in practice," Ferret explained with a wink.

"Well how did you get yourself captured in the first place, Ferret?" Tyveris asked.

"A minor miscalculation," Ferret replied, looking decidedly uncomfortable. "I had decided to relieve one of those spineless lords of a portion of his rather considerable store of gold. Unfortunately, I had the bad luck to pick one who had managed to get himself on Ravendas's bad side. Just as I was about to leave his tower, the Zhentarim broke down the door and threw the lord in chains, hauling him off to the dungeons. They captured me as well, even though I was merely an innocent bystander."

"'Innocent bystander?'"

Ferret shot Caledan a sour look. "Anyway," he said in his raspy voice, "Ravendas has quite an operation going on down beneath the tower's dungeons. The tunnels go on for miles. She must have close to a thousand cityfolk slaving for her against their wills. I don't know what it is she's digging for down there, but it must be something pretty important."

Caledan nodded intently. "I'd pay handsomely for that information."

"Really?" Ferret asked, a gleam in his beady eyes. "I might be able to . . . ask around."

Caledan grimaced, reaching for his purse. "All right, Ferret," he grumbled. "How much is it going to cost?"

* * * * *

It was midnight. Caledan and Mari stood in the shadows of a deserted intersection in the Old City, waiting. "Where is he?" Mari said in a whisper. "You don't suppose he ran off with the gold we gave him, do you? He is a thief, after all."

"He'll be here," Caledan whispered back. Unless the rogue ends up with a knife in his back, Caledan added silently to himself. "Ferret may not be strictly honorable, but there is a certain consistency to his actions, and we've been friends a long time. Besides, he wants the Zhentarim

gone from the city just as much as we do, and I'm sure the
thieves' guild does as well. They must be losing a fortune to
Ravendas."

"I'm still not certain petitioning a thieves' guild for help is
a good idea," Mari said.

Caledan disagreed. "Thieves are as much a part of city
life as temples, schools, and markets are. They keep the
merchants from getting fat and lazy, and give the city
guards something to do besides troubling honest folk. Now
what could be wrong with that?"

It was scant minutes later when the shadows stirred, and
Ferret abruptly appeared. "So did you have any luck?" Caledan asked.

Ferret nodded. "A little, I think. I tried all day to find out
if there were any thieves in the city who had done work for
Ravendas since she's been here, someone who might have
heard what it is she wants, or know something concrete
about her underground operations."

"And?"

"Most thieves have been avoiding her," Ferret explained.
"No one wants to do work for someone who's likely to dispose of you when the job's finished. But I did hear of one
old fellow, named Tembris, who did a job for her when she
first came to Iriaebor. He may know something."

"So where is this Tembris?" Mari asked.

Ferret cast a nervous glance over his shoulder. "Uh, I'll
tell you on the way. I don't think it's such a good idea to
stand around here for long." He started off at a brisk pace
down the street, and Caledan and Mari hurried to keep up.

"All right, Ferret. Who did you kill?" Caledan asked the
rogue sternly.

"No one," the thief answered in his raspy voice. "Er, no
one you know, that is." He gave Mari a sheepish look. "People can be so uncooperative sometimes."

The Harper glared at the weasely thief. Caledan, however, didn't care how Ferret had gotten his information as long as it got them some answers.

"This Tembris is a member of the Purple Masks Guild," Ferret explained as they made their way through the darkened streets.

"Well, that's going to complicate things," Caledan muttered.

"How so?" Mari asked.

"Ferret and his family are independent thieves, Harper," Caledan replied.

"He means we're not aligned with the guild," Ferret added. "Guilds don't usually tolerate independents like us. They generally give independents two choices—either join or be killed."

"Why hasn't your family joined?" Mari asked with a puzzled frown.

Ferret laughed nastily. "You don't know my grandmother Jewel, the head of my clan. She refuses to answer to anybody. Even a guildmaster would think twice before tangling with her."

Soon they stood before a temple built of pale marble. Graceful columns supported an intricately carved facade, behind which rose a lofty, tapering spire. An elaborate frieze glimmered in the moonlight beneath the temple's cornices, depicting a woman with flowing hair holding the reins of a chariot that rode through the sky, bearing the orb of the moon.

"The Purple Masks Guild is in the temple of the goddess Selune?" Caledan questioned Ferret.

"Of course not," the rogue protested. "It's *beneath* it. The Moon Goddess is revered by all who walk the night, you know."

They stepped through massive doors of polished mahogany into the shadowy temple. Within was a long, column-lined hall. Moonlight poured through windows high in the pale walls, caught and reflected by mirrors so that the entire temple glowed with an unearthly light. A few priests and worshipers moved quietly about the temple, but none seemed to take notice of the three newcomers.

A row of teakwood prayer boxes lined one wall, each large enough for a person to kneel in while making a silent, private plea to the goddess. Ferret counted the boxes as they passed by. When he had counted to thirteen, he stopped. He opened the door and stepped into the small, dark space, gesturing for Caledan and Mari to follow. The Harper protested, claiming they couldn't possibly all fit inside.

"You can wait outside if you like," Caledan told her, stepping into the cramped space.

She swore under her breath, tossed her dark auburn hair, then stepped into the prayer box. Caledan shut the door. The only light came from a grate in the box's roof. The three barely fit, and Caledan was forced to take shallow breaths. The Harper was pressed close against him, and for the first time he noticed how small she really was. Her head barely came to his shoulder, and her hands, each cupping an elbow of her crossed arms, seemed half the size of his own.

Ferret rapped three times on the wooden back of the prayer box, paused, then knocked twice more. Suddenly the wooden panel slid to one side, revealing a corridor beyond. The three stumbled into the larger space.

Caledan froze. A swordpoint glittered in the torchlight an inch from his chest. A man clad all in gray except for a silken violet mask held the hilt of the sword, watching him warily. Caledan looked to either side and saw that Mari and Ferret had been similarly greeted.

"Well, if it isn't the famous Ferret," one of the thieves said with an unpleasant smile. "The guildmaster is going to be pleased to see you, my friend." Caledan looked questioningly at Ferret, but the thief only shrugged.

They were led down a long flight of stairs and then through a labyrinthine network of corridors and chambers that must have spread beneath the entire temple. Caledan had known the thieves of Iriaebor were organized, but he had no idea the guild had such an elaborate headquarters. Finally they were escorted into a lavishly decorated chamber. Many-hued silks hung from the walls, and the floor was strewn with thick rugs and embroidered cushions. On a heap of pillows in the chamber's center reclined an enormous man. He was dressed in maroon and silver silk and held a goblet of wine in a fat, ring-covered hand.

"Guildmaster Bock," Ferret said, nodding his head. The little man sounded calm, but Caledan knew he was nervous. His pointed nose was twitching furiously.

"My good Ferret, what a pleasant surprise," the guildmaster said in a surprisingly rich, clear voice. "Do drink some wine with me."

"Er, I don't think we're really all that thirsty," Ferret said, eyeing the three goblets a servant carried on a tray.

"But I insist," Bock intoned. Caledan felt the swordpoint poking into his side.

"Now that I think of it, though, I *could* use a drink," Ferret said, grabbing a goblet and swilling down the contents. Reluctantly, Caledan and Mari did the same. The vintage was excellent, but Caledan detected a slight bitterness in the wine's aftertaste. He set the goblet back on the servant's tray and regarded the guildmaster.

"Which poison was in that, Bock?"

The guildmaster laughed. "Very good, Caledan Caldorien. Yes, I know who you are, and you as well, Harper Mari Al'maren. Neither of you are very inconspicuous, after all. And might I add, Ferret, that your taste in friends has gone downhill again. I thought your grandmother Jewel told me you had outgrown this disturbing practice of befriending Harpers."

Ferret shrugged. "Old habits are hard to break."

"You still haven't answered my question," Caledan said.

"Ah, yes, the poison," Bock replied with a smile, displaying a row of surprisingly even, white teeth. "It's sindari, a native herb of Thay. A very unusual substance. It shows absolutely no effects for an entire day, and then, without warning, the victim lapses into violent convulsions. I'm told they're quite painful. However, they are also quite brief. Death comes within but a few minutes. But not to fear, Caldorien. It is a precaution only." He waved a chubby hand, and the thieves sheathed their swords, retreating from the room.

"You see," Bock went on, "I also have the antidote. You might call the sindari a bit of insurance for my safety, that's all. Harm me, and you shall never have the antidote. Conduct yourself as civilized guests, and the antidote is yours."

Caledan shook his head. He had to admit, it was a clever method of ensuring good behavior.

"We're looking for a thief named Tembris," Caledan explained, deciding to lay all their cards on the table. Deception at this juncture could easily prove fatal.

"Interesting," Bock said. He stroked his numerous chins with a pudgy hand. "Let's see what I can extrapolate from this," he mused. "Tembris is one of the few thieves in the city who has done work for the Zhentarim, Lord Ravendas—though it was a mistake, to be sure. You yourself are a Harper no longer, Caldorien, but you come to me in the presence of one who is. Knowing there is little love lost between the Harpers and the Zhentarim, I can only assume you are working against Ravendas, trying to discover her weaknesses to see if she can be defeated. And what has Tembris to do with this?" A calculating expression crossed his face. "Ah, yes, perhaps the work he did for Ravendas may shed some light on what it is she seeks deep in the heart of the Tor."

The guildmaster's logic was flawless. Caledan flourished his road-worn cloak and bowed deeply.

"Did Ferret tell you I enjoyed flattery, Caldorien?" Bock snapped. Then he chuckled, a deep, bubbling sound. "If he did he was correct. Very well, Caldorien. You may see Tembris. He is here in this very guildhouse. However, you may be disappointed after you meet him."

"Thank you," Caledan said, but the guildmaster waved the remark away.

"Don't thank me. I'm doing this purely out of my own interests. When a city falls on hard times, so do its thieves. It's difficult to rob people who are destitute, you know. I would like nothing more than to see Ravendas ousted from the tower. However, if the Harpers and the Zhentarim manage to annihilate each other in the process, that would be so much the better."

Bock clapped his hands twice. Moments later a servant arrived bearing three small vials—the antidote to the sindari. Caledan drank his down quickly, surprised at the trembling in his hand. It figured that the antidote would taste far worse than the poison. Mari's face was pale as she glared at him. It was apparent she hadn't enjoyed this little transaction with the thieves' guild.

"Now, Ferret," Bock said, "won't you give up your poor taste in company and come work for me? I can always use a thief of your caliber."

Ferret shook his head. "I'm flattered, Guildmaster Bock, but somebody has to keep on eye on the Harpers."

Bock nodded. "Good lad. Give my greetings to your grandmother. And let me know if she's reconsidered my proposal." Ferret promised he would, and then the three followed a thief who led them out of the chamber and down a twisting corridor.

"What 'proposal' to your grandmother was Bock talking about?" Mari asked Ferret.

"A marriage proposal," he replied. "Bock's been asking her to marry him for the last twenty years."

"But she keeps saying no?" Mari asked.

"No," Ferret said with a sly expression. "She keeps saying maybe."

Bock's servant led them to a door at the end of a narrow corridor. "This is Tembris's room," she said as she opened the door.

They stepped into the small, dim chamber. The room was sparsely yet comfortably furnished. On a pallet in one corner sat a thin spider of a man dressed in a simple black tunic. His skin was wrinkled with age, his long hair iron gray. The old man turned his head when they entered the room. Where his eyes should have been there were only two deep, shadowed pits bordered by loose folds of skin. The old thief was blind.

"Ravendas did this to him," Bock's servant explained. "I'm telling you because he can't. Tembris is also mute. He has been since birth. That was why Ravendas hired him, because he wouldn't be able to talk after the job was done. He stole something for her, and you see how Ravendas rewarded him. She had his eyes cut out."

"But he can hear us?" Caledan asked, and the servant nodded. She left the three in the room with the old thief, shutting the door behind her.

"Greetings, old father," Caledan said, kneeling down to touch the thief's fine, wrinkled hand.

Tembris nodded, smiling placidly.

"We need your help against Lord Cutter," Caledan explained. Tembris clenched his jaw tightly. He was listening.

"Iriaebor is dying under her rule, Tembris. She's draining the life out of it. Even at midday the streets are filled with shadows and ghosts. The people have lost hope. You may be their last chance." Mari gave Caledan a look of surprise, but he concentrated on Tembris. "Will you help us?"

The old thief reached out, searching until he found Caledan's hand, gripping it tightly. Tears glimmered beneath his ruined eyes. Tembris nodded.

"We need to know what it was you stole for Cutter," Caledan said gravely. Another nod, but followed by a shrug. Tembris gestured to his mouth. He could not tell them.

Mari knelt down. "Can you write, Tembris?" she asked. The old thief grinned then and gestured with his hand. A little, he indicated.

Mari pulled a blank sheet of parchment and a piece of charcoal from her pocket. She spread the paper before the old thief and placed the charcoal in his fingers. She guided his hand over the parchment. "Write for us, Tembris. Write what it was Lord Cutter had you steal for her."

The old thief nodded, biting his lip in concentration as he slowly moved the charcoal across the parchment. Caledan and Mari exchanged glances. Tembris seemed to grow confused after a minute. He scribbled fiercely at the first lines he had made, marking them out.

"It's all right, Tembris," Mari said, reaching for the charcoal, but the old thief held on to it tightly, shaking his head. He put the charcoal to the paper again and started over. He slowly moved the charcoal over the page, concentrating as he tried to summon the letters. Finally he finished and nodded, setting the charcoal down.

Caledan picked up the parchment. Scrawled across the page were several letters. They seemed to spell a word, but it was not one he recognized. *Malebdala*. He showed it to Mari and Ferret, but they shook their heads. Still, maybe it was a clue. Caledan carefully folded the parchment and put it in his pocket.

"Thank you, old father," he said, gripping the thief's hand. Tembris gestured to his eyes, to the air above his head, and then made a fist. The message was clear.

"We'll do our best to stop Cutter," Caledan told him. "I promise." The old thief nodded, then lay down on his pallet, weary. Caledan, Mari, and Ferret left the small chamber, shutting the door softly.

"Do you think the word he wrote means anything?" Mari asked the others.

"It has to," Caledan replied grimly. "It has to."

* * * * *

He was having the dream again.

He moaned, a low sound of fear deep in his throat, struggling against the tangled silken sheets of his bed. The chill night air coming in through the chamber's window did little to cool his fevered brow. It was the dream that had set him afire, as it always did. He could not escape it.

He was running through the labyrinth of sewers and drains beneath the city's dungeons, his feet splashing through foul, murky water. He was dripping with sweat, and his breath came in ragged gasps. He could hear the sound of booted feet echoing in the corridors above him, but he knew that the dungeon guards would not catch him. His fate lay deeper down, farther into darkness.

The mouth of the empty drainage pipe loomed before him. Shadow seemed to pour thickly from its lip, as if the pipe carried not water, but darkness itself. He knew what horror awaited him down there, but he could not resist its pull. He began crawling down the dry, dusty pipe. He couldn't breathe in the cramped space and could hear the staccato beat of his own heart bouncing off the crumbling tiles around him. The sound was driving him mad.

Suddenly the floor gave way beneath him. Even though he had known it would, it did not lessen the terror of it. He fell down into endless darkness for what seemed an eternity. Finally a bloody, crimson light sprang to life all around him. He lay on a polished floor of darkest jet in a vast, columned chamber. His body was twisted and broken, and he could see his own hot blood oozing out to pool on the dark floor.

Weakly, in great agony, he lifted his head and gazed up at the massive throne he knew would be there before him. The throne was constructed entirely of dark steel, its edges as sharp as knives. Upon it sat a figure lost entirely in shadow, save for its gleaming crimson eyes. The dreamer moaned. That bloodred gaze filled him with such horror he felt it would rend his mind.

The figure upon the cyclopean throne lifted a hand. Its eyes pulsed in time with the dreamer's fading heartbeat. Then the throned figure spoke.

Be made whole, thief!

The dreamer screamed in agony as searing fire coursed through his body. His back arched off the stone floor, his fingers clawing helplessly at the dark marble.

Then he woke.

The lord steward of Iriaebor, the man named Snake, sat up suddenly in bed, clamping his jaw shut against a scream. For a moment his close-set eyes were wide in utter fear. In them shone a look of purest madness. Then it was as if a veil descended over those eyes, making them once again as hard and dark as polished stones. The madness of the dream slipped away. There was something Snake had to do.

He rose from his bed and, clad in his green silken nightrobe, moved to an ornate wooden cabinet near the window. He could see the city outside far below the tower, dark in this hour of the night. He opened a drawer in the cabinet and took out a small ebony box. Inside was an opaque polished crystal as large as an egg. He spoke a single arcane word, and suddenly the crystal darkened. An image appeared within its heart.

The image showed a moonlit ridgetop above a windswept

plain. In the center of the image stood a figure clad in heavy black robes.

"Report," Snake whispered harshly into the crystal.

"Both with the shadow magic are in the city still," the figure's hissing, strangely accented voice emanated from the crystal. "Caldorien left the walls for a time, but he returned before I could take him."

"Then you must wait. And when he leaves the city again, be ready. I will concern myself with the other."

Snake spoke another ancient word of magic, and the image in the crystal vanished. He slipped it into its box, but he did not return to bed. For the rest of the night he watched the darkened city outside his window. With sleep would come dreams. And Snake did not want to dream again.

Nine

"That is by far the most idiotic idea you've had yet, Caldorien. And that's no mean feat."

Mari tossed her thick, red-brown hair as she peered at Caledan across the table. Morning sunlight streamed through the window of the Dreaming Dragon's private dining chamber, highlighting the edges of her wide cheekbones and too-square jaw.

Caledan sighed in frustration and leaned back in his chair. Had the Harpers trained Al'maren to be so contrary? Or had she simply been born that way?

"Listen, Harper," he said slowly, trying to explain it all once again. "You don't understand the Zhentarim as well as I do. There isn't enough loyalty flowing in the veins of the lot of them to fill a thimble even halfway. Without Ravendas, the Zhents in the city would start slitting each other's throats trying to figure out who's the top boss. They would do our dirty work for us."

"And what about Cormik's report?"

Caledan picked up a rolled parchment from the table, glanced at it, and tossed it back down. According to the report, Ravendas had requisitioned more warriors. The Zhentarim fortress of Darkhold in the Far Hills was only six days' hard ride north of Iriaebor. Soon there would be more Zhents than ever in the beleaguered city.

Caledan ran a hand through his dark hair, pushing it back from a furrowed brow. "I don't know, Harper." He shook his head slowly. "I think that, given time and a little of our help, Cormik's rebels might overcome the Zhentarim. But then, maybe not. Besides, Ravendas is still digging for something beneath the Tor, and it may not be long before she finds whatever it is. Time is something we don't have all that much of."

He took a deep breath, fidgeting with the braided copper bracelet on his wrist. "Of course, Ravendas will never have the chance to dig up anything if I confront her alone in the tower." He looked Mari in the eyes. "You should be able to understand that, Al'maren. Isn't that how the Harpers operate? They send one person to slip in and do a job where an army can't go. If that agent fails, they've lost only one. But if the agent succeeds . . ." He struck the oaken table with a fist. "You're the person they sent to Iriaebor, Harper. Let me be the one to go into the tower, to end this all."

Mari regarded him for a moment. She laughed bitterly. "And what makes you think Ravendas won't simply toss your body down the tower steps, Caldorien?" She hesitated as if she was going to say something more, then bit her lip in silence.

"Why, Harper. You almost sound like you're worried. Don't tell me you actually care about me."

This time Mari's laugh rang with genuine mirth. Caledan winced. "All I care about is this city, Caldorien, and my mission for the Harpers. Don't forget that."

It was midafternoon when Tyveris came to the inn. Cale-

dan had been enjoying a rare moment of solitude, Estah
was with Jolle in the kitchen preparing the evening meal,
and Mari was upstairs, trying to keep Pog and Nog out of
trouble. Caledan had no idea where Ferret was. One typi-
cally didn't see the thief during daylight hours.

Tyveris had thrown a patched peasant's cloak over his
broad shoulders, concealing his loremaster's robes. Priests
of Oghma did not usually frequent taverns, and it was best
not to draw any undue attention to the Dreaming Dragon.

The big loremaster slung a bulging satchel onto a table
and began pulling out heavy leatherbound books. Caledan
filled two clay mugs with foamy red ale—Estah's own
brew—from a cask in a corner. He started to hand one to
Tyveris, then paused.

"You haven't given up ale as well as your sword, have
you?"

The monk shook his head emphatically. "Brewing beer is
a most holy art, Caledan. Surely you know that." Tyveris sat
down and took the mug, drinking deeply. "Ah, but then I'm
forgetting what a heathen you are."

Caledan drank to that. "What did you find in the abbey's
library?"

"Quite an interesting search it was," Tyveris replied. He
pushed his gold-rimmed spectacles up his broad nose with
a dark finger and began sorting through the various tomes
and codices. Yesterday Caledan had shown the big monk
the scrap of paper the thief Tembris had written on—their
one clue hinting at what Ravendas was searching for
beneath the city. Caledan had asked Tyveris if he could
research the peculiar and unfamiliar word the old thief
had scrawled, and the loremaster had readily agreed, his
dark eyes gleaming at the prospect of pursuing a scholarly
mystery.

Mari descended the narrow back staircase then, clad in
doeskin breeches and her customary green velvet jacket.

She poured herself a cup of pale sweet wine and joined the two men.

"What's this?" she asked, pointing to one of the moldering books that Tyveris had opened before him.

"A history of the lands west of the Sunset Mountains," the loremaster explained. He ran a big hand affectionately over a yellowed page, then drew out quill, ink, and parchment from his satchel to scribble a few notes. It was clear he was in his element. Still, Caledan couldn't help but remember the days when Tyveris had held a sword as comfortably as he now did a pen.

Caledan leaned over to peer at the faded words carefully scribed on the page. "I can't read a word of that."

"That's not surprising, given that it's written in a language that hasn't been spoken in a thousand years," Tyveris replied with a rumbling laugh. "It's called Talfir." He picked up the wrinkled scrap of paper on which the thief Tembris had scrawled the single word: *Malebdala*.

Mari arched a single eyebrow in curiosity. Caledan motioned for the loremaster to go on.

"The Caravan Cities—Iriaebor, Berdusk, and Elturel—were founded about three centuries ago," Tyveris continued. "That may seem like quite a long while, but against the full sweep of history it's really quite a recent development. People have lived in the lands along the banks of the River Chionthar for millennia. They raised kingdoms that had fallen to dust centuries before the first folk crossed the Sunset Mountains from Cormyr to the east to resettle these lands. And those ancient people spoke a different language than the one your ancestors brought with them. That language was Talfir."

Mari picked up the scrap of paper bearing the strange word. "Can you translate it?"

Tyveris nodded. "I think so. A number of books written in Talfir have survived over the centuries. We have a few in the abbey's library, and I've been studying them." He took the small piece of parchment from Mari. "*Mal* signifies shadows or twilight, and *dala* is a book or tome. *Mal'eb'dala. The Book of the Shadows*. That's how I would translate it."

Caledan frowned. "Ravendas had Tembris steal a book for her?" He had never known the Zhentarim lord to be the literary type. How could a book be so important to her?

"It would seem so," Mari replied, rubbing her square chin thoughtfully.

"I asked the other loremasters at the abbey if they had ever heard *The Book of the Shadows* mentioned before. One of them, Loremaster Avros, showed me this." Tyveris opened another book, this one bound with two flat pieces of wood. The pages were darkened with time.

"You can read that?" Caledan asked dubiously.

"This will help," the loremaster said. He took a pinch of white powder from a small clay pot and sprinkled it across the page. Then he blew gently. The powder seemed to stick to the parchment but not to the faded ink. The words stood out more clearly now, written in some archaic tongue Caledan could not make out. He looked at the Harper, but she shook her head doubtfully.

"What does it say, Tyveris?" she asked.

The monk pushed his spectacles up and studied the passage. "It's a story about a book," he said in his deep voice. "'A tome writ upon enchantments myriad and shadowed.'"

"*The Book of the Shadows*?" Caledan asked.

Tyveris nodded. "I think so. It's a long passage, which tells of all the various copies of the original *Book of the Shadows* and what became of them over the course of time. The original was destroyed in a fatal battle between two mages. Almost all of the other copies have since been lost or ruined. But there is said to be one copy still in existence, kept under lock and key in the library of Elversult to the east, where it has lain for the last two centuries or so."

"And is it there still?" Mari asked.

Tyveris shook his head. "Loremaster Avros journeyed to the library in Elversult recently and found things in a bit of a stir. It seems the *Mal'eb'dala* was stolen about a year ago."

Caledan swore. "So Ravendas has the one and only copy." He turned to Mari. "We're going to have to break in to the tower, Harper. Right now that book is the only clue we have that might tell us what Ravendas is digging for beneath the Tor. I don't see that we have any other choice."

"Wait," Tyveris said, holding up a hand. "We may have one other choice. Loremaster Avros told me about a friend of his, one Loremaster Erill, a disciple of Oghma who resides in a monastery in the Sunset Mountains to the east. It seems this Loremaster Erill has made a life's hobby of copying as many rare and decaying tomes as he has been able to find, to preserve them for future generations. Loremaster Avros isn't certain, but he thinks Loremaster Erill might once have journeyed to the library of Elversult to copy the *Mal'eb'dala*."

A triumphant grin crept slowly across Caledan's face. "The Sunset Mountains, you say?" He looked at Mari and then back to the monk, his pale green eyes dancing. "How do you two feel about going on a little journey?"

* * * * *

The Zhentarim Lord Ravendas ran a hand lightly over the cool steel spikes protruding from the machine. It was a curious device. There was a flat table beneath the needle-sharp spikes where an uncooperative prisoner might be bound, lying upon his back. At the foot of the table were a number of small wheels. Each one could be spun to raise or lower a single spike. The dozen spikes were positioned so that lowering them would cause terrible pain long before they caused fatal injury. Once Ravendas had been able to

lower nine of them into the flesh of a captain who had failed
her before his screams had ended in death. One day she
hoped to lower all twelve into a subject without actually
killing him. It was a great challenge, and Ravendas enjoyed
challenges. But so far nine was her best.

The circular stone chamber was filled with other malevo-
lent devices formed of twisted steel, sharpened wood, and
leather straps. All were different, yet all had the same func-
tion—to maim and cause agony, without causing death.
This was her torture chamber, deep among the foundations
of the city lord's tower. It was a favorite refuge when she
was in a rage, a place of peace. And Ravendas had been in a
rage much these last days.

Cityfolk had dared to stand against her.

True, not many so dared. And while persons had stolen
from her caravans and slain her guards, no real damage
had been done. But that was not the point. The point was
that cityfolk had dared to oppose her. The rebels would be
punished for that.

So far the resistance groups had eluded her attempts to
find them. They were well hidden in the city, like rats cow-
ering in the filth of a sewer. But now the rats had made a
foolish move. They had tried to discover something about
her. In turn she would discover something about them.

The heavy, iron-bound door opened with a grating of
rusted hinges. Two guards entered, cruelly dragging a prisoner between them. Behind them strode the lord steward,
Snake, in his poison green robes, eyes emotionless as
always.

Ravendas, clad in a robe as dark as an executioner's,
approached the prisoner. He was an old man, his limbs thin
and frail, his bony shoulders slumped, his head hanging
downward in despair. She lifted his chin with a finger and
found herself gazing into two empty pits of wrinkled skin
where his eyes had once been.

"Greetings, dear Tembris," she said softly.

Terror rippled across the old thief's face as he recognized her voice. His spidery limbs began to tremble.

She ran a finger slowly along his cheek. "Did you think that because your work for me was finished that you were no longer my servant, Tembris?" She spoke in a sickeningly sweet voice.

The thief shook his head in mute reply.

"Once my servant, always my servant, Tembris. That is my rule. And I hate it when one of my servants betrays me." Her long crimson fingernail dug into his flesh. A bead of dark blood trickled down his cheek like a tear. "It seems I should have taken your hands as well as your eyes." The thief was shaking with fear, and Ravendas bared her teeth in satisfaction.

Ever since the insurrection had begun in the city, she had been routinely capturing members of the Purple Masks Guild and interrogating them. There were few, if any, who knew more about what occurred in a city than its thieves, and the torture sessions had proven informative, as well as entertaining. A slowly descending, razor-sharp blade had convinced one of the thieves to speak of two strangers she had taken to visit Tembris in the guildhouse of the Purple Masks. Unfortunately, the thief had died just when her story was proving interesting. That had been Ravendas's own mistake. She had been so caught up in the thief's tale that she had forgotten to pay attention to the descent of the blade.

Thus Ravendas had ordered Tembris captured. Now she would discover what she wished to know.

She gestured for the two guards to lead the old thief to a chair in an alcove. Unfortunately, she would not be able to use any of her remarkable machines. They were designed for victims whom agony could compel to speak. Yet Snake had other methods at his disposal.

The guards strapped Tembris into the chair and at a harsh glance from Ravendas retreated.

"Are you prepared, my lord steward?"

"Yes, Lord Ravendas," Snake replied in his dry voice. From his robes he drew a silver knife and a small round dish of polished green stone. He muttered a few arcane words, then with the tip of the knife pricked the third finger of Tembris's right hand. The old thief winced in pain. A thin stream of blood trickled into the stone dish.

When the small dish was full, Snake dipped a finger into the dark blood and drew an intricate rune upon the old thief's forehead. Then he held a splay-fingered hand over the dish.

"*Azahk el gahzrabak!*" the lord steward hissed.

With a swift motion Snake turned the dish on edge and pressed its bottom against Tembris's chest, directly over his heart. A mild look of surprise crossed Ravendas's pale face. The blood did not spill out of the dish. Instead it seemed to be frozen in place, a smooth, dark circle absorbing all light.

"Ask him your question now, my lord," Snake instructed.

"Who came to visit you in the guildhouse, Tembris?" she demanded. "And what did they want of you?"

Tembris shook his head, his expression defiant. But Snake's magic did its work. The dark circle of blood began to glow with an unearthly crimson light. An image appeared within it, a bony hand holding a lump of charcoal, scrawling something upon a piece of parchment. A word. *Malebdala*.

So whoever they were, they too were seeking *The Book of the Shadows*, Ravendas thought. Of course, they would not find it. She possessed the only copy, stolen by Tembris from the library at Elversult. No one else would learn the secrets within its pages. No one.

The image flickered and changed. Now it showed a woman with red-brown hair. Her heavy cloak had shifted just enough to reveal a silvery pin on her jacket, wrought in the shape of a crescent moon encircling a harp.

Rage flared hotly in Ravendas's cheeks. She turned her sharp gaze to Snake.

"I thought you said all the Harpers in the city had been dealt with," she snapped furiously.

No emotion registered on Snake's thin face. "Apparently this one escaped, my lord."

She clenched her fine hands into fists. "Apparently," she said acidly. She was about to say more to berate her lord steward for his failure when the image wavered and changed again. Ravendas froze. The image showed a man with dark hair, pale green eyes, and angular, wolfish features. It was a face Ravendas would never mistake. She should have known she would not be rid of that one so easily.

"My lord steward," she said, her voice calm but deadly. "Find the captain who reported to me that Caledan Caldorien had been driven from the city."

Snake nodded deferentially. "Shall I bring him to you, my lord?"

"No. Just his heart will do."

"And what of the old thief, my lord?"

Ravendas tapped her chin thoughtfully with a slender finger. "I shall think of something," she said.

A low, wordless sound of fear escaped Tembris's lips.

*   *   *   *   *

Dawn was still only a silvery glimmer on the horizon as Mari, Caledan, and Tyveris rode from the courtyard of the Dreaming Dragon. They kept the hoods of their traveling cloaks up, concealing their faces. Iriaebor's streets were empty at this hour, but all the same they took care not to be seen.

"You're sure you don't want me to come along?" Ferret had asked as they made their farewells at the inn.

"Thanks, Ferret, but not this trip," Caledan had replied. "We thought we'd try *asking* the monks to see the book first."

The thief had shrugged his thin shoulders. "Suit yourself," he'd said in a slightly wounded voice, fidgeting with a sharp-edged dagger. "It just seems like a waste of time to me, that's all. Asking is so . . . so indirect."

Tendrils of mist crept from the ground as they made their way down the Tor into the New City. When they rode into the wide plaza of the free market, Caledan laid a hand on Mari's arm.

"Look above that archway," he whispered softly, "but don't be obvious about it."

She did as he instructed, and her breath caught in her throat. A spear had been wedged atop a stone wall bordering the plaza. Thrust upon the tip of the bloodied spear was a human head. It was a man with empty, wrinkled sockets for eyes.

Quickly Mari averted her gaze from the awful spectacle. "Tembris," she whispered. "But why. . . ?"

"It's a warning," Caledan growled softly. "Ravendas must know now that we're still in the city. But obviously she doesn't know where. Otherwise we'd both be up there with him."

A sick feeling settled in Mari's stomach. Serving Ravendas had first cost Tembris his eyes. In the end it had cost him his life. There was nothing to do now but ride onward.

The three companions made their way out Iriaebor's west gate, then left the main road shortly after midmorning, cutting overland to the northeast toward the distant, gray-green peaks of the Sunset Mountains. The mist had burned off the rolling plains, and the day had grown fine and warm. Mari pulled a felt-covered bundle from a saddlebag and carefully unwrapped it, revealing a very old-looking baliset. It was a beautiful instrument, built of ash inlaid with darker maple and reddish cherry. She strummed the four strings and smiled at the pure sound. The baliset's voice was as true as the day Master Andros had given it to her.

She had not played in several weeks, but her fingers plucked the strings with practiced ease, and she began a simple song. Tyveris, riding close by, smiled at the music. After a while, Mari added her rich, burnished voice to that of the instrument, singing one of the first songs Master Andros had taught her, a rollicking air about a sparrow in flight, and a man returning home to his true love.

> "I spy her far above me,
> Against the wide blue sky.
> She's whirling swift and graceful,
> A sparrow soaring high.
> But my love is no less lovely.
> Her eyes are just as bright.
> And while she may wear no jesses,
> She'll be my bonny bird this night.
> Aye, fly my love, and sing your song
> Like a sparrow on the wing.
> Don't be shy, for I won't be long,
> And I'll bring your wedding ring!"

When she finished, Tyveris applauded enthusiastically. "Truly, the gods have blessed you with the gift of music, Mari," the big loremaster said, smiling broadly at her. "Why, Caledan himself couldn't play a better tune than that, could you Cal—" Tyveris stopped short, his dark eyes going wide as he realized what he was saying. Mari bit her lip and cast a glance at Caldorien, who rode on in silence, gazing at the far-off mountains.

Mari played a few more songs as they rode, but soon she packed the baliset away. She found she had little heart for it, at least not that day.

* * * * *

It was verging on midday when the attack came.

They had just crested a low, rocky ridge. Below them at the foot of the ridge rushed a small river, muddy and swollen with the runoff of melting snow from the nearby mountains. The ridge was crowned with a jumble of massive granite boulders. As Caledan rode by, something dark dropped down from above them, knocking him from Mista's back.

He fell hard to the ground, the assailant on top of him. Caledan tried to struggle, but he was tangled in the assassin's heavy black robes. He didn't even have the chance to shout out to the others. Smooth gloved hands closed swiftly about his neck. In moments he was gasping for air, white hot sparks buzzing before his eyes. He tried to pry the assassin's hands off his throat, but his fingers might as well have been scrabbling against stone. The pain was terrible. Darkness began to close around him.

Suddenly a cry of rage shattered the air.

The assassin's hands were ripped from Caledan's neck. He watched in dulled amazement as Tyveris picked up the attacker bodily. The Tabaxi lifted the assassin above his head and hurled him through the air. Dark robes fluttered like strange wings. The assassin struck a boulder with a sickening thud, rolled to the ground, and then lay still.

"Caledan, are you all right?"

It was Mari, helping him to his feet, her face white with fear.

He nodded weakly. "I think so," he said. He swore to himself. After seeing Tembris in the free market they should have expected an ambush. Most likely the assassin had followed them out of the city. But why had Ravendas sent only one?

"Is he dead?" Caledan asked, climbing back onto Mista. The others remounted as well.

"I think so, Cale—" Tyveris halted. All three watched, stunned, as twenty paces away the black-robed assassin stirred and then slowly rose. Face lost in the deep shadows of the hood's cowl, the figure took a step toward Caledan. Then another, and another, each one faster than the last.

A hiss like a viper cut the air. An arrow abruptly appeared in the mysterious assassin's chest, stopping the figure dead in its tracks. "That should finish the job," Mari said grimly, lowering her short bow.

But instead of falling, the assassin slowly reached down with a black-gloved hand, gripped the shaft of the arrow, and pulled it out, casting it aside as if it were a piece of straw.

Ten

"By all the bloodiest gods," Caledan whispered, a chill prickling the hairs on his neck.

Tyveris muttered a hasty prayer.

Mari slung her bow over her shoulder. "Let's get out of here!"

The three whirled their mounts and cantered down the steep slope of the ridge toward the frothy river. The assassin pursued them with a strange, fluid swiftness, black robes billowing out behind.

The three pushed their mounts into a gallop, a perilous move on such a steep slope. The horses snorted, their nostrils flaring. The assassin—even though on foot—was gaining on them.

Caledan swore another oath. What kind of being did not feel the pain of an arrow's bite? Perhaps some fanatic of a dark god, caught in a religious frenzy. He had heard of such things but never expected to witness them firsthand.

Just as Caledan felt a gloved hand grope his heel, Mista plunged into the turbulent river. Muddy water swirled wildly about her flanks. The mare nearly lost her footing, then recovered. Spray slickened Caledan's face and the roar of the water deafened his ears. The other two struggled to keep their mounts upright to either side of him as the current carried them all downstream.

For a moment all thoughts of his strange attacker were forgotten. There was only the rushing of the river, angry and frigid with water from the spring snowmelt. Once Mista rolled onto her side, and icy water closed darkly over Caledan's head. His lungs began to burn. Then he was thrust back above the surface as Mista fought to stay upright, and air filled his lungs. The gray mare scrabbled up the slick stones of the opposite bank. Astride their own mounts, Mari and Tyveris followed.

Caledan leaned against Mista's neck, shivering and coughing up gritty water. The gray mare's flanks were heaving. The others were in a similar condition. He turned around, expecting to see the black-robed assassin fording the raging river, ready to close dark-gloved hands about his neck.

There was no one in sight.

The three galloped hard across the rolling terrain, letting the warm sun dry them as they rode. But the spring sunlight could not counteract the chill in Caledan's chest.

*   *   *   *   *

The three companions stopped for the evening as the golden orb of the sun dipped toward the horizon. They made camp in a low hollow beneath a hill and took turns keeping watch throughout the night. But they saw no further sign of the mysterious black-robed assassin.

They reached the monastery of Oghma late in the afternoon of the following day. The road leading into the foothills was simple enough to find. Two tall, weatherworn standing stones marked the way like sentinels at the mouth of a narrow, wooded valley. The road climbed steeply through sun-dappled groves of aspen and pine until finally the trees gave way to a grassy meadow at the foot of a sharp, iron-gray peak still tipped by snow.

"That's a monastery?" Caledan asked in astonishment, staring at the massive stone edifice hulking on the rocky mountain slope above them. "It looks more like a fortress."

"It *is* a fortress," Tyveris said with a deep laugh. "This was wilderness only a short time ago, remember, and monks have to protect themselves too, every bit as much as ordinary folk. Ravendas wouldn't hesitate to attack this place if she knew a copy of *The Book of the Shadows* was here."

The steep, winding path that led to the monastery's gate was too narrow for the horses, so the three climbed up the last part of the trail on foot. Caledan let fall the massive bronze knocker, and after a long while a panel in the gate opened, revealing the face of a wizened old loremaster.

"Hail, brother," Tyveris said, holding his palms open in greeting. "Hallowed is the name of Oghma, the Binder of all things."

The wizened old loremaster smiled and nodded. "Indeed, hallowed is the Binder's name."

The old loremaster opened the gate and led them across the tiled courtyard into the monastery. Despite the starkness of the outside of the stone building, inside it was warm and comforting, its walls paneled in dark wood and its floors covered with finely woven rugs. The loremaster left them in a small receiving room.

Minutes later the abbot of the monastery shuffled forward to greet them. Abbot Derevel was a tall, gray-haired man with bright eyes and a kind smile. Derevel sent a pair of monks to see to the companions' horses, then led the three to his study, offering them wooden cups of warm, spiced wine. They accepted gratefully. The air was crisp and chilly in the mountains despite the advent of spring.

Tyveris did most of the talking, bringing Abbot Derevel up to date on all of the happenings in the Realms which might be of interest to the disciples of Oghma.

"I appreciate your patience in telling me all the latest news, Loremaster Tyveris," Derevel said finally, "but surely you did not journey all this way simply to pay a kind visit to an old loremaster who does not travel as much as he used to. Is there some matter in which I might help you?"

Tyveris nodded. "Indeed there is, Abbot Derevel. You see, we're looking for an ancient book, one written in Talfir."

Derevel nodded. "Our library is not large, but it does contain some rare tomes written in that tongue. What do you seek?"

"It's called the *Mal'eb'dala, The Book of the Shadows*," Tyveris said. "I'm told your Loremaster Erill might have made a copy from the original in the library of Elversult."

Abbot Derevel raised an eyebrow in surprise. "That's true. Old Erill did make a copy of the *Mal'eb'dala*. That was several years ago, not long before he passed on to Oghma's halls."

Caledan grinned eagerly. "Can we take a look at it? It's important."

The abbot stood up, a frown on his face. "I'm afraid not," he said, shaking his head as the three companions stared at him. "You see," Derevel went on, "the *Mal'eb'dala* is no longer here.

"It's quite odd, really," the abbot continued. "Had you come here asking for the same tome a month ago, I would not have even recognized the title. But just last tenday a traveler came from the city asking to borrow the book. He seemed a scholarly man and offered to leave us several rare volumes in trade. I saw no reason not to let him borrow the tome and take it with him." Derevel looked at Tyveris in concern. "Have I unknowingly done some wrong?"

"I'm not certain, Abbot Derevel," Tyveris said, pushing his spectacles up. "These are dark times in Iriaebor, and there are wicked folk who seem interested in learning about ancient mysteries."

"Do you know the name of the one who borrowed the tome, Abbot Derevel?" Mari asked.

"I wrote it down. It's here somewhere." The abbot rummaged through the papers strewn across his desk. "Tall, quite stern-looking fellow . . . Ah, here we go." He lifted a scrap of paper and held it up to the fading light coming through the window. "Yes, I lent the book to one Morhion Gen'dahar of Iriaebor."

Caledan stood abruptly and snatched the paper from the abbot's hand, staring at it with hard, unblinking eyes.

"Is this someone you know?" the abbot asked, taken aback.

"Yes, I know Morhion Gen'dahar," Caledan said in a low voice, as if the name were a curse. "I know him too well, that treacherous mage."

*   *   *   *   *

"I won't do it," Caledan said in disgust, pacing the back room of the Dreaming Dragon. "I will not go begging at the tower of Morhion the mage. Not for *The Book of the Shadows*. Not for anything. Is that clear?"

Mari glared at him hotly, her arms crossed tightly across her chest. "You're being utterly unreasonable, Caldorien. So far that tome represents our only chance to learn what Ravendas is digging for beneath the Tor. I don't care if you and this wizard had some sort of fight years ago. What could he have done that's so bad you're afraid to see him again?"

Caledan shook his head and laughed, a hard, bitter sound. He ran a hand through his dark hair."If I'm afraid to pay a visit to Morhion the mage, it's only because I fear I will kill him the instant I lay eyes on him." Caldorien turned and stomped upstairs, leaving her alone.

He had been like this ever since their visit to the monastery in the Sunset Mountains three days before. It had rained in heavy, cold sheets the entire journey back. At least they had not encountered the black-robed assassin again, but then it would have been impossible for anyone to follow their tracks in the torrential weather.

Mari sighed and sank into a chair by the fire, resting her head in her hands. Caldorien could make her feel so weary. Sometimes she wished she could forget him, forget Iriaebor, forget the Harpers and simply return to Elturel. But she had knelt on the cold earth by Master Andros's tomb the day she had left, and she had promised her mentor she would be strong. How could she give up now?

Mari felt a hand grip her shoulder. She looked up in surprise to see Ferret regarding her with his dark, close-set eyes.

"Ferret, I didn't know you were here. I thought . . . I thought Caledan and I were alone."

The wiry thief smiled crookedly. "I'm sorry. It's a habit. Sneaking around, that is."

She tried to return his smile but failed miserably. His pointed nose twitched, his expression speculative.

"You heard?" she asked.

Ferret shrugged. "Of course." He pulled up a chair and drew out a dagger, carefully sharpening the edge with a small whetstone. Mari regarded him curiously, wondering what the thief wanted. Of all the members of the old Fellowship, Ferret was the one she understood least. Why the rogue had ever thrown his lot in with a Harper in the first place she couldn't imagine.

The room was dim save for the flickering glow emanating from the hearth. Ferret continued to sharpen his knife. Suddenly Mari realized he was waiting—waiting for her to ask something. "Tell me about the mage Morhion," she said finally. "I need to know, to understand why Caldorien hates him so."

Ferret set down the whetstone. He tested the dagger's edge with a thumb, spun the blade experimentally on a fingertip, and nodded in satisfaction. He scratched his stubbly chin thoughtfully, his dark eyes glimmering in the firelight.

"Hate is a simple thing, Mari," he said finally in his raspy voice. "If you hate someone, you act on it." He thrust the dagger into the wood of the table for emphasis. She flinched at the sudden motion. "That's what I do anyway. Of course, I'm just a thief. But then, I think the same is true for anybody." He worked the dagger free and slipped it into a hidden sheath inside his brown tunic. "But you know, I don't think Caledan does hate Morhion. After all, once they were the best of friends." He brushed the scar the knife had left on the surface of the table. "It's just that sometimes old wounds are hard to erase."

"Tell me, please," Mari said, leaning forward.

"I'm no storyteller."

He started to rise, but Mari reached out and gripped his hand. "Please."

He looked at her in surprise, then shrugged and sat back down. "You know about Kera?" For a moment Mari thought she saw a look of sorrow flicker across the thief's usually imperturbable face. But it was only the firelight, she supposed.

"Yes. Estah told me. Ravendas murdered her."

"There's not much to tell after that," Ferret went on. "After her army disbanded, Ravendas fled back to Darkhold, the Zhentarim fortress in the Far Hills. Caledan followed."

"But why?"

"To kill her, of course. I was ready to go myself. I had my daggers all sharpened and poisoned." Ferret sighed wistfully. "But Caledan forbade me, and I . . . well, I figured it was the least I could do, to obey his wishes. He wanted to punish Ravendas alone. I can't really blame him for that, though I myself wouldn't have minded sticking a knife in her." The thief's words sounded nonchalant, but there was a murderous look in his dark gaze that startled Mari.

"Caledan actually made it into Darkhold," Ferret continued. "That's no mean feat, by the way. There isn't a fortress in a thousand leagues more heavily guarded. But there was one who ignored Caledan's orders and followed after him."

"Morhion?" Mari whispered.

Ferret nodded. "The mage Morhion. And it was the fault of the mage that the two of them were discovered within Darkhold. They were forced to flee before Caledan could confront Ravendas. And by what secret route they managed to escape the fortress, I would give my left hand to know. There are any number of thieves who would pay quite a sum in gold in exchange for that particular information."

"Why did Morhion follow Caledan to Darkhold?"

Ferret shook his head. He didn't know. "To help Caledan? To hinder him? Who can say, with the mage? Thieves may be treacherous, Mari, but at least with us you always know where you stand. No one ever really knew what Morhion's motives were, except himself, I reckon."

Mari bit her lip in thought. "So Morhion's actions prevented Caledan from gaining his revenge upon Ravendas?"

"Exactly."

"And Caledan has never forgiven the mage for that?"

"Or himself."

The two were silent for a time. Finally Mari reached out and touched the gouge that Ferret's dagger had made in the wood of the table. "Estah will be mad at you for this, you know."

The thief smiled, displaying crooked teeth. "I know. But she'll forgive me."

Mari paused a moment. "Do you think Caledan will ever forgive Morhion?"

Ferret gazed at her flatly.

"No."

* * * * *

Mari barely saw Caledan at all the next day. He shut himself in his room upstairs after breakfast and did not emerge. Mari helped Estah in the kitchen during the morning and occupied the afternoon with her baliset, strumming softly as Pog and Nog listened drowsily until finally they drifted to sleep on a rug before the fire. It was verging on evening when Caledan appeared suddenly at the foot of the stairs, walking purposefully into the inn's back room.

"Get your cloak, Harper," he said.

"Where are we going, Uncle Caledan?" Pog asked in a sleepy voice, looking up at him.

"Finish your nap, Pog. You, too, Nog," Caledan told the halfling children. "Mari and I are going to visit someone, that's all."

Mari looked at Caledan in curiosity.

"Well, we have to get a look at that damnable book, don't we?" he told her gruffly.

Mari set down her baliset and pulled her cloak about her shoulders. "I wasn't arguing."

"That's a change."

The two slipped down the back alley behind the inn and into the city, making certain they weren't observed.

Mari was thankful Caledan had changed his mind. Now they just had to find the mage. None of the companions had

seen Morhion in the last seven years, but they knew the
place to start looking for him was the laboratory tower to
which he had moved after the Fellowship disbanded. The
tower stood on the eastern side of the Tor on the Street of
Runes, not far from the Temple of Selune. By the time they
reached the quiet avenue, the westering sun had sunk
behind the tower of the city lord, casting a premature twilight over the Street of Runes.

Caledan brought Mari to a halt.

The tower was dilapidated. Dead vines clutched at the
timeworn stones like skeletal fingers trying to pry the walls
apart. Weeds and witchgrass grew wildly amidst the piles of
rubble that had tumbled down from the tower's crumbling
buttresses. The high windows stared out over the city like
dark, empty eyes, and the peaked roof looked as if it had
caved in years ago. A pall hung over the place, a mantle of
dusty silence, of decay.

"This is it," Caledan said grimly. "Or *was* it, anyway."

Mari shook her head. It looked as if Morhion's tower had
been long abandoned.

"Maybe he's dead," Caledan said with a mock laugh. He
gathered his patched cloak about him against the evening
chill.

Mari circled the base of the tower, looking for a way
inside. The arched doorway had collapsed into a pile of
jagged rubble, but there was a dark, gaping crack to one
side of the doorway. It looked almost wide enough for her
to squeeze through. She shrugged off her heavy cloak.

"What are you doing?" Caledan demanded.

"Something useful," she snapped.

She ducked her head to peer into the crack—and stars
flashed before her eyes. She cried out in pain, taking a
dizzy step backward as she rubbed her aching head.

"You're right," Caledan said drily. "That's the most useful
thing you've done in ages."

"Shut up, Caldorien." Something was wrong here. Very wrong. She began running her hands along the tower's wall. The cracked and weathered stones felt strange, smoother under her touch than they looked. An idea glimmered in her head. She tried to stick her hands into the crevice in the wall.

Her fingers met solid stone.

"It's an illusion!" she whispered in sudden understanding.

"What are you talking about, Harper?"

"The wall, scoundrel. I know it's difficult, but try not to be so dense. Here, feel it for yourself." She grabbed his hand and held it against the stones. "It looks like it's crumbling, but it *feels* solid."

Caledan's eyes widened in surprise as he felt along the wall.

"I'm willing to bet the rest of the tower is the same," Mari went on. "Someone is using magic to make it look as if it's moldy and abandoned."

Caledan shook his head, frowning.

They heard the sound of a heavy iron bolt, and suddenly a door swung open where a moment ago there had been only blank wall. Golden torchlight spilled out onto the street. Mari and Caledan stared in shock.

A man clad in a simple but expensive-looking robe of pearl gray stood in the doorway. He was tall—far taller than even Caledan—and his face was lost in the shadow of a cowl. The man stood in silence for a long moment, then lifted his hands slowly to push back the robe's heavy hood.

"Caledan Caldorien. It has been some time," the man said, his tenor voice as burnished as brass. He gestured to the open doorway. "Enter."

Minutes later Mari found herself sitting in the study of Morhion the mage, an octagonal chamber at the top of the tower, anxiously clutching a goblet of crimson wine in her hand. She had always thought a mage's work chamber would be a dark and cluttered place, littered with stacks of moldering scrolls and myriad jars filled with foul concoctions. However, Morhion's study was a surprisingly clean and pleasant room. Neatly kept bookshelves lined the walls, and intricate Sembian rugs covered the floors. A small fire burned on the hearth, and dozens of candles bathed the room in a warm glow of light. The air was sweet with the faint, dusty fragrance of dried herbs.

Caledan paced the room in agitation, having drunk the wine the mage offered him in one swift gulp. His shaggy eyebrows were drawn down over his pale eyes. The tension seemed to hang in the air between the two men, an almost palpable thing. Mari did not dare say anything.

Morhion sat at an uncluttered table of polished rosewood, sipping his wine calmly. The mage was a handsome man, one of the handsomest Mari had ever seen. His features were fine and noble, and his golden hair fell about his broad shoulders like a lion's mane. Yet his deep blue eyes were so cold and calculating that Mari found it disturbing to gaze at him for any great length of time.

"You have come seeking something, Caledan," the mage said. "Perhaps you can stop for a moment and tell me what it is before your pacing wears a hole in my floor."

Caledan snorted in disgust and sank down into a leather armchair, glaring at the mage. "That's one thing I never did like about you, Gen'dahar. You always pretended you didn't understand things you knew perfectly well. You know why we're here. It's the book, the one you took from the monastery of Oghma in the Sunset Mountains."

The mage nodded. "The *Mal'eb'dala*? I suspected as much."

"What do you want with it?" Caledan asked accusingly.

"The same as you, I imagine," the mage answered, unperturbed by Caledan's tone. He stood and walked to a narrow window, gazing out over the city. "Ravendas seeks something buried deep beneath the Tor, and in the past she has shown an interest in *The Book of the Shadows*. It is not so difficult a connection to make. I had hoped the book might hold the secret to defeating Ravendas, to driving her from Iriaebor."

"Why should you care, mage?" Caledan asked, gritting his teeth. Morhion turned to regard Caledan with his unblinking gaze, and Mari noticed that even Caledan could not bring himself to meet the mage's disturbing eyes.

"This is my home," Morhion said simply. "My life is here, such as it is." Caledan looked daggers at Morhion, but he did not contest the mage's words.

"Have you read the *Mal'eb'dala*?" Mari forced herself to ask. "Have you learned what it is Ravendas is searching for beneath the Tor?"

"I believe so." Morhion pulled a heavy tome bound in black leather from a high shelf and set it on the table. Mari and Caledan bent over the book as the mage turned to a page marked with a ribbon of black satin. The writing was clear, but Mari could make no sense of the words, written in the ancient Talfirian tongue.

"Well, what does it say?" Caledan asked in annoyance. The mage ignored him, directing his words to Mari.

"*The Book of the Shadows* is an encyclopedia, of sorts. Its author, whoever he or she was—and indeed, there may have been more than one over the centuries—describes many mysteries forgotten since ancient times. Some entries describe terrible creatures, abominations of magic, while others discuss swords of power, or enchanted rings and the like. But there is only one entry that Ravendas would be interested in." He touched the page lightly. "This is it."

The mage began to translate the passage. "'Long ago,'" the mage read in his resonant voice, "'in a land east of the mountains and west of the sea, there dwelt a king named

Verraketh, a ruler both feared and mighty.'" Morhion
flipped the page. "The tale of how Verraketh became a king
goes on for some time. It is not particularly relevant to what
comes after." He ran a finger down the page, then started
again. "Ah, yes. This is it. 'Skilled above all men was Verraketh in the art of sorcery, but such was the power of his
dark magic that slowly it did consume him, flesh and soul.
Verraketh was changed until he appeared as a man no
longer, but rather as a being most hideous, his maleficent
heart filled only with darkness. Thus it was that Verraketh
came to be called by a new name—the Shadowking.'"

"Sounds cheerful," Caledan noted wryly.

Morhion shot him an unfriendly glance but continued
reading. "'For a long age did the Shadowking rule over his
dusky realm, but ever he hungered for greater dominion.
Many were the lands that fell. . . .'" Morhion paused. "I am
afraid the ink is blurred on the rest of this page, but I think
we can imagine that many lands fell under the Shadowking's dominion." He turned the page. "This, I think, is the
important passage.

"'. . . so began the forging of the Nightstone. It was a gem
wrought by the hand of the Shadowking from his own
essence, but it was not beautiful to look upon. Rather it was
as dark and cold as death. With it the Shadowking meant to
gain sway over the spirits of men and bring countless
realms under his dire rule.

"'Yet when the Shadowking first took up the Nightstone
in his hand to wield it, he discovered that he had been
tricked. The mute troll who had worked the bellows of the
Shadowking's forge cast off his disguise, revealing himself
as the great bard named Talek Talembar.

"'In his rapture, the Shadowking had detected not the
enchantment which Talembar had bound subtly within the
Nightstone. The gem refused to obey its creator, but rather
heeded only the power of the magical song which Talembar

played upon his pipes.'"

Morhion turned another page. "'For seven days and seven nights the Shadowking wrestled with Talek Talembar, and the earth shook with the fury of their battle. But in the end victory belonged to Talembar. At the end of all things the great bard raised his pipes to his lips and played the shadow song, weaving its enchantment about the Shadowking and his dark creation, the Nightstone. The Shadowking bowed on bended knee to the bard who had defeated him. Then did Talembar bind his vanquished foe within a great crypt, and over the crypt he raised a cairn higher than a hill. And the power of the Nightstone was hidden away forevermore.'"

Morhion stopped then, shutting the book carefully.

"But what happened to Talek Talembar after he defeated the Shadowking?" Mari asked.

Morhion shrugged. "I cannot say. The passage remains unfinished."

Mari frowned. It disappointed her that the tale told nothing more about the hero named Talembar.

"I don't understand," Caledan said with a scowl, starting to pace once again. "What does any of this have to with Ravendas and Iriaebor?"

"The *Mal'eb'dala* says Talek Talembar raised a great mound over the Shadowking's crypt," the mage answered, "a mound as high as a hill. I think that hill of legend is the very Tor upon which Iriaebor stands. I think Ravendas is digging within, searching for the Shadowking's crypt."

"Then it's the Nightstone she seeks," Mari interrupted, and the mage nodded.

"Perhaps it is only a legend and nothing more," Morhion said, returning the book to its shelf. "But what if it is not? If the Nightstone was real, and Ravendas held it in her hand, she would have the power to enslave every man and woman in Iriaebor, perhaps even beyond."

Mari clenched her jaw. "The Harpers will never allow this," she said grimly.

"Damn the Harpers," Caledan said angrily. Mari looked at him in surprise, but he glared back defiantly. "*I* will not allow this."

* * * * *

Caldorien and the Harper were gone. The mage, Morhion Gen'dahar, sat alone by the fire in his tower. He studied the runes he had scattered across a wooden tray lined with dark velvet. There were nine of them, each a small square of fired clay embossed with a single rune. Sometimes he saw hints of the future in the patterns they formed. It was these very runes that so far had kept him from moving against Ravendas. And now Caldorien had come, just as the runes foretold. In his heart he found he was gladdened to know that Caldorien yet lived. There had been madness in the man's eyes the last time the mage had seen him. But that had been long ago. He supposed Caldorien considered him an enemy now, but that did not matter.

What mattered now was the Nightstone, and nothing else.

These last seven years had been trying. They had been long years, years of waiting. Morhion had been forced to stoop to working as a court magician to support himself and his work. How much time had he wasted, advising foppish lords and entertaining petty nobles? How many times had he been forced to create a disguise for an adulterous husband, or conjure frivolities of illusion for a tittering contessa, when his time would have been so much better spent here among his books? But it was the curse of life that one had to eat, and so Morhion had performed these petty services in return for gold.

All that would be over soon. The waiting was done. Ravendas sought the Nightstone, and she was near her goal. Now Caldorien had returned, to help or hinder the mage as the fates decreed. Morhion wondered which it would be.

Morhion rose and knelt by the hearth, banking the coals in the ashes for the night. Suddenly a cold draft of air fanned the flames, bringing with it the dank scent of earth and rot, the sweet fragrance of death. Tonight was the full moon. It was time.

He stood up and watched as a pale, luminous form materialized before him, just as it had once each month for the past seven years. Thin strands of silver spun upon the empty air, outlining the shape of a man dressed in ornate, archaic armor. The silver strands grew brighter, weaving their glimmering magic, tracing the sharp lines of the man's face, his cruel mouth, and high cheekbones. Finally the silver strands plunged into the darkness where the man's eyes should have been. Two small specks as fiery as coals appeared.

Morhion felt his knees weaken, but he did not bother to sit. Even after all these years, no matter how many times the spirit came, he was never prepared for this sensation.

"It is time," the ghostly man whispered, his voice as insubstantial and chilling as mist. "The pact we forged beneath the fortress of Darkhold is binding. I demand my due."

"The pact is binding," Morhion whispered with a nod. His fingers trembling, he pulled a small bronze knife from the pocket of his robe and drew it across the flesh of his left arm. He grimaced with pain but made no sound as the dark crimson blood welled forth, sizzling where it fell upon the hot stones of the hearth.

The spectral man cried out in ecstasy, an inhuman sound, and knelt, bringing his cruel mouth to the pool of blood on the floor. The hot, crimson blood vanished from the stones as Morhion watched with all too familiar horror.

"More, mage," the spirit whispered, clutching Morhion's wrist with fingers as chill and numbing as ice. A low sound of terror ripped itself from Morhion's throat, but he could not break free.

The spirit bent the cruel mouth to the mage's arm to drink. "Yes, mage, the pact is binding. . . ."

Eleven

Caledan and Mari walked in silence back toward the Dreaming Dragon. Night had descended, and the full moon rising above the city's towers seemed to cast more shadows than light. The gloomy setting suited Caledan's mood. The conversation with Morhion Gen'dahar had left him edgy and preoccupied. Why was the treacherous mage so interested all of a sudden in *The Book of the Shadows*?

When they reached the narrow alleyway that led to the inn's back entrance, Mari laid a hand on Caledan's arm, halting him. "Caldorien, tell me something," she said, her brown eyes intent. "You're not going to act a fool and break into the tower to confront Ravendas, are you?"

Caledan shrugged, annoyed at her question. "Why would I tell you if I was? Do you confide everything in me, Harper? Or are there matters your precious Harpers have discussed with you that you've neglected to share?"

Mari's eyes widened, her face pale. Caledan allowed himself an inward smile. He had struck a blow. It seemed that the Harper was hiding something from him.

"You don't understand anything about the Harpers, Caldorien," she replied, shaking her head sadly. "I think you've forgotten everything it means to be one."

He laughed harshly. "No, I remember all too well. Everything's a game to you and your kind, isn't it? You manipulate people as if they were pieces on a gameboard. Don't tell me the Harpers really care about Iriaebor, or any of its people. They want to show up the Zhentarim, that's all."

"Think whatever you like, Caldorien."

Caledan opened his mouth for a bitter retort, but then he swallowed the words. There was something in her usually proud expression, a hint of a sorrow he had never seen before. His anger drained away.

Suddenly she was in his arms, clinging to him tightly. Their lips met, and Caledan felt a dizzying wave of fire inflame him. He held her close, and for a single crystalline moment the darkness around them was forgotten.

Then they heard the hiss of a sword being drawn.

Caledan and Mari broke free of each other. Caledan pushed her behind his back, spinning around. He found himself facing a swordpoint inches from his chest. A Zhentarim warrior held the hilt, an evil leer on his scarred face. Caledan considered reaching for the dagger concealed in his boot, but he knew he would never have the time to grab it. Behind him Mari had started to move, but he held her by the wrist. He didn't want her to do anything foolish. The Zhent couldn't kill them both at once. At least she would have time to escape down the alley.

"Harpers." The Zhent sneered. "Looks like I'm going to be popular with Lord Cutter tomorrow."

The Zhent raised his sword—and then hesitated. His leer dissolved into a look of confusion. He shook his head slowly. The words he uttered were lost in a stream of foamy blood gushing from his lips. The warrior's eyes went dull as he slumped to the cobblestones. Caledan and Mari stared at the lifeless Zhent.

A small, wiry form stepped out of the shadows.

"Good thing I was out for a walk," Ferret said, his crooked smile showing in the moonlight. Caledan could only nod. "Terrible, isn't it, the garbage people leave lying about the streets these days?" the thief went on nonchalantly. He wiped his dagger clean on the dead man's cloak. "I'll find a more appropriate place to dispose of this refuse. The wharfs are always a good choice. They already stink. Why don't you two hurry on inside?" Caledan patted the thief's thin shoulder in thanks, then Ferret vanished once again into the shadows. Caledan turned to see how the Harper was doing, but the alley behind him was empty. She had already vanished inside.

* * * * *

Caledan watched the sunrise through the panes of the window in his small room. Then he dressed and headed downstairs. Estah and Jolle were both seeing to customers in the common room. But Mari was in the kitchen. Caledan winced when he saw her.

How the kiss last night had happened, he was not at all certain, and he was even less certain about what it meant. The Harper was stubborn, self-righteous, overly critical, and she hardly fit any common definition of beauty. Caledan did not even remotely like her. So why couldn't he forget the warm sensation of her lips against his?

Mari was busily scouring a table. Her sleeves were rolled up, her hair was tied at the nape of her neck, and her cheeks glowed as she vigorously scrubbed at the wood with a rag and a scattering of sand. So intent was she on her task, she did not notice him watching her. Her jaw was

clenched tightly, her brow furrowed with a scowl. Suddenly
Mari looked up. Their eyes met briefly, then each looked
away.

"Listen, Harper—" Caledan began after a moment of
awkward silence.

"It's all right, scoundrel," she said, turning back to her
work. "You don't have to apologize."

"Apologize?" he said, a bit puzzled. Then he shrugged.
"Very well, Harper. I just wanted to let you know that, about
what happened . . . I mean, you and I . . ."

"I said you don't have to apologize, Caledan. It was an
accident, that's all. I know it didn't mean anything to you."
Mari seemed to be scrubbing a particularly stubborn spot,
practically scraping a hole in the tabletop.

"No—no, of course not," Caledan said, forcing a grin.
"I'm relieved you feel the same way. I guess we can just forget about it then."

Mari nodded. "I think that would be best." A silence followed. Thankfully Estah bustled into the kitchen then, dis-
pelling the awkwardness.

It was early evening when Tyveris arrived at the inn after
spending the day in the library of Everard Abbey. The loremaster had been searching for references to the bard Talek
Talembar and his battle with the Shadowking. If Ravendas
truly was searching for this "Nightstone" the mage had
spoken of, then Talembar's shadow song might represent
their only chance to stand against it.

Estah, Jolle, Ferret, Mari, and Caledan followed Tyveris
into the private dining chamber, and the companions gathered around a table.

"I'm afraid there isn't much," Tyveris said as he pulled
out a pair of books from his leather satchel. Caledan looked
at the tomes curiously. The first had the title *Talfirian
Eddas* emblazoned in gilt across its spine. Tyveris opened
the book.

"The eddas have been translated," Tyveris explained. "Unfortunately, none of them concern this Talek Talembar directly. However, one of the eddas is intriguing."

"How so?" Estah asked.

Tyveris flipped through the pages. "Here it is. Whoever penned this saga tries to convince the reader of the greatness of his hero by comparing him to heroes of the past. The skald lists about a hundred names out of legend. I don't recognize most of them. But one of the heroes he mentions is Talek Talembar."

Tyveris pointed out the passage, reading aloud. "'. . .and as brave as Talek Talembar, who in the Year of the Lion, in the reckoning of Cormyr, lamentably did fall to a craven goblin's arrow in the Duchy of Indoria.'"

Caledan frowned. "That's it?"

"I'm afraid so," Tyveris replied, shutting the book.

Ferret scratched his stubbly chin. "I've never heard of this 'Indoria.'"

"You're not the only one," Tyveris said with a rumbling laugh. "I spent hours going over every map in the abbey's library, and I couldn't find any trace of it. Until I looked in this book." He held up the second book. "It's a history of Calimshan."

"You mean Indoria is somewhere in Calimshan?" Caledan asked. He had journeyed to that arid southern kingdom on a few occasions and didn't much care for it.

Tyveris shook his head. "No, but it is in a history of one of the ancient noble houses of Calimshan that Indoria is mentioned."

Briefly the monk sketched what he had learned. Five or six centuries ago, the land to the west of Iriaebor, between the Winding Water and the River Chionthar, was a favorite battleground for kingdoms seeking control of the western lands of Faerun. Over the centuries, army after army clashed there in titanic battles. Many of those armies came from Calimshan, for this was before the founding of Calimshan's northern neighbor, Amn.

"I found a passage in the journal of a Calimshite lord who led an army across the River Chionthar," Tyveris explained, "where the lord notes in passing that they camped one evening in a place called Indoria. Bless the man, he even drew a map of his journey."

"Then we know where Talembar must be buried," Caledan said, his eyes glimmering.

Tyveris nodded. "At least the general vicinity. There's a village called Asher where Indoria used to be. Only nowadays the land between the Winding Water and the Chionthar is called the Fields of the Dead. Hardly a patch of earth can be plowed there or a well dug without turning up ancient bones or rusted armor. Reminders of the long-ago battles are everywhere."

Ferret gazed at the book speculatively. "What does it gain us to dig up old Talembar?"

"Maybe Talembar's shadow song was buried with him," Caledan replied. "According to the *Mal'eb'dala*, the only way to counter the magic of the Nightstone is by playing the shadow song."

"Then it's settled," Mari said firmly. "We must journey into the Fields of the Dead, to Indoria and Talembar's tomb."

"There's no reason to delay," said Tyveris.

"Tomorrow at dawn," agreed Caledan.

"It's a bit early, but I guess I can make it," Ferret added.

Estah smiled at them all. "It's almost like the old Fellowship," she said wistfully. "Almost." Jolle gazed at his wife, and for a moment Caledan thought he saw a sadness reflected in his usually merry brown eyes.

"Then let us see to the provisions, wife," he said, and she nodded, standing up.

"We need to pack food enough for four," she agreed.

"You had best make that five, friend Estah."

The companions all looked up to see a tall, imposing man step into the room. His long blond hair fell against the shoulders of his pearl-gray robe, and his cold blue eyes bore no trace of emotion.

"Morhion," Caledan said, as if the word was poison.

The mage approached. He nodded slowly in greeting to each of the companions before returning his attention to Caledan.

"What do you want?" Caledan said, standing to face the mage.

"These matters involve ancient magics, Caledan," the mage said unhesitatingly. "The Nightstone is an object of fell sorcery, and the shadow song itself an enchantment of great power. You will need me if you wish to truly understand their nature."

Caledan opened his mouth to protest, but Mari stepped forward and spoke before he could say anything. "We leave from the inn at dawn," she told the mage. Morhion nodded and then lifted his cowl, plunging his face into shadow.

"I will be here. At dawn."

Caledan clenched his fingers into a fist, but the Harper's hand on his arm restrained him.

"Until then," the mage said. He turned and left the room. A chill seemed to linger in his wake.

Silence reigned for a long moment. Finally Caledan spun around to glare at the Harper. "Why did you do that?" he demanded hotly.

"We need the mage, Caledan," she said defiantly. "You know we do. Think of someone other than yourself for a change."

"I think Mari's right, Caledan," Tyveris said solemnly, watching Caledan intently.

Caledan glared at the others. He knew they didn't bear the same enmity for Morhion he did—they were a forgiving lot, maybe to a fault. "I won't deny we are dealing with things—with magic—that we know little about, Harper. But I've already warned you once that the mage does things for his own purposes."

"And what purposes might those be, Caldorien?" Mari responded.

Caledan looked at the others grimly. "Maybe he wants the Nightstone for himself."

Twelve

Mari rose in the dark, before even the first gray light of morning had touched the sky. She dressed quickly in her small room, donning her soft doeskin breeches and a rust-colored coat, over which she threw a thick woolen traveling cloak of her favorite forest green. She gathered the few items she would need on the journey, packing them in a leather saddlebag. Briefly she considered bringing a roll of blank parchment and a quill, then realized there would be no time—or opportunity—to send another missive to the Harpers of Twilight Hall.

Downstairs she found Caledan already up. Estah and Jolle were helping him gather the gear they would need for the journey. Jolle had brought down a number of swords, daggers, crossbows, and stiff leather jerkins from the attic.

"Good morning, Harper," Caledan said with his wolfish smile. "So you decided to get out of bed and join us on this quest after all."

Mari held her tongue. She tried on several of the leather

163

jerkins. Finally she found one that appeared to be the right size, but the buckles were stiff and unbending.

"Here. They go this way," Caledan said, reaching roughly around her waist to fasten one of the straps.

Mari jerked away from his grasp. "I can do it myself," she said crisply. Caledan backed off, looking somewhat miffed.

Both Ferret and Tyveris arrived at the inn's back entrance just as Estah was setting breakfast on the table in the kitchen. The monk's timing was impeccable when it came to meals. Afterward, the others sorted through the attic equipment. Ferret selected several sharp daggers, tossing them experimentally in the air to test their weight. Tyveris came across a worn leather jerkin that had once been his. He grinned and pulled it on, then frowned. Unless a miracle were performed, he wouldn't be able to fasten the laces across his stomach.

"I guess being a monk agrees with you," Caledan commented wryly.

"I never liked this ratty jerkin anyway," the loremaster grumped, discarding the garment for a somewhat roomier choice.

Cormik slipped into the inn's back room to bid the companions farewell. Beneath his plain, unobtrusive cloak he was clad in a silken, gold-embroidered tunic. His opulent attire always looked a bit out of place in the rustic inn.

"Any idea how close Ravendas is to finding the Nightstone?" Caledan asked.

Cormik shook his head. "None of my people have gotten close enough to Ravendas to find out."

Mari nervously adjusted the silver Harper's sigil on her jacket, making sure it was concealed for the journey. "She's been digging for months now. She must be close."

Cormik patted her shoulder with a chubby, ring-covered hand. "Don't fear, Mari Al'maren. My associates and I will keep Ravendas occupied while the Fellowship is away." He smiled broadly, his eyes gleaming wickedly. "Of course, if you wanted to stay behind, my beautiful Mari, I'm certain I could find some . . . er, shall we say 'suitable tasks' you could help me accomplish while your friends here are gone."

Mari patted Cormik's cheek fondly and deftly extricated herself from his grasp. "Not in a thousand years," she said with a sweet smile.

"That's impertinent of you, Mari," Cormik said chidingly, and then he laughed. "I like that in a woman. Take care of her, Caledan."

Caledan regarded Mari sourly. "I'll try," was all he said.

After Cormik departed, the companions gathered in the garden behind the inn. As the first amber rays of dawn streaked across the sky, changing it from burnished silver to brilliant azure, Ferret kept watch for any city guards that might wander down the lane. Jolle had retrieved their mounts from the inn's stable, and the companions saddled their horses and loaded their saddlebags. Mista stamped a hoof impatiently.

"Patience. We're almost ready," Caledan told the gray mare, affectionately scratching her chin. She responded by trying to nip his fingers.

As they mounted their horses, Mari took in a sharp breath of surprise. There were five riders assembled in the garden, not four. The mage Morhion was there, clad in midnight blue leather and a cloak of misty gray, sitting astride a black gelding. But she had not heard him and his horse approach. Nor, by their reactions, had the others.

"I see you didn't change your mind," Caledan said, making no attempt to disguise his dislike of the mage. If the words stung Morhion, he did not show it. His regal visage was placid, his blue eyes like iced sapphires.

"I gave you my word I would come," Morhion said. "My word is binding."

Caledan snorted but said nothing more. Mari nudged her chestnut gelding, Farenth, toward the mage.

"I am glad you've decided to come with us," she said to Morhion, trying to keep her voice steady under his disconcerting gaze.

"Is that so, Harper?" the mage asked. His tone was not hostile, but neither was it especially friendly.

Mari shifted uncomfortably in her saddle, doing her best to meet Morhion's eyes. "Yes, it is," she said firmly. "The Nightstone is an artifact of legend, Morhion, of magic. It's simple. We need a mage on this journey."

"Is it as simple as that?" Morhion asked with a faint smile.

Mari gathered her cloak more closely around her shoulders to ward against the damp morning air. "Caledan thinks that you're coming with us for your own purposes. He thinks you wish to obtain the Nightstone so you can wield it for your own ends. Should I listen to him?" She searched the mage's face carefully for any trace of a reaction. His face, however, was as smooth and unreadable as a marble statue's.

The mage shrugged, his golden hair glimmering in the sun. "You yourself must choose what to believe, Harper."

It was time to be off. Estah was scurrying busily about. Every few moments she remembered one more thing the companions just might need and hurried to tuck it away in a pack or saddlebag.

"Enough, wife," Jolle chided her gently, holding her hand firmly. "If you put anything more in those packs, the poor horses are going to collapse."

Estah sighed and nodded. "I suppose you're right, husband. I've packed some balms and bandages, Tyveris. You know how to use them if . . ."

"Of course, Estah," the big loremaster said warmly, reaching down to grip the halfling healer's hand.

Estah nodded with a smile. Then the expression faltered. "But what will you do without a healer?" she said, worry showing in her brown eyes. "If one of you were to get hurt, and I wasn't there to . . . and especially you, pretty one." She reached up to touch Mari's hand. Mari didn't know what to say. "I just don't know what I'd do. I don't think that I could bear it."

"Go," a voice said softly. A hand fell gently on Estah's shoulder.

It was Jolle.

Estah turned to gaze at him, shaking her head softly. "Go," Jolle repeated. "It means everything to you. And it might mean everything to all of us as well."

"But I can't," Estah said softly. "Why, who will run the kitchen in the inn? And tend the garden? And take care of the children? And who will light new candles for you, husband, when the old ones burn too low?" Jolle raised a finger to her lips to silence her protests. "Go," he said one last time. They embraced. His eyes shone with sorrow, but also with pride and love.

Scant minutes later Estah sat in her pony's saddle, and the Fellowship of the Dreaming Dragon, reunited, was ready to take up where they had left off.

"I'll be here when you come back, wife," Jolle cried. Estah only nodded, as if even that was more of a farewell then the two of them could bear.

"Take care of yourself, Jolle," Caledan advised the halfling innkeeper. "If any of Ravendas's men come around asking questions, you don't know anything about where we've gone. Be careful. Don't get yourself into trouble."

"Don't you worry about me," Jolle said, a hard glint in his eye. "I can take care of myself. It's you who ride into danger, not I. May the gods watch over you."

The riders made their way single file down the alley behind the Dreaming Dragon. Ferret rode at the fore, scouting ahead. When he indicated the way was clear, the companions made their way out of the alley, riding through the city streets in the early morning light.

As they approached the city's west gate, they fell silent. They were about to pass through when a rough-looking guard stepped into their path, halting the companions. He didn't look to be Zhentarim, but his hand rested on his sword hilt with practiced ease.

"All right, mates. Show me your papers," the guard said, eyeing them distrustfully.

"Papers?" Caledan asked, apparently taken by surprise.

"That's right," the guard growled. "It's a new rule, come down from the tower just yesterday. No one's to leave the city without papers bearing Lord Cutter's seal. Seems some city guards have been getting badly cut up, and Lord Cutter doesn't want the rats who are doing it to sneak out of Iriaebor before she rewards them properly. Now, you got papers or don't you?"

Mari saw Caledan's hand creeping down toward his boot—and his concealed dagger. "Sure, I'll show you our papers," Caledan said, his body tensing.

Suddenly his horse was jostled aside as Morhion rode forward. "Here they are," the mage said, handing the guard several pieces of parchment. Mari's eyes widened. The papers were completely blank! The mage was going to get them all killed. She started inching her own hand toward the saddlebag where she had stashed a crossbow.

"Well, everything seems in order here," the guard said. Mari stared. The man wore a vacant look on his face, and Morhion watched him intently as he folded up the blank parchment and handed it back. "Well, get on with you," the guard barked. "I haven't got all day."

Morhion spurred his horse through the gate.

"Come on," Caledan whispered to Mari, and she nudged her horse to follow. Whatever magic Morhion had used to trick the guard, it had worked.

They rode swiftly for a league or so until Iriaebor, the City of a Thousand Spires, disappeared behind a low hill. They turned west across rolling plains that were green with the new growth of early spring. Pale, tiny flowers dotted the grass, their fragrance sharp in the air. The sun was warm, and Mari threw her cloak back over her shoulders. It felt good to be away from the oppression of the city. She had forgotten how bright and lovely the world could be.

They had a long journey before them. Even riding hard, the city of Berdusk was almost four days' away, and the Fields of the Dead lay another hundred leagues to the northwest, nearly a tenday farther, and that only if the weather held.

Shortly after midday, Ferret, who had been scouting up ahead, came galloping back toward the companions on his skinny roan stallion, his nose twitching. "I don't know if any of you were expecting company," the thief said, "but it looks like we've got some. There's someone keeping watch on a hilltop about half a league ahead."

Mari knew the thief's sharp eyes were seldom wrong. "Just one person?"

The thief nodded. "It could be either a man or a woman. It's hard to tell, with the black robes."

"Black robes?" Caledan spoke up, casting a glance at Mari.

She looked worried.

"What is it, Caledan?" Estah asked in concern. "Is it someone you know?"

"Maybe," he said grimly, gripping the hilt of the sword resting at his hip. "It sounds like that would-be assassin we ran into on the road to the Sunset Mountain monastery."

Ferret led them farther northwest, following a narrow valley that circled out of sight some distance from the rise where he had glimpsed the black-robed assassin. They rode hard for over two hours, pushing their mounts to their limits as the land, green and damp with the new spring, rolled by. But as the sun sank toward the western horizon, Ferret once again saw a black silhouette on a low ridge in the distance.

"It's no use," Caledan said. "This fellow can move fast. Mari, Tyveris, and I know that from experience. I'd rather face him now than later, in the dark." He eyed the westering sun nervously.

"Then we should find a defensible place and wait for him," Morhion said coolly. "Let the choice of where we meet be ours, not his." Caledan nodded grudgingly.

They found a low rise that dropped off into a rock-strewn ravine. A clear stream flowed swiftly in the ravine's bottom, toward the Chionthar, now three leagues to the south. Mari, Caledan, Ferret, and Tyveris formed a semicircle on the top of the knoll, backs to where Morhion and Estah stood with the horses. Caledan reached for his sword and Mari her crossbow. Ferret gripped a dagger in each hand; Tyveris was ready to fight with fists alone. Even Estah clutched a small knife, though all knew she was loath to use weapons. Morhion seemed calmest of all, waiting and watching.

"There he is!" Ferret exclaimed, pointing with his knife. They watched as a figure clad in jet-black robes appeared atop a ridge, striding toward them. The assassin moved with uncanny swiftness, and Mari had to force her hand to remain steady on the crossbow. In moments the black-robed man was ascending the low knoll where the companions stood. Mari waited until she was certain the figure was within range. Then she fired.

The crossbow bolt whistled through the air, landing with a sickening *thunk* directly in the chest of the assassin. The figure stumbled backward, clutching at the arrow with a black-gloved hand, then toppled to the ground.

"He's dead—" Ferret started to say, but then he choked on the words as the assassin rose and started back up the hill. A gust of chill wind whipped over the knoll. It caught the heavy cowl of the assassin's robe and then tore it aside, revealing the attacker's horrible visage.

"By all the gods!" Tyveris swore. "What is it?"

The figure that approached them was not human. The beast's face was misshapen, covered with thick, iron-gray scales. Two obsidian-dark tusks curved like scimitars from its maw, and a single, serrated onyx horn sprang from its brow. But most revolting of all, where the creature's eyes should have been, there were only two shallow depressions. It could not see. Rather, it swung its head from side to side, taking in air through its two slit-shaped nostrils.

It followed them by scent, Mari realized, not by sight. "I have read of creatures such as these," Morhion said in a low voice. "It is called a shadevar."

Ferret let loose a dagger, but the shadevar lifted a hand. Razor-sharp talons sprang from its fingertips, shredding its black leather gloves. The creature batted the knife away. Uncannily, it did not need eyes to fight.

Then the shadevar was upon them. The horses neighed in terror as it lunged. Mari barely ducked those deadly talons as the creature swung at her. Caledan brought his sword down hard on the shadevar's arm. The blade sliced through the thick black robe, then bounced aside, barely scratching the beast's metallic scales.

Almost carelessly, the shadevar struck back toward Caledan. His swing had left his side unprotected, and now the creature's talons dug deep, cutting through leather and flesh as though they were butter. Caledan cried out in pain, stumbling backward.

Suddenly there was a pounding of hooves as Caledan's mount, Mista, lunged forward. The gray mare reared onto her hind legs, then brought her forehooves crashing down

on the shadevar full force. The creature tumbled backward,
rolling halfway down the hill. It lay still for a moment, then
slowly it stirred and began to crawl up the slope.

Caledan groaned, sinking to the ground in Estah's arms.
He clutched his side as blood welled up thickly through his
fingers. Mari fumbled with her crossbow, her hands numb.
It took Ferret's help to get it loaded again. Tyveris was
chanting a prayer to his god, a powerful ward against evil,
but Morhion held up a hand, interrupting him.

"Do not waste your breath, monk," the mage said. "The
shadevar's magic will smash your ward as if it were made of
glass."

"I suppose you have a better idea?" Tyveris growled.

Morhion lifted his hands, the queer, dissonant language
of magic tumbling from his tongue. The shadevar was on
its feet again, picking up speed as it lumbered toward them.
The mage pointed a finger directly at the creature's feet as
he spoke the last word of the spell. There was a clap of
thunder, and then the earth beneath the shadevar shook,
tearing apart. The creature stumbled on the edge of the pit
that had opened just behind it, but somehow managed to
keep its balance. It took another step forward.

The hiss of a crossbow bolt sliced through the air, and
the shadevar clutched at a shaft protruding from its throat.
The force of the blow knocked it backward. The shadevar
lost its balance and tumbled into the rift in the earth that
the mage's magic had created.

"*Kalgava*!" Morhion shouted, and the rift groaned shut,
sealing the shadevar deep inside. The sound of thunder
faded.

"Is it . . . is it dead?" Mari asked in a weak voice.

The mage shook his head. "No. It will take far more to
slay the shadevar. Look." He pointed. Already the earth was
churning. The creature was trying to dig its way out.

"We have to flee," Tyveris urged. He lifted Caledan to his

horse. Estah had bound his wound with a makeshift bandage, but already it was stained crimson. Caledan's face was pale.

The others mounted, then guided the horses down the steep slope toward the ravine. "We must ford the river," Morhion shouted to the others. "By its nature the shadevar cannot cross water. Its magic prevents it."

The horses splashed across the stream, clattering up the far bank. Mari cast a look over her shoulder. There was nothing there.

The companions rode hard into the westering sun, their shadows stretching out on the land behind them.

*   *   *   *   *

They made camp in a hollow beneath a low hill as the purple veil of twilight descended over the land. Morhion arranged several flat stones around the camp's perimeter, and on each he set a leaf, a blade of grass, or a bit of moss. He spoke several words in the eerie, fluid tongue of magic, and a pale green nimbus sprang to life around each of the stones.

"I suppose a few glowing rocks are going to keep that foul creature away?" Tyveris asked the mage skeptically. The Tabaxi had never placed great stock in sorcery. He didn't much care for the trickery of wizards.

Morhion shrugged, his face impassive. "Speak your prayers if you think it wise, monk. No ward I might conjure would be strong enough to keep the shadevar at bay. This enchantment will disguise our camp, that is all. To anyone outside the nimbus, it will seem as if there is nothing here but a patch of grass and wildflowers. But I would be the first to say this is a temporary solution."

Tyveris grunted, as if this confirmed his low opinion of wizardry.

They had laid Caledan gently on a cloak on the ground. His head was foggy from loss of blood and the hard ride, but he seemed to have control of his senses.

"I am really far too old for this lunacy," he said through gritted teeth. He cried out in pain as Estah removed his shirt.

"I see this isn't the first fight you've ever lost," Mari commented. His lean, muscular chest was crisscrossed with a dozen scars, pale white lines that stood out sharply against a dusting of dark hair.

Deftly and efficiently Estah cleaned the dried blood from the wound with a cloth soaked in hot water steeped with medicinal herbs. The shadevar's talons had cut four furrows into Caledan's flesh. Luckily the gouges were not so deep as all the blood indicated. When the wound was clean, Estah carefully pulled out her silvery medallion bearing the likeness of the goddess Eldath. She held it in one hand, while the other hand she placed over the wound. The medallion emitted a faint, sweet humming, and Caledan felt a strange tingling sensation in his body.

When Estah lifted her hand away the blood and pain were gone. The marks had closed; already scabs had formed over the cuts. Caledan shook his head in amazement. It was not the first time Estah had used the medallion of Eldath to heal one of his wounds, but its power in the healer's hand was miraculous.

"It's going to leave a scar," Estah said.

Caledan didn't care. "What's one more?" he returned. Estah rummaged in his pack, handing him a clean shirt. The evening air was cold.

"Now there remains only one question," Morhion said. The mage sat on a low stone, leaning on a staff of ashwood before him. "Who is it who is so eager to see you dead, Caldorien?"

"I don't understand," Estah said in confusion. "Isn't it

Ravendas who commands the shadevar?"

Morhion shook his head. "Ravendas does not possess the power to summon a creature of such fell magic. There are few, if any, sorcerers among the Zhentarim who would have the ability to gain mastery over a shadevar. The shadevari are ancient creatures, as old as the world itself by some accounts. As far as I know, their kind has not walked the land in a long age. Once they were thirteen in number. Some scholars argue it was the evil god Bhaal who created them, but that is not so. He discovered them, but even then they were already ancient, as ancient as time itself. For thousands of years they served Bhaal, but eventually even the Lord of Murder in all his power could not control the shadevari. It was Azuth, the High One himself, who banished them far from the worlds of both humans and gods."

Morhion directed his piercing gaze toward Caledan. "Whoever the creature serves, he is a lord to be feared, that is certain."

The companions ate a cheerless meal as the stars appeared one by one in the sky. They took turns keeping watch during the night, but as Morhion had hoped, dawn came without any evidence of the shadevar. The creature's inability to cross water seemed to have worked to their advantage.

All that day, they pressed their mounts as the gray-green plains slipped by. Caledan's wound still ached dully, but thanks to Estah's medallion the pain was fading. Shortly before noon they came upon another small river flowing toward the Chionthar. They guided their horses down the riverbed for a half league before climbing the far bank. There was no sense making their trail obvious for the shadevar.

The sun was beginning to sink toward the western horizon and the light had taken on the thick amber hue of late afternoon when the Harper guided her horse next to Caledan and Mista.

"So how are you feeling, scoundrel?" she asked him. The wind blew her thick dark hair from her shoulders, the sunlight setting its auburn highlights afire.

"You'd better be careful, Harper," Caledan said wryly. "That sounds dangerously like concern in your voice."

She started to nudge her mount away, but he reached out to grab the bridle of her chestnut gelding. Their horses came to a stop. The others riding ahead seemed not to notice. "I just wanted to say . . . I just wanted to say thanks for worrying about me, all right? It's been a long while since anyone's really done that."

Mari was silent for a long moment. Finally a smile touched the corners of her lips. "Don't mention it, scoundrel." She nudged her mount's flanks, and the chestnut broke into a trot, catching up with the others. Caledan followed after.

"I don't know, Mista," he said to his mount as they rode. "There's simply no understanding women sometimes." The gray mare snorted, giving a sudden sharp kick, and Caledan had to clutch her mane tightly to keep from being thrown out of the saddle.

"Traitor!" he said through clenched teeth. "You females always stick together, don't you?" The gray tossed her pretty head in defiance, and Caledan swore under his breath. That was all he needed—another headstrong female to make his life miserable.

Thirteen

The lord steward Snake slipped the dim crystal into its velvet-lined box. His servant, the shadevar, had just made a disturbing report. Snake was going to have to take action, and he would need Ravendas's help. But first he had to decide how much to tell her.

He paced across his private chamber to a window high in the tower of the city lord and gazed out over the night-mantled city. A thousand lights glowed below him. This was the time of evening when Snake felt most alert and alive. The sunlight only caused him pain of late, and during the hours of brightness he felt constantly weary, his mind dulled. He hated the daytime. It had been that way ever since his ascent upward from the sewers below Iriaebor.

He closed his eyes, and for a moment he was back in the sewers, crawling through the dank pipes and foul-smelling passageways.

After escaping the dungeons, he had fallen, and the fall left his body broken and dying. But then he had made a bargain and become whole—no, more than whole. The blood sang through his veins, and a strange tingling in his fingers bespoke his new power. He remembered journeying in the darkness beneath the city, wondering what had happened to him in that cavernous, crimson-lit chamber deep in the heart of the Tor.

This is impossible, Snake, he recalled saying to himself over and over. You should be dead. Dead! You are going mad. . . .

But gradually another voice had intruded on his thoughts, growing in power, drowning out his panic. It was the voice that had spoken to him when he lay dying at the chasm's edge. Now the voice whispered in his ear, giving him understanding, purpose—reminding him of the bargain. Eventually his own thoughts drifted into nothingness. After that the voice was everything.

Finally he had crawled through a sewer grate into a dank alley of the Old City. Though the daylight was dim and gray, it seared his eyes all the same. He had been down in the blackness below for too long. He cowered in a shadowed alcove until twilight. Then he moved through the city streets once again.

He was desperately hungry. Once he had been a thief, and that instinct still pulsed within him. He came upon a baker who was just closing his shop, and slipped inside. Just as he confronted the rotund baker, he realized he had no weapon. But his hand moved instinctively. The baker's shout of protest was silenced in a dying gurgle as a livid bolt of emerald brilliance crackled from Snake's fingertips. The green fire burned a hole through the man's heart. The baker slumped to the floor with a look of horror on his face.

Snake stared at his hand. It was unmarked by the fire. The tingling of power was stronger now. His head spun as if he were drunk. Slowly a smile spread across his face. Then he stepped over the baker's body, picked out several loaves of bread, and began to eat. All the while the voice whispered in his ear. . . .

A cool breeze blew through the window, its touch bringing the lord steward Snake back to the present. He looked at his hands resting on the windowsill. The power in them had grown over the last two years. And the voice still spoke to him. It was the voice that had told him to seek out Ravendas when she came to Iriaebor. It had told him how to make himself useful to her, how to help her gain control of the city. Snake had never questioned the voice. The voice was always right.

Snake cocked his head, as if listening to a far-off sound. His dark eyes shone dully, like two black stones. Yes, even now it was telling him what to do. He must hurry to see Lord Ravendas.

He found her in her chamber, reclining languidly on a velvet-covered lounge in a robe of silk as pale as her alabaster skin.

"My lord, I must speak with you," Snake said in his sibilant voice.

"You are disturbing my rest, my lord steward," she said with irritation.

Snake's reptilian face remained expressionless. "It is important, my lord."

Ravendas glared at him, then abruptly stood. She moved to a table and poured herself a goblet of red wine from a crystal decanter. She drained it. "Well?" she demanded.

Snake moved closer to her, his green robe hissing like a serpent's scales against the marble floor. "Caldorien has left the city, my lord. Five travel with him, one of them the Harper."

The goblet crashed against a wall, breaking into tiny shards of glass. "Is that so?" Ravendas said with perfect calmness. "Caledan and his precious Fellowship—I should have known they would still be following him like a band of drooling puppies. Tell me, my lord steward, where are they journeying?"

"To the Fields of the Dead, my lord. That can only mean one thing. Somehow they must have found a copy of the *Mal'eb'dala* we did not know about. They must have learned about the Nightstone, and now they seek to discover the shadow song to counter its magic."

Ravendas laughed, a sound like breaking glass. "Let them try, my lord steward. I doubt they will fare any better than we. They will be unpleasantly surprised by what they find in the Fields of the Dead. And meanwhile we shall continue our excavations." She reclined upon the lounge once again. "Caldorien is more a fool than ever."

"Shall I send a party of your men after them, anyway, my lord?"

"Very well." A secret, wicked smile curled itself about Ravendas's lips. "But remember, my lord steward—I want Caldorien alive. The rest you may do with as you please, but Caldorien must not be slain."

Snake backed from the room, leaving her alone. He made his way down the tower's central staircase to give the orders for an attack party to ride hard to the Fields of the Dead. As Ravendas wished, he would instruct them to capture Caldorien alive.

But the shadevar had no such orders. A smile like the blade of a knife made a slash across Snake's severe visage.

* * * * *

The little room high in the city lord's tower was dark and quiet. Kellen lay in his bed, covered by fine woolen blankets. But he was not asleep. He was waiting. He clung tightly to a small wooden soldier. It was a crudely carved toy, dressed in a torn cloth napkin of royal blue. One of the servants had made it for him, a kind old man who had looked at him sadly when he learned Kellen had no toys other than the exquisite musical instruments his mother gave to him. Mother had ordered the old servant put to death when she learned of the gift, but she had let Kellen keep the toy.

"All gifts have a price, my son," she had said to him, leading him to a window where he could look down upon the old servant, hanging from a gibbet. The kind old man's face had been purple and swollen. It had made Kellen feel sick inside. But she had let him keep the soldier.

The square patch of moonlight falling through the open window spilled slowly across the floor, lengthening as he waited. Suddenly Kellen heard the outside bolt being drawn. He held the wooden soldier more tightly. "Don't be frightened," he whispered to the doll. "It will be all right." He closed his eyes, feigning sleep, as the door opened.

"Rise, Kellen," a sibilant voice whispered. It was the lord steward, Snake. "Your mother has sent for you."

Kellen sat up in bed, nodding wordlessly. He hated the lord steward. It was always Lord Snake who came in the middle of the night, like a phantom, to wake Kellen and take him to Mother if she had called for him. Kellen wished he could run from Lord Snake, but he had to obey, else Mother would be angry with him.

An attendant entered to help Kellen dress, and soon he was shown to his mother's chamber high in the tower. He shivered in the thin silken tunic the attendant had made him don. Wool would have been better on a frigid night like this, but Mother fancied him in silk, so that is what he wore.

His mother, the Zhentarim Lord Ravendas, reclined on a velvet lounge, her blue gaze lost in the flickering fire. "Come, my son. Play for me," she said, not looking away from the flames.

Kellen nodded wordlessly. He picked up the set of polished reed pipes that rested on a low table and knelt on the carpet at his mother's feet.

Sometimes Mother made Kellen drink wine before he played. It was always strange-tasting, bitter, and made him have queer thoughts. The room would go all funny, and his head would feel heavy and dull. Worst of all were the shadows on the walls. If he played for a long time, sometimes it seemed as if they were moving, reaching for him, hungry for a taste of him. Those were the times Mother would talk to him, her red lips smiling. The things she said frightened him, but afterward he could never seem to remember the words, as if everything had been a dream.

This time there was no wine, and he did not feel so afraid. He lifted the pipes in his small hands and brought them to his lips. The notes sounded pure and clear. Soon he forgot Mother, and Lord Snake, and the shadows, and thought only of the music. He loved music, even when it was Mother who made him play.

"Enough," his mother said finally, striking the pipes from his grip. They clattered across the cold marble floor. Kellen stared at her, his green eyes wide. Her cheeks were flushed with too much wine. Something had angered her. "Why did you play those vile pipes, Kellen? They make me remember. You know I do not like to remember."

"But you asked me to," he said in a small voice. She glared at him, her face pale and hard. Kellen cringed. Don't be frightened, he said inwardly to the wooden soldier hidden in his pocket. She raised a hand as if to strike him, then suddenly she laughed, a crystalline sound.

"Ah, my dutiful son," she said, caressing his cheek with the hand that had been poised to strike him only a moment before. "Of course I did. You are good to obey me, my son, my sweet son. Now you must go and get your sleep. Your important day is coming. You must be ready." Kellen rose and started for the door.

"What have you forgotten?" Mother said to him. He reluctantly shuffled to her, then leaned forward and pressed his lips against her cheek. She hugged him, squeezing him so tightly it hurt, but he did not cry out. Then she let him go. Her gaze fell back to the fire, as if he were already gone. Lord Snake appeared to show him back to his chamber, and Kellen ran ahead of him so that the steward would have no opportunity to touch him.

Lord Snake left him alone in his bedchamber, shutting the door and drawing the bolt. Kellen would not be let out of the room until morning, if they did not forget to let him out. Sometimes they did, not coming for him until evening or, once, even the next day. But Kellen did not mind. He might grow hungry and thirsty, but it was worth it to have some time away from *them*.

When he was absolutely certain that Lord Snake was gone, Kellen knelt down and pried up a loose tile from the floor beneath his bed. In a hollow beneath the tile was a small tatter of cloth. Kellen carefully unwrapped the rag and pulled out a small object. It glimmered brightly in the moonlight falling through the window.

"This was Father's," he explained to the wooden soldier. He did not take the object out often, for he feared its discovery, but it comforted him on nights when he felt particularly lonely. He had found it in a box in Mother's chamber, and for some reason had fancied it and slipped it into his pocket. It was the only thing he had ever taken from her. Later he had heard Mother shouting at Lord Snake, demanding that the object be found. That was when he learned that it had been Father's.

Kellen did not know who Father was. Mother said he was dead, but at night, in secret, Kellen would whisper to Father, regardless. In that way Father had become his friend, along with the wooden soldier. Sometimes Kellen would lie awake all night, just imagining what Father

looked like, wondering what it would feel like if Father held
him in his arms. He did not believe Father was dead, otherwise Mother would not look so angry on those rare occasions when she mentioned him. Mother was never angry
with dead people. Kellen knew that. She had nothing to fear
from dead people.

"Someday," he said to the wooden soldier, "Father will
come and take us from this place, and things will be so
good. . . ."

Kellen climbed into bed then, tucking in the wooden soldier carefully. He held the memento of his father tightly,
then let the darkness of sleep finally blanket him.

The square of moonlight from the window crept across
the floor and up the bedcovers. It moved across the small
boy's sleeping form, touching his dark hair, his pale
cheeks. It reached his hand which had fallen open in the
peace of sleep. The light shone softly on the object that
rested there.

It was a small silver pin, wrought in the shape of a crescent moon encircling a harp.

*   *   *   *   *

The companions rode into the village with the long shadows of sunset, weary and ready for rest. They had been
traveling for over a tenday now. It had taken four days of
riding west from Iriaebor to reach the trade city of Berdusk.
The distance might have been covered faster, but they had
avoided all roads, traveling overland instead. So far they
had seen no further sign of the shadevar.

They had spent one night in a disreputable inn on the
outskirts of Berdusk. The bustling trade city was where
Twilight Hall—one of only two permanent meeting places
kept by the Harpers—was located. Caledan had asked Mari
if she wished to contact any of her colleagues. Oddly, she

had seemed disinterested, but Caledan did not push the point. He had no desire to meet with the Harpers himself. One was enough.

They had not lingered in Berdusk, and the ride to Elturel had taken six days more. The spring weather had turned fine and clear, and Caledan had found himself beginning to enjoy the trek. Each of the members of the Fellowship had fallen comfortably into his or her old familiar habits. Estah and Tyveris took charge of meals, Ferret constantly prowled the terrain, and Morhion kept to himself, perpetually studying his spell books in silence—the curse of being a mage. Everything was almost exactly as it had been during the days of the Fellowship, almost as if the Fellowship had never disbanded. Except there was one glaring difference: Mari Al'maren rode with them, and Kera . . . Kera did not.

Just a glance from the Harper, and Caledan could feel his heart beating faster. Yet each time he resolved to speak with her alone something stopped him, forced him to turn away. And something seemed to be restraining the Harper as well.

Mari had not wished to pass through Elturel, even though it was the city where she had grown up. "There's nothing there for me now except memories," she had said as they skirted around the city's walls. Caledan hadn't known how to respond. He knew that, sometimes, memories were all a person had left.

Now Elturel lay three days behind them, and they trod on the very edges of the Fields of the Dead. Somewhere in the vast rolling plains before them lay the tomb of Talek Talembar—and, they all hoped, the key to fighting the dark magic of the Nightstone.

The village was little more than a sparse huddle of stone houses with thatched roofs. A few peasants picked their way through the churned mud of the village's one and only street, but these looked up in fright as the companions approached, hurrying indoors. Wary eyes watched from cracked shutters as the companions rode down the street, but no villagers came out to greet them.

"Friendly place," Caledan noted. "Ferret, did you notice any inns or taverns while you were scouting?"

"I saw a large building on the far side of the village," the thief said. "If the owners aren't willing to accommodate us, I'm sure we can convince them somehow." He idly spun a sharp dagger on the tip of a finger.

"Ferret, there is such a thing as *paying*, you know," Tyveris commented. The thief gave the monk a nauseous look.

The big structure Ferret had spied turned out to be, in fact, an inn. It was a tidy, two-storied building of wood and stone. Tyveris and Ferret saw to the horses while the others went inside to inquire about lodging. The common room was austere but neatly kept, and the freshly scrubbed tabletops warranted a look of approval from Estah. "Yes, this will do nicely," the halfling said.

The innkeep, a man named Brandebar, was a jovial fellow of middle years, a widower who kept the inn with the help of his two daughters. The inn had no guests at the moment, and the innkeep was grateful for the business. When the Harper gave him three heavy gold coins, his eyes widened.

"I'll show you to my finest rooms, milady," he said, sketching a rough bow as he pocketed the coins. "If you don't mind my saying, you seem like important folk. We don't get many lords and ladies riding through these parts. I hope you'll find my modest rooms to your liking."

"I'm sure we'll like things just fine," Mari said reassuringly.

The innkeep showed them to a pair of comfortable adjoining rooms on the second floor.

"There you go, *my lady*," Caledan said wryly as he tossed Mari's saddlebags onto a bed.

"Don't expect me to start calling you, 'my lord,'" she replied smartly, hands on her hips.

After they stowed their gear they headed back to the common room to see what was in store for supper. Tyveris and Ferret had already finished with the horses, and each held a clay pot of ale in his hand.

"That's not fair, starting without me," Caledan said in a hurt tone. He ordered two more pots of ale from one of the innkeep's daughters, a stout woman with ruddy cheeks and a cheerful smile. He had some catching up to do.

The innkeep himself brought them their supper—a rich meat stew, loaves of fresh, crusty brown bread, and a crock of soft, pale cheese. It was without doubt the best meal they had eaten since leaving the Dreaming Dragon, and Caledan felt his spirits lifting.

"Where's Morhion?" Mari asked as they ate.

"That mage," Estah said with a scowl. "He isn't the least interested in eating. He's upstairs with his nose buried in one of his musty old books. He mumbled something about needing to be ready."

"Ready for what?" Ferret asked.

The halfling shrugged. "Why, for battling the shadevar, I suppose."

"I'll take him a plate," Mari said, dishing up some of the stew and slicing several pieces of bread.

"Good luck, Mari," Estah said, patting her hand. "The gods know, I tried for years to get that man to eat enough without much luck. I don't know what he subsists on. Ink fumes or some such thing, I suppose."

Caledan watched Mari as she ascended the stairs, plate in hand. Why was the Harper so concerned about that infernal mage?

After a time Mari returned downstairs. She sat back down at the table where the companions were eating and picked at her stew.

After the supper dishes had been cleared they sat near the fire, discussing their plans for the next day. According to Tyveris's map, the village of Asher was no more than a day's ride to the northwest.

Mari sighed and told the others she was going to turn in early. Estah noticed that she was rubbing her temples, as if she had a headache.

"Is something wrong, Mari?" Estah asked in concern, but the Harper shook her head.

"I'm tired, that's all," Mari answered with a thin smile. "Thanks, Estah." Mari left the common room.

"Why don't you go after her, Caledan?" Estah said softly, touching his arm gently. Ferret and Tyveris were engaged in a friendly argument of some sort and paying little attention to Estah and Caledan.

Caledan should have known he couldn't hide his emotions from the healer. "I can't, Estah," he said almost angrily. How had he gotten himself into a situation like this? "Maybe the Harper and I do feel . . . something for each other. But both of us know that it's not going to work."

"Why?" Estah asked simply. "Why turn your back on love, Caledan?"

He shook his head, fidgeting with the copper bracelet on his left wrist. "I loved once, Estah. And I think maybe once was enough."

"I've never heard such nonsense," Estah said, her brown eyes flashing fire. "Why, you're every bit as stubborn as she is." She stood up, her hands resting firmly on her hips. "We all loved Kera very much," she said quietly but firmly. "But someday, Caledan, you are going to have to take that bracelet off."

Caledan stared at her in surprise, but the halfling turned on a heel with a flounce of her gray dress and marched up the stairwell.

* * * * *

The moon had not yet risen; the night was dark. It was Tyveris's watch. The loremaster stood by the window while the others slept, gazing out over the village streets. He yawned, keeping his eyes peeled. He was determined not to fall asleep during his watch.

So intently was the loremaster's attention focused outside, however, that he did not hear the faint stirring in the shadowed room behind him.

A form quietly slipped from one of the beds and stood in the dimness, clad only in a light robe of white. It was the Harper, Mari. Her eyes were open, but they stared blankly into the darkness, unblinking. Slowly, Mari reached down to the leather pack that lay next to her bed. She slipped something silently from the pack, then gripped it tightly in her hand. Sharp steel shone dimly in the dusky air.

Mari trod almost soundlessly on bare feet past the bed where Estah lay, deep in slumber. Tyveris did not turn from the window, nor did he see Mari step through the open doorway into the adjoining room. Moving stiffly, Mari strode past the bunks where Morhion and Ferret slept until she reached a low cot against the far wall.

Caledan lay sleeping before her.

He shifted in his slumber, making a low sound, but did not wake. Still staring blankly ahead, Mari lifted the dagger. She hesitated, her brow furrowing. But after several heartbeats her face hardened once more. Her grip on the hilt tightened as she poised the blade over Caledan's bare chest.

And then she thrust the knife downward.

Fourteen

Caledan woke to the sound of a scream. It was a terrible, wordless cry of primal rage.

He leaped from the bed and stared at the scene before him. Tyveris was grappling with the Harper. She struggled furiously, trying to stab Tyveris with her dagger, but the loremaster held her tightly. Again Mari cried out in fury.

"By the gods, Tyveris, what is going on?" Caledan shouted. The others had risen now and were also staring at the strange scene in astonishment. Then Morhion spoke a word of magic, and the room was suddenly flooded with silvery light.

The big loremaster shook his head. "I was hoping someone could tell me, Caledan. I went to wake Ferret for the next watch and saw that Mari's bed was empty. When I came in here, I found her ready to bury this knife in your heart. I caught her hand just in time."

Caledan shook his head disbelievingly, his mind reeling.

The Harper had meant to kill him?

"But Mari would never do such a thing," Estah said, the halfling's voice trembling.

"Wait," Morhion said. "Can you not see it in her eyes?"

Indeed the Harper's eyes were empty. Normally glowing with life and fire, they were instead as dark and dead as stone.

"What is it, Morhion?" Estah asked, wringing her hands. "What's happened to her?"

The mage did not answer immediately. Gazing at the Harper, he muttered a few strange words as he touched her forehead. Suddenly she went limp in the loremaster's arms, the dagger slipping from her fingers.

"She is under an enchantment," the mage said.

Caledan helped Tyveris lay Mari down on the bed. Her eyes were closed now, her face was pale, her breathing shallow and rapid. "Enchantment?" Caledan wondered, turning toward the mage. "By whom? The shadevar?"

Morhion shook his head. "No, I do not think such would be within its powers. A Zhentarim sorcerer is the more likely culprit."

Caledan swore.

"Estah, is there something you can do for her?"

The halfling healer laid a hand upon the Harper's brow, then shook her head. "She's burning with fever, but none caused by any sickness. It's the magic that's setting her blood afire." She looked hesitantly at the mage, then back at Caledan. "Magic must be fought with magic."

Caledan clenched his jaw, not looking at Morhion. The Harper moaned in the enchanted slumber the mage had cast upon her, her hands clutching at the bedsheets. "All right, mage, do what you must." If you harm her . . . Caledan almost said, but he swallowed the words.

Morhion drew a small pouch from the pocket of his gray robe. He removed a dried leaf from the pouch, then opened the Harper's mouth, placing the leaf beneath her tongue.

Caledan looked worriedly at Estah, but the halfling shook her head. She had no idea what the mage was doing. They would have to trust him.

Morhion rummaged in his pack until he found a flask of wine. He dipped his finger into the flask, then let three ruby-colored drops fall onto Mari's brow. As the third drop fell he spoke several eerie, flowing words of magic. Suddenly the Harper cried out in pain.

"You're hurting her!" Caledan cried, grabbing the mage's arm, but Morhion shook off Caledan's grip.

"*Madrak ul madrakel*!" the mage intoned, and Mari's eyes flew open. They were wide with confusion, but glimmering with life.

"What . . . what happened?" the Harper said weakly. She frowned and spit out the bitter-tasting leaf. She looked at the mage and Caledan in puzzlement.

Estah shook her head ever so slightly. The others exchanged meaningful looks. This incident was something Mari need never know of.

"We're not sure," Caledan told Mari. "The mage thinks there might be a sorcerer outside the inn, someone who means to do us ill. Whatever he was doing was making you . . . uh, sick. But the mage's spell took care of that."

Mari nodded weakly. "Thank you," she said to Morhion, but the mage had already turned to gather his things.

"We must leave here immediately," Morhion said, and for once Caledan agreed with him.

In minutes the companions were packed and ready to leave. Mari still looked a bit drawn, but she was standing firmly. "Can you make it?" Caledan asked

She nodded, her face grim.

They found Brandebar in his nightshirt in the common room, a look of concern on his face. "What is it?" he asked.

"We've got to go, Brandebar," Caledan told the innkeep.

"I want you to lock the door behind us. Don't open it again until daylight. Do you understand?"

"Is there someone out there who means you harm, milord?" Brandebar asked.

Caledan hesitated. "I believe so."

"Then I think you should follow me." The innkeep beckoned for them to go into the kitchen. Caledan looked at the others and then followed. In the corner of the kitchen Brandebar pulled up a wooden trapdoor. Caledan could see a ladder leading down into shadows.

"It's a tunnel leading to the stables. Winters are bitter here, and I dug this one year so I could see to the horses without having to venture outside."

Caledan grinned. "Brandebar, we owe you a debt."

"You've paid me quite enough already, milord," the innkeep said, beaming. "I'm just glad I could be of small service to such important folk. Now take care. I expect you to come calling at the inn again one day soon."

They bid Brandebar farewell and then descended, one by one, into the earthen tunnel. It was crowded and damp inside, but after perhaps a hundred yards there was another ladder, this one leading up through a trapdoor in the stable's floor.

When the horses were ready Ferret quietly opened the stable doors, and they rode out into the dark, windswept night. The moon had set; dawn was at least two hours distant. The only light was the faint glow of the stars. They rode north, avoiding the road that led from the village. They had covered half a mile when Ferret pulled his horse up next to Caledan's.

"I don't mean to worry you or anything," the little thief said, "but I thought you might like to know that there are some shadows following us on the hills to our right and left."

"Horsemen?" Caledan asked, and Ferret nodded.

"My guess is they're waiting for us to ride into a ravine or gully—someplace good for an ambush. That's what I'd do, anyway."

"What do you propose we do about them?" Caledan asked.

Ferret smiled, his crooked teeth glowing in the dimness. "Be ready," he said, drawing a dagger from his belt. Caledan nodded, loosening his sword in its sheath as Ferret moved away to warn the others.

The attack came swiftly. The low trough in which they rode had gradually narrowed until finally ending in a steep wash. Before they could spur their mounts up the rocky slope, the night was shattered by battle cries.

In the dimness Caledan saw a dozen dark shapes rushing at them from the ridges to the right and left. Men on dark horses drew their swords, which glimmered dully in the starlight. One of the horsemen tumbled from the saddle as he rode, Ferret's knife in his throat. Another fell to the ground next to him, clutching weakly at the crossbow bolt embedded in his side. Mari had hit her target and was frantically trying to reload.

Then the first of the horsemen reached them. Two lunged at Caledan. He parried one swing, then Mista reared up on her hind legs. She came crashing down, adding her strength to Caledan's blow. His sword cleaved deep into one of the riders. Hot droplets of blood struck Caledan's face. The rider slumped forward in the saddle as his mount galloped away. Caledan turned his attention to the other horseman.

Behind him, Tyveris ducked a horseman's blow and then reached over, pulling the man bodily from the saddle with his massive arms. The loremaster's shoulders bulged as he lifted the man and hurled him through the air. The man landed in a crumpled heap and did not rise again. Another attacker took the opportunity to swing at Tyveris, but a dagger appeared abruptly in his chest, and he fell screaming to the ground. Ferret was already drawing another dagger from his seemingly endless supply.

Mari guided her mount between Estah and the attacking horsemen, trying to aim her crossbow. She fired, but the bolt whistled harmlessly through the air. She took aim again, then swore in frustration. It was too chaotic, and she couldn't be sure she wouldn't hit one of her companions instead of one of the horsemen.

Caledan managed to fell his second attacker, then looked up to see a horseman fly from his mount as a brilliant, cobalt blue bolt of light exploded against his chest. Caledan cast a glance at the mage, but Morhion was deep in concentration, readying another spell. Caledan grunted. At least the mage could carry his own weight in a battle. There were only five horsemen left now, and Caledan sensed the tide was turning.

Suddenly a sound split the air. A sphere of searing crimson brilliance burst apart in the night. Then came a boom like thunder. The companions scattered, their mounts skittering away from the magical inferno. It was sheer luck that the flames did not engulf them.

"Beware sorcery!" Morhion shouted above the din of the battle. Caledan glanced up and saw a figure silhouetted against the dark sky on a low rise. So that was the source of the magical fire. He tried to break Mista away from the battle, to ride up the hill, but his opponent rained a flurry of fierce blows upon him, and Caledan was forced to stop and parry.

He heard Morhion muttering another spell, but the mage's words were cut short as a horseman bore down on him. Morhion drew a small dagger, prepared to defend himself. Caledan looked up to see the sorcerer on the ridgetop gesturing wildly.

Abruptly the sorcerer staggered backward, his spell

going wild. A trail of fire arced high overhead, bursting in a flash of crimson light that momentarily illuminated the battle scene as though it were day. Then the magical fire faded into darkness. Sparks drifted down like fireflies. On the hilltop, the sorcerer crumpled. Caledan glanced to his side and saw Mari lowering her crossbow. He reminded himself to compliment the Harper on her good aim.

Without any further interruptions, it was scant minutes before they dispatched the rest of the attackers. Estah examined the companions in turn. Each had suffered nicks and bruises, and Tyveris had wrenched his shoulder.

"That last one was a bit heftier than I thought," he said, wincing as Estah probed his shoulder to make sure it was no more than a strained muscle.

"Well, next time knock the rider down, not the horse," Estah quipped, and Tyveris grinned sheepishly.

Caledan dismounted, kneeling by one of the fallen horsemen. The man was wicked-looking, his cheekbones outlined by raised, jagged scars. Caledan pulled off the man's black glove, then nodded. The horseman was missing the tip of one of his fingers.

"They're Zhentarim," he told the others.

"As was their sorcerer," Morhion said gravely as he came down the grassy slope after having examined the fallen Zhent on the top of the rise.

"But how could the Zhentarim have followed us?" Mari asked, her brow furrowed in concentration. "How would Ravendas have known to lay an ambush for us here, so far from Iriaebor?"

Caledan turned to look at Morhion. The mage returned the gaze, giving no clue to his thoughts.

"I don't know," Caledan said, gritting his teeth. "I don't know."

* * * * *

Much as Caledan hated the delay, they spent the following day camped in a low grassy hollow, sheltered from the wind. Dawn had broken shortly after the battle with the Zhentarim, but they had decided not to ride on. The horses were exhausted, and the fact was, so were the rest of them. None of the companions had fought such a wild battle in years. Although Caledan knew none of his old friends would admit it, the fight had depleted them. So they rested, with Caledan spending most of the day pacing nervously. He wanted to get this journey over with and get back to the city.

The next day dawned clear, and they spent it riding deeper into the Fields of the Dead. Ferret periodically spurred his horse ahead, scouting the terrain and keeping watch for any more Zhentarim—or the shadevar. However, they encountered only a few peasant farmers.

Despite their ominous name, the Fields of the Dead were beautiful, grass-swept plains broken occasionally by lines of low rolling ridges. Ancient oak trees grew atop some of the gentle hills, like hoary old sentinels keeping watch. The spring sunlight was warm and golden, the air above filled with the wheeling and diving of meadowlarks.

It was difficult for Caledan to imagine that, centuries ago, these grassy plains had been trampled and torn up by the booted feet of vast armies. It was said that rivers in the Fields ran red with the blood of the thousands who had perished here, and that some of the low hills were not hills at all, but were instead huge burial mounds where entire armies had been entombed.

Several hundred years had passed since those tumultuous days. With the rise of the city of Waterdeep to the west, the empire of Amn to the south, and the Caravan Cities to the east, the Fields had gradually lost their strategic importance in the struggle for power in the western half of the continent of Faerun. Now the land was sparsely populated by villages and farms, and most of the scars of ancient battle had been turned beneath the soil by the activity of countless plowshares.

There were still some reminders of how these plains had acquired their name. Caledan had lost count of all the overgrown stone barrows and grass-covered burial mounds they had passed as they rode. He found himself hoping the dead slept soundly in the Fields. He couldn't imagine a worse place to start believing in ghosts.

It was shortly after midday when the Harper guided her mount near Caledan. The two rode in silence for a long time before the Harper broke the silence.

"Tell me about Kera," she said in a thoughtful voice. Caledan looked at her sharply, feeling a momentary flash of irritation. But then, why shouldn't the Harper want to know about Kera?

"What do you want me to say?" he asked her softly.

Mari shrugged. "I don't know," she said simply. "When did you learn that Ravendas and Kera were sisters?"

Caledan raised an eyebrow, but Mari did not meet his gaze. One of the others must have told her, he realized, or maybe even the Harpers had. "It's strange," he said, thinking back. "It was Ravendas I knew first, not Kera. It must have been twelve, thirteen years ago. I was sent on a mission by the Harpers to the city of Baldur's Gate. Rumor had it that an assassin had been sent to wipe out the Council of Four which governed the city. That would have been disastrous. The Zhentarim would be all too happy to step in and take control. Anyway, it was an ambitious young commander in the city's secret police who helped me infiltrate the council so I could spy on them. I discovered the would-be assassin who—and this isn't much of a surprise—turned out to be Zhentarim."

"And that young commander was Ravendas?" Mari asked.

Caledan nodded. "Even then, she was an ambitious woman, daughter of a famous mercenary, proud of her ability as a warrior and as a commander, and determined to rise up in the world. But at the time I didn't have an inkling of her true nature." He shook his head. No, he had underestimated Ravendas every step of the way. "I met her sister before I left the city, though I didn't think much of Kera at the time. She was little more than a girl, about five years younger than Ravendas. Ravendas didn't think much of Kera either. Her little sister was quiet, shy, and thoughtful. Those weren't traits Ravendas much respected."

Caledan swallowed hard. "Some years later, my travels brought me back through Baldur's Gate. By that time Ravendas had become leader of the Flaming Fists, yet even that position didn't satisfy her. I spent some time with her, as an old friend, but I grew weary of her delusions of power. Before I moved on, however, I ran into her sister again, and . . ."

"And time had done its work on Kera," Mari said.

Caledan grinned. "It had done its work well. Let me tell you, this time she was definitely more than a sweet, shy girl. After my last visit to the city, Kera had spent her time gathering as much information as she could about the Harpers. Kera wanted to help people as much as Ravendas wanted to control and dominate them, and she wanted to join the Harpers. She asked me to take her to Berdusk, to Twilight Hall. I agreed.

"The next time either of us saw Ravendas was several years later, perhaps eight or nine years ago. We ran into her in Berdusk, and it was clear that she had changed for the worse. While she had always been power-hungry, now she seemed consumed by her visions of greatness. She tried to convince us to join with her and her allies in a scheme she boasted would make us all rich.

"As it turned out, those 'allies' of hers were the Zhentarim. Of course, we refused her offer and left the city. Kera put on a brave face after that, but I know it devastated her to learn that her sister had thrown her lot in with the Black Network. I don't think she ever really got over it."

"And the next time you saw Ravendas?"

"She was raising an army of goblinkin outside of Hluthvar. The Harpers sent Kera and me, along with the Fellowship, to stop her." He looked at Mari sadly. "You know the rest."

Mari nodded. She was silent for a long time. "You're never going to let go of her memory, are you?" she asked finally, her voice husky.

Caledan shook his head. How could it still hurt so much, after all these years? He was going to make Ravendas pay. "What would be left of me if I did?" he asked.

The Harper sighed, then amazingly she smiled at him. "I hate to say this, scoundrel, but for once I actually understand you." Caledan could only watch in wonder as she spurred her mount ahead, leaving him to ride on alone.

At sundown they reached the village of Asher. The hamlet, a small cluster of fieldstone houses with thatched roofs, was set in a vale between two tree-covered hills. The folk here seemed a bit friendlier than those at the last village, and they directed the companions to the village's lone inn, a rambling one-storied building set against a hillside.

After a filling supper, Tyveris asked the grizzled old innkeep if there was anyone in the village who knew any tales of elder days. Much to the companions' delight, the innkeep himself professed to be an expert on the Fields of the Dead. When Caledan asked him if he had ever heard the name Talek Talembar, the innkeep scratched his narrow chin thoughtfully.

"Aye, that I have," the innkeep said in his country drawl. "He was a great hero long ago, or so the stories go. Some say he turned back entire armies with a song, though in the end I can't say that helped him much. He died with a goblin's barbed arrow in his back, he did."

With the prompting of a gold piece, the innkeep was happy to describe how they could find Talembar's death site, in a valley not a half-day's march away.

That night the companions' sleep went thankfully uninterrupted, and after breaking bread the next morning they rode north from the village across the plains.

It was early afternoon when they came upon a massive, gnarled oak tree standing alone in the middle of a vast field. "This must be the 'Lonely Oak' the old innkeep described," Caledan said, the cool air ruffling his dark hair. "If he's right, the valley where Talembar fell should be just over the next rise."

Ferret rode up the hill to scout out the terrain, but in a few minutes he came riding back. "Well, I've got good news and bad news," the little thief said.

"Why don't I like the sound of this?" Tyveris groaned.

"What is it, Ferret?" Caledan asked, not much in the mood for guessing games.

"Well, first the good news. It looks like the valley the innkeep spoke of is just beyond that last ridge."

"And the bad news?" Caledan prompted.

"I think you may want to see that part for yourself," Ferret said in his raspy voice.

Caledan glowered at Ferret but knew it would take longer to wring more information out of the thief than it would to simply ride ahead and see for himself. He spurred Mista forward, and the others followed. When he reached the top of the ridge he stopped.

"By all the gods," he swore, and the others followed his gaze.

Before them stretched a long, narrow valley fading into the hazy distance. The sun filled the valley with a green-gold light, and Caledan caught the faint, sweet scent of wildflowers on the breeze rising up from below.

"What are all those queer round lumps on the valley floor?" Estah asked.

Tyveris shook his head. "Those aren't lumps, Estah. Those are barrows."

"But there must be hundreds of them!" Estah said in dismay.

"No—thousands," Caledan corrected her without relish. "Thousands of barrows." He turned to the others, his expression grim. "It looks as if Talek Talembar has some company."

Fifteen

"This one looks like it's got more Calimshite soldiers," Tyveris said in disgust. He threw down the spade next to the hole he had dug in a low barrow and pulled out a helmet that bore the crest of the southern land of Calimshan. A human skull, its blankly staring orbits filled with dirt, still rattled around inside the helmet. Muttering a prayer to appease the dead, Tyveris set the skull back in the pit.

"We could try that barrow that Estah noticed last night," Mari said, though without much enthusiasm. "She said it looked more weathered than the others."

"We've been digging up barrows for three days now, Mari," the big Tabaxi said in annoyance, picking the spade back up and filling in the hole, "and not a one of them seems to date from the time before Indoria fell. By Oghma himself, if I turn up another Calimshite skull, I'm going to march south to Calimport, barge into the Emperor's throne room, and brain him with the blasted thing as punishment for all the soldiers his predecessors sent up here to die and torment me."

"Now what good would that do us?" Mari asked.

"None, I suppose," Tyveris grumbled, "but it would make me feel a bit better."

It was growing late as the two made their way across the grassy floor of the valley back toward camp. The valley itself was beautiful, the verdant ground scattered with pale, tiny flowers. Yet there was an eerie silence that Mari had found increasingly disturbing these last days. She hadn't seen a single bird since they arrived at this place, and the only sound was the ceaseless hiss of the wind through the long grass.

The barrows themselves were of many different kinds. Some were little more than small piles of dirt overgrown with grass, while others had been built up with walls of rock and were surrounded by circles of massive standing stones. Some of the standing stones bore runic inscriptions carved into their surfaces, but almost all of these were too weathered and overgrown with lichen to decipher.

Mari and Tyveris reached their camp only to discover that the others had fared little better. A feeling of despair was steadily descending over the companions. Even Mari was starting to give up hope that they would ever find Talembar's tomb. They had made camp some distance from the valley, beneath the sheltering branches of the ancient, solitary oak tree.

They made a cheerless supper of dried fruit, supplemented by the last of the cheese and some stale unleavened bread Estah had bought in the village of Asher. As the twilight deepened, the companions gathered around the glow of the fire—all except Ferret, who was perched on a nearby knoll keeping watch. Mari pulled her baliset out of her pack. Perhaps some music would lift their spirits.

She strummed a few soft chords, then broke into a

gentle song about a maiden seeking her lost lover by the shores of a misty lake.

"That was just lovely," Estah said when Mari had finished.

Mari smiled and started to ask the halfling what she would like to hear next when her eyes were caught by Caledan's intent gaze. He sat across the fire, his face lost in shadow, his pale green eyes locked on hers.

Caledan stood up. "I'm going to go stretch my legs," he told the others. He walked away from the ring of firelight. Mari watched him until he vanished into the deepening purple twilight.

The healer requested a lively tune next, one called "The Dragon and the Dormouse." After that, Mari played several more songs, but finally her hands fell from the polished wood of her baliset.

"I'll . . . I'll be back soon," she told the others, setting down the instrument. She gazed into the dusky night and walked in the direction Caledan had taken earlier.

What are you doing, Mari Al'maren? she asked herself. But she had no answer. She knew she ought to stay away from Caledan. She had known so from the moment she first looked at him and felt the tingling in her skin when he touched her. She had fought those feelings with all her strength, as if they had been demons trying to gain control of her.

She knew it was wrong, even dangerous, to fall in love with Caledan. She had sworn to be true to the Harpers, and she couldn't love Caledan and perform her duty at the same time. She could not compromise herself as a Harper. And yet . . .

"Who's there?" a voice spoke softly in the dimness. It was Caledan.

"It's only me, scoundrel," she said, stepping from a shadow into the silvery light of the rising moon. They stood

atop a low hill. The land stretched out beneath them in all
directions. In the distance Mari could spot the brightness
of the companions' campfire, but they were out of earshot.

"What do you want?" Caledan asked, his voice neutral.

Mari shook her head. "I don't know. Nothing, I suppose."
The moonlight glimmered off her silver Harper pin. "No,
that's not true," she added after a heartbeat. "I do want
something. Foolish as it may be, I want you, Caledan."

He was silent for a long moment. "I want you, too . . .
Mari," he said finally, his voice unusually husky. "But . . ."

Mari took a step forward, placed her hands on his broad
shoulders, and kissed him soundly. He tried to pull away,
but she held on with all her strength and did not let him go.
Then, slowly, his lips melted against hers. Finally he
reached out and pulled her close, her head resting against
his chest.

"You may live to regret this, you know."

"I know," she said, smiling wryly. "But I'll love you even
then."

He spread his cloak out upon the dewy grass, and the
two sank down to the soft ground.

*   *   *   *   *

"One more day," Caledan said when the companions
were all mounted, ready to ride again into the valley of the
ancient, numberless barrows. Dawn had come; the sky was
gray and the light gloomy. "After that, we've got to get back
to Iriaebor. For all we know, Ravendas has found the Nightstone already."

"If that is so," Morhion said, "then there is little point in
our returning at all." Caledan looked darkly at the mage but
did not answer him.

They made their way to the north side of the valley and
spent the morning exploring among the overgrown burial

mounds. There were fewer barrows here, but they seemed to contain the same as all the others they had examined— mostly the remains of Calimshite soldiers.

"Calimshan must have lost a major battle here at some point," Tyveris said, tossing down another helmet in disgust. "Serves them right." The loremaster was beginning to develop a serious dislike for Calimshites.

Mari glanced over at Caledan, who was refilling the hole Tyveris had dug in this latest barrow, and saw that he was looking at her. He smiled, the expression lighting up his green eyes, then he winked at her mischievously before returning to work. Mari couldn't help but grin. He was a scoundrel, that was certain, but at least he seemed to be *her* scoundrel.

"Caledan, Mari, come look at this," Tyveris said then. He was examining a large barrow not far from the one they had just excavated. It was a low, circular mound, its doorway filled with dark stones. "This one looks a little different than any of the others we've investigated so far."

Morhion walked around the barrow, examining it critically. "It is different, loremaster. That could mean it is older, dating closer to the time Talembar fell. Or . . ."

"Or what?" Caledan asked.

"Or it may mean that this tomb was built for a different sort of occupant."

"Like a king, you mean?" Ferret asked, his beady eyes lighting up. "And kings are usually buried with treasure, am I right?"

"I suppose there's only one way to find out," Caledan said.

They set to clearing away the stones from the barrow's low, circular entrance. Within minutes they found that the entrance to the barrow had been sealed up with daub and wattle. Strange symbols had been drawn in the mud of the seal, but centuries of dampness had worn them down so that they could barely be seen, let alone read.

"Allow me," Tyveris said. The big loremaster stood before the barrow's entrance. He closed his eyes and spoke a soft, rumbling prayer. "Just apologizing in advance," he explained when he finished.

"Apologizing for what?" Mari asked.

"This." In one swift motion, Tyveris gathered up his brown robe around his knees and landed a powerful kick on the daub and wattle seal. The dried mud shattered. There was a faint hiss, and a puff of foul-smelling air issued from the entrance.

"I don't think I want to be the one to crawl in and see who's buried in there," Tyveris said, grimacing as he held his nose.

"I'll go," Ferret said eagerly, bounding toward the barrow's entrance. Abruptly he stopped short.

A spray of dirt and stone burst outward from the barrow's entrance, showering the companions. Mari watched in horror as something began clawing its way out of the tomb. Its fiery red arms were massive and gnarled. It scrabbled at the dirt with yellowed talons as long as daggers. Its face was that of a beast, its ears large and pointed, its snout strangely flattened. Its fangs were long and sharp, and it had two hot eyes as crimson as fresh blood.

"Ready yourself, Tyveris!" Morhion called out loudly. "We've got to force it back into the barrow. Once it is free, we will not be able to defeat it." The beast continued to inch its way out of the tomb's narrow entrance. It let out a piercing scream.

"Can you call on the strength of your god or not, loremaster?"

Tyveris nodded.

"Then do so," the mage snapped. "Use your prayers to drive the creature back into the barrow. I will attempt to seal the entrance again."

Caledan drew his sword to defend the loremaster and mage should their spells fail, but he knew his blade would be futile against this horrible beast.

Tyveris began to chant a fervent, rapid prayer to Oghma. The mage wore a look of concentration on his face as he struggled to recall the words of some arcane spell.

"*El atha cul Oghma, el faltira kempar min Oghma yar!*" Tyveris shouted, gripping a bronze holy symbol that hung about his neck, his deep voice booming like thunder. Caledan didn't see anything happen—no crackle of magic or burst of fire—but suddenly the creature screamed as if it had been struck a dire blow. The light in its fiery eyes flickered. The creature snarled and writhed in agony, then retreated back inside the barrow.

At the same time, the mage released his spell. A shimmering blue nimbus appeared where the mud seal had been. "Quickly, help me replace the stones," the mage said, and the others rapidly piled the dark stones back, sealing the entrance tightly.

When the last stone was in place, the mage sank to the ground, breathing hard. Tyveris slumped nearby, his head in his hands.

"Are you all right?" Estah asked them concernedly.

"I am weary, that is all," Morhion said, and Tyveris nodded in agreement.

"It's been a while since I asked my god for that much power," the big loremaster said with a wan grin.

"What was that thing?" Caledan asked the mage.

Morhion shook his head. "I cannot truly say. Some beast of magic created by sorcerers long ago, I would imagine. Mages often took part in the battles fought here in the Fields, sending creatures of dark magic to ravage an enemy's army. This was one such creature, I would guess, bound and buried by a victorious mage."

"But not dead," Caledan said.

"No. It is a thing of magic," Morhion said, his breathing still rapid. "It will never die."

"Then we had better leave a marker here, so no one makes the same mistake we did," Caledan said. He paused then, as if he was struggling with something. "Thanks, mage," he said gruffly after a moment of silence, then he turned to mount Mista. "Let's put some distance between us and this barrow."

They rode to the north edge of the valley, then broke for a meal at midday, The distant sound of thunder echoed over the valley. The wind rattled through the tall grass, and the clouds looked as heavy and dark as lead.

Tyveris looked forlornly at the rather pitiful array of foodstuffs Estah had pulled from the saddlebags. There was a little dried fruit left, a few bits of cheese, and barely enough stale bread for each of them to have a piece.

"I really hate to ask this question," the big monk said, "but what exactly are the rest of you going to eat?"

"Tyveris!" Estah said chidingly.

"It was a *joke*, Estah," the loremaster protested lamely.

"I'm not laughing," the halfling healer said, her eyes flashing fire. She watched carefully over the food to make certain each of them got a fair share.

"What do you have there, thief?" Morhion asked as they were readying themselves to set out again after lunch. Ferret was performing tricks with a dull, tarnished coin, sending it dancing over his knuckles and leaping into the air.

"It's just some old coin," Ferret said, flipping it deftly toward the mage. "I found it on the ground when I was scouting maybe a half-league back."

Morhion snatched it precisely out of the air. He studied the coin intently, turning it over in his hand. "You may wish to see this," he said to Caledan and Mari.

"What is it?" Mari asked.

"I'm no expert, but it just looks like some old copper coin

to me," Caledan said with a shrug. "And a badly stamped one at that."

"That is true," Morhion said, holding up the crudely made coin. Its edges were rough and uneven and seemed to be thicker on one edge than the other. "I cannot even say what the symbol it is embossed with is intended to represent, but there are words beneath it. I can still make them out. They read, *Altaro'eb'Telkadra*."

"What does it mean?" asked Mari.

"It is written in the tongue called Talfir," Morhion said, his blue eyes glittering. "It means, 'The Year of the Lion.'"

"'The Year of the Lion,'" Mari repeated, then her eyes widened in realization. "That was the year Talek Talembar was slain."

Caledan took the antique coin from the mage. "Ferret, I think you'd better show us where you found this."

"Sure," Ferret said. "But I'll tell you one thing. If the barrow I found it by was Talembar's, he didn't have many friends when he died. It's not much to speak of."

The thief was not exaggerating. The barrow he led them to was little more than an irregular heap of dirt about six paces across and knee high at its center. "I found the coin sticking out of the dirt near the base of the mound," Ferret explained. "The barrow looks fairly eroded. I suppose the coin was washed out."

"This barrow isn't shaped like any of the others," Mari noticed. "All of the Calimshite barrows are almost perfectly round. Whoever built this mound seems to have just tossed the dirt on haphazardly, probably just enough to cover whoever fell here. I can't imagine it holds anyone who was very important."

"Let's find out," Caledan said, taking the spade and sinking it deep into the soft turf covering the barrow.

He had dug down barely a foot when the spade ground against something hard. He knelt down and brushed away the dirt from the hole. He pulled out the object that had caught the spade. It was a bone, yellowed and cracked with age, gnarled and knotty-looking.

"What sort of bone is this?" Caledan asked.

"Let me see," Ferret said, taking the bone from Caledan's grip. He turned it over in his hands, studying it carefully with his beady eyes. "It's a thighbone," he said after a moment. "But it's not human." The others stared at him in amazement.

"How do you know that?" Mari asked him.

"Isn't it obvious?" Ferret rasped. "Whoever this bone belonged to, he wasn't all that good at walking upright. See these small bumps here? They'd be much bigger on a human, or a halfling for that matter. And look at the shape of the knee joint. It's all wrong. No, whoever this was, he had dreadful posture. I imagine his arms dragged the ground when he walked."

"Like a goblin?" Caledan asked, and the thief nodded.

"That's a good bet. Goblins have never been very good at standing up straight. What's more, this bone has knife marks all over it."

"You mean from a battle?" Mari asked.

The thief shook his head. "No, more like from a butchering. I'd say that, after he died, our friend here was the guest of honor at a big feast—and the main course as well."

Mari gagged in revulsion.

"Goblins!" Tyveris spat like a curse.

"Ferret, how did you come to have so much knowledge concerning anatomy?" Morhion asked. If Mari hadn't known better, she would have thought she saw a flicker of amusement dancing in the mage's eyes.

"A good thief needs to know how the human body is built, Morhion," Ferret explained cheerfully. "How else would you know just where to slip the dagger in when you need to kill someone quickly and silently?" The companions regarded the thief with vaguely disgusted expressions, all except for Morhion.

"Interesting," the mage mused. "Very interesting."

Caledan's spade turned up more gnarled, knobby bones and flakes of rusted metal that might have belonged to weapons of some sort. It was clear from the number of bones that there were at least a dozen individuals buried in the mound.

Finally Caledan unearthed a low-browed skull with two nubby horns and a protruding snout. Its thick jawbone was lined with sharp, yellowed teeth.

"That's a goblin, all right," Caledan said. He had seen enough of the foul, twisted creatures in his lifetime to recognize that, given a little hairy, warty flesh, this skull would suit a goblin quite well.

"You don't suppose these are some of the goblins that killed Talek Talembar?" Estah asked.

"It's possible," Caledan mused. "But even if they were, I'm at a loss for how that could help us."

"Give me the skull," Morhion said. Caledan looked at the mage questioningly, but handed over the goblin skull.

"What are you going to do with it?" Mari asked.

"I'm going to speak with it," Morhion replied.

"No offense, Morhion," Ferret said, "but I've found that you tend to have more luck interrogating subjects when they're a little, er, *fresher* than this. I think you're a few centuries too late with this fellow."

"We shall see," the mage replied. He set the skull on a flat stone along with several items he drew from the small, mysterious pouch he always kept hidden in a fold of his robe: a bit of silver thread, a small chunk of yellow sulfur, and six pomegranate seeds. He held his hand over the skull and spoke several guttural words in the tongue of magic. The items the mage had set on the rock flared brightly with a deep purple light, then suddenly they dimmed and vanished. Mari gasped in shock, but before she could say anything a rough voice interrupted her.

It was the skull.

"Leave me alone, you bloody mage!" it said in an eerie voice.

The companions stared at the goblin skull in astonishment. It had not moved when it spoke, but Mari had no doubt that the voice had issued from the weathered skull. It was the dead goblin speaking.

"You must first answer my questions," Morhion said firmly.

"Garn, but I won't do it," the skull snarled. "Now go away, nasty wizard."

"I shall scatter your bones to the four winds," the mage said in a voice that sent chills up Mari's back. "I shall let the buzzards peck at them, and you shall feel every moment of their desecration as an eternal agony."

"Oh, I'm scared, I am now," the skull said sarcastically. "You think I 'aven't already been desecrated? My mates made chow of me; it can't get any bloody worse than that."

"He has a point there," Caledan murmured to the others.

"Now put me back in the ground," the goblin skull whined.

"The wall that leads into the nether world of the dead is no barrier to my magic," Morhion said darkly. "I can cause such agony to your soul as you never dreamed of in life."

"You wouldn't dare!" the skull shrieked.

"Do goblins even have souls?" Mari whispered to Tyveris.

"I'm not sure," the loremaster whispered back. "It's an interesting theological question. If they do have souls, they've got to be awfully wretched, warty ones."

"Try me," Morhion said to the dead goblin, his eyes glittering.

"All right, all right, I'll talk," the skull whimpered. "But you got to promise you'll put me back in the ground."

"It will be done," the mage said. "Now tell me this: how did you come to be here?"

"I told you, my mates gnawed on my bones."

"*Before* that," Morhion said angrily.

"Oh," the skull said. It paused a moment, apparently thinking. "It all started when that shadowy man killed my tribe's chief. Now, no one 'as a right to do that. It's every tribe's privilege to murder its own chief. Why, what sort o' tribe is it, if you can't slit your leader's throat when you get tired of listening to 'im?"

"Stick to the story," Morhion warned.

"All right, don't get touchy," the goblin skull said in a hurt tone. "This shadowy man, he came from some place far off, but that weren't no excuse for sticking a sword in our chief. Me and some of the boys snuck up on 'im and put an arrow in 'im right neat. Taught 'im a lesson, we did. But when we got back to tell the rest o' the tribe what we done, we got a nasty surprise. Ol' Glok, he thought he should be chief now, but he knew we would just as soon tear 'is guts out. So's Glok laid an ambush for us. We beat him, only all that got kilt were et at the victory feast."

"Like you?" Morhion asked.

"Don't remind me!" the skull exclaimed.

"One more question."

"This 'ad better be it."

"What did you do with this 'shadowy man' after you put the arrow in him?"

"We shoved shadowy man in a hole, you know, to let 'im age a while before we et 'im. 'Twas in the west end of the valley. There's a ravine there, good for ambushin' travelers and slittin' their throats. We stuffed shadowy man in a cave up top o' the cliff. But Glok saw to it we never got to go back for 'im. I suppose he's still there, though I don't know what good he'd do you. I bet 'is bones ain't much good for gnawin' on by now."

"I suppose you're right," Morhion said. "I thank you for your help."

"I didn't do it 'cause I liked you, blasted wizard!" the goblin skull barked. Morhion murmured a few arcane words as he sprinkled a handful of ashes over the skull. As they fell, the ashes spiraled about the skull, glowing until they were transformed into a swirling purple mist.

"Hey!" the goblin cried indignantly. "Wot's all thi—"

Abruptly the skull was silent. The purple mist faded, leaving no trace of the ashes. Tyveris muttered a final prayer.

"I know he's just a goblin," he explained in answer to the curious looks the others gave him. "But he did help us."

The companions quickly reburied the goblin skull and bones, then mounted, setting off west across the valley. Excitement surged through their veins. Talembar's tomb was almost within their grasp.

The rumbling of thunder grew louder as they rode past the countless barrows. Even though it was early afternoon the air was as gloomy as twilight. After a half-league the valley narrowed, leading into a steep, rocky wash. The hills rose up more and more sharply to either side until they became sheer sandstone cliffs.

"This has to be the ravine the goblin spoke of," Caledan said. They guided their mounts carefully over the loose jumble of talus at the foot of the cliffs. "Where do you suppose the cave is?"

"From the goblin's words, I'd say at the far western end of the ravine, at the top of the cliff," Morhion replied.

"I'll go scout it out," Ferret said, urging his horse ahead. He disappeared around a curve in the ravine, but came galloping back scant minutes later.

"You'll break that horse's legs riding on these rocks like that," Tyveris said with a scowl.

"I'm sorry, but I thought you all might be interested to

hear this," the thief said, scratching his stubbly chin nervously.

"What is it, Ferret?" Mari asked.

"From around the corner you can see the end of the ravine," Ferret told them. The weaselly man swallowed hard. "I caught a glimpse of an old friend of ours on the cliff top."

"An old friend?" Caledan asked dubiously.

The thief nodded. "The shadevar."

Sixteen

 As a booming peal of thunder rent the clouds, and the first chill drops of rain came pouring down, the companions and their horses huddled by the sheer sandstone cliff on one side of the ravine. A shallow rock overhang gave them scant shelter against the cold, driving rain. Jagged streaks of lightning lit the sky, each followed by the rolling crash of thunder.

"All right," Caledan told the others grimly. "We're going to have to face the shadevar sometime. It might as well be a time and place of our choosing."

The companions nodded in agreement. "We know this thing can survive dagger wounds, crossbow bolts, and being buried alive," Caledan went on. "But this ravine gives me an idea I think is at least worth a try. I'm going to lure the shadevar toward me. But once it's close, I need something to distract it, something that will make it forget me, at least momentarily. Anybody have any ideas?"

"I believe I can arrange something," Morhion said. The

mage's eyes were as impassive as ever.

Caledan scowled. He knew the others were watching him intently. Finally he nodded. "Be ready, then," he said through clenched teeth.

"As you wish."

Caledan swore inwardly. Sometimes he wondered if a heart even beat inside the mage's chest.

Ferret remembered seeing a game trail at the mouth of the ravine. He thought it would lead them atop the southern cliff while keeping them downwind of the shadevar. They guided their mounts into the storm. How Ferret found the faint track in the blinding rain, Caledan couldn't guess. The trail wound its way haphazardly up the slope. Soon the ravine gaped below them to their right, a great dark maw in the earth.

Caledan blinked the cold rain from his eyes and noticed that Mari rode next to him. She reached out a hand. He gripped it tightly for a moment, then let go.

"We're getting close," Ferret shouted, though his voice was almost drowned out by the roar of the wind. "We should be downwind of it still."

"There's a small knot of trees near the top of the ridge," Caledan said, pointing to a cluster of stunted cedars twisted by a lifetime of scouring winds. "Let's leave the horses there. We can climb to that jumble of rocks on top of the ridge. Do you think you can cast your spell from up there, Morhion?"

The mage nodded.

"Good," Caledan said. "As soon as the shadevar is within ten paces of me, cast your spell."

"Very well," was all the mage said.

They tied the horses in the scant shelter of the ancient cedars and scrambled up the rocky slope. At the crest they hunched behind the cover of a pile of granite boulders. The wind whistled across this high place. Caledan peered into the hollow. He felt his heart lurch.

The shadevar stood upon a mound of rock a hundred paces from the ravine's edge. The tatters of its black robe fluttered like wisps of shadow upon the air. Its monstrous face was upturned toward the leaden sky, seemingly oblivious to the pelting rain. It moved its head slowly from side to side.

It's trying to catch the scent, Caledan realized with a shiver. *My* scent. But they were almost directly downwind from the creature. It could not possibly realize they were so close. Caledan started cautiously down the slope. He reached the bottom, moving swiftly to the edge of the ravine. He could see a jumble of jagged rocks far below. He continued along the cliff's edge.

The creature caught scent of him much sooner than Caledan expected it to, and when it did it moved with a speed that amazed him.

The wind seemed to be whirling in all directions now, and some eddy must have borne his scent to the shadevar. The creature let out a high, inhuman scream that cut across the noise of the storm and made Caledan's blood run cold. Its scaled, muscular legs pumping with blinding speed, its taloned feet gripping the stone, the shadevar hurled itself forward.

Caledan looked for a place to stand his ground. The shadevar had already covered nearly half the distance between them. It screamed again, baring its obsidian tusks, a viscous, ruddy ichor drooling from its gaping maw. Caledan saw a flat-topped boulder and made for it. He drew his sword and leaped onto the rock.

The heel of his boot skidded on the wet granite. The rain had made the stone slicker than he thought, and he shouted a curse as he lost his footing. He tumbled backward, landing hard on the edge of the cliff and grunting with pain. The sword skittered away from his fingers.

Suddenly a shadow loomed over him. Another high, soulless scream sliced through the air. Caledan blinked the blinding rain from his eyes. Out of the corner of his eye Caledan saw his sword, just out of arm's reach, balancing precariously on the precipice. He wanted to turn to grab it, but could not break his gaze away from the shadevar.

The creature raised a clawed hand, preparing to strike a blow that would gut Caledan. "Damn you, mage!" he shouted above the raging storm. "Damn you to the Abyss!"

The shadevar's talons descended.

Suddenly another scream rent the air, only this one was a cry of agony. Caledan opened his eyes. The shadevar reeled above him. Its razor-sharp talons were clawing at its own face, at the hollows where its eyes should have been. It screamed again in fury and pain. Caledan watched in horror as the creature writhed above him.

A brilliant flash of lightning sliced across the dark sky, and the shadevar screamed again, clawing at its eyeless face even more furiously. Hot, dark droplets of blood fell against the stone, sizzling before they were washed away by the rain.

Suddenly Caledan understood. The creature could *see*. The shadevar had seen the lightning, and the brilliant illumination had caused the thing pain! Somehow the mage had given the sightless creature the power to see, and it was driving the shadevar mad.

The shadevar stumbled, on the verge of losing its balance. Caledan did not waste more time. He snaked out a hand and grabbed his sword. He thrust it upward into the shadevar's gut. The creature's scaly armor was nearly impenetrable, and the blade did not bite very deeply. But it was enough.

The shadevar slumped forward over the sword point. Caledan kicked out, grunting with effort as he used his foot and the sword to lift the creature above him.

The shadevar's claws flailed wildly, one talon tracing a hot, crimson line across Caledan's cheek. With one last blood-chilling scream it sailed into the ravine.

There it struck a jagged, razor-edged column of granite. Even the shadevar's scales could not withstand the impact of the fall. The creature's hideous cry was cut short as the shard of rock was driven through its body. Dark blood sprayed out in a hissing, steaming fountain.

Caledan nearly slid over the edge after the shadevar, but he caught himself at the last moment, wedging his fingers in a crack and dragging himself back up. He lay on his side, panting, gazing down at the shadevar impaled below. The wind tugged at the shreds of its black robe, but this time the creature did not stir. The torrent of blood gushing from its body gradually slowed to a trickle, then stopped, and soon the rain washed the dark stain away. Caledan groaned, his head sinking to the stone in weariness just as the companions reached him.

The shadevar was dead.

* * * * *

The storm was over.

It was late afternoon, and all that remained of the storm were a few ragged shreds of clouds scudding along against the azure sky. Morhion had ridden back down the game trail and into the ravine to examine the shadevar's body. Now the mage was returning astride his black gelding.

"The shadevar will not rise again," Morhion said when he reached the others. "The stone driven through its body pierced its heart, shattering the magic that gave it power. Already its body is decaying. By nightfall nothing will be left of it but cinders." The mage drew something from a pocket of his gray robe. "However, I did find this."

In his hand Morhion held an egg-shaped crystal, its myriad facets dim and opaque.

"What is it?" Caledan asked.

"I cannot say," Morhion replied. He muttered several words in the tongue of magic. Suddenly the gem began to glow with a crimson light.

"Magic . . ." Tyveris whispered.

Morhion nodded solemnly. "I will be able to study it further when I return to my tower." The mage spirited the crystal away into a hidden pocket of his robe.

"Your magic was greater than the shadevar's, Morhion." Mari said. "We saw the creature ready to strike Caledan, and the next moment it was writhing in pain."

The mage nodded, his long, pale hair blowing in the wind. "The shadevari were sightless from the moment of their creation. Their spirits were never meant to be touched by light. I think the lightning burned it from within. I doubt it had ever known such pain."

Caledan regarded Morhion carefully. He could never let himself forget how dangerous the mage could be.

"Do you think there will be more of them?" Tyveris asked. "More shadevari, I mean. We still don't know who sent the thing after Caledan in the first place."

The mage gestured noncommittally. "That even one of these ancient creatures yet remained in the world surprises me. For all we know, we have killed the last of their kind."

"Then good riddance," Caledan growled.

Ferret called to the others then. He had gone off wandering as usual and now was standing by the low heap of rock where they had first seen the shadevar. The little thief was gesturing wildly.

"What is it?" Caledan asked when they reached him.

"Take a look," Ferret said, pointing to the bare rock at the base of the small hill. "It looks like a fissure that's been filled in with stones."

Caledan knelt down and picked up one of the loose

rocks. "I think you're right, Ferret." The fissure, filled with a jumble of rocks and dirt, was perhaps a half-dozen feet long and several feet wide. "This has to be it—Talembar's tomb." He started clearing the rubble away from the fissure. Tyveris joined in, flinging huge stones aside as easily as if they were pebbles.

Caledan grinned as Tyveris helped him heave another heavy chunk of granite from the fissure. All of them felt their spirits lifting.

They had been working only scant minutes, however, when Caledan felt a sudden chill. The golden sunlight dimmed as if a cloud were passing overhead, and the wind carried the scent of dry, stale dust to his nose. That was strange after all the rain that had fallen.

"Caledan. Look above you." Something in Mari's voice made the hair on the back of Caledan's neck stand up. He and Tyveris looked up, and both of them froze.

A man stood on the side of the small hillock no more than ten paces away, gazing down at the companions. He was a noble-looking man with a strong, aquiline nose and eyes of pale gray. His attire—a brocaded longcoat over a ruffled shirt, tightly fitting breeches, and high leather boots—was fine, even opulent, but it looked strangely archaic, bespeaking the fashions of another age. Oddest of all were his silvery cloak and his long, onyx-black hair, for neither of these stirred in the brisk wind that whipped across this high, open place.

"By Oghma above, I can see right *through* him," Tyveris whispered, and Caledan realized he could do the same. The outlines of a gnarled cedar tree were hazy but clearly visible through the man. The loremaster gripped the holy symbol that hung about his neck and muttered a prayer to appease the dead.

Morhion stepped forward, bending slowly in a regal bow. "Hail, Talek Talembar," the mage intoned in his burnished voice. Caledan stared at Morhion in shock.

With ethereal elegance the spectral man mirrored the mage's bow. The motion was accompanied by a faintly audible sound, like the tinkling of tiny, distant bells. Tatters of mist drifted about the phantom, glowing in the bronze light of the westering sun.

"Indeed, mage," the spectral man spoke in a voice that was so deep as to be thunderous, yet musical at the same time. "It is I, Talek Talembar. Or at least the shadow of one who once was so named."

A look of wonder crossed each of the companions' faces. Caledan felt a shiver ripple up his spine. It was not every day he found himself facing a man who had been dead for over a thousand years.

The phantom nodded his head solemnly toward Caledan. "Greetings, Caledan Caldorien."

A tendril of mist reached out to softly encircle Caledan. He could feel its chill, gentle touch. "How . . . how do you know me?" He somehow managed to give voice to the words. His breath fogged on the strangely cold air. He realized he was trembling but could not help himself. He had been prepared for uncovering the dusty remains of Talembar's long-dead bones. This . . . this was something altogether different.

The phantom made a shrugging gesture. "How do I know that it is daylight? That a storm has just vented its anger here? That a thousand years have fled since the day I fell in this valley? I do not know how I know, only that I do know. I know who each of thou art, and even why thou seeketh me, though in truth I could not tell thee how I came to be here, standing before thee. Perchance thy need was great enough to summon me. I must confess to thee, Caldorien, death has proved most mysterious." A faint smile touched the phantom's lips.

Ferret took a timid step forward, though he kept close to

Caledan. "You aren't angry that we've . . . ah, disturbed your eternal rest, are you?" the thief asked in a tremulous voice.

The phantom laughed, a haunting yet lovely sound, like the call of a far-off horn. "Fear not, my good, cunning rogue. The only danger that awaited thee at my tomb lies now at the bottom of the precipice, quite dead, as I might well know. No more harm will come to thee, at least not in this place."

Caledan managed to regain a semblance of composure. He nodded in solemn respect, then dared to speak again. "Then you know why it is we have come seeking your tomb, Talembar."

Slowly Talembar nodded. "Yes, I do know. But I cannot tell thee the secret of the shadow song, Caldorien. For the simple reason that I have forgotten it."

"Forgotten it?" Caledan said incredulously. "But how could you forget something as important as that?"

"The spirit world is far removed from ours, Caldorien," Morhion interposed. "The veil that separates this world from that is heavy and obscuring. Eventually the dead must forget the world of the living, else they would never be able to leave it behind."

"Alas, what the mage doth speak is true," Talembar said sadly. "And I think had thou arrived a century later than thou hast, I may not have come to greet thee at all. Most of my memories of the daylit world are as if viewed through a hazy mist, muted and dimmed by the centuries that have passed. A few memories stand out clearly like glimmering jewels, but even these are growing fewer. I remember creating the shadow song, Caldorien. I remember playing the song upon my pipes to wrest the Nightstone from that being of darkness, the Shadowking. But alas, what the precise notes of the song were eludes me now. I am sorry."

Caledan sighed, swallowing his frustration. There was

little use in shouting at a ghost.

"Is there anything at all you can tell us?" Mari asked the phantom. "Anything that might help us to understand the secret of the song?"

The shadow of Talek Talembar paused for a long moment, his gray eyes lost in thought. He seemed to be growing dimmer as the sun sank toward the western horizon. Finally he made a gesture of regret. "Of that, I can tell thee nothing except . . ." Talembar frowned in concentration, then he shook his head. ". . . except that thou might look for its echo in the place where last it was played. That is all."

The phantom had grown more transparent and was beginning to fade.

"Do not despair yet, Caldorien," Talembar said. His voice sounded hollow and distant, as if echoing down a long corridor of stone. "It is true that a great darkness awaits thee beneath this city you call 'Iriaebor.' I know, for I have faced it. But I defeated it. It is in thy power to do the same, Caldorien, for thou doth possess the shadow magic."

Caledan frowned in puzzlement. "The 'shadow magic'? You mean that trick of making shadows move on the walls?"

Talek Talembar glowered angrily, and for a moment Caledan shivered. "It is far more than a trick to amuse children, Caldorien. The shadow magic is the key. None dare play the shadow song unless he be a friend of the shadows. It is a gift most rare and precious, Caldorien. It is for thy shadow magic that the shadevar was sent to slay thee. How is it thou didst not come to know this? Why, even the maiden who stands beside thee knows that what I say is true."

Caledan felt a coldness slice through his chest. He turned to stare at Mari in disbelief. Her face was pale, her eyes wide. Mari knew about the importance of the shadow magic?

"'Ware the darkness within the hollow Tor, lest it be freed to wreak grievous ruin upon the land," Talembar warned. Little remained of the phantom now but a faint, blurring outline. "Remember, Caldorien, only thou mayest stand before it. Yet do not forget how the strength of each of thy companions may steady thee."

The ruddy orb of the sun dipped beneath the western horizon. The tendrils of mist scattered in the wake of a sudden breeze. The phantom was gone.

Like a mantle on the land, purple twilight descended. The companions were silent. All faces were turned toward Caledan. Mari's dark eyes were wide. "Caledan, let me explain," she said, reaching out and gripping his arm.

He shook her hand off. "What's to explain?" he said acidly. He felt sickened; his head ached fiercely. "You and the Harpers have been using me all along, I see that now. You knew that Ravendas was searching for the Nightstone, didn't you? Just as you knew that only someone with the shadow magic could reclaim it from the Shadowking's crypt." Mari shook her head but did not deny his words. The others stared, dumbfounded. "That's why you sought me out," Caledan growled. "Not because I was familiar with Iriaebor or Ravendas, but because the Harpers knew about my shadow magic."

Mari bowed her head. The wind caught her dark auburn hair, lifting it from her troubled brow. Then she looked up. Her dark eyes shone with sorrow. Caledan glared at her, his lip pulled back almost in a snarl.

"Is it true, Mari?" Tyveris asked softly, his voice heavy.

"I did know," she said. "The Harpers knew. We didn't know any of the details, of course—certainly not about Talek Talembar or the shadow song. All that our spies had learned was that the Zhentarim Lord Ravendas was searching beneath Iriaebor for an object of power called the Nightstone, and that she had—at least at one time—expressed interest in finding someone who possessed something called shadow magic. A few older Harpers remembered your ability, Caledan. That was when the Harpers decided to send me to seek you out."

Estah watched worriedly. Ferret nervously fidgeted with a dagger, flipping it from hand to hand. Tyveris started to say something to try to break the tension in the air, but then Mari went on, the words tumbling from her lips. "Thantarth, the Harper who gave me this mission, feared that you would never have agreed to help us, Caledan, not if we had simply come straight to you and told you that we needed you and your magic."

Caledan grunted. "Thantarth was probably right on that account. He knew I would have laughed in his face if the Harpers had come begging to me. But tell me this, Harper. Did Thantarth order you to pretend to love me as well? Or was that a little bit of improvisation you came up with on your own to get me to do what you wanted?"

"No!" Mari shouted.

"Don't worry, Harper," Caledan said sharply. His eyes were hard and cold. "You've accomplished your mission perfectly. I'm going back to Iriaebor, and I'm going to keep Ravendas from getting her hands on the Nightstone. But it's not for you, or the Harpers."

He shot a dark glance at Morhion. As always the mage's handsome visage was impassive. "This time," Caledan said, "I'm going to get my revenge against Ravendas. So send a missive to Thantarth, Harper, and inform him that everything has worked out just as you hoped. You've done your job. And when this is all over, you can go back to Twilight Hall in Berdusk and be with your precious Harpers, and I won't ever have to look at you again." Caledan spun around, his boot heel grinding against the cold stone. Tyveris laid a hand on his shoulder, but Caledan jerked free and stomped away.

"Caledan!" he heard the Harper cry behind him. He did not let himself hear the anguish in her voice. "Caledan, come back!"

He kept his back to her as he walked away.

Seventeen

"You have failed me, Snake."

Ravendas prowled about her chamber, clad in a gown of midnight black. She held a polished, gold-hilted stiletto, twirling it absently in her hands. She paused before an intricate tapestry depicting two lovers embracing in a greenwood. "You know what I do with servants who fail me."

Snake watched her with his hard, flat eyes. "It is true Caldorien escaped your Zhentarim sorcerer in the Fields of the Dead, my lord," Snake said in his dry voice. "Yet he must find his way back to Iriaebor. We shall have all the gates into the city guarded. He will not escape us."

"That is not good enough!" Ravendas snarled. She plunged the stiletto into the priceless tapestry and slashed downward, tearing open a gash that passed directly through the serenely smiling lovers. She threw the knife down disgustedly, her face twisted into an expression of fury and madness. "I want Caldorien now. Do you understand me,

Snake? *Now*! If you fail me again, I personally will cut out your heart." She slumped into a chair. The rage bled from her face, leaving it pale, but the madness still swirled in her blue eyes.

"My lord, I will—"

"Silence," she said broodingly. "Leave me, Snake." She stared sullenly at the ruined tapestry, scratching at the arms of the chair.

"As you wish, my lord."

Snake bowed, drifting from the room. He made his way through the tower to his private chamber. These black moods were overwhelming Ravendas more and more often of late. She was beginning to speak of Caldorien as much as she did of the Nightstone and her ambition to rule all of the Caravan Cities. She was growing erratic in her judgment, and foolish as well. That could put everything in jeopardy. Soon Ravendas would outlive her usefulness.

Snake shut the door to his chamber. He was alone. He took the dim crystal from its wooden chest. It was time to contact the shadevar. Caldorien had escaped the Zhentarim Snake had sent into the Fields of the Dead, but that was hardly a surprise. Their only purpose had been to harry Caldorien. Then the shadevar could do its deadly work. But he needed to contact the shadevar to confirm that it had been successful.

Snake spoke the word that unlocked the magic of the crystal. It glimmered briefly in his hand, then went dark. A frown crossed his thin face, and he repeated the key word. Again there was a faint glimmer, then the crystal went dull.

Something must be interfering with the crystal's magic. Snake tried other spells, all to no avail. It was possible that the crystal's enchantment had faded. It was an ancient device, and such was not an impossibility. Regardless, Snake would have to wait until the shadevar returned to the vicinity of Iriaebor to make direct contact. It annoyed him, but he could not believe the shadevar had failed in its task.

Snake put the darkened crystal away. He had another task to perform. He opened a drawer in an ornate wooden cabinet, taking out a small crystal vial and a thin golden needle. The vial held a thick, purplish fluid. It was telsiak, a rare poison native to the southern empire of Amn. One drop in the blood caused the heart to stop beating instantly.

He dipped the needle into the vial and then, taking great care, slipped the needle into a pocket. He left his chamber and walked softly through the dim corridors of the city lord's tower. He passed a few Zhentarim, who only nodded to him respectfully and did not block his passage. Soon he stood before a door. He carefully unlocked it, pushing the door open. He stepped into the darkened chamber, shutting the door softly behind him.

A child slept soundly in a bed near the chamber's window, bathed in the silvery moonlight. Without a sound, Snake moved to the bed and drew out the poisoned needle. He held it so that the point was a hairbreadth above the boy's small hand. One prick, and the child would be dead.

Suddenly Snake cocked his head, his hard eyes going distant for a moment. He nodded then, a new understanding filling his mind. He put the needle carefully away and slipped from Kellen's room. The boy never woke.

Kellen must still die, Snake knew as he crept softly back to his chamber. But his death could wait. The child might yet serve a certain purpose.

* * * * *

"The gateway is ready," Morhion said to the companions, stepping away from the intricate circle he had laid out on the ground beneath the oak tree. The circle of silvery dust was perhaps a dozen paces wide, and the mage had scattered the interior with wild mint and dandelion. In the middle of the circle were two small pyramids of white stones, set far enough apart that a horse might walk between them. The mage had used a piece of burnt ocher to draw arcane symbols on the stones of the two pyramids, and atop each he had laid a single hawk's feather.

"Below my tower in Iriaebor there is a magical portal," the blue-eyed mage told the others. "It was fashioned by a powerful conjurer who dwelt there many years ago. I have cast an enchantment that links this portal with the one in my tower."

"It looks more like a bunch of rocks and weeds to me," Ferret commented skeptically, his beady eyes glittering.

Morhion regarded him icily. "That is why you are a foolish thief, Ferret, and I am a mage." Estah interposed herself between the two of them, wanting to make certain one of them didn't end up a toad and the other a corpse.

"I'll go first," Caledan said roughly, "just in case there's trouble on the other end." He swung himself into Mista's saddle as the others followed suit.

Caledan nudged Mista into a walk, guiding her toward the circle Morhion had drawn. Mari watched Caledan's mare step into the circle. Suddenly the silvery symbol drawn upon the ground began to pulse with an unearthly light. Horse and rider approached the two stone pyramids, then moved in between them.

Mari gasped.

Mista's head vanished! The rest of the gray mare was still there, Caledan in the saddle, but her head—no, now her entire neck up to her withers—was gone.

Caledan turned around in the saddle to glance at the others, but suddenly he, too, was gone. All that remained were Mista's hindquarters, and in a moment they disappeared as well. There was one last swish of Mista's gray tail dangling by itself in midair between the two small pyramids, and then there was no trace of either Caledan or his mare.

"We must follow quickly," Morhion said. His smooth brow was beaded with fine droplets of sweat; his skin looked ashen. "I cannot hold the gateway open for long."

The companions cast looks of trepidation at each other but did as they were told. One by one they rode into the circle. Mari was first. She swallowed hard and guided Farenth between the stone pyramids.

She felt a sudden chill slice through her. It was almost as if she were riding through an icy cold waterfall, frigid water passing over and then behind her. She felt her heart pound in her chest, and for a panicked moment everything went dark. The rolling plains vanished. She couldn't breathe. She couldn't feel the reins in her hands. She was lost in nothingness and tried to scream but found she had no voice.

Then a warmth broke over her. Her lungs drew in a shuddering breath as her heart lurched into motion once again. Farenth's hooves clattered loudly against a slate floor. She realized she was in a dimly lit circular chamber of stone.

The spell had worked. She was in Iriaebor once again.

She watched in amazement as one by one the others rode through the portal. It was as though they were riding out of an impenetrable darkness into light, but Mari knew it was solid stone, not darkness. Finally they were all through. Estah breathed a sigh of relief as Tyveris mumbled a prayer to his god. Ferret simply looked nauseated.

Caledan seemed to have no desire to tarry at the mage's tower, and soon they were outside, guiding their mounts through the cobbled streets of the Old City.

Iriaebor had grown even more shadowed in their time away. The sun was just now setting, yet already the streets were deserted. All along the avenue, doors were tightly closed, shutters securely drawn against the approaching night. A scrawny, mangy-looking dog slunk across the street. It pawed through a pile of rotten garbage, then moved on, finding nothing edible among the refuse.

"Nice place to come home to," Ferret said, and Mari thought she noticed a hint of sadness in the thief's normally merry black eyes. "I'll ride ahead and warn the rest of you if I see any city guards coming our way." The thief spurred his roan stallion and disappeared into the twilight.

The companions waited until full darkness before slipping into the garden behind the Sign of the Dreaming Dragon. Even so, Jolle had seen them coming.

"The inn was a dark place without you, wife," Jolle said, embracing Estah tightly in the warm glow of the kitchen.

"Mother! You're home!" Pog shouted, with Nog echoing her, though as usual his words were unintelligible. Estah hugged them tightly, but after a moment they squirmed free and bounded toward the others.

"And none too soon, I might add," Cormik commented. The corpulent, elegantly attired man was seated by the fire with a glass of wine clutched in his hand. "Some of us have been hard at work while the rest of you have been off on your leisurely travels."

"Leisurely?" Tyveris rumbled.

"Should I kill him now or later?" Ferret asked casually.

"Both," Tyveris replied.

Cormik's one good eye widened, and he shifted uncomfortably in his chair. "A little sensitive, aren't we?"

Mari smiled wanly. "I think you'll understand a little better after we tell you what happened."

Cormik nodded. "Good. I have some news for you as well. But I don't think you're going to want to hear it."

*　*　*　*　*

It was late. The companions, along with Cormik, sat around a table in the inn's back room. Pog and Nog lay curled up on a rug before the hearth. The halfling children were fast asleep. Jolle was out in the common room, not that there were many customers to serve. No one ventured about the city this late at night anymore. Instead the halfling innkeeper was making certain that if any city guards happened upon the inn unannounced, they would see nothing out of the ordinary.

"Things are worse," Cormik explained flatly, his face grim. "Much worse. The guards aren't waiting anymore for folk to wander out on the streets after dark to abduct them. Now they simply break into people's homes and take however many they want for the work gangs. Anybody who resists is killed." Cormik sipped at the glass of wine absently, for a change not seeming to notice that it wasn't the best vintage. "But that's not even the worst of it. Ravendas is allowing fewer and fewer trade goods to remain in Iriaebor. Virtually everything that comes to the city from the west and south is loaded onto caravans bound for the eastern kingdoms. The free market in the New City closed last week for lack of goods to sell. Soon people will begin to starve."

"It doesn't make sense," Mari said angrily. "What is the point of presiding over a dead city? There's nothing to be gained in that. It's almost as if Ravendas is punishing Iriaebor. For what?"

Cormik turned his one eye toward Caledan, yet said nothing.

Caledan sat with his back to the fire, his face lost in shadow. He had been silent and brooding all evening, but now he spoke. "Has she found the Nightstone yet?"

"My agents have been unable to discover that," Cormik replied.

"If she had gained the Nightstone, we would certainly know it," Morhion interposed. "For one thing, all of our efforts at concealment would be meaningless. There would be nowhere in the city we could hide from her."

Mari swallowed hard.

"What of the resistance groups?" Tyveris asked Cormik.

Cormik sighed. "Paralyzed. For a time we were making progress against the Zhentarim. We were taking a serious bite out of their trading operations, and we were managing to smuggle some goods into the city." He shook his head, absently twirling the rings on his stubby fingers. "Not anymore. Ravendas has captured too many cityfolk and pressed them into her work gangs deep in the Tor. At night they are locked in the dungeons below the tower. You'd have a hard time finding anyone in this city who doesn't have a son or daughter, a brother or sister, a friend or loved one imprisoned by Ravendas. I'm afraid no one is going to fight against Ravendas when she could kill a thousand people with a single order."

A despairing silence settled over the room. Then a thought struck Mari. "What if the prisoners were somehow set free?"

"That's a fine idea," Tyveris said, the firelight reflecting off the loremaster's dark skin. "But just how do you propose we manage to get into the dungeons below the tower, let alone free the prisoners?"

Mari sighed. "I don't really—"

Ferret interrupted her. "I think I might be able to manage something, Mari, provided Guildmaster Bock would be willing to cooperate. But I'm certain I can make him see the profit in it. After all, an all-out rebellion would mean a fair number of Zhentarim corpses. And Zhentarim *always* carry gold. I imagine Bock will find the temptation of so many gold-laden bodies to loot too great to resist."

Tyveris shook his head, glowering. "You're a nasty man, Ferret."

"Why, thank you, Tyveris," the thief replied cheerfully.

"Well, Mari," Cormik said with a wicked chuckle. "It

looks as if you're onto something."

Cormik left to return to the Prince and Pauper, and Morhion departed as well, intending to study the mysterious magical crystal he had found on the shadevar's body. Tyveris picked up the two sleeping halfling children and went with Estah to help bundle them into bed.

For a moment Caledan and Mari were alone.

"I wish you luck with your plan to free the prisoners, Harper," he said, his tone frosty. "But there's really only one thing I care about at this point. Revenge against Ravendas."

He rose and made his way up the staircase, disappearing into the shadows. Somehow Mari managed to wait until she was alone before the tears started rolling down her cheeks.

* * * * *

Caledan sat alone in his room. Sunlight streamed heavily through the window, gleaming dully off the copper bracelet encircling his left wrist. Sometimes the thing looked more like a shackle than a piece of jewelry.

He sighed, trying to push the thought out of his mind. He had been stupid to believe that he could fall in love—again. The Harper had her mission, and he had his own. Ravendas was finally going to pay for what she had done to Kera.

He turned his mind back to that windswept day in the Fields of the Dead, when the phantom of Talek Talembar had appeared and spoken to him. He tried to recall the words the ancient hero had spoken—the one clue he had given them to the secret of the shadow song.

Talembar had said something about finding the echo of the song in the place where it was last played. Unfortunately, Caledan had no idea where that could be. The history of Talek Talembar in the *Mal'eb'dala* had been frustratingly incomplete. After defeating the Shadowking, the ancient bard could have traveled almost anywhere in the Realms. He could have played the blasted shadow song anywhere, Caledan thought in frustration. For all I know the secret of the song is somewhere in Sembia, or Thay, or the gods know where.

Yet that didn't really make sense. The purpose of the shadow song was to counter the power of the Nightstone. Why would Talembar have needed it once the Nightstone was sealed in the Shadowking's tomb? Most likely, Talembar had never played the song again. And that would mean that the last place the song was played was in the crypt of the Shadowking itself.

Even if the secret of the shadow song is buried with the Shadowking, I can't see how that really helps, Caledan thought sourly.

He doubted Ravendas was going to let him search around the crypt hoping to hear the echo of the song. Still, he couldn't quite rid himself of the feeling that there was more to Talembar's clue than he gleaned on the surface.

A knock at the door interrupted his concentration, and he looked up. "Come in."

It was Tyveris, filling the doorway with his massive shoulders. For some strange reason, Caledan found that he was almost disappointed it wasn't the Harper.

"I'm sorry to bother you, Caledan, but you may want to come downstairs. Morhion just came back from his tower. There's something he wants all of us to hear."

A grimace crossed Caledan's face. He had hoped his dealings with Morhion were over now that they had returned from the Fields of the Dead.

Caledan stepped into the inn's private dining chamber and found the others already there. While he couldn't say that he had ever seen Morhion excited—he had watched the mage engulf whole bands of attacking goblins in magical fire without so much as blinking an eye—there did seem to be a hard, bright light shining in the mage's usually indifferent gaze.

"I have learned the purpose of the magical crystal I took from the shadevar," Morhion said when Caledan sat down. The mage pulled the opaque gem from his pocket.

"I believe it is a communication device of some sort. By means of the crystal, one might speak across great distances to the one who holds the gem's twin."

"That must be how the shadevar kept in contact with whoever its master was," Caledan mused.

"You want to use the stone, don't you, to speak with whoever will answer?" Mari asked the mage.

Estah scowled. "That sounds rather dangerous."

"Perhaps," the mage said, "but it would not be the first danger I have ever risked. The same would be true for all of you."

All eyes turned to Caledan. Much as he did not care for it, everyone had fallen into the old habit of looking to him as a leader. Even the Harper seemed to be waiting for him to say something.

"Do it," he said to Morhion finally, an edge of steel in his voice.

Morhion lifted the cowl of his robe, concealing his face. He was wearing black, just like the shadevar. The companions watched as Morhion spoke several sibilant words of magic. The crystal began to glow with a pale luminescence.

Suddenly an image appeared in the heart of the crystal. It was the gaunt, severe-looking face of a man with eyes as hard and dark as stones. It took several heartbeats for Caledan to recognize the man. An image of a procession riding into the High Tower of the city lord flashed before his eyes. It was the day when he had first seen Ravendas in the city. And on a black horse before her had ridden . . . the lord steward Snake. The man who was rumored to be Ravendas's lackey. He was the shadevar's master.

Caledan looked up at the Harper involuntarily. She nodded. Apparently she had recognized the lord steward as well.

"Why has it taken you so long to make contact?" Snake demanded in a voice as dry as bleached bones. "I have been attempting to communicate with you for the last two days."

Morhion drew in a breath to reply.

"Never mind," Snake interrupted impatiently. "It does not matter now. All that concerns me is Caldorien. Is he dead?"

Without hesitation Morhion nodded.

"Excellent," Snake said, his voice pure venom. "Now no one with the shadow magic can stand against us. Things are moving toward an end. Perhaps I will let you deal with the fool Ravendas yourself." A cadaverous smile touched Snake's mouth. "You have done well. Our lord who is to come will not forget that."

Again Morhion nodded.

"I must go," Snake hissed. "I shall make contact again when all has been—"

Snake's words were cut off by a sudden high-pitched commotion. Caledan swore under his breath and sprang toward the stairs, but he was too late.

Pog and Nog had burst into the room.

"Mother! Nog hit me!" Pog wailed before Caledan could quiet her. Nog's piping voice rose in denial.

The damage was done.

In the image inside the crystal Snake's hard eyes glittered with suspicion. "Who are you?" he demanded.

Morhion laughed. "A foe!" he cried. He passed a hand over the crystal. "*Bahtra!*" he spoke as the gem went dark. The image of Snake vanished.

They all stared at the darkened crystal for a long

moment. Pog and Nog clung to Estah for comfort, sensing they had done something wrong. Finally Tyveris cleared his throat.

"Well, Caledan," he said, his deep voice rumbling, "at least now we know who wants you dead."

"Comforting thought," Caledan growled in reply.

Eighteen

"I don't like this, not one bit," Caledan said, pacing agitatedly before the hearth. Night had fallen outside. The room was bathed in the warm glow of the candles Jolle and Estah were lighting. Pog and Nog had been sent to play upstairs, and the other companions sat around the oaken table.

"Snake said that soon he's going to be rid of Ravendas," Caledan went on. "If he's powerful enough to summon a shadevar, he can probably make good on his little boast."

"Perhaps this Snake fellow is just a fool who's a bit too full of himself," Tyveris offered.

"I don't think so," Caledan said, shaking his head.

"He is only pretending to serve her," Morhion agreed. The magical jewel sat on the table before him, dark now. "He is only waiting for the right moment for betrayal."

Caledan gazed intently at the mage. "I suppose you would know about things like that, wouldn't you?"

No one spoke for a tense minute until Ferret broke the

silence. "There's still one thing I don't understand. Why is Snake going to so much trouble to kill everyone in the Realms with the shadow magic? Talek Talembar told us that only someone who possesses the shadow magic can utilize the Nightstone."

Caledan scratched the disreputable-looking growth of beard on his chin. "Your guess is as good as mine."

"The Harpers know for a fact that Ravendas has been searching for someone with the shadow magic for years," Mari ventured. "That may be why she has been trying to capture you alive, Caledan. She needs someone with the shadow magic for when she gets her hands on the Nightstone."

"Well," Tyveris said finally, "if Snake doesn't serve Ravendas, then who *does* he serve?"

No one had an answer for the loremaster's question.

* * * * *

Caledan and Ferret waited just inside the mouth of the cramped, musty-smelling storm sewer. Caledan had not enjoyed crawling through the narrow, debris-cluttered tunnel. Ferret had wriggled his way through the pipe like a snake, but Caledan's broad shoulders had proven a liability, and more than once he had nearly gotten stuck.

Now the walled courtyard surrounding the High Tower of the city lord lay just on the other side of the rusted iron grating that covered the pipe. The others had protested earlier that morning when Caledan had told them he intended to sneak into the tower, but he had waved their caution aside.

"I'm not going in to confront Ravendas," he had growled. "At least not yet. All I want to do is try to find out how close she is to locating the Nightstone."

Caledan had planned to try to bluff his way through the

tower's gate disguised as a Zhentarim warrior, but Ferret
had suggested the ancient, forgotten storm drain as a less
conspicuous method.

Caledan watched as black-booted feet marched by on the
other side of the iron grate. After a minute Ferret motioned
that the coast was clear. Quickly the thief shifted the grate
to one side, slipping out. Caledan swiftly followed, replacing
the grate behind him. They brushed the dirt from their
black leather garb. They had stolen the uniforms from a
pair of guards whose corpses were still cooling in a dim
alleyway not far from the tower.

"I look like a buffoon!" Ferret swore softly as he futilely
tried to adjust his swordbelt. Even though one of the
guards had been nearly his size, the little thief looked ill at
ease in the stiff leather uniform.

Caledan himself had fared quite a bit better than the thief
in terms of fit. Unlike Ferret's, his uniform included an
embossed, black enameled breastplate and an ornate helm
with a visor that concealed his face.

As Ferret had promised, the two found themselves
inside the wall that surrounded the tower. The sun was just
on the verge of setting. Streaks of angry crimson and
molten gold crossed the evening sky, silhouetting the
single, unblemished spire.

Ferret nudged Caledan. A half-dozen Zhentarim were
marching across the barren courtyard toward them. Caledan clenched his jaw and kept walking, doing his best to
look as if he were at home. However, the guards did not
accost them as he feared. Instead, much to his astonishment, they saluted him as they marched past. Hurriedly
Caledan returned the formal salute—a fist clenched before
the forehead.

"It looks like I've got the livery of someone important,"
he noted under his breath. "You'd better act like my subor-
dinate so we don't attract undue attention."

"Lucky me," Ferret replied acidly.

Eight guards stood, swords drawn, to either side of the tower's massive bronze doors. Just as Caledan and Ferret approached, the great doors swung open, and a flock of gaudily attired men and women, followed by pages and scribes, began to exit the tower, streaming down the expansive stone steps. Some of them wore self-important expressions on their faces, a few wore looks of disgust, but most simply looked like small, frightened animals.

"The city's lords," Ferret whispered.

Caledan nodded. "They must be getting out of a session in the Hall of Argument."

The two took advantage of the confusion to thread their way through the crowd and slip across the threshold.

Nearly the entire base of the tower was taken up by the vast Hall of Argument. Its high ceiling was supported by countless arches soaring up in graceful vaults. The ceiling was covered with luminous frescoes, and the light of a hundred torches reflected off the hall's polished stone floors. Ferret allowed Caledan little time to gaze at the splendor of the place, however. He ducked into a side corridor, roughly pulling Caledan with him.

"That's no way to treat your superior," Caledan snorted under his breath.

"I thought you'd like it better than a knife in your back," Ferret replied.

They moved swiftly down the corridor. Several more Zhentarim passed the pair, saluting Caledan. Caledan returned the gesture, trying his best to keep his bearing stiff, as one would expect of a commander. They soon reached a spiral staircase leading up to the tower's higher levels.

"Breldurn, there you are!" a voice suddenly exclaimed behind them.

Caledan felt his heart lurch in his chest. "Keep walking," he hissed to Ferret.

"I say, Breldurn, wait there!" the rough voice called out again. "It's me, Drim!" Booted footsteps sounded behind them, and Caledan reluctantly came to a halt.

He turned around to find himself looking into the eyes of a grizzled, powerfully built sergeant. "Say, I'm glad I caught you, Breldurn. Lord Cutter would've had my head if I missed you. She wants to see you right away." He winked then, a wicked smile crossing his face. "You lucky devil. I told you she had an eye for you. Now come with me. I'm to see you to her chambers myself. Milord's orders."

Caledan glanced in panic at Ferret, but the thief's eyes were wide. He didn't know what to do either. Caledan swore inwardly. Apparently he had had the misfortune to steal the uniform of some man Ravendas favored. Thank the gods he was wearing a visor.

"Right now?" Caledan said, keeping his voice husky.

"Yes, now," the man called Drim said. "Do you want to keep Cutter waiting?"

"I suppose not," Caledan said hoarsely. Drim frowned. "What's the matter with your voice, Breldurn?"

Caledan gave a cough. "Cold," he explained.

Drim grinned slyly. "Well, I hope you'll have enough vigor to handle Cutter properly. Now, let's go before she strings us both up. Our master's a pretty one, but she doesn't like it when she's kept waiting."

Caledan sighed, resigned to his fate. A score of guards were marching down the corridor. He and Ferret would not be able to fight their way out.

"I'll meet you later," he said to Ferret. The thief looked at him with surprise. "That's an order!"

"Yes, sir," Ferret said, saluting. Without another glance, he hurried away down the hall. At least Ferret would escape. Caledan could be confident of that.

"All right, Drim," Caledan said, taking a deep breath. "Take me to Lord Cutter."

* * * * *

The heavy, iron-banded door shut behind Caledan, and he heard the sound of a lock turning. The two Zhentarim warriors outside the portal had taken his sword. There was nothing to do now except to wait for Ravendas.

The chamber he found himself in was circular, about twenty paces across. The dark stone floor was strewn with silvery furs, and the walls hung with richly woven tapestries. The furniture was ornate and expensive-looking. A fire burned brightly in the great archway of a marble fireplace. There were windows facing to the south and west, but it was a good distance to the courtyard below. Jumping would be a desperate option indeed.

Suddenly Caledan heard the faint sound of music. It was coming from near the fire, the sweet, rich voice of a lute. The melody was none Caledan recognized, but it was both lovely and sorrowful, filled with a sense of longing.

Curious, he walked slowly toward the source of the music. It was a boy, sitting in a large armchair that had concealed him from Caledan's immediate view. The boy was small—no more than eight or nine, Caledan guessed—his feet dangling several inches above the floor. His smooth hair was raven-dark, his skin as pale as snow. His green eyes were widely spaced, bordered by dark lashes, and his cheeks were lightly touched by blooms of pink from the heat of the fire.

The boy strummed the lacquered lute with small, perfect hands, gazing absently into the fire. Caledan simply stood there, entranced, listening to the music. Finally the song ended on a long, wistful note, and the boy's hands fell from the instrument. "Hello," he said in a pure, sweet voice, though he barely lifted his gaze from the fire.

"Hello," Caledan stammered, a bit startled by the calmness of the boy's tone.

"You've come to see my mother, haven't you?" he said, gazing up at Caledan. Behind his visor a look of shock passed over Caledan's face. *My mother?*

"You didn't know she had a son, did you?" the boy said.

"No, I didn't," Caledan replied truthfully enough.

The boy shrugged. "Most people don't. I think she keeps me a secret."

Fascinated, Caledan knelt by the boy's chair. "Why does she keep you a secret?" he asked, his voice gentle.

The boy smiled, yet it was a melancholy expression, making his face seem wise beyond his years. "You don't know my mother terribly well, do you? Everything is a secret to her."

Caledan shook his head. There was something peculiar about this boy, but something compelling as well. He could only guess how terrible it must be to grow up under Ravendas's care.

The boy's eyes shone. "She'll break me when she's done with me, you know. That's what she does with everybody, once she's used them. She'll break you, too, as soon as you finish whatever it is she wants you to do. I've seen her do it to others."

Caledan shuddered. "It doesn't have to be that way, you know," he said. "You don't have to do what she wishes. She can't break you, not if you're strong."

For a brief moment a light glimmered in the boy's eyes like a flicker of hope. Then it vanished. "I used to dream of things like that," he said abjectly. "I don't dream anymore."

Before Caledan could say anything more, he heard the lock of the door turning. Quickly he stepped away from the boy. The chamber door opened, and Ravendas stepped through. Caledan felt a hot wave of hatred rush through his body but forced himself to stand firm.

She was dressed in a gown of crimson and gold, hues accented by her red lips and shimmering hair. She was exquisitely beautiful, like a too-perfect rose which, upon closer inspection, reveals a rotting, loathsome center within its petals.

Ravendas stepped blithely into the room. "I see you received my summons, Captain Breldurn," she purred in a voice as thick and cloying as honey. "You may greet me," she said imperiously.

Though he was unsure what the proper greeting was, Caledan dared not hesitate. He strode to her and knelt as she presented her hand. He bent his head over her proffered hand and raised his visor just enough for a kiss. He hesitated a scant second. This is the hand that strangled Kera, he thought. He clenched his jaw, swallowing bile. He pressed his lips against the smooth skin of her hand. He stood then, letting the visor fall back into place.

She smiled, displaying her perfect white teeth. "You're a bashful one, Captain Breldurn," she crooned. "I find that charming in a man. But then, innocence can grow tiresome after a time. We shall cure you of this soon enough."

She glanced toward the chair where the boy sat, silently watching. "Leave us, Kellen," she said coldly. "Find Snake and practice your music for him."

"Yes, Mother," the boy said. He picked up his lute and walked to a side door, turning the knob with a small hand. He cast one backward glance at Caledan, then stepped through the portal. Caledan made a silent oath to himself then. If it was at all possible, he was going to rescue that child from Ravendas.

"Come with me, my shy soldier," Ravendas said with a sultry laugh. She took his hand and led him to a divan covered with snowy white furs. She sat down, the crimson silk of her dress spilling bloodlike over the white fur. She leaned forward to fill two crystal glasses with ruby-colored wine from a decanter resting on a black lacquered table.

For a heartbeat, time seemed to cease for Caledan. He

realized this was the moment he had been waiting for these last seven years. This was the perfect chance to exact his vengeance upon Ravendas. As she leaned forward her graceful neck was extended like a swan's, and the large vein that ran in her throat stood out clearly against her pale skin. The guards at the door had taken his sword, but the boots he wore were still his own. Inside the right boot was a small throwing knife. In less than the time required to take a single breath, he could produce the knife and slit Ravendas's throat.

He knew there would be little chance of escaping. Even if Ravendas died without a sound—something he could not count on—there was no way to slip by the guards outside the door. They would know something was awry, and his life would be forfeit.

But did that matter? All he had lived for these last seven years was revenge against Ravendas. Once he had revenge, his life would mean nothing to him. His hand inched its way down his leg, toward the hidden knife. You will be avenged, Kera, he vowed to himself for the final time. His fingers brushed the hilt of the knife.

Suddenly his hand froze.

After a moment he sighed, his hand dropping away from the concealed knife. Ravendas turned and handed him a goblet of the deep red wine. The moment for vengeance had passed.

Why didn't you kill her? a part of his mind screamed at him, but he pushed the question aside. He knew the answer.

Ravendas's death was exactly what Snake wanted.

He forced himself to remember that Snake was the greater danger now, not Ravendas. Perhaps he should use this opportunity to warn her. If anyone had the power to defeat Snake, it was she. At least he had to try.

Forgive me, Kera, he whispered inwardly.

"Come, Breldurn, speak a toast to me," Ravendas said in a lilting voice, lifting her glass.

I can't believe I'm going to do this, Caledan snarled to himself. This must be the Harper's bad influence on me.

"To you, Ravendas," he said as he lifted his goblet, the words dripping like poison from his tongue.

He flipped up his visor.

Shock flickered in her azure gaze for only a second. Then a dangerous smile coiled about her red lips.

"It has been some time, Caledan Caldorien," she said, her voice as cold as steel. Swiftly, before he could react, she snaked out a hand and reached deftly inside his right boot. She drew out the small knife concealed there.

"Right where you always kept it," she said with a smile that would have been enchanting had it not been so devoid of warmth. "If nothing else, you were always predictable, Caledan."

"Do you mean to say you were expecting me, Ravendas?" He made no effort to hide the revulsion in his voice. He pulled off the hot, uncomfortable helm.

She stood and moved to the window, gazing out for a long moment. She sipped her wine delicately. "No, but I should have known my lord steward would fail once again in his efforts to capture you." She moved to a chair opposite him and sat, arranging her gown precisely.

"So who *was* this 'Captain Breldurn'?" Caledan asked casually, emphasizing the past tense. The meaning was not lost on Ravendas. "How did he compare with Maderon?" Caledan allowed himself a vicious smile. Maderon was the nobleman who had intended to murder Cormik years ago. He had also been Ravendas's lover. "You know, I never would have taken Maderon for a screamer. You should have heard the way he begged for mercy on the end of my sword before he died. Shameful."

Caledan saw the briefest ripple of annoyance flicker

across Ravendas's placid visage. He had struck home with
that one.

"Ah, yes. Maderon," Ravendas said frostily, recovering
her perfect composure. "He was an entertaining toy. Pretty
but stupid. I was growing weary of him, however. I should
thank you for disposing of him."

"My pleasure."

"Did you enjoy your little journey to the Fields of the
Dead?" Ravendas asked, quickly changing the subject. "I
trust you weren't disappointed when you arrived at the val
ley near Asher. There must be ten thousand barrows there.
You're a clever man. I'm sure you realized that finding Tal
embar's tomb is an impossibility."

"Did you journey there yourself?"

"Of course," she replied calmly. "I've been far ahead of
you from the beginning, Caledan. Don't you see? It is point
less to struggle against me." Her expression darkened.
"You know," she went on, "stealing my jewels from the
countinghouse made me very . . . angry."

"I hope you're not expecting me to apologize," Caledan
said, refilling his wine glass.

Ravendas regarded him for a long moment, absently fid
geting with the strand of pearls about her throat. "All right,
Caledan, what is it you want ?" she demanded flatly.

"I've come to warn you, Ravendas," Caledan said simply.
"Your lord steward is planning to betray you. While I don't
know who he is, I do know that Snake serves another mas
ter, a powerful one." He went on in a dire tone. "What
Snake and his master are planning, I can't really say, but I
think it involves the Nightstone. At any rate, he's gone to
great lengths to kill everyone who possesses the shadow
magic. You're in grave danger, Ravendas. We all are. What
are you going to do about it?"

She laughed, a sound utterly devoid of mirth.

"I would not have expected so feeble an attempt at decep

tion from you, Caledan," she purred. "Have the years been so hard that your wits have left you?"

Caledan felt anger flare inside him. "It's the truth, Ravendas. You're foolish if you don't listen to me."

She rose and paced smoothly before the fireplace, the crimson silk of her dress rustling against the marble floor. "Snake is my servant. I fear him no more than I would a lapdog. Of course, he is not without cunning. That was why I elevated him to his present position. He has proven quite useful a number of times. But when I first met him he was little more than a common cutpurse. He is hardly capable of defeating *me*." Her blue eyes flashed.

"You're wrong," Caledan said, standing. "Dead wrong. Do you know what a shadevar is?"

"A shadevar?" Ravendas repeated, a frown creasing her brow. "What, pray tell, is that?"

"An abomination," Caledan growled. "A sightless monster that follows by scent, not by sight, and that can kill in a heartbeat. The shadevari were ancient creatures, maybe older than the world itself. Once they served the god Bhaal, but in the end even he was powerless to control the shadevari, and Azuth himself banished them. It would have taken a sorcerer of incredible power to summon a shadevar into the world again. And that's exactly what Snake did."

"If this shadevar was so powerful, why is it you're not dead, Caledan?" Ravendas demanded.

"I managed to kill it with the help of a few others in the Fields of the Dead. But it was more by luck than anything else. Believe me, this thing was powerful enough to lay waste to an army."

Ravendas sighed. "I'm growing weary of this talk, Caledan. There's nothing you can say that could make me fear Snake. You see, there's really no time left for him to do anything that could interfere with my goal."

"What are you talking about?"

"I have found the crypt of the Shadowking," Ravendas replied gloatingly. "In two days' time I will be able to open the doorway into the tomb beneath the Tor. My sorcerers tell me that the dark of the moon is the most propitious time." Caledan stared at her. "In just two days, the Nightstone will be mine, Caledan. Nothing—not you, not Snake, not the Zhentarim—can stand in my way then. With the power of the Nightstone, I will rule this city and a dozen others like it. I will not stop until all the Realms kneel before me.

"But I will need a prince consort to stand beside me and give me strength," Ravendas added in her dulcet voice. Her gaze drifted over Caledan like a caress. "That could be you, Caledan. Would you stand beside me and rule the Realms with me? You have only to kneel and pledge your life to me as your queen."

"You're mad," Caledan said simply, shaking his head. "Besides, what you really want is my shadow magic. I know that you need one with the shadow magic to take the Nightstone from its resting place."

Ravendas laughed again. "You think you're terribly clever, don't you, Caledan? Then again, you always did. However, I'm afraid you're wrong this time. Oh, once you would have been right. Years ago I did seek to win you over for your shadow magic. You see, I first learned of the Nightstone more than a decade ago. I was weaving my plans even then. You proved stubborn, however. Whatever you saw in that fawning sister of mine I cannot say, yet you chose to spurn my advances. In the meantime I have discovered another way in which I might gain control of someone blessed with the shadow magic, and he is mine even now."

Caledan made a sudden intuitive leap. "The boy? Kellen?"

"Indeed," Ravendas purred wickedly. "I think he inherited his coloring from me. But his hair, his eyes, and his shadow magic—all come from his father."

Caledan felt a sudden numbing coldness grip his heart. He stared at Ravendas.

"Yes, Caledan," she said with chilling calm. "Kellen is your son."

Caledan's gaze went to the door where the boy had disappeared. His gut instinct was to shout out in denial, but he remained silent. As unbelievable as it was, somehow he knew it was true. Even when he had spoken with Kellen he had felt drawn to the boy, as if there was some unspoken bond between them. He sank back on the fur-covered divan. "How old is he?" he asked finally.

"Eight. He'll be nine soon." Ravendas's eyes shone. Caledan looked at her, but he could not ask the question that lay bitterly on his tongue.

"How?" Her voice was exultant. "It was all very simple, really. It was that last time I met you and my insipid sister, Kera, in Berdusk. After you spurned my advances, I finally realized I was going to have to devise some other plan. . . ." She smiled evilly. "Do you remember the night you spent with Kera at the Running Stag, that inn in Berdusk? You and Kera had separate rooms—she was always such an annoyingly proper young woman—but that night she wasn't able to stay away from you. She stole into your room in the darkness and . . . well, the natural thing happened."

Caledan watched Ravendas with a growing feeling of disgust. "How did you know that?" It was one of his most private memories. He and Kera had made love the entire night without ever speaking a word. It had been wonderful.

Ravendas's eyes narrowed, like those of a cat about to pounce. "It was not Kera in your arms that night, Caledan. It was I. I drugged Kera, donned her clothes, and slipped into your room. Earlier that night I had poured something into your ale to make you a bit more . . . pliable, shall we say? I left your bed before dawn, and nine moons later Kellen was born. And just like his father, he possesses a talent for music—and the shadow magic."

Caledan gazed at her in horror. He could find no words.

"How like Kera, that she never did tell you," Ravendas crooned.

"She knew?" Caledan said hoarsely. His throat tightened; he felt as if he was going to be sick.

"Of course. Sisters cannot hide such things from each other. But she was the sort of fool who chose to bear the pain alone to protect you. Nobility was always one of Kera's most tiresome traits."

The room seemed to be spinning in a haze of crimson. "Damn you," Caledan cried. "Damn you to the Abyss."

"Spare the dramatics, Caledan," Ravendas snapped. Her voice was like a slap to his face, clearing his head. "You see now that there is nothing you can do to stop me. I do not need your shadow magic. But I would still have you stand beside me. You are strong, brave, and not without some charm. Though you should shave more often." Her eyes glittered hungrily. "Will you kneel before me as your queen?"

Caledan gazed at her in revulsion. "Never."

Scarlet blotches bloomed on Ravendas's cheeks. "Then you will die," she hissed. She pulled a cord that hung from the ceiling. Moments later the door to the chamber opened, and her guards stepped through.

"Take this lowlife to the dungeon," she commanded. "But take care not to kill him right away. I want that pleasure for myself."

* * * * *

Kellen leaned away from the door in the small anteroom adjacent to his mother's chamber. He had been listening to

the loud discussion on the other side of the doorway. He
had not understood much, but he had understood enough.
Tears streaked his pale cheeks, and the look of calm melancholy in his green eyes was replaced by one of deep sorrow. He pulled something from the pocket of his dark tunic.
It was the small wooden soldier.

"It's *him*," he whispered softly to the doll. "He's come for
us. But she won't let him take us away. I know she won't."

He heard the kind man's voice speaking to him again.

She can't break you, not if you're strong.

He brushed away his tears then, his expression growing
hard. He put the wooden soldier back in his pocket and left
the small anteroom. It was time to practice his music for
Lord Snake.

* * * * *

Caledan leaned against the rust-covered iron bars of the
cell. The cramped room was damp and cold, the floor covered with sour, decaying straw. Moans of despair and agony
drifted down the dim stone corridor. He felt his spirits sinking. He wished Ravendas would have simply killed him and
gotten it over with. He didn't relish the idea of rotting to
death in this cesspool of a dungeon.

He slumped down in a corner of the cell, resting his face
in his hands. His was going to be an utterly meaningless
death. He had let his one chance to take vengeance against
Ravendas slip away, and what had he gained by it? Nothing.
She had not even credited his warning about Snake.

"Are you just going to sit there looking gloomy?" a voice
rasped. "Or do you want to get out of this rat's nest?"

Caledan looked up in surprise. A guard dressed in an ill-
fitting uniform stood in the shadowy corridor outside of
Caledan's cell. The guard lifted his torch higher, and the
light flickered across his face. Caledan laughed aloud.

"Ferret!" he cried hoarsely, scrambling to his feet.

The thief used the tip of his stiletto to pry open the cell's lock. Caledan couldn't help but notice that the knife was stained with blood. The cell door opened, and Caledan followed Ferret into the dimly lit corridor. He suddenly noticed there were shadowy figures all around them.

"Friends?" he whispered to Ferret.

"No. Thieves," Ferret replied as they started down the corridor. "You have a problem with that?" Caledan shook his head. "This way," Ferret said, gesturing toward a narrow corridor. "The thieves of the Purple Masks Guild have a private entrance to the dungeons that the guards don't know about. Bock was kind enough to let me use it. For a price, of course. You owe me quite a bit of gold, you know."

Caledan was not about to haggle.

Nineteen

As the lord steward Snake spoke a harsh word of magic, the pale, egg-shaped crystal went dark in his hand. A leering smile touched his lipless mouth. He was most pleased with this surprising turn of events. Neither Ravendas nor the Harpers could dare stand against him now.

Snake wrapped the crystal in a velvet cloth, tucking it into the pocket of his poison green robes. He walked from his room and ascended the tower's spiral staircase until he reached Ravendas's chamber. The guards permitted him to enter, and he found Ravendas sitting by the west window, gazing out over the city with her azure eyes. She was dressed entirely in black velvet—shirt, doublet, and breeches—a man's clothing.

Her chamber was neater than it had been earlier in the morning. After Ravendas had learned of Caldorien's escape from the dungeon, there had not been a breakable object in the room that had escaped her wrath. The servants had cleaned up the shards of crystal and porcelain, however, and now Lord Ravendas's face was as pale and placid as alabaster. But there was death in her cold blue eyes, Snake noted. Hatred and death.

"My lord, may I speak with you?" Snake said in his sibilant voice. Ravendas was silent for a long moment, until finally she nodded, turning her head and her cold gaze upon him.

"Speak."

"My lord, there is a plot of insurrection in your city."

"Is this so, my lord steward? And who might I ask are the perpetrators who dare to attempt such a bold affront against me?" She smiled, red lips pulling back from white teeth. "As if I might not guess."

"It is not only Caldorien, my lord, but also his cohorts."

"Ah yes, Caledan's 'Fellowship.'" Ravendas sneered.

Snake nodded. "The Harper woman plots to free the prisoners in your dungeon. If this were to happen, the entire city would erupt in rebellion."

Ravendas tapped the fine line of her jaw. "This is intriguing news, my lord steward. Do you know where this Harper, Al'maren, can be found?"

"No. She is hiding somewhere within the city, my lord. The traitor was reluctant to reveal any further details."

"Traitor?"

"One who is close to Caldorien," Snake explained. "Any more than this the traitor would not reveal to me."

Ravendas stood and paced before the window with cat-like grace. With her shoulder-length golden hair and the black doublet and breeches, she looked almost like a fair young man, a prince from a Cormyrian court perhaps. "What else has this traitor told you?"

"The attempt to free the prisoners will be made tomorrow, on the night of the moon's dark."

Ravendas turned this news over in her head. "Very well, my lord steward," she said crisply. "Let them plan their little insurrection. I shall be ready for them. But do keep in contact with this traitor of yours. I shall be eager for more information."

"As you wish, my lord." Snake bowed his head, starting to walk from the chamber.

"And, Snake," Ravendas called after him, "send Kellen to me. I want to be certain that my son is fully prepared for tomorrow."

Snake hesitated for a moment. "Yes, my lord," he said, then walked from the room, leaving Ravendas smiling with self-satisfaction.

* * * * *

The hour was late. The Dreaming Dragon was silent. Though the moon was but a thin, faint sliver, the pure light of the stars spilled in through the window of Mari's room like liquid silver. The Harper lay in her bed, wakeful, her eyes gazing out the small round window. She could see the spindly shapes of the city's towers looming dimly in the starlight like gray ghosts. Or like tombstones, she thought.

Tomorrow night was the dark of the moon. Tomorrow night everything would be decided, for good or ill.

That evening she and Cormik had finalized their plans in the secret chamber beneath the Prince and Pauper. She had expected a representative of the Purple Masks Guild to be in attendance as well but had been surprised when Guildmaster Bock himself arrived.

These last days of planning had been wearisome for Mari. Tyveris had proved a great help to her with his tactical advice, but she could have used Caledan's support. However, Caledan had been silent and brooding ever since his return from the tower the day before. Something had happened to him there, something he wasn't telling the others. His eyes had a haunted look. A dozen times she had wanted to reach out to comfort him, but each time she had pulled back.

Once, for a heartbeat, she had almost thought she recognized the identical desire in his eyes. But the bitter words they had spoken at the tomb of Talek Talembar hung on the air between them, and neither had spoken.

Mari tried to turn her thoughts away from Caledan. Her mission was everything now. I hope what I'm doing is right, Master Andros, she murmured inwardly.

She sighed and slipped from the bed. She was clad only in a thin nightdress and pulled her woolen cloak about her for warmth. There was going to be no sleep for her, not this night.

She opened the door of her room quietly and slipped softly down the hallway. She heard a floorboard creak above her head, probably Jolle or Ferret steadfastly keeping watch on the narrow lane that led to the Dreaming Dragon.

When she started down the stairwell to fix herself a cup of tea, she was surprised to see a flicker of firelight from below. Somebody must still be up, she realized. She stepped into the warm, firelit common room and found herself greeted by the chill gaze of the mage, Morhion.

He sat in a chair by the fire, the shadows playing across his proud features. He held a glass of pale wine in his hand, but it was full, as if he had not taken even a sip. Mari hesitated for the space of a heartbeat, then moved to a chair opposite the mage. He inclined his head slightly, but said nothing.

For a time both of them sat in silence, watching the coals glowing on the hearth. Finally Mari gathered her courage and spoke. "There was no sleep for you tonight, either?"

"I have a momentous decision to make, Harper." The mage spoke softly. "Such decisions preclude sleep, I fear."

"Decision?" Mari asked. She almost thought she heard a tinge of regret in the mage's voice.

"Yes, a decision. Perhaps you can offer some guidance, Harper. Does one do what he feels is his duty, what he is bound to do? Or does one do what his secret heart whispers to him?" His eyes were intent upon her.

Mari looked away from the mage's piercing gaze. He seemed to have read her own inner struggle perfectly. She had fought long and hard to decide whether to accept her love for Caledan, even though she knew it would compromise her duties as a Harper. "I too have tried to make a decision, Morhion. But sometimes such decisions are made for you by someone else."

The mage nodded. He understood. She had pushed duty aside in favor of her heart, but the decision had been made too late.

"Caledan is not the kind who ever forgives betrayal," Morhion said. The mage did a surprising thing then. He reached out and touched her hand gently.

"*Did* you betray him, Morhion?"

"Yes."

They were silent for a long moment. "Tell me," she finally dared to say.

The mage stiffened. "This is something of which I have never spoken, not to anyone," he said gravely. "Never did I think there was one who might understand." His gaze flickered to her dark eyes. "Until now." Mari could not help but shiver.

The mage went on. "After Kera's murder, there was but one thought on Caledan's mind: vengeance. It was an obsession that gradually consumed him. He followed Ravendas as she fled to the Zhentarim fortress of Darkhold in the Far Hills. Somehow he managed to slip through the Darkhold defenses. This is no small feat, for these are many and perilous." A note of admiration edged Morhion's voice. "But far greater dangers awaited him within the fortress itself. He had gone to meet the spider in her lair. It was a confrontation he would never survive. Of that I had no doubt."

Morhion sighed, sipping some of the pale wine. "I followed him. Such was my decision. I allowed myself to be captured by the Zhentarim, and they took me to Ravendas for questioning. Then I revealed to her that Caledan was within the walls of Darkhold, intending to slay her."

"Did she reward you?"

"Yes," the mage said. He smiled bitterly. "She allowed me to keep my life. As the guards escorted me from the keep, I cast a spell of enchanted sleep upon them and got away. With the aid of my magic, I was able to find Caledan. He was hiding deep among the foundations. I told him what I had done. He was furious, yet he did not try to kill me—not then. Perhaps it was because, until that moment, we had been the closest of friends. Of course, that is no longer so."

"But you were trying to save him, weren't you?" Mari asked. "You knew that you couldn't convince him to leave Darkhold unless he realized it was hopeless to attack Ravendas in her lair."

"That is so. But the truth is, he wished to die, Harper."

Mari stared at the mage. Morhion paused momentarily, then went on. "He knew he would never be able to slay Ravendas and then escape Darkhold, yet that suited him. He wished to join Kera in death. I denied him that wish—I forced him to choose life. For that he has never forgiven me."

"How did you escape Darkhold?" Mari asked finally.

Morhion gave a slight start. For the first time Mari thought she understood the mage's expression. In his eyes was the look of fear.

"Tell me."

The mage's countenance turned impassive again. "Long before I journeyed to Darkhold, I had learned in an ancient tome of a black spirit that was said to haunt the caverns beneath the keep. Darkhold has a long history, Harper, stretching back through the centuries. It was built long before the Zhentarim ever set foot within its walls. Once it marked the southernmost border of a kingdom now long forgotten.

"In life, this spirit had been a knight of that kingdom, a man named Serafi. He had sought to usurp the throne, but his plot was discovered, and he was sentenced to death. Such was the dark power of his ambition that even in death he knew life, and so he was doomed for all eternity to drift through the caverns beneath Darkhold, craving that which he might never attain.

"I realized that, if anyone knew of a secret way leading out of Darkhold, it would be the undead spirit of Serafi. By means of a dark spell I summoned Serafi to me. He agreed to reveal to me a secret route through the caverns that led out of the keep. It was by means of this underground passage that Caledan and I escaped from Darkhold. But there was a price."

"A price?"

The mage lifted an arm. Slowly he drew back the sleeve of his gray robe. Mari gasped, clamping a hand over her mouth. The mage's forearm was crisscrossed with fine, pale scars. She looked up at him, her eyes wide.

"Such is the fate of the restless dead that they are envious of the living," the mage said. For a moment, there was a trembling in his voice, and again the fear in his eyes. "Once each month, when the moon is full, the spirit of Serafi comes to me and drinks of my fresh, hot blood. Such is the pact I made with the vaporous spirit in payment for the knowledge he imparted to me."

Mari shuddered. "When will the pact end?" she managed to gasp. She felt ill.

The mage's eyes grew icy once more. "When I die."

* * * * *

The shadows of twilight crept through the narrow streets of the Old City like ghosts. It was time to go. The companions readied themselves as best they could in the warm firelight of the common room.

As Caledan adjusted his swordbelt, he saw the Harper and Morhion exchange a meaningful look. Something has happened between them, he thought, clenching his hands into fists. He swore softly under his breath. Yet why should whatever went on between those two be of concern to him?

"I wish I were going with you, wife," said Jolle regretfully as he hugged Estah close. His broad, usually cheerful face was troubled.

"You have two rather good reasons to stay," Tyveris said as he picked up Pog and Nog and tossed them, shrieking with laughter, into the air before setting them back down.

Mari spoke then. "Once Tyveris and I begin freeing the prisoners, guards will most likely be summoned to the dungeons. The tunnels beneath the Tor should clear out. With luck you will be able to find the entrance of the crypt of the Shadowking."

"Don't worry about me, Harper," Caledan growled. "You do your part tonight, and I'll do mine. After that, I never expect to see you or the Harpers again. You can save your meddling for somebody else. I've had enough of it."

For a moment the proud look on Mari's face wavered. She cast a brief glance at Morhion, her dark eyes troubled, then turned her gaze back to Caledan and thrust her chin out defiantly.

"Let's go, then," Tyveris said gruffly, breaking the uncomfortable silence.

They kept to shadowed lanes and dim alleyways, hoping to avoid any confrontations with the Zhentarim. A silence hung over the city. There was not a trace of wind. It was as if the city itself knew that its fate hung in the balance this night and was holding its breath.

They were near the rear wall of the Temple of Selune when two dark forms suddenly separated themselves from the shadows of an alcove to join the companions. Caledan started to draw his sword in surprise, but Ferret's hand on his arm stayed the action.

"These are friends," the thief hissed.

"Well met, Ferret," one of the thieves, a slender, dark-haired woman with large, catlike eyes, whispered.

"Greetings, Kyana," Ferret answered the woman.

Kyana spied the big Tabaxi. "What is this?" she asked mischievously. "A disciple of Oghma sneaking around the city like a common criminal? A rather large disciple of Oghma at that."

Tyveris's face darkened. "I was a warrior long before I was a loremaster, thief," he said dangerously. "Don't forget it."

Kyana tapped her cheek thoughtfully. "Very well, I won't." She turned to Mari. "Talim and I will be going with you into the dungeons." She nodded toward the other thief, a young man—hardly more than a boy—with a mop of red hair. Mari started to protest, but Kyana held up a hand. "No arguments, Harper. If you want to use our entrance to the dungeons, you have to play by our rules. Besides, you're going to need some help springing all those locks on the prisoners' cells."

Kyana led them down a dank, foul-smelling alley. She stopped at a peeling wooden door, knocking three times before pausing, then twice after that. After a long moment the door opened. Caledan felt eyes watching them from all around.

Kyana led the way into the ill-lit building. There were numerous thieves inside, but it was difficult to count them all, for they kept to the shadowed corners. Kyana paid them no heed as she led the companions down a flight of rickety stairs into the basement. The small stone room was littered

with broken crates and rotted furniture. Against one wall
slumped an ancient oaken wardrobe. Kyana opened the
wardrobe's doors. Inside was blackness, pure and perfect.

"In there?" Tyveris asked, uncomfortably eyeing the narrow opening.

Kyana nodded. "You're not afraid of the dark, are you, my
overfed monk?"

Tyveris glared at her. Then he gathered his robes about
his knees and stepped into the wardrobe. Kyana gestured
for the others to follow.

Caledan had taken this way before, when Ferret had
helped him escape from the dungeons, so he knew what lay
ahead of them. Still, it did not make the utter darkness of
the narrow, confining tunnel any more pleasant. He
breathed a sigh of relief when they finally stepped out of
the passage into an abandoned part of the dungeon beneath
the tower.

Kyana shut the entrance behind them. It blended seam-
lessly with the rough stone wall. The portal would be
absolutely impossible to detect if one didn't know before-
hand where it was.

Kyana led the way down the debris-littered passageway.
Cells lined the corridor, but their iron bars were rusted,
their doors hanging on their hinges at extreme angles. No
one had used this part of the dungeon in centuries. They
would encounter no guards down here.

Soon they reached an intersection. Caledan could see
golden light glowing down each of the passageways to their
right and left. Moans of pain and the dull clanging of iron
drifted faintly on the dark, fetid air.

Here was to be a parting of ways.

"There are prisoners down each of these corridors," Ferret whispered. "Both eventually lead to the tower. The tunnel leading to the excavations is a short distance down the
left-hand passage."

"Tyveris, you head down the corridor to the right," Mari said gravely. "Free as many prisoners as you can. Kyana, go with him. Talim and I will take the left-hand passage and do the same. We'll catch up to you by the stairs leading up to the tower—if at all possible."

Tyveris nodded solemnly. "May the gods be with you this night," the big loremaster said in his rumbling voice.

"Don't worry, Harper, I'll take good care of him," Kyana said as she and the loremaster started off down the right-hand corridor. Ferret didn't hesitate, quickly leading the others down the other passageway.

They were nearly to the tunnel that led to the excavations when Ferret called the others to a halt. He cocked his head. Caledan could see his ears twitching. "There are guards coming," he whispered. "Seven or eight at least. I can hear the clanking of their armor."

Caledan listened. At first he could hear nothing, then the faint sound of booted feet against cold stone drifted down the passageway. They couldn't risk a fight. At best, it would delay them, and at worst . . .

"This way," Morhion said, gesturing to the shadowed mouth of a side passage. "It may be our only chance."

Caledan hesitated, but there was no time to think. "Come on," Morhion hissed, starting down the side corridor. The others followed. There was a foul, vaguely sweet odor in the air. The passageway gave Caledan a bad feeling.

Without warning the passage opened up into a small, darkened chamber. It was a dead end, Caledan realized. He swore, sensing something was very wrong, and gripped the hilt of his sword. Too late.

Torches burst into life all around the companions. Caledan stumbled backward involuntarily, blinded by the glare. When his vision cleared, he realized they were surrounded by Zhentarim.

There were at least a dozen warriors, each holding a

crossbow trained on one of the companions—all except for
Morhion. The mage stepped forward, joining two dark-
robed figures who stood alongside the Zhentarim.

Morhion had betrayed them.

"You'll pay for this, mage," Caledan spat. He lunged forward, only to be brought up short as several Zhentarim lev-
eled their swordpoints at his chest.

"I wouldn't do that if I were you, Caledan," a clear voice
said as one of the black-robed figures pushed back its cowl.
Ravendas. "Yes, Caledan, it is I. You did not think you would
escape me so easily, did you?" She turned to address the
other black-robed figure. "Your traitor has done exceed-
ingly well."

Ravendas's companion also pushed back his heavy cowl.
It was Lord Steward Snake, his dark eyes glittering in the
torchlight. "As I promised, my lord."

"Twice now you have done me a great favor, Morhion
Gen'dahar," Ravendas crooned. The mage did not meet her
gaze. He stared blankly forward, his attitude unfathomable.
"This time you have outdone yourself. I had not expected
you to bring me the troublesome Harper as well."

Ravendas approached Mari. "Who will lead your little
rebellion now, Harper?" Mari stiffened, yet remained silent.
So Morhion had betrayed them, informing Ravendas of the
plan to free the prisoners.

"What are you going to do with us?" Caledan demanded
hotly.

"Kill you, of course," Ravendas said flatly. "But I wish you
to live long enough to see me wield the power of the Nightstone. It will make your failure all the more bitter." She
turned to one of the Zhentarim warriors. "Bind them."

Caledan, Mari, Estah, and Ferret were each bound
tightly. Suddenly Caledan noticed that the young thief,
Talim, was not among them. He must have slipped away in
the darkness. The four were dragged out of the passage-

way, and for a brief moment Caledan found himself next to Morhion.

"If ever it is in my power," he whispered harshly, "I will kill you for this treachery, mage."

"I know," was all Morhion said.

Twenty

"Where are they?" Tyveris muttered repeatedly. He paced the small stone antechamber. Kyana watched him, her arms folded across her doeskin jerkin. A score of prisoners huddled in the cold, dank chamber behind her. Their clothes were in rags, their faces dirty and haggard, many of them gaunt with hunger. However, they clutched makeshift weapons in their hands, along with several short swords and crossbows Tyveris and Kyana had brought with them.

"I know the Harper is your friend, monk," Kyana said, "but we can't afford to wait much longer. We've been lucky so far that we haven't run into any guards. But eventually our luck is going to run out. I'm afraid we have to assume that something has happened to the Harper and the others."

"You can assume what you like," Tyveris growled. The prisoners watched him with worried eyes. "Where *are* they?" he muttered one more time.

Much as he hated to admit it, he knew Kyana was right.

It had been nearly an hour since he and the thief had freed a score of men and women in one of the dungeon blocks. It was only a matter of time until the escape was discovered, and then they would lose their only advantage—surprise. Cormik's agents were poised outside the tower, ready to send the signal to the bands of cityfolk waiting throughout the city that the prisoners had been safely freed. Then the rebellion would begin in earnest.

Tyveris could feel Kyana's eyes on him. She was pressing him to make a decision. Tyveris had hoped Mari and the others would catch up with him before it was necessary to make the final assault on the tower. I'm a priest now, not a warrior, Tyveris swore inwardly.

Suddenly Kyana stiffened. She lifted a hand to her lips for silence. Tyveris caught the faint sound of footpads echoing off cold stone. Someone was hurrying toward the antechamber. Kyana loosened her saber and moved to the door. Tyveris prepared himself to spring. A shadow moved outside the doorway.

"Wait, it's me—Talim!" a voice gasped just as Kyana raised her saber. Tyveris sighed in relief as the young, red-haired thief rushed into the room. His freckled face was pale, his gray eyes wide.

"What is it?" Kyana asked him, concerned.

"I have bad news," the young thief said, swallowing hard. He told his story: Mari, Caledan, and the others had been captured by Ravendas and taken to the crypt of the Shadow-king. "It was the mage who betrayed them," Talim said sadly. "But I was at the rear of the party, and I managed to melt into the shadows. They didn't notice me."

"You did well," Tyveris said somberly. His heart felt as cold as the surrounding walls. Almost instinctively he started for the door.

"Where do you think you're going?" Kyana demanded.

"To help my friends," he declared fiercely.

"And what do you propose we do with them?" she asked quietly, nodding her head toward the prisoners gathered in the antechamber. "Return them to their cells?"

Tyveris glared at her. Then his shoulders slumped. Again, the thief was right. He couldn't turn his back on the prisoners. No, he had to trust that Mari, Caledan, and the others could take care of themselves. He had his own job to do now.

"All right," he said gruffly. "We'll go on as planned, without Mari. But I'm not much of a warrior nowadays, Kyana. You're going to have to take charge."

"Oh, no, you don't," Kyana said slyly. "They're looking to you, monk, not me." All faces turned expectantly toward Tyveris.

He swallowed hard. I will lead them, but I will not kill, he vowed inwardly. I gave you my promise, Tali, my sister. I promised you there would be no more killing.

"All right, then," he growled. "Let's go."

Despite the weeks and even months each of them had spent laboring beneath the Tor, the cityfolk moved with a speed and energy that amazed Tyveris. With Kyana and Talim scouting ahead, they made their way past the slime-covered walls of the corridor, toward the heart of the dungeon. They moved as stealthily as they could, with the brave, though pale and haggard, faces of people determined to win their freedom or die.

The group came to a corridor leading off to a block of cells, and Talim and Kyana swiftly picked the locks on the iron doors. Tyveris quickly explained to the newly-freed prisoners what they intended to do. "If you do not wish, you do not have to come with us," the loremaster said. When they left the block, however, not a prisoner chose to remain behind.

It was at the next block of cells that they encountered several guards, three dungeon warders, gambling with dice of polished bone. The first two died before they realized what was transpiring, one with Kyana's saber in his heart, the other with Talim's dagger in his back. The third tried to shout an alarm as he scrambled for his sword, but his cry was strangled into silence as a trio of crossbow bolts buried themselves in his throat and chest.

Tyveris whirled in surprise to see three of the cityfolk reloading their crossbows. He reminded himself not to underestimate these courageous people.

One of the guards had a ring of keys at his belt, and these made the task of freeing the prisoners quicker. The thieves of the Purple Masks Guild had hidden several caches of weapons in lesser-used parts of the dungeon, and one of these was nearby. Soon Tyveris found he had over a hundred cityfolk crowding the corridor behind him, each with a weapon in hand, be it sword, knife, cudgel, or crossbow. Some of the cityfolk were but children, others were gray and weathered. There were as many women as men. All of them were ready to fight, and none were afraid to die.

One of the prisoners, an older woman with steel-gray hair and eyes to match, said something when Tyveris helped her from her cell that seemed to speak for all the cityfolk. "The wheel is turning," she said in her worn voice. "The captors become the captives, and the prisoners fly free once again. If one soul perishes in the wheel's turning, such is the way of things. The wheel cannot be stopped. We must shed our tears, and then go on."

And go on they did.

"We need to be even more careful now," Kyana said to Tyveris as once again they started down the corridor. "The dungeon's central chamber is not far ahead. That's where there are likely to be the most Zhentarim."

"How many?" Tyveris asked gravely.

"According to Ferret's reports, at least a score of them," Kyana said. "The numbers are on our side."

They encountered another pair of guards as they approached the central chamber, but the cityfolk dispatched them swiftly and silently. Tyveris motioned for the prisoners to hang back while he, Kyana, and Talim crept forward toward the glow of torches.

From Ferret's reports, they knew that most of the cell blocks were arranged around the dungeon's central chamber almost like the spokes of a wheel. Tyveris and the two thieves moved silently as they approached the open doorway. Beyond was a walkway with a stone balustrade. Staying close to the floor, the three eased forward until they could peer down toward the large, circular chamber below them. Tyveris barely managed to stifle an oath.

The stone-walled room was filled with guards.

There was not a score of them, but rather five times that number. And all of them were armed. Tyveris could see the stairwell leading up to the tower no more than fifty feet away, but it might as well have been a hundred miles for the sea of guards blocking their way. He looked at Kyana in desperation. The thief shook her head.

"It appears we were expected," was all she said.

* * * * *

Caledan was not certain how far beneath the Old City they had descended, but he knew they must be deep within the heart of the Tor.

Ravendas moved through the rough-hewn tunnel at a swift pace, Snake following subserviently on her heels. Caledan, Estah, Ferret, and Mari stumbled along after Ravendas. Their hands were bound tightly behind their backs with leather thongs; their ankles had been hobbled with heavy rope so that they could not run. A dozen cruel-faced Zhentarim warriors trod behind the four, pushing them roughly onward each time one of them hesitated. Behind the warriors walked Morhion, his face as cold as granite.

Without warning the rocky passageway widened, and the odd party of friends and enemies came to an abrupt halt. They stood in a sort of antechamber, a roughly square room perhaps two dozen paces in width. Acrid, smoking torches lined the walls of dark, jagged stone, and piles of rubble littered the corners. However, Caledan barely saw any of this, for instantly his attention was fixed on the door.

The portal dominated the far wall of the antechamber. It was a slab of perfect, unblemished onyx, as tall as two men and as wide as six abreast.

"The crypt of the Shadowking," Caledan whispered in awe.

"Indeed," Ravendas purred. "My greatest triumph lies within." She tossed aside her dark robe and stood before the door resplendent in a silken gown as deep and rich in hue as dried blood. "The time has come."

She clapped her hands, and two Zhentarim stepped from a dim alcove Caledan had not noticed. By their deep purple robes and the disturbing, misshapen symbols that hung about their necks, Caledan guessed these Zhents were priests of some sort. Between them stood a small figure clad in a velvet tunic.

It was the boy, Kellen.

Caledan felt his throat tighten. The boy looked up at him with his wide, dark-lashed eyes. *He knows!* Caledan thought suddenly. He was certain of it. For a moment he saw a look of pleading in the boy's deep green eyes. Then Ravendas approached her son and brushed his pale cheek with a solitary finger.

"Your time draws near, my son," Ravendas said in her crystalline voice. Kellen nodded slowly but said nothing. He clutched a set of polished reed pipes tightly in his hands. Mari, Estah, and Ferret regarded the boy with surprise. None of them had known Ravendas had a son. But they still don't know the full truth, Caledan thought bitterly.

"There is one last thing," Ravendas said. She stepped forward and reached inside Caledan's leather jerkin, drawing out the set of pipes that he had concealed in an inner pocket. "I know you still have not discovered the secret of the shadow song, but then, I do not care to take unnecessary chances." She dropped the pipes on the stone floor and ground them under her heel until they were nothing more than splinters.

Caledan could not help but wince. That was the first set of pipes he had ever made, and the truest. He had brought them along as a last-ditch hope, in the event he somehow managed to discover the secret of the shadow song.

"You're a fool, Ravendas," Caledan said harshly. "You've always been a fool. You'll do anything for power. But it's a desire that blinds you." He nodded his head toward Snake. "So how do you intend to kill her, Snake?" he asked in a cutting voice. "I suppose you don't need her or the Zhentarim any longer, now that the crypt has been found. Ravendas would just stand in the way of your ultimate plans, wouldn't she? Why don't you just kill her now and get it over with?"

"I am afraid you are quite mistaken," Snake replied in his sibilant voice. His eyes were flat, his face emotionless.

"Stop this idiocy!" Ravendas snapped. "I will hear it no longer. All my servants obey my will and my will alone, Caldorien. As will you." A blotch of color touched each of her pale cheeks.

She is uncertain, Caledan thought. He had planted the seeds of doubt in her heart, and they had taken root.

"Tell me, my lord steward," she said, turning to the green-robed man. "Is there any truth to this base accusation? Do you intend to cross my wishes?"

"By all the powers that be, I swear not. I serve only to see the Nightstone placed in your hand, my Lord Ravendas. That is my sole purpose."

Ravendas nodded in satisfaction. "You see?" she said smugly to Caledan. "I own him, as I own all of you. Once the power of the Nightstone is mine, I will own far more. Now the door must be opened." She lifted a hand and pointed a finger at Morhion. "You, mage, shall perform this momentous task for me."

Morhion nodded, stepping toward the onyx door. He spread his arms wide and closed his eyes. He spoke a single guttural word of magic, and a small, silvery ball of light burst into existence before him. Caledan watched as thin, glowing tendrils began to stretch from the orb of light. Like silvery threads, the tendrils caressed the door and began to trace their way across its dark, flawless surface.

Caledan realized that the silvery threads were outlining strange symbols and weird runes. In moments the entire door was covered with their glimmering decoration. Morhion spoke another word of magic, and the ball of light vanished as abruptly as it had appeared. The magical tendrils faded, yet a curious luminescence remained. The symbols and runes could be faintly observed.

For long moments Morhion studied the ancient writing. Finally he nodded. He gestured to a dark, perfect circle in the center of the doorway, a place where the smooth stone was untouched by rune or sigil.

"The circle is as dark as the moon is this night," Morhion intoned. He gazed at Ravendas. "One who desires to enter need only touch it." He stepped away from the door.

Caledan saw Ravendas hesitate only briefly. Then she thrust her chin outward and boldly stood before the door. "All that lies beyond this portal, I claim for my own," she proclaimed. She reached forward, laying her hand full upon the dark circle.

There was a sharp sound like ice cracking, and Ravendas took a startled step backward, staring at the door. The writing on the portal flared brilliantly. Then it went dark. A faint, sharp line appeared in the portal's center. The line darkened, growing into a crack. Then, propelled by some unseen force, the two halves of the onyx slab swung silently inward. A puff of stale air rushed out of the open doorway, bringing the smell of death. Beyond lay only impenetrable darkness.

"The portal is open," Morhion spoke softly.

"Then let us enter the crypt of the Shadowking." The fear had left Ravendas's face, replaced by a look of exultation. She took a torch from the wall and stepped through the portal.

"Follow," Snake said harshly, and the warriors pushed the four companions through the portal. Caledan felt a momentary chill as he passed through the doorway, then he blinked in surprise. He could see. He had expected the room to be utterly dark, or at most to be faintly lit by the single torch Ravendas carried. Instead the vast chamber was filled with a peculiar, ruddy illumination.

The crypt of the Shadowking was a vast, circular chamber. The floor was fashioned of the same flawless dark stone as the doorway, and the perimeter of the tomb was lined with massive buttresses of basalt, thirteen in number. The spandrels between them were carved with nightmarish friezes, the bas-relief gargoyles leering evilly down at the companions. Beneath each stone buttress was a shallow alcove. Those few into which Caledan could see were filled with burial offerings: one with ornate jewels, another with casks of wine and cups of gold, still another with ivory figurines, servants to wait upon the dead in the afterworld. The Shadowking may have been Talembar's foe, but he had been a king also. Talembar had given him a burial deserving of royalty.

Farther into the chamber stood a circle of huge columns, surrounding the center of the crypt like a ring of sentinel giants. The tomb was deathly silent. The stale, ancient air seemed to smother all sound, as if it resented the intrusion of living beings in a place where nothing had stirred in a thousand years.

When they reached the ring of columns Ravendas stopped. She clapped her hands, a signal for the Zhentarim warriors and priests to withdraw from the crypt. The Zhents, especially the warriors, seemed more than willing to leave the eerie chamber.

"Don't get any rash ideas," Ravendas said to Caledan. "What will transpire within this circle is not fit for simple eyes to behold, so I have sent my servants away. But they will guard the portal with their lives. I needn't remind you there is only one exit from the crypt."

"I really don't think we'll be going anywhere," Caledan said sarcastically, glancing meaningfully at the rope that hobbled his ankles.

With a gesture of mock politeness, Ravendas gestured for the others to follow her. They passed between two of the gigantic columns and entered the circle within.

Caledan could see now that there were seven of the massive columns, each resting on an enormous basalt plinth as big as a small house. The surface of the columns was without carving or sigil, except for a single word that had been incised into the stone of each column perhaps twenty feet above the floor. Caledan squinted at the words through the hazy crimson light, but he could not discern them.

He let his gaze drift upward. The columns supported a domed ceiling about a dozen fathoms above his head. A mosaic covered the ceiling, but in the half-light all Caledan could see were pale, cruel-looking eyes staring down at him from above. He noticed a dark, jagged line running across the center of the domed ceiling. It was a crack, the single flaw he could detect in the construction of the crypt.

In the very center of the tomb stood a dais of basalt bearing a huge sarcophagus of flawless onyx. Upon the coffin's

lid was carved a figure that could only represent the
Shadowking. The figure was manlike in shape, but massive
and twisted, the gnarled arms ending in claws, the legs in
cloven hooves.

But the face of the Shadowking was the face of a man.
Unlike the rest of the figure's body, the visage was smooth
and perfect, even beautiful. This was how the sorcerer Verraketh had looked before dark magic had twisted him into
the being of maleficence called the Shadowking. His features were crowned by a pair of dark antlers springing from
the unfurrowed brow of the death mask, a bestial symbol of
violence.

Caledan could not help but shiver. Within that sarcophagus lay a being of terrible malevolence. But the Shadowking is a thousand years dead, he reminded himself.

"Cheerful-looking fellow, isn't he?" Ferret whispered.
Caledan winced. How could the thief joke at a time like
this? "By the way, did you notice those words on the
columns are written in Talfir?" Ferret said softly. "I thought
you might be interested to know. . . ."

Caledan stared at the thief in surprise, then he jerked his
head up to look at the runes carved high on the basalt
columns. He squinted through the dimness and saw that
Ferret was right. By now the ancient language was familiar
enough to recognize, though he cursed himself for being
unable to read it.

He thought back to that day when the phantom of Talek
Talembar had appeared on the windswept cliff top. What
had the phantom told him? What were the words he had
used? The *exact* words?

For a long time his mind was empty. He almost swore
aloud in frustration. Then abruptly, like a dam bursting, the
memory came to him. It was as if Talembar was speaking
once again, only this time inside his mind.

    . . .*thou might look for its echo in the place where last it was played.* . . .

"Ferret," Caledan whispered hurriedly, his voice barely audible. "I understand the secret of the shadow song. Don't ask how. There isn't time for that. But I need those pipes the boy has."

Ferret did not nod, but by the glimmer of excitement in his beady eyes Caledan knew he understood. Caledan returned his inspection to the seven words of Talfir inscribed upon the columns. His knowledge of the ancient language was sorely limited. He wished Tyveris was here.

His concentration shattered as Ravendas spoke. "Come, my son." She held out a hand to Kellen. "It is time." Slowly the boy reached out a small hand. Ravendas led him up the steps of the dais. Caledan could see the terror in his eyes, but the child did not falter. He is brave, my son, Caledan thought. His hands strained reflexively against his bonds.

For the first time Caledan noticed that there was something standing at the foot of the massive sarcophagus. It was a small wooden box of simple, almost crude construction. The box seemed oddly out of place amidst the magnificence and grandeur of the rest of the crypt.

"Open the box, my son," Ravendas said when they stood atop the dais. Her voice was gentle, but her lovely face was twisted with desire. Kellen hesitated. "Open it," Ravendas repeated, her voice more harsh. The boy winced and knelt before the box. Slowly, he reached out a small hand and opened the lid.

Shadows leaped forth.

Kellen screamed as he fell backward. Around the box whirled a small maelstrom of rippling shadows. Caledan almost thought he could glimpse faces amidst the swirling tatters of darkness. They were forlorn faces, hopeless and hateful, faces of death.

"To touch the shadows which surround the Stone is to die," Snake proclaimed.

Ravendas did not appear alarmed. "Play, my son," she instructed. "This is the time for which you have prepared all your life. Play your song. Make the shadows disappear. They will do your bidding, if only you play." Kellen stood frozen, clutching the reed pipes tightly as he stared at the whirling shapes of darkness.

"Remember what I told you, Kellen," Caledan called out, his voice cutting across the wail of the shadows. "You don't have to do this, not if you don't want to!"

"Silence!" Ravendas yelled.

Kellen cast a desperate look at Caledan. Then he turned his round face toward his mother. The pipes slipped from his fingers to fall against the hard stone.

"I won't do it!" he said. His voice trembled. "I won't pipe the shadows away!"

Ravendas cast a venomous look at Caledan. She knelt before Kellen, gripping his shoulders cruelly. "Listen to me, my son," she said in a cloying tone. "I am your mother. You must obey me. If you do not, there will be a price to pay. And do you know what that price will be?" Kellen's eyes widened in horror. "That is right, my son. I will kill Caledan—your father—even as you watch." She stood and folded her arms. "Are you prepared to pay that price, Kellen? Or will you obey me?"

Kellen hung his head. Caledan's companions, even Morhion, stared at him at this revelation. Finally Kellen looked up at Caledan. There was a deep sorrow in his eyes. Kellen knelt to pick up the pipes and lifted them to his lips.

You don't have to do what she says, Caledan wanted to shout out again, but he knew it would be no use. He had become the weapon Ravendas now wielded against the boy.

The sweet notes of Kellen's song seemed muffled at first, as if the ancient air was trying to subdue them. But as Kellen played on the music grew in clarity and strength. Caledan felt his skin tingle. He recognized the power of the shadow magic. It ran in the blood of his son even as it did in his own veins.

The whirling maelstrom of shadows slowed, then began to fade. In moments the darkness surrounding the box was gone. All could now clearly see the object that lay within. It was a rough, uneven Stone, unusual only because it looked so completely ordinary. But Caledan had no doubt of what it was. Even from this distance he could feel the pulsing of dark energy emanating from the thing, washing over him in sickening waves. It was the Nightstone.

* * * * *

"They want to go on, Tyveris," Kyana said softly. She and the monk stood slightly apart from the mass of prisoners who huddled in the dim dungeon corridor. Not two hundred paces down the passageway was the dungeon's central chamber—and the Zhentarim.

"By all the gods, they'll be killed, every one of them," Tyveris rumbled as quietly as he could. Tyveris cast a glance back at the cityfolk. They stood in the corridor, their faces pale, their hands gripping their weapons tightly. "If we head back to the thieves' entrance now, at least some of these cityfolk will be able to escape," he growled.

Kyana shook her head. "They're not going to retreat," she said fiercely. "Look at them, monk. These folk are ready to fight. All you have to do is give the word."

"I can't," Tyveris said, shaking his head. His dark eyes were mournful behind his spectacles. "Maybe Mari could have, but I cannot."

"Then we have no hope of driving the Zhentarim from the city," Kyana said flatly.

The two returned to the crowd of prisoners. However, when Tyveris told them of his intention to turn back, a burly man with the calloused hands of a blacksmith stepped forward.

"Begging your pardon, sire," he said hesitantly, "but I don't think there's any here who want to turn back." The crowd murmured in agreement. "You see, it wouldn't be right for us to escape while all the others are still caged up like so many animals. Besides, we've had enough of Cutter and her guards." He shook the stout cudgel he gripped in his hand. "We've acted like frightened pups long enough. Now's the time to fight."

Tyveris opened his mouth to protest, but the sound of quickly padding footsteps stopped him. Talim pushed his way through the crowd of prisoners, breathing hard.

"There are a dozen guards patrolling the corridors not far from here, and they're headed this way," the young thief said hoarsely.

Tyveris groaned in dismay. They couldn't get back to the thieves' entrance without fighting the patrol. And if they did that the other Zhentarim were bound to hear the noise and rush to join the fray.

"It seems your decision has been made for you," Kyana said, watching Tyveris carefully.

Tyveris was silent for a long while. Finally he spoke. "To the stairs," was all he said.

Tyveris was forced to admit that when the cityfolk rushed into the dungeon's central chamber it was a glorious moment. "Iriaebor!" the prisoners cried as they raised their weapons high. "For the Thousand Spires!"

They poured down the ramp which led into the large, circular chamber. Those prisoners who bore crossbows loosed a rain of bolts down upon the Zhentarim from the high walkway that circled the room.

Yet the Zhentarim had been warned there would be a battle that night and were not caught unaware. A few fell with arrows quivering in chest or throat, but far more blocked the flurry of deadly bolts with wooden shields. The rest of the prisoners streamed into the chamber, and the room erupted into chaos.

Abruptly two score prisoners came rushing out of one of the cell blocks, knocking several spear-wielding guards aside. Talim was with them. Somehow the wiry young thief had slipped past the guards and freed the prisoners. They dashed into the chamber, grabbing weapons from fallen Zhents or fighting with the very chains that bound their wrists. Even so, the battle-hardened Zhents pushed them back with almost comic ease.

It's not enough, Tyveris realized, standing numbly on the edge of the battle. They have the hearts of lions, but their hands are those of merchants and artisans, not warriors. He tried to say a prayer to his god, but his lips were unable to form the words. Already the cityfolk were faltering. In minutes, it would be over.

The battle surged before him. A prisoner, a young woman hardly more than a girl, was clumsily brandishing a rusty sword, fending off the hard blows of a grinning guard. Even as Tyveris watched, the sword spun from her hand to clatter against the slate floor. The Zhent's grin broadened luridly as he readied a killing blow.

Forgive me, Oghma, my god, Tyveris said inwardly. Forgive me, Tali, my sister. This is something I must do.

Tyveris let out a roar of fury as he leaped forward and grabbed the young woman's fallen sword. Tyveris swung the blade with lightning-quick skill. The Zhent's grin faded as he slipped off the blade and into a pool of his own blood.

Tyveris stared at the corpse dully, but he did not drop the sword. There was no more time for prayers or regrets. Now was the time to fight.

He reached down a powerful hand to help the young woman to her feet. Her eyes were filled with gratitude. "Here, you're going to need this." He pushed the blade

back into her hand. She nodded fiercely. Tyveris bent down
and pried the saber from the guard's fingers.

"What's your name?" he asked the young woman.

"Erisa, sire,"

"All right, Erisa, I want you to stay by me," Tyveris rumbled. With his bare hand, Tyveris ripped the livery—the
azure river and silver tower with Ravendas's crimson moon
above—from the fallen guard's jerkin. He hastily tied the
piece of cloth onto the end of a broken spear he found
nearby, fashioning a makeshift standard. "May Oghma and
all the gods grant us strength this night," Tyveris said
solemnly. As Erisa watched in wonderment, the symbol of
the crimson moon suddenly burst into flame, flared brightly,
and then went dark. At the same time the outlines of the
river and the tower, the traditional symbols of Iriaebor,
began to glow with an unearthly silvery light.

"You're going to be my standard-bearer, Erisa," Tyveris
said, handing the stunned young woman the banner. "Hold
it high for all to see. And do not let the standard fall, not at
any cost."

Erisa stared at the glowing banner for a moment, then
nodded, lifting the standard high. "I won't fail you, sire!"

"Then I'll try to do the same," Tyveris said gruffly. He
joined the throng making for the flight of dark stone stairs
that led up toward the tower and freedom. He swung his
sword with easy, practiced strokes, cutting a swath through
the Zhentarim. Erisa followed close on his heels, holding
the gleaming standard high in one hand, and protecting
Tyveris's back with the sword he had given her in the
other.

"To me! To me!" Tyveris bellowed in his enormous voice.
Despite the din, all around him the cityfolk looked up to see
him striding through the battle, his sword flashing under
the magical illumination of the banner. Hope ignited in their
eyes. Heartened anew, the prisoners hacked at the Zhen-

tarim ferociously, fighting to make their way to the lore-master.

A fierce grin spread across Tyveris's face as he swung his sword tirelessly. Zhent after Zhent fell beneath his blade. "To me!" he cried again. "To the stairway! To freedom!"

Whatever the outcome, he was determined to make this a battle the gods would never forget.

Twenty-one

Ravendas snatched the pipes from Kellen and tucked them into the sash of her gown. "Out of my way, child," she snarled. "I have need of you no longer." She struck Kellen sharply across the cheek. The boy cried out in pain and tumbled backward, rolling down the steps of the dais.

"You will pay for that," Caledan swore, clenching his hands into fists behind his back.

"I pay for nothing," Ravendas replied, her cheeks flushed. "I *take* what I want."

"Talembar said that only one with the shadow magic can take up the Nightstone," Mari called out desperately. "You must not touch it!"

"And why, by all the gods, would I believe *you*, Harper?" Ravendas spat. Without any further hesitation she bent down and closed her fingers around the dark stone. With an exultant smile Ravendas lifted the Nightstone above her head. "You see?" she cried. "You are wrong! The power of the Nightstone is mine. With it, I shall rule the greatest empire Toril has ever known!

"Now kneel before me," Ravendas declared, her voice ringing in the subterranean chamber. "Kneel and pay homage to your new queen. Kneel and perhaps I shall—"

Ravendas winced, faltering as a momentary spasm of pain crossed her features, but she quickly regained her composure.

"Kneel," she repeated, "and perhaps I—"

This time the pain showed clearly on Ravendas's beautiful face. The blood drained from her cheeks, her eyes widening as she stared at the Stone. "No!" she cried out in horror. She shook her hand, trying to drop the Nightstone, but she could not loosen her grip.

"It's burning me!" she shrieked. Ravendas screamed in agony. The pale skin of her forehead was undulating, as if something was writhing beneath the surface, something alive. Kellen had regained his feet, and he stood by Snake at the foot of the dais, watching his mother in horror.

"Kellen, don't look!" Caledan cried out. "Don't look at her!" Caledan tried to lunge forward, but the hobbles about his ankles tripped him, and he nearly fell to the hard floor. Kellen slowly turned away from the grisly spectacle.

Ravendas let out one last, soul-wrenching scream, and suddenly two dark objects burst from the smooth skin of her forehead. They were antlers of onyx, thrusting and branching like saplings from her brow. Ravendas's eyes went blank, her face twisted, and Caledan knew that she was dead.

But whatever writhed inside her was not.

The form that had been Ravendas began to crack like ancient porcelain. Without warning the shell exploded outward in a spray of pale shards. Her silken gown was ripped to shreds. The reed pipes clattered down the steps of the dais.

A shadow unfurled itself from the shattered remains of Ravendas's body, a thing of utter darkness. The shadow was shaped vaguely like a man, except for the antlers sprouting from its head. With every moment it rose higher off the dais, its outline coalescing, growing clearer and sharper. And in the center of the shadow hovered the Nightstone, pulsing rhythmically with a vermillion glow.

"By all the gods," Caledan whispered hoarsely. "It is the Shadowking."

"Yes, and he is the master of us all!" Snake cried out in rapture. "Bow down before the darkness that will rule forevermore!" Snake abased himself before the dais, lying prostrate before the undulating form of the Shadowking.

Caledan saw something moving to his left, and he turned to see Morhion standing behind the Harper, a small knife in his hand. Was this to be the mage's final treachery? Then to Caledan's amazement, he watched as Morhion deftly cut the leather thongs that bound Mari's wrists, then bent down and cut the rope that hobbled her ankles. She stared at him, but he had already hurried on to free Estah and Ferret. Snake saw none of this. His attention was upon the form of the Shadowking.

In moments Morhion stood behind Caledan, who felt the mage's knife slit his bonds. "Why are you doing this?" he whispered savagely. "What more do you seek to gain, mage?"

"We do not have time for explanations," Morhion said with infuriating calm. The mage also cut the rope binding Caledan's ankles.

Free of her bonds, the Harper had started toward the dais. She closed her hand about the reed pipes. Snake looked up, fury blazing in his eyes.

"Caledan!" Mari shouted as she threw the pipes in his direction. Even as the instrument arced through the air Snake reached out an arm toward the Harper and spoke a word of magic. A jagged stream of poisonous light burst from his fingertips, striking Mari full in the chest. The force of the blast hurled her backward, and she crumpled without a word, her face white. She did not move.

Caledan caught the pipes but stood as if frozen. At that moment he knew he had been a fool. He loved the Harper as much as he had ever loved Kera. Perhaps even more. But he had been prideful and realized his true feelings too late. Now Mari was gone as well. His shoulders slumped in defeat.

"Will you let her sacrifice mean nothing?" Morhion whispered in his ear. Caledan turned to the mage. More than ever he wanted to kill Morhion. But that could wait. With one last glance at the runes inscribed upon the seven columns, he lifted the pipes to his lips.

"Play a single note, and the boy dies," a soft, sibilant voice said. Snake stood before the dais, holding Kellen tightly by the shoulder. A bare inch from the boy's neck Snake held a thin, golden needle. "The needle is coated with a poison called telsiak. Believe me when I tell you that the child will be quite dead before you can play a second note."

Caledan stared at the thin, hard-faced lord steward for a long moment. He sighed, lowering the pipes. He could not do it. He had lost Kera. Now Mari lay unmoving, almost certainly dead. How could he let himself lose his newfound son as well?

"No, Father!" Kellen cried out. "You don't have to do what he says. Isn't that what you told me?" The boy's voice was plaintive, but there was something different about his eyes. . . .

"I'm . . . I'm sorry, Kellen." Caledan let the pipes slip from his fingers.

"In the name of the Abyss, look above!" Ferret shouted, pointing to the crypt's domed ceiling. Involuntarily, Snake turned his gaze upward. There was nothing there but shadows. Too late the lord steward realized he had fallen for the oldest trick of all.

He winced in pain as he looked down at the golden needle protruding from his chest. In the instant when he had looked away, the boy had grabbed his hand and turned the needle into the lord steward's body.

"Master . . ." Snake said as he pulled out the needle. But that was all. In the space of a heartbeat his lips turned blue, and his hands stiffened into rigid claws. He toppled to the floor. His hard eyes stared blankly forward, as dull and lifeless as stones. The lord steward Snake was dead.

But the Shadowking was not.

"Thanks for the distraction, Ferret," Caledan said grimly to the thief.

"Don't mention it." the thief replied. "Though you might want to start worrying about *that*." He nodded toward the dais.

The Shadowking was nearly complete. Muscles and veins writhed like serpents beneath skin as dark and smooth as night. Its legs were as thick as columns, ending in cloven hooves. It flexed its powerful arms; long, dark talons sprang from its fingertips. A tail lined with jagged, saw-toothed barbs cracked like a whip in the air. All that remained indistinct was the Shadowking's face. And slowly, inexorably, that too was taking shape.

"Do something, Father!" Kellen cried, running forward.

"Play the shadow song, Caledan," Estah said, her voice strong and reassuring.

"Now would be a good time," Ferret added.

Caledan reached down and picked up the pipes. His fingers felt numb, and he fumbled, nearly dropping the pipes. It had been so many years since he had played music. He feared he would not remember how. He feared that he had read incorrectly the Talfir letters inscribed upon the columns. Then a hand reached up and touched his own, a hand that was small but strong. He did not need to look to know it was Kellen's. Suddenly all his fear slipped away, all his regrets and bitterness. And then there was only music.

He played a first, clear note—a wistful, almost optimistic sound. Talek Talembar had not told him to *listen* for the echo of the song in the place it had last been played. Talembar had told him to *look* for the echo of the song. That was the key.

He played the second note of the song, higher in pitch, a pure, ringing note. What the words written in Talfir said, Caledan wasn't certain, but he knew enough of the ancient language to recognize what letters the runes stood for, and that was enough. The first letter of each word was a note of music. It had been so terribly obvious, a puzzle so simple any apprentice minstrel would have seen it, yet anyone who could not read music would never have understood.

Caledan played the third note, this one lower, more ominous, a note of power. The pipes felt warm in his hands.

"I don't mean to be pushy, but you might want to hurry it up," Ferret whispered, jerking his head toward the dais.

Slowly the Shadowking had begun to draw itself up to its full, towering height, spreading its arms wide. Two batlike wings unfurled from its back. The Nightstone pulsed lividly in the center of its misshapen chest as hot and red as blood. Now the Shadowking's visage was coming into focus, but its face was not the face of a man, not like that of the death mask on the sarcophagus. Instead it was the face of a beast. Fangs like obsidian knives protruded from its maw, oozing dark ichor.

Caledan almost faltered as he played the fourth note, but he clenched his fingers tightly about the pipes and forced himself to breathe. The music continued. The entire chamber was beginning to resonate with it. Each of the notes echoed off the dark stone, interweaving with the others. He played the fifth note, then the sixth. He was trembling now. The sound of the echoing song was growing deeper, more complex.

The Shadowking took a step forward. Its cloven hoof cracked the stone of the dais. It took another step, and more stone crumbled beneath its ponderous stride. It reached out a claw, straight toward Caledan. The last outlines of its twisted face coalesced. It opened its maw to let out a roar of triumph, and a crimson flame burst to life in its eyes. After a thousand years of entombment, the Shadowking lived again.

Bow to me! a vast and ancient voice thundered within Caledan's mind. Terror clawed brutally at his heart. *Bow to me. I am Darkness!*

Caledan shook his head against the crushing power of the voice, struggling to stay upright. Summoning his last few shreds of will, he played the final note of the shadow song.

The vast harmony that echoed about the crypt was suddenly complete, becoming a single chord of deep and ancient power. The music soared to a deafening volume. Caledan fell to his knees, dropping the pipes and covering his ears. The others did the same.

The Shadowking shrieked with a fury so monstrous and incomprehensible Caledan thought the sound of it would drive him mad. Then, with a clap of thunder, the Nightstone that beat in the Shadowking's chest burst asunder in a spray of dark, crystalline shards. The Shadowking began to waver and grow indistinct. Its darkness faded into a hazy translucence.

Finally, with a last shuddering sigh, the Shadowking flickered and was gone, like a shadow on the wall banished by the light of a single candle.

*   *   *   *   *

Caledan looked up to see Kellen. The boy's face was expressionless. Caledan gripped his hand, then Kellen flung himself into Caledan's arms, sobbing. Caledan held him tightly. "It's all right, Kellen," he said softly. "I'm here now. It's all right."

"Caledan, I think you'd better come here."

It was Estah. Her voice sounded tight. Gently, Caledan pushed Kellen away and rose.

The healer knelt at Mari's side. The Harper lay unmoving, her fiery hair spread out beneath her on the dark stone, her face deathly pale.

"Is she. . . ?" Caledan managed to ask, choking on the words.

"She is not dead," Estah said.

"Then you can use your medallion," Caledan said urgently, kneeling beside the halfling. "Use it, Estah. Please. Heal her for me. For all of us."

Estah shook her head sorrowfully. "I don't know if my magic can help her, Caledan. She is not dead, nor is she alive. It's almost as if her spirit is somehow caught in the gateway between this world and the next."

"It is the enchantment of the tomb," Morhion said. He ran his fingers across the stone of one of the basalt columns. "I can feel it lingering in this place."

"Then let's get her out of here," Caledan said. He lifted Mari's limp form in his arms, taking a few steps forward. Suddenly the floor lurched beneath him. Only Ferret's hand kept him from falling. There was a cracking sound, followed by the tumult of falling stone.

Caledan gasped. The crack in the dome of the ceiling gaped wide and jagged now, and other cracks spread outward from it. Suddenly one of the buttresses lining the perimeter of the tomb slumped, sending massive blocks of basalt crashing to the floor. The onyx shattered like glass beneath the force of the boulders.

"The crypt is collapsing!" Caledan shouted above the roar of the cave-in.

"The vibrations of the song must have weakened the dome," Morhion cried.

The floor lurched again. With a sound like lightning a crack opened in the center of the tomb. The companions scrambled away from the edge of the widening chasm. They watched as the massive sarcophagus listed like a sinking ship and then slid into the void.

"Stay close to me," Caledan shouted to Kellen above the deafening noise. Kellen's face was white with fear, but he nodded, following behind. Caledan stumbled on, clutching Mari.

They ran for the open doorway and had nearly reached it when the greatest tremor yet shook the crypt. Two of the basalt columns tilted crazily and tumbled off their plinths toward the tomb's center. A huge chunk of the ceiling gave way, and the mosaic exploded against the floor. Caledan dropped to his knees. Chunks of flying stone and shards of tile cut into his skin, yet he kept his grip on Mari.

"Look at the door!" Kellen shouted.

Caledan jerked his head up to see the two massive slabs of onyx slowly closing. He could see now that it was not magic that had opened the doors after all, but a simple lead counterweight hanging from a chain. With that last tremor, the iron chain had snapped and was now slipping freely through a pulley.

With impressive quickness Ferret dashed forward, sprang into the air, and caught the rising end of the chain. The onyx doors continued to swing shut. The chain carried the thief higher. Then the doors began to slow. Finally they came to a halt, leaving an open space barely two feet wide between them. Ferret dangled at least a dozen feet above the floor, swinging slowly from side-to-side, a crooked-toothed grin on his face.

Another tremor shook the tomb. With a groan the doors swung shut a few more inches.

"I'm not sure I can hold on much longer," Ferret shouted down. "Get through the door. I'll follow."

"Crazy thief," Caledan muttered, but with Mari in his arms, he slipped through the narrow opening with Kellen on his heels. Estah and Morhion followed moments later. Caledan peered back through the doorway at the thief still dangling from the chain.

"All right, Ferret, we're on the other side," Caledan called through the doorway. "Now you—"

"Caledan, don't you see?" Estah said fearfully. "Once Ferret lets go of that chain, the doors will shut. He'll be trapped. Ferret, don't let go!" she cried through the doorway.

"It's all right, Estah," Ferret called to them. He still wore his grin, but there was sorrow in his dark eyes. "It's just my greedy nature. You see, I want to keep all of the treasure in the tomb for myself. You understand, don't you?"

Tears streamed down Estah's cheeks. "Yes, Ferret. I do understand."

"Don't do this, you idiot thief!" Caledan shouted. He laid Mari down, ready to dash through the doorway, but he was too late.

"Tell Tyveris good-bye for me," Ferret called out in his raspy voice.

The thief let go of the chain, and the onyx doors closed with a boom.

"*Ferret!*" Caledan screamed. He slammed into the doorway, trying to dig his fingers into the crack to pry open the ponderous slabs of stone. But it was no use.

"You cannot open those doors, Caldorien," Morhion said solemnly.

Caledan slumped, bowing his head against the door. He knew the mage was right. The blasted mage was *always* right. Another tremor shook the stone around them. Dust rained down from the ceiling.

"We have to go, Caledan," Estah said, her voice thick with grief. "Mari needs you now. And Kellen, too."

Slowly, Caledan stood up, nodding grimly. He took Mari's form in his arms once again and looked at Kellen, who stood bravely beside him.

"Let's get out of here," he said.

* * * * *

Their flight upward through the dark, labyrinthine tunnels was like a nightmare, a nightmare Caledan thought would never end. His lungs burned as if they were on fire; his heart felt as if it was going to burst. But he did not slow his pace. He clutched Mari against his chest, his knuckles as white as her pale face. Estah, Kellen, and Morhion followed close behind.

Finally they reached the dungeons below the tower. They came to a large, circular chamber and saw the remnants of what looked to have been a ferocious battle. Corpses littered the slate floor, which was dark and slick with blood. Many were Zhentarim, but many looked to be cityfolk as well. Caledan could not be certain of which there were more. The air was hazy and stifling with the reek of torches. He dashed up the flight of stone steps, two at time.

After what seemed an eternity of climbing, Caledan burst outside into the blessedly clear night. Kellen, Estah, and Morhion were only paces behind him. Each of them was coated with dust, covered with bruises and scratches, but they were alive.

"Caledan!" a deep bellow rang out in the tower courtyard.

Caledan looked up, blinking the dust from his eyes. He saw that the gates in the tower's outer wall had been thrown open. Between them stood a massive, hulking figure with a broad, familiar face. Behind him was a throng of cheering cityfolk.

"At least the Zhentarim aren't here to greet us," Caledan said, his voice weak. He coughed. Tyveris came striding toward them. "The cityfolk have done it, Caledan!" the big Tabaxi announced joyously. "Mari and Cormik's plan worked. The Zhentarim are gone. We've driven the curs from the city, those that we didn't lock up in the dungeon, that is!"

As soon as Tyveris reached them, his exuberant expression vanished. "Let me," he said softly, helping Caledan ease the Harper to the ground. The loremaster looked at Estah with deep concern.

"You must act swiftly," Morhion said. "The enchantment of the tomb will no longer preserve her spirit."

"I'm not going to be able to do this alone, Caledan," Estah said, drawing out her silver medallion inscribed with the sign of Eldath. The healer brushed Mari's dark hair from her face, laying an expert hand on her brow. The Harper's features looked deathly. "I can make her body whole, but her spirit has already gone far away," Estah explained. "You must give her a reason to return to us, Caledan."

"Me?" Caledan said, staring at the healer. "But the Harper hates me now, Estah. You know that."

The wise halfling woman scowled at Caledan. "Must you always act like such a child, Caledan? We really don't have time for that now. Mari needs you." She laid the medallion on Mari's chest.

Caledan swallowed hard. Tentatively he reached down and held Mari's hand. What could he say to her?

Suddenly he knew.

This time he *did* have the power to save the one that he loved. He would not let this second chance pass him by. Slowly he slipped the copper bracelet from his left wrist.

Farewell, Kera, my beloved, he whispered in his heart. He slipped the bracelet over Mari's hand.

"I love you, Harper," he said simply, knowing it was the truth. "Come back to me."

For a single, terrifying moment nothing happened. Then suddenly the medallion hummed with a faint, sweet sound, like the song of running water. But the sound faded, and still Mari did not move.

I have failed, Caledan almost whispered.

Then the Harper's fingers closed tightly about his hand, and he stared at her in wonderment. Mari's eyes fluttered and flew open. She looked around in confusion, and her gaze locked on Caledan. A surprised smile touched her lips.

"So you didn't leave me after all, scoundrel," she said, her voice husky.

"I'll never leave you, Mari." He looked up at Kellen, and for the first time Caledan saw the boy smile. It was a hesitant, almost fragile expression. Still, it was a smile all the same. Caledan grinned in response. "Never," he said gruffly. He bent down and touched his lips to Mari's.

Suddenly Mari began to laugh.

"What is it?" Caledan asked her, a bemused expression on his face.

She reached up a hand and brushed his cheek. "You need a shave, scoundrel, that's what."

Epilogue

It was the first day of summer, and all of the windows in the Sign of the Dreaming Dragon were thrown open to let in the fresh air and sunlight. It was still early in the afternoon—the usual crowd of customers would not start arriving until the shadows grew longer—and save for Caledan and Mari, the common room was empty.

Jolle was out behind the inn working on the garden, and Estah had taken Pog and Nog, along with Kellen, to the free market. In the last weeks merchant ships had streamed freely in and out of Iriaebor's port, and the merchant stalls in the market were filled with goods, both ordinary and exotic, from every corner of the Realms.

Caledan and Mari sat at one of the inn's freshly scrubbed wooden tables. Between them rested a small package which had been delivered earlier along with a sealed parchment scroll.

Mari deftly broke the wax seal and unrolled the scroll. Caledan watched her face carefully as she scanned the words on the page. Her hair glowed with a deep, rich hue in the sunlight streaming through the door, and blooms of color touched her cheeks. In the weeks since they had fled from the destruction of the crypt, she had already regained much of her strength.

"It's a missive from the Harpers," Mari said, rolling up the parchment. "From Belhuar Thantarth, the Master of Twilight Hall."

"And?"

"*And* this is for you," she said, pushing the package toward Caledan.

He looked at her questioningly. Her smile was mysterious. He sighed, swallowed hard, and undid the leather ties that bound the small parcel. He upended the pouch over his hand. A small, silvery object slipped out.

It was a pin, wrought in the shape of a crescent moon encircling a harp.

"Congratulations, Harper," Mari said.

Caledan stared at the pin in amazement. At most he had expected a word of thanks from Thantarth for helping Mari complete her mission. But this he had most definitely *not* expected.

"Here. You *wear* it," Mari said wryly, when it was clear all Caledan was going to do was stare at the pin. She carefully fastened the symbol of the Harpers to the shoulder of his new slate blue tunic. The pin glimmered brightly in the sunlight, a twin to the one that adorned Mari's forest green jacket. Caledan laughed and took Mari in his arms. The two embraced for a length of time that might have seemed improper were they not alone.

Suddenly the sunlight that spilled through the doorway darkened. Caledan looked up in surprise to see a hulking shadow standing in the open door. The shadow took a step forward.

"Tyveris!" Caledan exclaimed. "It's about time you came

by for a visit."

The big loremaster smiled, pushing his gold-rimmed spectacles up on his nose. "Things have been busy at the city lord's tower," Tyveris said, joining the two at the table. He sighed ruefully. "*Really* busy."

Caledan laughed. Tyveris was working as an advisor to City Lord Bron, helping to plan the restoration of Iriaebor. It was a position Tyveris had taken reluctantly. After leading the victorious battle in the dungeons, the big loremaster had become nothing less than a hero in the city. The day following the battle the citizens had called for Tyveris to enter the High Tower as city lord. It was a job he did not want. He was a priest, and perhaps even a bit of a warrior still, but he was most certainly not a bureaucrat.

Luckily for Tyveris the old city lord, Bron, was discovered that same morning locked in a small, hidden chamber in the dungeons beneath the tower. Though pale from lack of sunlight and weak from over a year of confinement, Bron was still a man of considerable presence, and the cityfolk were overjoyed to see him alive and well.

However, despite Bron's reappearance, a significant number of citizens still called for Tyveris to take up rule. It was Bron who had proposed Tyveris accept a position as his advisor, and the loremaster, realizing he had little choice in the matter, had agreed. Everyone in the city was thereby made happy—except Tyveris, but apparently he did not count.

"You're looking almost respectable today, Caledan," Tyveris remarked, eyeing Caledan curiously. Caledan had finally traded in his worn black leather traveling gear for newer, less unsavory attire, and he had even taken to shaving regularly. However, much to Mari's chagrin, he still hadn't given up his road-worn, faded blue traveling cloak. He had to draw a line *somewhere*. "Nice pin, too," the big monk noticed.

"Thanks," Caledan said, almost surprised at the pride in his own voice.

"I thought you might like to know that the last of the Zhentarim from the dungeon have been sent in a caravan to Darkhold," Tyveris told them.

"I'm still not certain that was such a good idea," Caledan remarked with a frown. "Why give the Zhents their own warriors back? We may have to fight them again someday."

"Bron didn't want them filling up the dungeon indefinitely," Tyveris explained. "They're a rather dangerous bunch to have hanging around, and, what's more, they eat a lot. Besides, Caledan, I think you know how the Zhentarim treat those of their number who fail them." He drew a finger meaningfully across his neck.

"I'd forgotten about that," Caledan admitted.

Jolle came into the common room after a time and joined them, and not long after Estah returned from the market. Pog and Nog squealed in delight at the sight of the big Tabaxi Chultan and immediately scrambled to their favorite perches atop his massive shoulders. Kellen sat quietly at the table, though he did flash a brief smile at Caledan and Mari. Caledan reached out and tousled the boy's dark hair.

My son, he thought, as he did numerous times each day. Kellen was still a very serious child. Caledan supposed he always would be. Yet somehow being raised by Ravendas had not left as great a scar on Kellen as Caledan would have imagined. The boy had about him an air of gentleness that made folk forget the odd things he sometimes said.

He looks like Kera, Caledan suddenly realized. The resemblance was clear, in the line of his jaw and the fine shape of his nose. Indeed, he looked far more like Kera than he did his mother, Ravendas.

Tyveris stayed for supper, and for a time the common room was filled with laughter. Their mood saddened only once, when they drank a toast to Ferret, but even then they couldn't help but smile at the recollection of the thief. "Would that there were as many men in the world as full of greed as Ferret," Caledan said as he lifted his mug. Everyone knew exactly what he meant.

Finally the shadows began to lengthen outside the inn, and Tyveris bid them all farewell, promising to return soon. He stepped outside into the gathering twilight.

"There's something I need to do," Caledan said then. "Something I've been meaning to do for a while." He stood and threw his multi-patched cloak over his shoulders against the cool onset of night. Estah, her eyes sparkling, nodded in approval.

"Come back soon, Father," Kellen said, holding Caledan's hand tightly for a moment before running off to entertain Pog and Nog.

"Yes, come back soon," Mari said softly. She stood on her toes and kissed him fleetingly.

"I will, Harper," he said gruffly. "I promise."

Caledan retrieved Mista from the inn's stable. The pale gray mare tried to nip his shoulder as he saddled her. Apparently she felt she had been neglected of late.

"Well, I'm sorry," Caledan said in mild annoyance. "I've been rather busy, you know."

Mista snorted. Apparently she cared little for excuses. However, despite her surly mood, she allowed Caledan to mount, and soon the two were making their way through the streets of the Old City.

Iriaebor was a much different place than it had been when Caledan had first ridden across the bridge that gray, rainy day in late winter. Free of the oppression of Ravendas and the Zhentarim, the cityfolk had set to the task of restoring their city. Streets had been swept clean, buildings repaired and painted, wells dredged so the water ran clear, and stains scoured from the city's stone walls.

Of course there were some wounds that would take

longer to heal. Willowy saplings now grew in gardens where ancient oaks and ash trees had once stood, before they were hacked down and burned by the Zhentarim. But scars such as these only served to remind cityfolk how much their homes meant to them and how valuable their freedom really was.

The evening air was sweet and clear, and the stars began to come out one by one in the slate-colored sky, winking above the tops of the towers like jewels. Torches lined the streets, filling the city with light, and despite the coming night the avenues of the Old City were alive with people bustling about their business.

As Mista walked on, Caledan drew out a baliset and began to play a soft melody. The baliset, fashioned of maple and ash, had been a gift from Mari. Caledan smiled. After seven years, he had forgotten what a simple pleasure making music could be. He was glad Mari had reminded him of that. It seemed the Harper had reminded him of a good many things he had forgotten in his wanderings.

Caledan and Mista made their way past the Temple of Selune, and finally he brought the gray mare to a halt before a well-kept but stark tower.

"Do you mind waiting out here?" Caledan asked the mare as he dismounted.

She answered him by stepping on his foot.

"Tough," Caledan replied, tickling her knee so that she would lift her hoof. Mista snorted in indignation, and Caledan slapped her flank affectionately. The mare laid her ears back and bared her teeth.

"I'll be back soon," Caledan said with a laugh. Mista let out an indifferent whinny, then leaned forward and nuzzled her soft, velvety nose against his cheek.

Caledan shook his head, bemused, then turned to lift the knocker on the tower's door. The full moon was just rising over the city's towers, filling the streets with its pure, silvery light.

The tower's door opened, and Morhion stared out in apparent stupefaction.

"Well, can I come in?" Caledan asked. "Or are you simply going to stand there staring at me?"

The mage blinked his eyes. "I am sorry, Caledan . . . I mean, Caldorien." There was a trembling note in his normally smooth voice. "Please, come in."

Caledan followed Morhion up the tower's steps into the mage's study. He sat and accepted a glass of wine, from which he drank deeply. All the while Morhion regarded him with an expression of confusion mixed with amazement.

"I suppose you're wondering why I've come here," Caledan said finally.

"I know why you've come," Morhion replied gravely. "You've come for satisfaction, to gain vengeance against me. I cannot say that I blame you. I have betrayed you twice, Caldorien."

"I'm sorry to disappoint you, but it's not vengeance I want," Caledan said flatly. He set down his glass and stood before the mage.

"Then what is it you wish?" Morhion asked, his blue eyes troubled.

"To tell you that I understand," Caledan said simply. He walked toward a narrow window, gazing out at the city for a moment. He heard the sound of music and laughter drifting through the night. He turned to regard the mage. "You saved me twice with your 'betrayals.' Once in Darkhold, and once in the Shadowking's crypt. For that I thank you."

Morhion gaped. For the first time Caledan could remember, his face did not seem cold and imperious, but rather tired and lonely. "I have never . . . I have never allowed myself to hope that you would ever understand."

Caledan reached out and laid a hand on the mage's

shoulder. "Believe it."

Slowly, almost imperceptibly, a faint smile crept across Morhion's face.

Caledan bid the mage farewell and let himself out of the tower, stepping into the warm summer night. "Come on, Mista," he said as he mounted the ghostly gray mare and nudged her into a trot. "Let's go home."

* * * * *

Morhion sat at his desk, sipping a glass of pale wine. The wooden surface before him was littered with scrolls and parchments filled with scribbled notes. He had been deep in study earlier, but now the parchments lay untouched. They could wait.

"To you, Caledan Caldorien," Morhion whispered to the silence of his study, lifting his glass. "To you, my friend." He drained the wine and smiled again.

Suddenly, despite the balmy air coming through the window, Morhion shivered. His smile faded as he set the glass down. A shadow appeared before him, and as he watched it gradually began to take shape, its outlines growing clearer.

Fine crystals of frost appeared on the empty wine glass, and Morhion's breath began to fog in the chilly air. He watched the apparition before him with a familiar feeling of dread.

"It is time," the dark spirit said in a voice that made Morhion's blood run cold. "Do not forget the bargain we made beneath the fortress of Darkhold." The apparition's eyes glowed a deep, bloody red. "The pact is binding."